THE
SALT
MARSH

CLARE CARSON

HEAD of ZEUS

First published in the UK in 2016 by Head of Zeus Ltd.
This paperback edition first published in the UK
in 2016 by Head of Zeus Ltd.

9 7 5 3 1 2 4 6 8

A catalogue record for this book is available from
the British Library.

ISBN (PB) 9781784081003
ISBN (E) 9781784080976

Typeset by Adrian McLaughlin

Printed and bound by CPI Group (UK) Ltd,
Croydon, CR0 4YY

MIX
Paper from
responsible sources
FSC® C020471

Head of Zeus Ltd
Clerkenwell House
45–47 Clerkenwell Green
London EC1R 0HT

WWW.HEADOFZEUS.COM

To Andy

'And oftentimes to win us to our harm,
The instruments of darkness tell us truths.'

—Banquo in *Macbeth*, Act i Scene iii

Monday 1 May 1978

JIM DID HIS vanishing act the day of the spring fair. Sam was sitting in her room reading, the last of the apple blossom drifting past her window, Jim and the dog downstairs, her mother Liz and her sisters visiting the new baby of one of Liz's old friends. Liz often went out on the days that Jim was at home. Her mother's departure had been preceded by an argument. Sam had half heard Liz shouting, Jim shouting back, but hadn't taken much notice because she had her head stuck in a book and, anyway, they always argued these days. Liz laughed, and that did catch Sam's attention because there was something manic about the cackle. She clocked Liz yelling, 'So if I want to know where you are, I'm supposed to call the fucking Home Secretary, am I?' The front door crunched.

Sam was glad to hide in her room, curled up on her beanbag with her book. As she read, she was vaguely conscious of Jim clattering around in the kitchen below, tasked by Liz with cleaning the sink's U bend while she was out. He was crap at DIY. Approached all domestic repairs with a rubber mallet, a bottle of Guinness and a stream of four-letter words – arse, piss, shit.

'Fuck.'

The fuck was followed by the noise of china shattering. Then silence. She lifted her head from the pages again,

1

wondered whether she should go downstairs and check that he was OK but was distracted by the auburn flash of a fox, visible through her bedroom window as it slunk along the railway track at the bottom of the garden. There was a den in the brambles that smothered the embankments of the London commuter line. Rabies threat, according to *John Craven's Newsround*. She focused on the gap in the thicket where the fox's brush had disappeared; if she watched long enough, perhaps she would see the cubs emerging to play in the unexpected warmth of the spring sun. She waited. A train rattled past. No sign of the cubs. She was about to return to her book when the notes of Jim's whistle floated on the air, growing louder as he clomped up the stairs; the tune familiar – 'The *Third Man* Theme'. His good-mood whistle. She loved that film, *The Third Man*. So did Jim. They had watched it together and he had promised her that one day they would go to Vienna where the film was set and they could ride on the Reisenrad, the giant Ferris Wheel. The whistling ceased. Jim's face appeared around her bedroom door and he smiled in his conspiratorial way.

He said, 'I'm taking George for a walk.' She decided it was probably best not to ask him about the sink. Or the broken crockery. He disappeared, then he obviously had an afterthought because his face reappeared around the door.

'How old are you now?'

'Nearly twelve.'

'Oh. I suppose you'd better come with me then. I don't want to get done for negligence.'

She sat in the back of the Cortina with the dog. George was large, black, part German shepherd, part hound from hell, and had failed the police sniffer dog test. Jim loved the dog, the only other male in the household. He shouldn't have been allowed to become a family pet, but one of Jim's mates in the

2

Force had bent the rules, as coppers do. Jim worked for some strange part of the Force – half spy, half cop, secret missions away from home. God only knew what he was doing, Liz said. Well, God and the Home Secretary, apparently.

He swung the car around the roundabout, feeding the steering wheel through both hands, second exit along an oak-shaded lane.

'I'm in the dog house,' Jim said.

'Why?'

'Because I've got to go away again.'

'Where are you going?'

Jim threw her a glance in the rearview mirror. 'Over the hills and far away,' he said.

He always talked like that, in evasive riddles.

'Will you come back?' she asked.

She watched his shoulders heave. 'I've always come back before, haven't I?'

'Yes. I suppose so.'

'Well then.'

He didn't sound particularly convinced, but then he never did. She gazed out the car window; the hawthorn was flowering. The dog slobbered in her ear as they passed the golf course, forged deep into the criminal belt. That was what Jim called it. London's dirty tidemark where the city's mobsters washed up in their mock haciendas and kept a concrete mixer ready on the patio. He parked the Cortina by the graveyard at the edge of the village, the last stop on the bus route through the south London suburbs.

The dog leaped out as soon as Jim opened the car door, cocked his leg against a dumped mattress lolling on the pavement and bounded off. Jim strode after George, whistling the familiar tune as he went. She ran to catch up. Every now and then he stopped to identify a bird's song. Blackbird. Mistle thrush. The harsh call of the jackdaw. She named the wildflowers: violets, white star wood anemones glinting in the undergrowth. George ran loops around her and Jim, herded them along the lane, growling impatiently when they lingered.

The lane levelled off, merged with a freshly tarmacked road, one side lined by ranks of conifers, the occasional glimpse of red bricks visible through the trunks. Retirement community for the south London mob, Jim said. Cash down, he added. A break in the pine barricade revealed a wooden-framed Larsen trap with a bedraggled crow imprisoned behind the chicken wire, a decoy, a call-bird waiting for a mate to fall through the false floor of the death box.

'God, they're breeding game birds,' Jim said. 'A predilection for guns and shooting – funny how much bank robbers and the upper classes have in common.'

He sneered. 'Pheasant killers. They trap the crows to stop them raiding the pheasants' nests and when the chicks have grown and can fly, they shoot them.'

Sam wanted to release the crow; the bird looked so miserable, huddled in a far corner of the trap. Jim told her to leave it – he didn't want to attract attention. Not in those parts. Best put George on the lead, he added. He whistled; the dog trotted up meekly.

'We've almost done the circuit anyway,' he said. He fought through a hole in the hedgerow and strode diagonally across a muddy field, away from the gangsters' villas. Jim hated retracing his steps. He was always determined to walk in a circle even if it meant clambering over barbed-wire fences and squelching through ditches. She trailed behind.

'Look.' He pointed at a grey church spire poking above a distant canopy of trees. 'We're almost back.'

They reached the Cortina eventually, jammed in now by a Fiat estate, a Mini and a line of motorbikes – Harleys and a couple of Kawasakis.

'Lot of cars here,' Jim said. 'I wonder what's going on.'

Sam spotted a poster pinned to an oak. 'There's a May Day fair on in the playing fields. Fun stalls and exhilarating rides it says. Maybe there's a big wheel. Can we go and look?'

'We might as well; there's nothing much else to do today.'

That must have been what everybody else thought too. George strained at his lead, unnerved by the thickening crowds – leather-jacketed bikers swinging dog chains, scabby punks with glue-sniffer eyes and red-faced golfers in plaid trousers shouting blahdy typical at each other. The periphery always attracted an odd mix of people. Past the lychgate, the chippy, the Green Man, the sweet smell of candyfloss and hotdogs hit her before they reached the fenced fields where the locals played in Sunday leagues. The fair was a mishmash, an odd mix of funfair and village fete. A couple of crapola rides – a carousel and a waltzer – a collection of throw the ping-pong ball into the bowl to win a goldfish stalls with striped awnings and lightbulb fringes and a line of trestle-tables displaying less gaudy fete-type wares.

'No big wheel,' she said.

Jim scoffed. 'That's not going to satisfy the punters. They've advertised excitement and it looks to me as if they've persuaded the lads from Peter Pan's Pool to drag their spare equipment over and set up a couple of dodgy carousels.' Sam knew all about Peter Pan's Pool, a small but permanent fairground in Catford – she had been taken there by her sisters. She hadn't been impressed by the dilapidated dodgems and the gold-toothed wandering fair-hands. Her sisters liked it there. A passing phase, according to Liz. Jim was right, she reckoned, as she watched the cranky waltzer jerking into life, this May Day fair was not going to please anybody who had come in search of excitement.

'Not sure Morris dancers will help,' Jim said.

He cocked his head towards a roped-off square between the funfair attempt and the trestle-table stalls. The bearded Morris dancers were loitering near the Maypole. Some girls in flimsy dresses were practising their dance routine and a bunch of adults decked out in green capes, tunics and face paint were fussing with the Maypole's limp ribbons.

'What do you think all those people in green are doing?' Sam asked.

'Probably some hippy Beltane nonsense.'

'Beltane?'

'Old pagan celebration to mark the start of summer.'

Jim had these odd pools of esoteric knowledge.

'What does Beltane mean?'

'Bright fire. Shepherds used to light two fires and pass between them with their flocks. A sort of blessing. Protection for the yearling lambs when they moved from the uplands of the Kentish Weald to the lowland marshes.'

The waltzer was blaring 'You Sexy Thing'.

Jim scanned the fairground. 'Bet the crow-men are here somewhere.'

'Who are the crow-men?'

'Dancers from the darkness. Men in black. Birds of death. They always turn up in these parts, looking for trouble. Oh well. At least there's something to drink.' He nodded at a sagging white marquee with a beer tent sign above its open flaps. 'Here, you take George. I could do with a beer. Won't be long.'

He handed her the lead and the dog plonked himself on her shoes, pinioned her to the ground. She couldn't be bothered to shift the beast, stood with numbing toes and watched the girls in floaty dresses rehearsing. They made her squirm. She would never wear a dress like that; never wear a dress at all in fact if she could help it. She wore trousers.

Jim emerged from the tent with a bottle in his hand.

'OK, where next?' he said as he approached.

She noticed his face cloud, but she ignored his changing expression – she was used to his mercurial temperament – and surveyed the trestle-tables furthest away from the dancing girls – a tombola, jam and cakes, bric-a-brac. She turned to tell Jim she wanted to try her luck with the tombola. He wasn't there. In the twenty seconds she had been looking away, he had disappeared. She must be mistaken. She gripped George's lead and cast her eyes around, certain he was somewhere nearby. He wasn't. Her stomach tightened. She looked again, scoured the cape wearers, bikers, golfers, Bromley Contingent safety-pin punks, everybody the worse for wear. No trace of Jim. Where was he? Perhaps he had dropped something in the beer tent and gone back to look for it. She yanked George's lead, stepped over to the marquee, peered inside. She couldn't see him. She retreated to the spot where she had been standing when Jim disappeared. Still no sign of him. She had a sick feeling in her gut. She had to think. He had done this before, the disappearing act. He sometimes vanished when he spotted somebody from his shadow life because he was worried about being seen with his family, blowing his cover and jeopardizing the safety of his wife and kids. So he would melt away, leave them to carry on as if nothing had happened. But every other time he had vanished, she had been with Liz or one of her sisters. And now she was alone. Or, at least, alone with the dog. Had he seen somebody dangerous who knew him? She glanced nervously around the fairground, searching the crowd not for Jim this time but anybody who looked shifty. Everybody seemed sinister right then, red faces leering, bellowing voices, beer-bellied sweaty men. She was alone in the jostle, enclosed yet exposed, sensing danger all around but unable to pinpoint its exact location. She was starting to panic. Her breath was coming in short gasps, and when she tried to catch it she couldn't, she only made the lack of oxygen worse.

She squatted beside George, put her arm around his neck for comfort. The dog panted too, meaty breath stinking in her nostrils. 'What shall we do?' she asked. The dog whimpered. Her eyes were welling. She was confused. Should she wait for her father to reappear or was it safer to move? She couldn't call her mum from a phone box because Liz would still be at her friend's house and she didn't know the number. Should she walk home? It was about five miles along a main road. Perhaps it was better to catch a bus – she had enough change in her pocket. She wavered. The waltzer switched to 'That's the Way I Like It'. She decided to do a circuit of the fairground to see if she could find Jim.

She picked her way across the tangle of waltzer cables, bypassed the Maypole, peering into the crowds. No joy. She headed toward the trestle-table stalls. There were fewer people here, but still no sign of Jim. She skirted the tombola, came to a stall piled with cellophane bags that she thought contained sweets until she saw the *Herbal Remedies* sign taped to the table top. The woman with dyed green hair sitting behind the table waved one of the bags at Sam.

'Here, take it. It's willow bark. Bitter withy.'

Sam didn't want to stop, but she was too polite to ignore the stallholder so she took the packet, eyed its brown fragments.

'Bitter withy?'

'The weeping willow, or withy as it used to be called, is

the tree of death and grief. It's cursed. The bitter withy is the only tree to perish from the inside out, heart first.'

Sam shuffled awkwardly.

'According to Culpeper,' the woman continued, 'the bark can be used to stop bleeding, and when mixed with vinegar it takes away warts.' Sam was wondering how she could end the conversation when she noticed the woman's face harden, her mouth pulled taut and thin. 'Don't look now, but there is a man standing behind us by the Candy Man Can candyfloss stall and he's staring at you.'

Sam twisted round, assuming it must be Jim, but was caught by the gaze of a stranger, colourless eyes locking hers. She tried to look away, frightened by the intensity of the man's icy stare, but could only shift her gaze down and found herself transfixed by a crescent-moon scar on his cheekbone.

The woman's voice pulled her back. 'Where are your parents anyway?'

'I came here with my dad, but he's disappeared.'

'Disappeared?'

'He went off somewhere.' Her neck prickled. She wondered whether she should explain the problem – Jim's vanishing act possibly to avoid the scar-faced man – but her family had a strict code; she should be careful what she said about her father. Talking was dangerous. Anyway, she wasn't sure what she thought of this woman. The stallholder leaned forwards. Sam caught a whiff of patchouli oil and tobacco.

'Is your dad in the beer tent?'

'Probably.'

The woman was scrutinizing her face, making her feel self-conscious.

'Are you OK?'

Sam hesitated. 'I'm fine.'

The stallholder was still staring at her face. 'You've got a birthmark on your cheek.'

Sam lifted her hand without thinking to the lumpy brown splodge shaped like a cat's head. She tried to keep it covered with her hair, especially when she was at school, because her classmates called her bogey face when it was visible.

'Couple of hundred years ago, people would have thought you were a witch if they saw that mark.'

Sam laughed nervously. She couldn't tell whether the woman was joking.

'Witch?'

'Witch isn't necessarily an insult. It was often clever women, cunning folk, who knew about herbs and plants who were accused of witchcraft.'

The stallholder waved her hand across her cellophane packets, gave Sam a meaningful nod. Sam was desperate to escape now, find her father. She checked over her shoulder; a small queue had formed in front of the candyfloss stall, the flustered black-aproned stallholder was bent over the silver drum, whirring sticks around to collect the sugar wisps. The scar-faced man was nowhere in sight. She clocked the crowds surging towards the roped area to watch the girls prancing around the Maypole, 'Jake the Peg' pumping through the tannoy. The leering carousel horses were chasing round and round. She had a sudden idea about where Jim might have gone: if he was trying to avoid being seen by somebody – the man with the scar – he could have slipped away and walked back to the Cortina. It was the one place where he knew Sam might look for him.

'I'd better go and see if I can find my dad in the beer tent,' Sam said. She was still holding the cellophane packet. She didn't want it, but she thought it would be less hassle to pay for it than to hand it back. 'How much is the willow bark?'

'Take it. It's yours for nothing.'

'Thanks.'

Sam pulled George's lead and made her way through the jostle around the roped-off area. A policeman was jigging along with the girls in floaty dresses; the lairy bystanders egged him on – guffawing, cameras snapping. The Morris dancers were warming up their instruments – a violin, an accordion, a penny whistle and drum. The green-cape wearers were huddled in a corner behind the Maypole. One of them lit a bulrush torch, leaned back as it ignited, jabbed the burning wand down his throat and exhaled a leaping flame. Petrol fumes filled the air. The dancing girls shied away from the fire-eater, startled.

The policeman stopped being jolly, shouted, 'Oi. Enough of that.'

The fire-eater shouted back, 'Fuck off. I'll do what I want. It's a free country.'

'This is my fucking patch. You do what I say here.'

The fire-eater's mates jeered, closed ranks. The audience surged, eager for a fight, bored with the waltzer, little girls and Maypole dancing. Sam pressed against the flow, dragging George. As she reached the beer tent, a bunch of stick-wielding men with blackened faces burst out through the open flap – ragged black cloaks flapping from their shoulders and top hats decorated with pheasant feathers. Crow-men, she realized with alarm, dancers from the darkness, birds of death. The crow-men hurtled into the crowd, barged over to the Maypole. Sam heard a shout behind – 'let's get 'em' – quickened her pace and headed to the gate, George straining on the lead. She had almost reached the exit when a man clutching a stick of candy-floss stepped into their path. He turned to face her and she saw his colourless eyes, the scar. She gasped, inhaled the sickly sweet smell of spun sugar. Her gut dropped, her legs tensed for flight, certain now this was the man Jim had been trying to avoid. What was he? A murderer? A terrorist? He smiled.

'Your dad gave me a message for you,' he said.

His words caught her by surprise – his voice calm and reasonable. She edged back. Noticed a badge pinned to his windcheater, a peace symbol. CND. She stalled. Her aunt was in CND, she was always going on about Aldermaston, the dangers of nuclear proliferation. She liked her aunt. Harmless commie, according to Jim. Could this man be dangerous if he was wearing a peace badge? Maybe he wasn't so bad after all. Maybe he wasn't the person who had prompted Jim to disappear, perhaps he was a friend of her father's. Up close he seemed quite normal. Tall, not broad. Mousey hair. Anorak and jeans. His stare made her nervous, and the scythe-shaped scar was scary, but she had a marked cheek too and the bogey-face comments upset her. It was wrong to judge people by their looks.

He said, 'Your dad asked me to keep an eye on you and make sure you didn't leave the fair until he got back.'

'Did he?'

She couldn't work it out. If Jim wanted to give her a message why didn't he just say something to her before he vanished? Why did he ask this man to tell her? But what if he was telling the truth? Jim would be angry if she didn't wait for him. Maybe it was sensible to wait.

'Do you know how long he will be?' she asked.

'Not long. Why don't you stay here with me? Here,' he pushed the candyfloss stick he was holding at her, 'have this. Your dad told me to buy you a treat while he was gone.'

The candyfloss did it. Instant reaction. There was no way Jim would have told some strange man to buy her a treat, he wasn't like that, he knew she would never accept candyfloss from a stranger. It was totally wrong. The scar-faced man was creepy. She ran. The man reached out to grab her as she passed, dropped the candyfloss on the ground.

'Stop.'

He lurched at her. She dodged him, broke into a gallop. George was faster, overtook her, pelted down the road, towing her behind, her heart hammering.

The man shouted, 'Tell your dad he should take more care of you, otherwise something nasty could happen.'

They reached the Cortina. Jim was there, waiting in the driver's seat. He saw her coming, opened the door for her. She clambered in with George; the dog's rank smell filled the car. Jim didn't say a word, turned the ignition, accelerator, swerve. Along the bypass, white gypsy caravans huddled on the verge, tatty ponies tethered to the fence. She was still clutching the gift from the green-haired lady.

'What've you got in that plastic bag?' Jim asked, looking in the rearview mirror.

'Willow bark.'

'Makes a change from goldfish, I suppose.'

He was trying to be jolly. Pretend nothing had happened.

She said, 'Why did you leave me?'

He shifted on his seat. 'I had to. I thought you would know I had gone back to the car. And you had George with you.'

The dog stretched his paws across her legs. 'I worked it out in the end,' she said. 'I was scared.'

He sniffed. 'You were safer without me.'

He said it brusquely. She went red, the tears of pent-up fear gathering. She blinked them back because crying always irritated her father, leaned her head against the side window. Watched the world go by. Eventually she sat upright again and said, 'A man tried to stop me leaving.'

She noticed the veins on the back of his hand as he gripped the gear stick.

'What man?'

'He was standing by the candyfloss machine and staring at me when I was looking for you. Then he tried to stop me when I was leaving and said you'd asked him to tell me to wait at the fair.'

'What did he look like?'

'He had a scar on his cheek.'

'Bastard. Fucking bastard.'

Jim put his foot on the accelerator.

'I hope you didn't say anything to him.'

'Well, I did because I thought he knew you and he looked normal – apart from his eyes and the scar – and he was wearing a peace badge, you know, like the one Aunty Hazel wears.'

Jim snorted, shook his head. 'A badge doesn't mean anything. Appearances can be deceptive. People aren't always what they seem. You should know that by now. Anybody can pick up a badge and wear it.'

He winced when he said that; she wasn't sure why. She felt upset because it wasn't her fault anyway. It was Jim's. Why was he telling her off?

'He tried to give me a stick of candyfloss.'

'He what?'

'He tried to give me a stick of candyfloss. That's when I knew he was a weirdo.'

'A stick of bloody candyfloss? Jesus fucking wept. What was he playing at?'

He shook his head, mumbled to himself. 'Talk about going for the soft target. A kid. What did he think he'd get from a kid? Wanker. Well, I suppose you don't always know what you know.'

She had no idea what he was going on about. *You don't always know what you know.* She turned the words over in her mind, thought about the candyfloss, the colourless eyes, the scar face, the tightness in her stomach. She sang to herself while she was thinking, not conscious of what she was singing. 'The Candy Man Can'. *Willy Wonka and the Chocolate Factory.*

'Will you stop singing that bloody song,' Jim said.

They drove on in silence, circled the roundabout, past the skinheads hanging out at the bus stop, the fairy-light-bedecked bungalow where the tattooed biker lived with his ageing mother, turned into their street. Jim pulled up, hair plastered to the sweat of his forehead, yanked the handbrake on.

She said, 'He told me to tell you that you should take more care of me, otherwise something nasty could happen.'

'Fuck him,' Jim shouted. 'Fuck him.' He opened the car door. 'There isn't a fucking handbook. I have to make it up as I go along. I get it wrong sometimes. Maybe this time I got it wrong.'

She wasn't sure whether he was talking to her or to himself. He got out of the car, slammed the door. She followed with the dog. He walked up the front steps of their house. At the top he stopped, turned.

He said, 'He's an evil bastard. He might look normal but he's a fucking evil bastard.' He paused, then he said, 'He is a candy man, that's exactly what he is. A candy man spinning his sickly deceits. Using kids, for fuck's sake. You'd better remember his face. If you see him again, don't think twice. Run.'

Jim went inside, left the front door open, left her standing on the pavement. She didn't want to remember the candy man's face, the icy eyes, the scythe-shaped scar. She wanted to forget him, bury it. Along with all the other things it was dangerous to remember about her father. A gust of wind carried a swirl of apple blossom along the road. She stretched, caught a white petal as the mini tornado passed, squished it in her fist, released the intense perfume of the blossom, sweet like candyfloss. The scent made her retch.

CHAPTER 1

20 June 1986

FRIDAY EVENING, ALONE in the house: Dave her old housemate away in Skell, Luke her boyfriend doing a bar shift at the Wag. The room overshadowed by the Oval gasholder, its grey lung full. In the middle of the weekly phone session with her therapist; the last one before the memorial service that she had planned to mark the second anniversary of Jim's death. The soft voice coaxed confession. She held the receiver to her ear with one hand and in the other she clutched a photo of her father, taken from behind, black and white. He had always avoided the camera's lens, he did not want to be identified. She conjured up a memory of his features, tried to hold the image steady, but it slipped and faded into a recollection of his blank eyes staring up from the mortuary slab. He had been identified then, in the morgue, by her.

The beat of sullen raindrops against the window filled the pause in the conversation. Another drencher; a washout of a summer. She sighed and dropped the photo of her father on the floorboards, wiped her mouth with the back of her hand. Tasted saltwater on her lips.

'Sam, are you still there?'

'Yes.'

'You were saying your father always whistled a particular tune. What was it?'

She attempted to replicate the melody into the receiver.

'Oh, now where have I heard that before?... I know it...'

Sam laughed. '"The *Third Man* Theme". Anton Karas played it on a zither.'

'Of course. What a great film. Set in Vienna, wasn't it? The swindler who fakes his own death.'

'Yeah, and then Philby was called the third man because he was the double agent working in MI6 who helped his two mates Burgess and Maclean escape to Moscow.'

'Of course. Philby, the third man. You know your spies, don't you.'

She didn't answer. She never did go to Vienna, she never went on the Reisenrad with Jim.

The therapist asked, 'So when was the last time you heard your father whistle this tune?'

'I can't really remember. Perhaps it was a couple of days before he was...'

Killed by two bullets in the back of his head. Up by the Thames, the patch of trampled grass behind the railway arches at Vauxhall Bridge. Officially, a car crash. Unofficially, the work of a contract hitman.

'Sam, I've lost you again.'

'Sorry.'

'Sam. We've been doing these phone sessions for over a year now and I still find it difficult to get you to talk in any depth about your father.'

Sam scowled at the invisible therapist somewhere down the line. The therapist had been her mother's idea, of course. Sam had managed the first term at university, still numb from the aftershock of her father's death, gliding along on a thermal of jokiness and uplifting indifference until an unsettling event had caused a crash. March, just before the Easter vac. She had volunteered to collect money for the local women's refuge and was standing in Cornmarket Street rattling a tin with little result, apart from a handful of insults. Domestic violence? Doesn't happen. Not to decent women, at least. An innocuous-looking man had sauntered up to her – posh Harrington, stay pressed trousers, glasses, mouse hair swept back, potato face. Hard to place him, he could have been the manager of the local Tesco, sub-editor of *The Sun*, solicitor. Anything. There was nothing in the way he approached her that tripped any of her alarm bells. He stuck his hand in a pocket, whipped out some small change, dropped it in the slot, whispered, 'I know you. You are Jim Coyle's daughter.'

She jumped, too startled to push him away or leg it, her reflection in his glasses, mouth gaping, rabbit-caught-in-headlight eyes. He strode off down the street without a backwards glance. She stared after him, replaying the words in her head, uncertain whether she had misheard. Although, she knew she hadn't. She closed her eyes for a moment, opened them again and then she saw that everything was the same but everything was different. The whispered words had unsteadied her. Who was he? How did he know who she was? She made it back to her college room, lay on her bed, tried to forget it. She stared at the plaster ceiling but it was fracturing and dissolving into atoms, as if the stranger's identification of her as Jim Coyle's daughter had given her clearer sight of the hidden patterns beneath the façade. Nothing was as it seemed. She could see the secrets, the truths, and she was filled with fear and dread. She needed a distraction. She grabbed a slim volume from the pile of history textbooks by her bed: *Daemonologie* – a treatise on witchcraft by King James the First of England. It wasn't a comforting read, but she couldn't put it down. Found her eyes glued to the king's malicious words, his insistence that the dark power ran in families, passed from parent to child. Look for the mark, find the witch, make her confess and burn her. Sam's hand went to the splodge on her cheek as she stared at the page and sensed her tormentors circling.

She had missed several tutorials and Liz had turned up to find out what was wrong. She said she thought she was under surveillance, for some reason she couldn't quite explain other than that they knew she was her father's daughter. Liz observed that she'd always had obsessive tendencies – listing birds, collecting beetles, had to finish the cryptic crossword – and now she was becoming obsessively morbid, tripped into paranoia by thoughts about her father's death. Sam decided to take a year out to recover. Liz urged Sam to find a therapist – as if talking to somebody about Jim's death might take her mind off the subject. Her mother had insisted, found a friend of a friend, but she worked in Oxford and Sam had left Oxford, moved into Dave's south London home. Liz suggested doing the sessions by phone, and the therapist agreed. Sam couldn't see the point, but she went along with it anyway because she didn't want to argue; better to do the passive thing and say yes. A one-hour telephone conversation every week, not such a high price for keeping Liz off her back. Although, the therapist's connection with her mother was inhibiting. One more reason, as if she needed another, not to say too much.

'Sam? Are you still there?' The therapist waiting patiently at the other end of the line.

'Yes.'

'This is a safe space for you to talk. If you don't talk about your feelings, if you suppress them, they will come out in more destructive ways. You won't necessarily be able to control your emotions. And in the end, the person who will be most hurt is you. Do you see what I'm saying?'

'Yes.'

'Sam, you know grief has five stages.'

Oh god here we go again. 'I know. Yes.'

She mouthed the list silently as the therapist went through it.

'Denial. Anger. Bargaining. Depression. Acceptance.'

Silence.

'Sam, I don't want to push you here, but maybe you're still in denial.'

'I'm not.'

'You don't express any feelings about the loss of your father.'

Loss. He hadn't been lost. He had been killed by a contract hitman.

'Sam, why can't you talk about the feelings you have about your father?'

'It's just that...'

Habits so deeply etched she barely perceived their existence. Hedging to avoid unknown dangers. Words played like sleights of hand.

'I'm not always entirely sure what my feelings about my dad actually are...'

'Well, that's what I'm here for, to help you work it out. Everybody has to go through the grieving process.'

'I didn't realize it was compulsory.'

The therapist sighed.

'Why don't you try saying the first thing that comes into your head instead of preparing your lines?'

She eyed the Oval gasholder through the storm-splattered window. 'OK. But isn't our time up anyway?'

'Almost. One last question. Did "The *Third Man* Theme" have any significance for Jim?'

'No. Not really.' She heard a click on the line. 'Are you recording this conversation?'

ED LEISURE+CULTURE

'Of course not.'

'I thought I heard a click.'

'I didn't.'

Perhaps it was the rain. 'I must have been mistaken.'

'OK. Well, I'll call again next week.'

She replaced the receiver, plucked the photo of Jim off the floor. Only the back of his head was visible because he was facing Harry, who was grinning at the camera with a megawatt smile that softened his hard man broken nose. Harry, Jim's one and only trusted mate. How old was she when she snapped the photo? Ten. Eleven perhaps. The camera was a Christmas present and she had bugged Jim with her attempts to capture him for her album. You, he said. You again. You're always there watching. Seeing things you shouldn't see. Sticking the details in that memory bank of yours. The Third Man – that was Jim's nickname for her, the invisible addition to his partnership with Harry. Jim's silent shadow. She leaned back, held the photo up above her head, as if that might give her a clearer view of her father, and attempted to whistle the familiar tune one more time. The notes came out in a squeak. She gave up, licked her lips and tasted the saltiness of her tears.

The conversation with her therapist gave her a bad night's sleep. She arose fuzzy-headed. Saturday morning, ten a.m. Time to head south, to London's periphery. Standing in the hallway, her brain checked the list of camping gear while her eyes followed a going nowhere snail trail that shimmered across the doormat bristles. She wondered why she had suggested the ceremony in the first place. She wished she could skip the graveyard, drive straight down to Dungeness. The phone rang. The second call that day: Luke had phoned her first thing. She wavered, pick it up or leave it? Unlikely to be

Luke again. Perhaps it was Dave, calling from Skell to tell her he had spotted a bittern in the reeds or something like that. She enjoyed talking to Dave, but she didn't have the time right now; she had to leave otherwise she would be late. Decided to ignore the call: if it was important they could leave a message.

The dog next door howled. The phone rang and rang again and then the answering machine cut in with her disembodied voice. 'There is no one at home to take your call. Please leave a message after the tone.' The tape whirred. Beeped. A pause. A heavy breath, and then the familiar tune. 'The *Third Man* Theme'. For a moment she thought Jim was on the other end of the line, whistling impatiently while he waited for her to pick up. Her hand reached for the receiver then stopped in mid-air when she remembered that was impossible. The whistling ceased. There was a clunk as a receiver at the far end was replaced. The cassette spooled backwards and left the red message light blinking. She retracted her hand, wiped the perspiration from her face, walked away, climbed the stairs, checked her bedroom window was closed. The floorboards lurched. She slumped, head down, knees up, covered her face with her hands. Who was whistling down her phone? She recalled her conversation with the therapist, the click she had dismissed as rain; perhaps somebody was listening to her conversations after all. Some weird knicker sniffer was letting her know they were out there. She didn't want to think about it, block it out. She took a deep breath, returned downstairs. The red light of the answering machine winked in the gloom. Her hand hovered, index finger over play. She pressed the message erase button. And it was only then that she recalled her conversation with Luke earlier in the morning, and she wondered whether he had given too much away.

*

Inside the house where she had grown up, two suitcases stood by the front door. Liz was shouting instructions to Jess about some Folio Society special offer she had paid for but still hadn't been delivered. Roger was leering in the background. Sam had realized, in the aftermath of her father's death, that Roger had been hovering for longer than she had suspected. Leafing through an old family album, it had become apparent that Jim was more or less absent from the photographs while Roger appeared in nearly every one of them. Spritzer in hand, lurking in front of the blackcurrant bush at a summer barbecue. Hand to hair on a windy afternoon's chance encounter in Greenwich Park. Why hadn't she noticed before? Roger the Todger, they used to call him. They couldn't any more, at least not within earshot of Liz. Partner was the coy term her mother used. Liz turned to her youngest daughter as she made her way into the front room.

'Sam.'

There was guilt in Liz's enunciation.

'Mum.'

'I was worried you wouldn't arrive in time for me to say goodbye.'

'Goodbye?'

'We're heading to the airport. The flight leaves early afternoon.'

'Aren't you coming to the graveyard?'

'I can't.'

'I thought you were leaving for Greece tomorrow. That's why I arranged the memorial service two days early. To fit in with your plans.' She hoped that sounded like an accusation. It provoked a marginally defensive response.

'Roger found some cheaper tickets. If it were just a holiday, I would have waited. But it's work and all the travel costs come out of the research grant.'

In the fuzzy margins of her vision, Roger was gliding closer. She ignored him.

'How is a cruise around the Greek Islands connected to your research on Marlowe?'

Roger intervened. 'Not Marlowe. We are doing a joint project on Milton.'

She sidestepped, inserted her back between him and her mother. Milton was an uncharacteristic departure for Liz – she usually went for spies of sorts. Marlowe, Jim. Even Roger had once worked for the Special Boat Service. There was nothing to suggest Milton had ever been a spy, although he had worked as a political propagandist for Oliver Cromwell.

'Milton? Isn't he a bit… boring?'

'Hidden depths.' Liz said it without looking at Sam.

'Really? I still don't see the Greek connection.'

Roger edged around Sam, pressed his hand against the base of Liz's spine and propelled her in the direction of the door. The possessiveness of the gesture made Sam want to puke.

'We'd better go,' he said.

'*Paradise Lost*. Classical references,' Liz said. She was halfway through the door. 'The Fall. I'll phone to see how it went with your father.'

Your father. Two years after his death and Liz still referred to Jim as 'your father' when he irritated her. She hovered on the threshold.

'Speaking of your father, Harry called.'

'Harry?' She couldn't disguise the shock. Liz seemed oblivious.

'He said he needed to talk to you.'

'Oh.' She managed to say the oh casually, despite her panic. Why would Harry want to speak to her? Now? Perhaps she had summoned him up by digging out his photograph. Then it occurred to her that it could have been Harry who whistled down the telephone line; a signal she would know. A comforting explanation for the eerie call – she'd hold on to that.

'What's Harry doing these days?' she asked Liz. 'Isn't he working for some weird part of Intelligence?'

'Intelligence? How would I know? He was your father's friend. Yours as well, it seems. The three of you...'

Liz opened her handbag, faffed, pulled out a slip of paper, snapped the bag shut, handed the scrap to Sam.

'Here's his number. I hope you're not involved in anything stupid.' Liz hauled her suitcase over the threshold. 'Roger says he thinks you can be a bit naïve sometimes.'

'He what?'

Her mother shut the door.

Helen and Jess lounged on the floor, dark hair curtaining pale faces, a cross of cards laid out between them. Sam was sandier than her sisters, khaki eyes to their sapphire blue, but you could tell they were related. Shared attitude if nothing else; the wayward sisters. Jess still lived at home, doing shifts at the local frozen-food supermarket, meagre earnings spent on her chopper that she used on weekend runs with the Outlaws, the local biker gang. Helen had moved out before Jim had died, scraped enough cash from the shop she managed for a deposit on a one-bed flat north of the river in Kentish Town. She sold trendy clothes to her nightclubbing friends. The poseurs, Jim used to call them. You can talk, Helen used to say. Helen reached for the card at the top of the cross, flipped it over.

'Tarot?' Sam asked.

'The Moon.' She held the card in the air, waved it in Sam's direction. 'Deception and shadows. Travel without a clear destination.'

'Not my card,' Sam said.

'I wouldn't be so sure.' Helen scooped the pack into a pile. 'So we're off to the graveyard then. Let's get on with it.'

'Do we need to take anything?' Jess asked.

'No.'

Sam said, 'Wait a minute. Are there any of Jim's old things lying around?'

'Why?'

'I want to leave something on his grave.'

Helen scowled. But then Jess said, 'Liz cleared out the last of Jim's junk before she left. She's stuffed it in a rubbish bag in the cupboard under the stairs in case you wanted to take anything.'

'Why has Liz cleared out Jim's stuff?'

'Two years. She probably wants to move on.'

'Or maybe she wants Roger to move in,' Helen said.

'Well, she might want him to,' Jess said. 'But she'll think twice about asking him because she'll lose her police widow's pension if he does.'

'Will she?' Helen said. 'That's so fucking typical of the Force. What a bunch of sexist gits. She should have the right to shack up with whoever she wants to shack up with.'

Sam silently disagreed. She had stopped off at the house a couple of weeks previously with Luke because she had wanted to introduce him to Liz. She had never been in the habit of introducing her boyfriends to her parents. Liz wasn't really interested and Jim couldn't be guaranteed to react to anybody in anything approaching a civil manner. She'd never been serious enough about anybody to want to introduce them to her parents anyway. But she thought she would give it a try with Luke. He was different. Roger had opened the door, much to her annoyance. Liz was there, but had taken a backseat. Roger had been ostentatiously hostile to Luke, subjecting him to a tirade of questions about his work as a photographer and the places to which he had travelled. Luke had answered Roger's aggressiveness with his usual good humour. Luke was difficult to rile. Or, at least, he didn't get mad about personal issues. Only politics. Injustice. Luke had laughed it off when Sam ranted afterwards. Roger's behaviour was out of order, his questions tinged with a possessiveness that gave her the creeps, trying to establish himself as the dominant male of the household, showing Luke who was boss. He could get stuffed. If Liz wanted to hang around with him that was her business, but Sam wasn't about to put up with him assuming he had some sort of responsibility for her. Ownership even. Jesus no.

'Don't let it get to you,' Luke said. 'Give him a break. It must be hard to be the new man edging his way into a family of feisty women.'

'Maybe he shouldn't bother then.'

'Liz must have invited him,' Luke reminded her gently.

She tried to dispel the image of Roger leering as she peered at Jim's relics, dumped in the black rubbish bag under the stairs. Full of rubble. Pieces of unidentifiable electronic equipment, bunch of Yale keys, aviator sunglasses with one lens missing, blue Chairman Mao cap, Che Guevara badge. All of it extraneous. The last traces of his undercover life – a bag full of props for his false identities. The remnants of his legends. Perhaps that was the essence of Jim; a replicant, nothing but fake memories. What did that make her? She pinned the Che Guevara badge on her coat, next to her yellow and red smiling sun nuclear power no thanks badge, stuck her hand in the bag again. Lucky dip. Her fingers closed on a pile of small black soft leather-bound notebooks squished together with a rubber band. He must have been handed them for note taking, observations on objects of surveillance. There was nothing obvious to indicate they had been issued by the Force, but they were all the same and she couldn't imagine Jim going out and buying one diary, let alone the same diary every year. She extracted one from the bundle and opened it at a random page. A doodle; Kilroy, the bald man with a big nose poking his head over a wall. Jim had scrawled 'Kilroy was here' below the picture. So much for diligent surveillance notes. She was touched by the casual scribble, a reminder of Jim's errant schoolboy side, a trace of the real person below the cover of cop bravado. She closed the diary, spotted the gold embossed date on the front cover: 1984. The year of his death.

'Are we going to do this or not?' Helen had appeared from nowhere, leaning against the front door, tapping her foot.

'Coming.'

She stuffed the diary in her pocket, and returned the others to the rubbish bag, jammed it back under the stairs.

Crow trap country, that was where Jim was buried, out in the grubby edgelands among the gypsies and the criminals. May Day fairs she'd rather forget. They walked together, the three of them, paused under the lychgate – the first time she had been back here since her father's funeral two years previously. She pulled her Oxfam raincoat tight, a comfort blanket she needed even when it was sweaty. Jim was buried on the north side of the church. A vast black bird was writhing on his grave, wings spread, lost in some avian anting ecstasy and oblivious to their approach. The crow lifted its head, caught Sam in its beady stare, flapped into a stunted rowan tree from where it continued its scrutiny. The bird's eye drew Sam in until she was the crow, the bird on the branch, watching herself down below. Helen pinched her arm.

'It wants to be your friend.' She sounded jealous.

The limestone tomb was already lichen-starred, the hard edges of his epitaph softened. 'Jim Coyle. 10th August 1937 – 23rd June 1984.' A shiny churchyard beetle was feeling its way across the engraved letters backwards, like a witch's curse, a name invoked the wrong way round. elyoC miJ.

She turned to Helen. 'Do you think Mum should have put something more on the tombstone?'

'Like?'

'Dunno. Rest in peace?'

'Why?'

'Might have helped.'

'Helped what?'

'The transition. The passage towards the light.'

Helen scoffed. 'The light? What light? There was no light with Jim.'

Jess lit the spliff she had been busy rolling. Sam traced the cracked earth on the grave with her plimsoll, jabbed the loose soil. 'How do we know he's still down there?'

'Where else would he be?'

'Maybe somebody dug him up.'

'Don't be a wally.'

'The earth has been disturbed.'

'Must have been the crow. And anyway, why would anybody want to dig up Jim?'

Sam didn't have an answer to that.

'You'd have to be bloody stupid to dig him up,' Helen said. 'Lord knows what's buried down there with him.'

Jess puffed blue smoke, passed the joint to Helen. 'What do we do now?'

Helen glared at Sam. 'Search me,' Sam said.

'It was your idea.'

'I know.'

She had suggested it months ago, marked in her head as the line under her father's death. And now they were here, it seemed pointless. Worse than pointless. She had no idea how to proceed. She squatted, eyes level with the yellow ragwort sprouting from the soil's fissures, plucked and twiddled a seeded grass stem. *Here's a tree in summer.* She ran her finger and thumb along the stem, pulled away the seeds, leaving a bare stalk. *Here's a tree in winter.* She thought of Jim then, the morgue, his corpse, the husk. She held the grass seeds between her finger and thumb. *Here's a bunch of flowers.* She sprinkled the seeds on the grave. *Here come April showers.* Death brings forth new life. Even the dodgy seed can reproduce.

'We could improvise a Ouija board,' Helen said. 'See if we can contact him. Ask him how he's doing.'

Sam said, 'The Ouija board only ever worked when you pushed the bottle with your finger.'

'I thought you were the one who was pushing it.' Helen cackled. Jess joined in. Sam said nothing. Helen jabbed Sam in the back with the tip of her ankle boot, leaned down, passed her the joint. 'Although you know what really did work?'

'What?'

'The House of Levitation.'

'You're right,' Sam said. 'God, that was strange.' The House of Levitation; the ritual had filled the long summer of '76, the year of the drought when all hosepipes had been banned and it was too hot to go out on their bikes. Everybody wanted to be the corpse, because being dead didn't require any effort. Of course, her sisters and their mates usually got what they wanted, so she had only played the cadaver once – lying on the warm soil, cardigan slung over her face, half dozing in the heat while Jess and Helen and three or so friends knelt around her and chanted. Welcome to the House of Levitation. This girl looks ill, this girl is ill, this girl looks dead, this girl is dead. And then suddenly she was up in the air, weightless, high above the heads of the chanting mourners, a fleeting sensation of flight and brilliant white light before she had looked down, screamed and fallen back to earth. She wasn't sure what she had experienced, but she couldn't dispel the nagging unease, the pull. Her hand touched the birthmark on the side of her face.

'What was the final line of that chant?' Jess asked.

'Light as a feather,' Sam said. 'Stiff as a board.'

'Weird.' Jess's eyes were fixed on Jim's headstone. 'Perhaps he is still here. Hanging around, unable to leave and rest in peace. Maybe something is weighing him down.'

The crow squatting on the rowan cawed, irritated, flew away.

Sam said, 'Do you ever see Jim?'

'What do you mean?' Helen demanded.

'Do you ever catch a glimpse of him in the street or propping up a bar somewhere?'

'No. I don't see him.' Jess narrowed her eyes. 'Do you?'

Sam let the smoke drift out of her open mouth, curl away. 'No.'

'So why did you ask if we had seen him?' Helen said.

'Just making conversation.'

'God, I'd hate to be stuck with you at a party.'

Sam wriggled her hand in her pocket, felt the soft corner of the police diary, removed and placed it gently on the ground in front of the headstone.

'What's that?'

'One of Jim's diaries.'

'Is that a good idea?'

She blanked her sisters' glares, stared at the diary, black rectangle against the brown earth, closed book. She searched for something to say, the right words, but they didn't come. Neither of her sisters spoke. They stood heads bowed by the grave and only the rooks could be heard. Eventually Helen said, 'Some things in this life will never be resolved. And Jim is one of them.'

Sam saw then that Helen had tears tracking down her face and so did Jess. They were as bad as her, if not worse. As bad as Jim. Never judge a Coyle by their cover. She thought Helen was about to let rip and bawl, but she held it in, wiped her cheek and said, 'I've had enough of this bollocks. Let's go.'

Helen looped her arm through Jess's and walked away from the grave. Sam slunk behind, dragging her feet through the deserted churchyard, her mind on the rotting corpses beneath, liquid mulch, pondering the half-life of a dead undercover cop, the toxicity of his remains.

'Sam, I'm talking to you.' Helen was scowling at her.

'Sorry. Somewhere else.'

'I was saying I'm off to Ibiza in a couple of days.'

'Oh. Holiday?'

'No. I'm setting up shop. There are all these new nightclubs opening over there. So I'm going to sell clubbing clothes to everybody who lost their suitcase at the airport.'

'Good idea. You should do a deal with the baggage handlers – share of the profit.'

'I don't think the baggage handlers need any encouragement from me to mislay suitcases. What are you doing now anyway? I thought you were going down to the coast. Weren't you supposed to be driving down with your boyfriend, old what's-his-face?'

'Luke.'

'Yes, him. Leftie Luke. What's happened to that plan?'

'I'm meeting him at six.'

'Isn't six a bit late?'

'Evening is the best time down there.'

'Really?'

Jess was assessing her sceptically now as well. Jess liked Luke; she thought he was good-looking and funny, but all men were congenital wankers in Jess's book, genetically programmed to think with their dicks, so best to keep expectations low to avoid disappointment. She didn't buy Sam's attempts to explain her relationship with Luke as meaningful, based on shared interests, a deep bond. More than sex. They passed under the lychgate.

'So which beach are you going to then?' Helen asked.

'Dungeness.'

'The one with the power station?'

Sam nodded.

'Dungeness,' said Jess. 'Isn't that the place where your housemate, what's his name, works? The one who fancies you.'

'Dave,' said Sam. 'He doesn't fancy me. He was my housemate, but he's gone to Norfolk for six months and he never worked in the power station. He used to be attached to the experimental research station next to the power station.'

'Research station. Power station. Same difference,' Jess said.

'No it isn't.'

'What are you going to do in Dungeness anyway?' Helen asked.

'Hang out a bit, have a drink. Look at the stars. Camp somewhere.'

'Why Dungeness?' There was an edge to Helen's tone.

'I like it there.'

Helen pulled her you're-a-crazy face.

'And there's a good place to buy fish and chips nearby,' Sam added.

'You're up to something.'

'No.'

'One of your political protests. Ban the bomb. You and leftie Luke.'

Helen gave the two fingers pointing I'm-watching-you gesture. 'I hope you're not thinking of doing anything stupid.'

Everybody was on her case today. First Liz and now Helen.

'I'm just spending the evening with Luke.'

'You're a useless liar.'

'I'm not lying.'

'Well, I hope Luke turns up. Because otherwise you're going to be pretty bloody miserable sitting on a stony beach in front of a nuclear power station with nothing but a portion of chips for company. Dungeness is such a scuzzy hole, even if the power station did explode it wouldn't make much difference. It already looks like a bomb hit it.'

'That's why I like it.'

They had reached the camper van. Jess stopped, hand on van door. 'You know, I'm not sure it's clever to leave that diary on the grave. Somebody might pick it up.'

'It didn't have much in it. A couple of doodles.'

'It makes me uneasy.'

Sam was about to argue, took a deep breath and realized it was stupid. She obviously wasn't thinking straight.

'You're right. Bad idea. I'll run back.'

She took the mossy path along the east side of the church, rounded the corner and spotted a movement, a flicker among the silver birches on the graveyard's southern edge. She halted. Silence. Yet she could sense a presence. She checked over her shoulder: nothing apart from the ghosts of her imagination and a spit of rain. She stepped cautiously, skirted the grassy hummocks, the diary in view now, lying in front of Jim's headstone. Exactly the same place as she had left it. Except it was open, its black leather cover uppermost, spread-eagled, fallen angel's wings. She had closed it when she placed it on his grave. She glanced around the limestone crosses, searched the dark spaces between the bone-white birch trunks. A shadow danced. She edged nearer the graveyard gate. A rabbit darted out from the trees, raced across the field, running for its life. Behind – a weasel, long and brown, gaining on its prey. The rabbit circled, searching for its burrow, confused by the hunter's zig-zag tactics. The weasel lunged. The rabbit screamed. High-pitched. Tortured. Sam covered her ears. Couldn't bear it. Stop. Stop. Let it be over. Quickly. The screaming subsided. The rabbit and weasel had vanished, the field returned to emerald tranquillity.

She walked back to Jim's grave, legs unsteady, raindrops stinging. She stooped, snatched the diary and examined the pages at which it had been left open. The week beginning 4 June 1984, about three weeks before Jim had died. There was something written in Jim's unmistakable spidery handwriting. 6 June. *Meet Flint 9 p.m.* In a pub, if she knew anything about her father. And below the scrawl one of Jim's doodles. What was it? He wasn't very good at drawing. A lolly on a stick? She stared at the page, squeezed her eyes, took a deep breath, inhaled something sweet, a fleeting sense of childhood fear, squirming, caught on a creepy man's gaze. She retched. Jim had drawn a stick of candyfloss. Now she had identified the doodle, there was no mistaking it. Jesus. She jammed the diary in her pocket, strode through the graveyard, the camper van in sight parked beside an oak tree. Habit. That was where they always parked when they took George for a walk in the woods. That was where they had parked the day of the Beltane fair, the day Jim vanished and the candy man had tried to stop her leaving: 1 May 1978. She'd worried he was a murderer, or a terrorist perhaps. The candy man, that was what Jim called him, a fucking evil bastard. *Meet Flint 9 p.m.* Was that the candy man's real name, Flint? Had Jim contacted the candy man in 1984, a couple of weeks before he was killed? What had he been playing at? She shouldn't be asking herself these questions. She didn't want to know. Fuck it. She had to block it. It didn't make any difference now. Jim was dead. Finished. Who cared now what he was up to in his last few weeks on earth? She shivered. She would be relieved to hook up with Luke, he would lighten her mood, stop her slipping into the past.

CHAPTER 2

SHE LAY ON the beach, ahead the retreating tide, and behind the marshland stretching away for ever. Only the power station radiated colour, its amber light an artificial sun in the dusk. She summoned Luke's image in her mind – easy smile, scruffy curls, sea-green eyes – and willed him to appear. She lifted her head, searched the shore, but all she could see were the ribcage hulls of long-abandoned boats. Luke wasn't there. Where was he? Why hadn't he turned up?

Luke loved Dungeness as much as she did, although it wasn't her who had sparked his interest in its desolate charm. It was Dave, her housemate, who had enticed Luke south with his descriptions of the power station on the shifting beach, the bleak magic of the shore. Luke and she had driven down with Dave one weekend in January. In retrospect, it was that trip to Dungeness that had sealed the awkward angles of the triangle. Dave was her friend, and she was happy that Luke and Dave got on so well, but Dave's unexpected snappiness with her that day on the beach suggested the truth of the old adage – two's company, three's a crowd. Jess was right even if she didn't like to admit it; Dave probably did fancy her. After that trip, she and Luke drove down to Dungeness by themselves, drawn back by the winter walks along the wind-blasted shore. The idea of a protest had come later, with the spring.

The original plan for this weekend had been for Sam and

Luke to drive down together. Luke was going to wait in the van while Sam went to the graveyard with Jess and Helen – he didn't want to intrude on a family occasion – and then on to Dungeness. A treat to lift her spirits. Another recce of the power station, an evening on the beach together, catch the sea bass that swam close to the shore in the warmer months. She was a vegetarian, but Luke had persuaded her to eat the fish he snagged, blackened on a makeshift barbecue when the weather allowed. The plan had changed at short notice that morning. He had called from a phone box. She could hear the conversation in her head, she had replayed it to herself countless times throughout the day.

'Sam, I'm here. I'm in Dungeness.'

'Oh. You're there already?'

'I've just driven down.'

'I thought we were driving down together.'

'I know. Something has come up. I'm really sorry. I didn't want to call you before I set off, it was too early. I've had an unexpected stroke of luck. A contact.'

'Contact? Power station?'

'Yes. I'll tell you about it later.'

'OK.'

'I'm going to meet him in fifteen minutes.'

'Sounds interesting.'

'I hope so. Let's meet at six. The usual place. I'll be waiting for you. I'll get a fire going.'

'OK. Six.'

'Sam, I'm really sorry. I don't like leaving you to drive down by yourself, but this is important.'

'I know, don't worry. The drive doesn't matter. I've done it by myself before.'

'It's a difficult day for you. I'll make it up to you.'

'Stop apologizing. Really it's fine. Six. See you later.'

'See you.'

She had put the phone down, and if she had felt a twinge of anxiety at all, it was because he was doing something without her. Not that she would have admitted it to him, because she didn't want to appear clingy.

The darkness was thickening. She sat up, listened to the waves chafing the pebbles, wind chimes carried on the breeze, the low hum of the power station. Slices of light fell from the windows of the experimental research lab where Dave had been based when he was doing his thesis. One of Dave's old egghead friends, she reckoned, pulling a late-night writing stint. No other signs of life. No footsteps. No headlights tracking along the road. No Luke. She dug her fingernails into her arm, glanced at her watch. Five hours measured in ten-minute intervals of time checking. She had sprinted to the rusted phone box by the pub every half hour and called his home number to see if he had returned to London. But nobody had picked up, not even his obnoxious housemate Spyder. The sun had dropped and the band of crimson sky behind the power station had broadened. Red. Violet. Indigo. She hadn't even had the sense to buy some fish and chips before the pub stopped serving food. You had to be hardy to survive in this environment, Dave had told her when he introduced her to Dungeness, and he pointed to the salt-eaten sea kale that topped the ridges, long black roots searching for moisture. She used to consider herself a survivor, but she was no longer so certain; she couldn't sit there much longer, on this barren beach with only the cries of the oyster-catchers for company.

She skidded down the shingle. Out in the Channel, ghostly terns flitted around the boil – the warm-water discharge from the power station. She crouched, selected a flat pebble, rusty brown, leaking warmth in her palm, high iron content perhaps. Radioactive? Not possible. She dropped it anyway, selected another, held it horizontally between her thumb and index finger. She had always been useless at skimming stones; they invariably sank on first contact, an inconsequential inability that had riled Jim. She curved her hand inwards. Jim sneered. *Not like that. Flick. Not throw. You cack-handed lummox.*

She flung the stone. It scudded, fizzed, then sank. Her father scoffed. She ignored him. She didn't want Jim occupying her mind, dragging her into the shadows, reminding her of his paranoid undercover world, making her worry about Luke when there was undoubtedly a simple explanation for his non-appearance. She twisted around and yelled into the night.

'Leave me alone.'

Her words were consumed by the slope behind. She stooped, groped for a rock, lifted it, hurled it at the waves, smiled as it landed with a satisfying splash and thud.

'Fuck you, Jim Coyle.'

An emerald moth flitted past her face. She blinked and as she brushed away the fragile wings, the scrunch of footfall caught her attention. Luke. He must have heard her shouting. She had been waiting at the wrong spot. He was searching for her.

'Over here.'

She ran in the direction of the advancing figure, stumbled on the pebbles rolling beneath her feet.

'It's me. It's Sam.'

Her eyes could see it wasn't Luke before her brain was prepared to acknowledge that the scrawny figure sloping along the beach was not her boyfriend. Not Luke, but as he neared, she realized she knew him. She smiled, tried to cover her dismay at finding he was not the person she was hoping to see. He spoke first.

'We've met. Nukiller trains.'

She was flattered by his recognition; she was more likely to remember other people's faces than they were to remember hers these days. She had become invisible since Jim's death, saying nothing and disappearing.

'Nukiller trains,' she said. 'That's right. The meetings.'

The meetings had been Luke's idea. Luke had talked it through with Dave, because Dave had contacts in Greenpeace and he knew about the power station. Dave had said, in his usual dismissive way, that he didn't think a protest would achieve much, but he could put Luke in touch with a couple of people if he thought it would help. Luke had sweet-talked the landlord of the local pub, persuaded him to let them use the back room. They had stuck up posters and dished out a few flyers in the insular towns scattered around the marsh. Lydd. New Romney. Rye. The meeting had attracted only a handful of people and over half of those had been from the archaeology group Sam had joined the previous June when she first came down to Dungeness with Dave. Not much local interest in protesting against a power station that provided jobs.

The man with the beaky nose and black ponytail had slipped into the back of the room late, unnoticed except by her, because she was sitting at the front, her mind wandering while Luke held the floor. His oily fisherman's jumper sagged off his bony frame and gave him the appearance of a scarecrow. At the end of the meeting, as everybody was shuffling around to leave, he had stood and announced he was there because he wanted to protect the ancient powers of the land from the destructive evils of capitalism and the nuclear industry. Luke rolled his eyes. After the meeting, Luke said he distrusted ageing hippies, the sixties generation who talked about revolution and the dawning of a new age while amassing personal fortunes from selling industrially produced natural products to the gullible and guilty middle classes. Softy sell-outs. Luke was concerned that the hippy's rambling might put other, saner people off – he wanted to stick to the science. She was less doctrinaire than Luke. She saw magic in a kestrel swooping and didn't see a contradiction between matters of science and the soul. Nature was her spiritual retreat, an escape from her own darkness, solid and real when all else around her vanished. And anyway, she nursed her private, nagging preoccupation with the occult, her dog-eared copy of *Daemonologie* always close to hand.

The hippy had reappeared at the second meeting in early May. The room was packed this time – Chernobyl had done a better job of attracting people than their posters. He spoke again. The waste transportation routes were negative leylines, he said, emitting bad energy, destroying the earth's natural magic. People nodded politely. Luke repeated the rational arguments, the risks of nuclear waste transportation, the impacts of exposure to radiation. Accidents happened at nuclear power stations – look at Chernobyl – so why should anybody believe the promises that transportation of nuclear waste was safe? He proposed a local protest at the railhead where the spent fuel rod containers were transferred from the lorries with their sinister black and yellow radioactive symbol to the train heading north to the Sellafield reprocessing plant. A small crowd, a few placards and, if they were lucky, a journo from the local newspaper. There wasn't much debate; everybody was in favour of the protest. Why not? It didn't require much effort, there was nothing illegal about it. The lorries weren't even well guarded. After the meeting, she and Luke had joked about the hippy and his leylines. But in her head, she had marked him down as interesting, tried to classify him. Two types of dark worshipper existed, according to King James and his *Daemonologie*: the treacherous witches that he despised so much and who were nearly always women, and then the male practitioners of magic – the Magi and necromancers who studied the heavenly sciences and summoned the dead. She had decided that the hippy was a Magus.

Up close, his eyes were solid black, iris and pupil indistinguishable. Stoned, undoubtedly, but something deeper there as well, a magnetic pull.

'Are you...' The endings of his words dragged. 'OK?'

She nodded, wiped her nose on her finger, sussed him out over the white line of her hand. About the same age as her father, she reckoned. Late forties. Or, at least, about the same age her father would have been if he were still alive.

'I thought you were somebody else,' she said.

He seemed thrown by her statement – as if he half thought he was somebody else too – and he turned away, waved his hand at the silver Channel. 'I'd be a bit careful down here at night. It can be confusing, the sand, the water. And the tide is...' His sentence drifted off.

'I'm not staying much longer. I just came down to see a friend.' She was wary of giving too much away. 'I'm driving back to London soon.'

He nodded. 'Would you like a cup of tea before you set off?'

Now she was thrown – the prosaic nature of the offer, the prospect of being alone at night with a man she hardly knew. What if he was a nutter?

'It's OK, thanks. I'm fine.'

'If you change your mind, I live...' He pointed north along the shore. 'The cabin with the grey window frames.'

He stepped away, respecting her space and solitude, she noted. She was the only nutter on the beach – shouting at the shingle, waiting for her boyfriend to turn up. She could do with a cup of tea. She had often wondered what the clapboard fishermen's cabins were like inside and, anyway, he wasn't a complete stranger; she'd met him twice before.

'Hang on a moment. I'll come with you.'

She ran after him.

'Alastair,' he said.

She was disappointed; she had half hoped he would be called something more romantic. Eagle. River. Thunder.

He said, 'It's easier to walk along the low tide mark, where the shingle turns to sand.' His drawl contained the trace of a Cornish burr. 'People used to wear flat wooden clogs so they could walk across the stones. Back-stays.'

She grinned, relaxed. She liked a bit of history, so long as it wasn't hers. So did he, it seemed: he reached the ends of his sentences when he talked about the past. He gestured at a rotting boat, beached above the high tide mark like a decomposing whale.

'There's been a fishing community here for centuries. There's never been a harbour, though. The boats are hauled across the shingle. The fishermen stayed here in the winter then sailed round the coast to East Anglia for the summer. They had fishing rights there too. Den and strand. Rights to land and dry their nets on the beach.'

'Do you fish?'

'Me? No. I wouldn't know where to start. The only time I've caught anything is when I won a goldfish at a fair when I was a kid.'

He turned inland, treading an iron boat rail track embedded in the stones, the path marked by bleached driftwood spears, shards of twisted metal. They clambered over the ridges until they were on the flatter ground where the shingle was

45

carpeted with prostrate broom and the beach blurred with flotsam gardens: poppies, blue glass floats, gale-battered roses, red-capped gnomes. They reached a black plank-clad cabin, its sombre windows overlooking the sea, bamboo wind chimes clinking in the breeze.

'Have you lived here long?'

'About a year. I rent it from an old lady, a fisherman's widow. She moved to a care home after she had a fall. She's not ready to sell the place yet.'

A rusty can with a long nozzle had been placed in front of the door.

She pointed. 'What's that?'

'It's a funt. A smuggler's lamp. You only see the light when you are looking directly at the spout. You can make Morse code signals with your hand. Places that are good for fishermen are good for smugglers. If you can land a fishing boat you can land a carrier.'

Smuggling. Drugs. Of course, that made sense – he was a small-time drug dealer, she reckoned; how else would an ageing hippy make a living out here at the end of the world if he knew nothing about fishing?

He said, 'I use the funt to let people know whether I'm in or not. If it's out the front, they can knock on the door; if it's round the back, I'm not at home.'

He produced a key from a pocket, twisted it in the mortise. 'I don't know why I bother locking up. The back door is buggered. Anybody could walk in that way if they felt like it. It's the damp rot. The older cabins are made from driftwood – some of the timbers must be ancient, reused down the centuries.'

He reached for a paraffin lamp hanging on a hook by the door, struck a match, twiddled the wick. The light guttered, flicked shadows around the timbered walls.

'The storm last week,' he said. 'It knocked my power out and nobody has been round to repair it. It's ironic, living next to a power station and being without...'

She finished his sentence. 'Electricity.'

'I'll put the kettle on. Milk?'

'Yes please. No sugar. Thanks.'

He walked through an arch to a tiny galley kitchen, sent the gas whooshing as he ignited the stove. She stood still and listened to the noises of the night; wind sighing under the floorboards, gulls crying, and then another sound she couldn't identify. Tap tap tap. Silence. Tap tap again, this time on the other side of the room. A call and answer. Alastair seemed oblivious, he was gazing out the back window, head haloed by the solar glow of the power station. The tap tap ceased. Ancient timbers creaking in the wind perhaps.

She surveyed the shadowed room; wooden apple crates and cardboard boxes stacked against one wall as if he had only just moved in, or was forever poised to pack up and run. Not much furniture apart from a couple of chairs and a hefty oak desk strewn with notebooks, magazines, glass ashtray probably swiped from the pub. A school science lab test tube rack complete with six cork-stoppered test tubes sat awkwardly among the papers. Amateur drug-making kit? Best not to ask. He walked through from the kitchen holding two steaming mugs and she looked away from the desk, didn't want him to catch her staring at his equipment.

'Death watch,' he said.

She twitched.

'Tap tap.'

'Oh. Death watch beetles. The tapping.'

'Yeah, they only call each other in the evenings. It's the old timbers, damp wood – an ideal home for death watch beetles.'

'Does the lady who owns the place know she's infested?'

'I don't think it's worth bothering her. You can have death watch for centuries before the timbers collapse. She'll be long gone before this place crumbles. Sometimes it's easier not to know.'

She parked herself in a dilapidated armchair by a makeshift splintery crate table, its surface cluttered with animal remains: a line of bleached bird skulls and a selection of feathered wings, carefully arranged in descending size order. Below the wings, an unmacerated skeleton of some unidentifiable small animal, the bones still fused, shreds of skin and cartilage attached. She poked the pile with a finger, flinched at the feel of the rubbery flesh. He walked over, removed the decaying carcass and placed it in his pocket before he set her cup down in the space he had cleared.

'It's a toad,' he said. 'I'm gonna leave the bones outside so the ants can strip them clean.'

She pulled a face.

He said, 'It was dead already. Like the birds.' He gestured at the beaky skulls and wings. 'I find lots of dead birds out on the marsh. I don't know what it is about the marshlands, they attract death. That's where the toad came from too – caught by a crow most likely – they can't stomach the skins. Toads taste as bad as they look. The crows only eat the innards. Even rats leave the skin of the toad.'

'Why do you want the bones?'

'I'll wait for a full moon and throw them in a stream. That's how the Toad Men acquired their magic powers.'

'Toad Men?'

'Old English sorcerers.'

Toad Men. Sorcerers. She had been right, he was a Magus, a practitioner of the occult. Her hand went to her birthmark.

She retracted it when she realized what she was doing, hoped he hadn't noticed.

'White or black magic?' she asked.

'Toad Men? They could be either. That's the thing with magic, the ancient powers. You can start off with good intentions, but you get drawn in, you have to defend yourself against the accusations and curses, find some way of turning them around, reversing them, and before you know it, you are on the dark side.'

He caught her eye. She looked away.

'It goes with the territory,' he said. 'You have to learn to live with it.' He retreated to the chair at his desk. 'Anybody who thinks life is black and white is kidding themselves anyway. Nothing is ever that clear.' He blew the steaming vapours across his mug and stared at its contents; a scryer searching for prophecies and omens in the tannin liquid. She selected one of the wings from his crate-top collection and examined its golden topside, ran her fingers over the outer blades, the comblike edge of the outermost feather. Barn owl, she decided, designed for silent, ghostlike flight. She brushed its downy softness against her cheek, realized Alastair had finished examining his cup and was watching her. She replaced the wing on the crate hastily.

'Spliff?' he asked.

She nodded. He opened a drawer, removed a plastic bag of weed and Rizlas, rolled in silence, flicked a lighter, leaned back in his chair and inhaled. The smoke gathered, hung around his brow. He flipped the joint, angled the roach to her. She inhaled, exhaled. Inhaled again. The weed hit her harder than she had expected. The room pitched, the cabin like a gently rocking boat, becalmed in mid-channel, going nowhere.

'Good stuff,' he said.

He twisted the silver skull ring on his left index finger, tipped his head at her coat, the Che Guevara badge she had fished out from the bag of her dad's belongings and pinned to her lapel above her nuclear power no thanks badge.

'Revolution,' he said.

There was something odd about the way he was looking at the badge, as if he could divine that she'd nabbed it from the dressing-up box of a dead undercover cop. The dope was adding to her paranoia.

'I reckon you've got the powers.' He rocked back in his seat, assessed her. 'I can sense that kind of thing.'

His observation took her by surprise; she opened her mouth to speak, emitted a puff of smoke.

He said, 'Some people don't know they've got them. I've known since I was a kid. I hear the voices. Calling me from the other side.'

A cold breeze brushed her neck.

'You can't deny the powers – all you can do is try to master them, otherwise they can be dangerous. You have to learn the techniques – sorcery, witchcraft. A spirit guide can help.' He lifted his head, gazed into space. 'We live with the dead. The ghosts walk among us. Some people are just better at seeing it than others.'

And as he spoke, the House of Levitation filled her head, the day of the corpse, crossing the threshold, bright light, flight, cold air on her skin. She could hear the dead calling, see the hands reaching. He was right; the ghosts were always present.

'I have a spirit guide,' Alastair continued. 'A person. It doesn't have to be a person, though; could be a bird, an animal of some sort. You need another being outside your head who can help you channel what's going on inside. Show you the way. Something to give you focus.'

Focus. She had to focus. Stop her mind wandering. She concentrated and gold-tinged wings fluttered in front of her eyes.

'If I had a spirit guide it would be a bird,' she said.

'I knew it. An owl, I bet.'

Good guesser.

He bent forwards. 'Let your mind travel; wherever it goes, your body can follow.'

She leaned away.

'So who is your spirit guide?' she asked.

'John Allin. He was a philosopher of the occult. A seventeenth-century sorcerer.'

A spider dropped from nowhere, landed on her hand, then launched away on a gossamer thread and disappeared.

'How did you find Allin?'

'I didn't. He found me. That's how it happens. You can't go looking, but you can't stop it either.' He nodded at her. 'Like you and the barn owl.'

Barn owl? She hadn't told him she was thinking about a barn owl. He must have seen her fondling the wing.

'I was at the local records office when it happened, searching for stuff about witchcraft trials. I got chatting to the librarian, and she dug out this box of old court papers. Accusations of maleficence – women turning their neighbours' milk sour, widows cursing newborns, cavorting with their familiars.' He pressed his chin with his index finger. His nails were long. 'At the bottom of the box I found a bundle of letters, each one sealed with a red wax skull and crossbones. Memento mori. I touched the seal, rubbed the skull, and I felt a presence.'

She jumped; a tingle on her arm, a fingertip running over her skin. She looked for a spider, but there was nothing.

'Did you sense something?' he asked. 'Somebody touching you?'

'No.' She rubbed her arm. 'So the letters were from John Allin?'

'Yes.'

'Did he live in Dungeness?'

'He lived near here. He was a dissenting priest in Rye during the Civil War, the years of Cromwell's Commonwealth. This area was a hotbed of radicalism, power to the people. These things, they go hand in hand. Dissent, smuggling, sorcery, witchcraft – rebellion. When the monarchy was restored after the Civil War was over, Allin had to go on the run. He disappeared in London, Southwark.'

His head was nodding to a silent beat, as if he had a Bob Dylan track playing in his brain, a hard rain's a gonna fall.

'1665. That was when the plague hit town. People thought it was a curse, blowback from the attempted revolution. Punishment from an authoritarian divinity for daring to rebel.'

'The Empire Strikes Back.'

He smiled. 'Exactly.' He toked, blew grey smoke slowly. 'Allin worked as a physician, a plague doctor.'

She pictured a caped figure in a black-beaked mask, a crow-man in a darkened street of red-cross-marked doors. She shook her head, trying to rid herself of the image, uncertain where it had come from.

'Allin concocted pills and medicines. But his real skills were on the mystical side. He had a gift for magic: seeing spirits, reading the signs, alchemy.'

She coughed, the dense fug of the spliff too much, reached for the barn owl's wing, fanned the air.

He said, 'That which is below is like that which is above, and that which is above is like that which is below. Hermes Trismegistus, the *Emerald Tablet*, the source of all alchemical wisdom, the godfather of science.'

She was finding it hard to follow his thread. 'The godfather of science?'

'Newton had a translation of the *Emerald Tablet*. He knew its importance, understanding the rules, the patterns that shape and govern.'

His drawl lulled her, his words washed around her brain.

'We are a microcosm of the universe. We are made of the same matter. Master ourselves, master the universe.'

Her head drooped, the owl's wing slipped, fell on the floor. She snapped back to her surroundings. He was still talking.

'Alchemy is the transformation to a higher plane. Purification.'

She managed to formulate a sentence in her head and transfer it to her mouth. 'I thought alchemists were interested in making gold.'

'Well, making gold from base metal was a means to an end. The real prize was spiritual growth, mastery of the supernatural powers governing ourselves and the universe. Allin was searching for spiritual cleansing and healing to soothe the pain of the failed revolution here on earth. Alchemy was the opposite of black magic, it was about purification, positive transformation.'

His features tensed, he raised a dirt-scuffed warning finger. 'Of course, alchemy is no different from any other of the occult arts. Once you unleash the powers, they can be flipped, used for malign purposes. What starts off as a blessing may become a curse.'

The word *curse* stirred her. 'Reverse alchemy,' she said.

He nodded. 'The downward spiral. The sinistral spin. That's when the spiritual becomes separated from the material, we lose control and become corrupted. The darkness takes over.'

He lifted a glass test tube from the school science rack,

chucked it in the air so it twisted, glinted in the flicker of the hurricane lamp, round and up, floated above the smoke cloud for a few seconds then flipped and plummeted, down and down. He didn't move and she thought he was going to let it smash, but he stuck his hand out at the last moment and caught it, cradled the vial in his palm.

'How do you contact Allin?' she asked.

'He comes and he goes. I can't always command it. Like a signal, an interference in my mind. Sometimes his voice is flaky and I can't tell what he's after. Sometimes it's clear. Insistent. When people are in trouble of some kind or another...' He stretched out an arm, selected a white tern's wing from the avian ossuary on the crate, fanned it in front of his face, scrutinized her through the wafting grey vapour. 'Do you want me to see if I can contact him for you?'

She folded her legs up in the chair, feet on seat. 'No thanks. I'm fine.'

She grabbed her mug of tea, slurped, swished the tepid liquid around her mouth, swallowed, conscious of the noises she was making.

'You've lost something,' he said. 'I can sense it.'

She shook her head, alarmed at his clairvoyance.

'Seriously. Maybe I can help. What are you searching for?'

She squirmed around in the chair, tried not to watch the white wing fluttering, and then she thought, why not give it a go. Perhaps he could help.

'A person actually.'

'Oh? Who?'

'Luke. My boyfriend. I was supposed to meet him down here this evening and he hasn't materialized.'

'Luke. The guy who organized the meetings?'

'Yes.'

'He's your boyfriend?'

'Yes.'

'You were supposed to be meeting him this evening?'

'Yes. We were going to drive down together but then something came up.'

'Drive? Did he drive down alone then?'

'Yes.' His questions irritated her, she couldn't see the need for his tone of surprise. 'He drove down this morning. I was going to meet him on the beach at six, but he didn't turn up. Misunderstanding, I think.'

'Misunderstanding, yeah, must have been.'

He sounded wary now. Uncomfortable. He thought she'd been stood up, she was sure. She wanted to correct him, let him know it was nothing like that. 'We missed each other. He must have had a different meeting place in mind.' She was annoyed with herself for blurting, her voice cracked with emotion.

'A different meeting place,' he repeated. 'Of course. Let me see if Allin can help.'

He took a deep breath, flicked the white wing in front of his face in rhythmic sweeps, stared at her through the feathers, mumbled, 'He's not on the beach. He is somewhere else.'

'Sorry?'

'He's in another place.' He paused. Flicked the wing. 'I can see a boat.'

Her stomach tightened, her eyes caught his; all pupil, no iris.

'A boat?' she demanded. 'Where?'

He fanned the wing again, stalled, looked embarrassed. She wondered whether Allin had let him down this time, failed to deliver any useful information.

'On the flatland.' He whispered the words.

'The flatland? The marsh?' A starburst flashed in her head, she shouted, 'The Lookers' Hut.'

Obvious. Now she understood. The Lookers' Hut on Romney Marsh, that's what Luke meant when he said they should meet at the usual place. Not the beach.

'I can taste saltwater,' he said.

She wasn't listening, eager to leave and drive to their secret camping spot, filled with a certainty Luke was waiting for her there. Alastair replaced the wing among his table-top mortuary, carefully avoided her eye.

'Did that help?'

'Well, you confirmed what I half knew anyway.'

He smiled, seemingly relieved by her answer.

'Sure. Communicating with the spirits is almost a way of accessing the subconscious. Our sixth sense. Things we instinctively know to be true but can't trust ourselves to believe.'

She couldn't be bothered with any more dope-fuelled hocus-pocus, she was back on firm ground, wanted to get going, find Luke.

'I see what you mean. Thanks.'

'No problem.'

'I'd better be leaving. Check out the Lookers' Hut. It's where we usually go.'

'You're going to the marsh now?'

'Yes.'

'In the dark?' He wrung his hands. 'No, don't do that. Crash here if you like. Wait until morning.'

She stood, her legs wobbled. 'I'll be fine. Thanks.'

'You can come back if you don't find him.' There was something pleading about his tone that put her on edge. What was he after?

'I know my way around the marsh,' she said. 'I'm not scared of the dark.'

He gave her a tentative nod, shrugged, crossed to the door,

held it open. A low black car was parked outside the next cabin along the track – a scarab in a clump of viper's bugloss.

'Porsche,' he said. 'I've seen it a couple of times recently. There's lots of new money around here these days. Dungeness is becoming too fashionable for the likes of me. Time to be moving on.'

He hunched his shoulders and stuck his hands in the front pockets of his fading jeans.

'Remember,' he said. 'You got the power, you just gotta learn to channel it. Don't forget the barn owl.'

'Right.' She smiled glibly.

'The birthmark,' he said. 'I spotted it. You can't escape your legacy.'

She opened her mouth, couldn't find a response, turned and walked away.

CHAPTER 3

SHE HAD LEFT the camper van in the pub car park, Belisha beacon tangerine in the darkness. She clipped a kerb as she swung on to the road and headed north into the marsh, her head more befogged than she had realized. She wound the window down to clear her brain, inhaled sea air – brine, kelp, dead fish – and saw stars reflected in the obsidian waters of the flooded gravel pits. Her eyes drooped, lids dope-heavy, the tarmac dissolved in the lapping roadside shrubs. Bright light behind made her start. She gripped the wheel, blinded by the dazzle, swerved, left tyre hitting uneven verge, van tipping at a mad angle before she found the tarmac again. She slowed, allowed the black Porsche to overtake, a fleeting impression of a thick neck and a shaved head behind the steering wheel as the driver sped away. Jerk. Probably the Porsche from the spit; there weren't that many flash cars down here, whatever Alastair's concerns about the tide of new money. Most of the marsh was takeaway and trailer-park country. Isolated, run-down houses with Alsatian dogs, pick-up trucks and boundaries marked by chainlink fences to keep out the bleakness. Southern badlands, nothing quaint nor pretty here. An owl shrieked as she crossed the Rhee Wall causeway into the waterlogged meadows of Romney Marsh. Alastair was right, at night the marsh felt like a place where death hung close – spirits easily summoned from the drifting vapours and black waters. She had said she wasn't scared of the dark, but she hadn't been out on the marsh at night before without Luke, and now she was travelling alone through its morbid contours.

She pulled up by the narrow turfed bridge, certain she would see Luke's dented blue Polo squatting on the tyre-rutted verge. It wasn't there. He could have parked on the other side of the field for some reason. She checked her pocket for her torch and pen-knife – the talismans she always carried – then fished around in the back of the van for her sleeping bag, water bottle. She stood and listened: sheep bleating, breeze rustling the willows, toads croaking. She knew in her gut she wouldn't find Luke waiting for her in the Lookers' Hut. She half wished she'd taken up Alastair's offer and stayed at his place, left it until first light to look for Luke. Too late, she was here now. She might as well investigate, see if there were any signs that he had been there earlier.

The Lookers' Hut was in a field surrounded by deep drainage ditches – sewers they were called locally – treacherous at night unless you knew where you were going. The barn owl swept over her head as she crossed the bridge, quartered the meadow, flying low, top-heavy body transformed in flight to silent grace. She held the owl in her mind, focused. For a moment she floated, looked down on the marsh from above; the silky backs of bats falling away as they swooped above the grid of water channels, wheat fields criss-crossed with muddy tractor trails. An emerald glint caught her eye – what was it? The roof of a car? She couldn't see clearly and felt herself falling. The night engulfed the barn owl and she released the bird from her mind. She fumbled with the torch. The thin beam cut a path through scattering lambs to the blackthorn-shrouded island rising from the meadow.

She had discovered the dilapidated shepherds' huts through the archaeological group she had joined the previous June – nudged, in some way, by the hand of her father. Archaeology was the career that Jim had suggested the night before he died.

Digging up ancient bones in the middle of nowhere, he said, had to be more rewarding than dealing with the skeletons in the office cupboard. The first time she travelled down to Dungeness with Dave to visit his research lab she had gone for a walk across the marsh while he yacked with his mates. She had spotted the line of cagouled figures pacing a fallow meadow, bamboo canes in hands, heads down, and thought it was a police search – murder, missing person. Curious, she had asked what they were doing. A woman said they were field walkers, looking for artefacts, signs of a medieval site below, and had invited Sam to join the higgledy line. Coins, cheap brooches, worked stones, bottles, buttons, pottery sherds, all churned up and thrown together on the meadow's surface. The mishmash of old and new had intrigued her; the ghosts and relics lying among the mundane and modern. After that day, she had travelled down with Dave regularly so she could join their excavations – a way of staying sane and maintaining her academic interests in the year out from her history degree.

When the weather became too bad for digging, she had initiated her own project – mapping the remains of the Lookers' Huts. It had become something of an obsession. The Lookers' Huts had first sprung up in the seventeenth century when nobody dared live in the malaria-infested lowlands. The isolated buildings provided shelter for the shepherds who had to keep an eye on the flocks during the lambing season. They were simple structures – red brick, rectangular, one room, one window, one door. Sam suspected the simplicity was deceptive; she reckoned they were two-faced – sheltering the Lookers while they watched the flocks, but also providing cover for late-night deals with the smugglers – owlers – who ran the wool to France.

This hut, the one she camped in with Luke, was more complete than most; roofless and open to the sky, but its wooden frames weren't rotten and the walls were complete, breaking the bitter winds that swept in from the sea. She pushed her way through the nettles, paused on the threshold and cast the beam around the bare earth floor. No Luke. Her light swept the ash and charred branches of their successive campfires, illuminated the willow stems drooping through the glassless window, the dark corners. Maybe Luke had waited here for an hour or so then driven home when he realized she wasn't going to appear. She sighed with frustration. Doubt.

She checked for signs to confirm her explanation of events. There were none. But they had been here so many times together she could sense his presence, his warmth, and it comforted her, made her feel safe enough to stay despite being alone. She wasn't in a fit state to drive back to London anyway. She unrolled her sleeping bag on the patch of ground she knew from previous trial and error to be the most comfortable place to rest, extinguished her torch, lay back, linked her hands behind her head. A shooting star fell down the blackness above. A fox screamed. She couldn't settle; she reached for her torch again, dug in the back pocket of her jeans and removed a photo, examined it in the beam. She had snapped it in the light of the campfire, sideways on, his face shadowed, mysterious smile, eyes half closed, the dreamy, unfocused gaze of the short-sighted. And the stoned.

They had ended up camping in the Lookers' Hut almost by accident. May Day bank holiday. Luke was driving the kombi – she had put him on her insurance. The road south had been slow, packed with Londoners heading for the coast, and when they reached the outskirts of Hastings, they came to a near standstill. Hastings was depressing. The once grand sweep of white Regency homes had been reduced to rotting social security B&Bs, clinging to the southernmost fringe of England. The Channel dishwater swirled around the beach, flecking shingle with brown foam. The promenade was awash with teenage girls pushing prams, men in vests hanging out drinking Tennent's. As they inched past the Old Town, she spotted a knot of people dressed in green, dancing – a spark of life, excitement, a parade. The traffic was at a standstill and the revellers were weaving around the cars. Her mind was wandering when she was startled by the hard thump of a fist on the van's front.

'Oi,' she shouted. 'Don't do that to my van.'

A blackened face snarled at her through the windscreen, red mouth gaping, arms flapping to reveal his rag-feathered cape before he vanished into a backstreet. Crow-man. The grotesque figure jolted her memory, knocked her back to the Beltane fair she had visited with her dad when she was eleven. Eight years ago. She hadn't thought about the fair for a long while, hadn't wanted to remember the events of that odd May Day. The van stopped and started, inched along the traffic-jammed road, and she had an uneasy sense of her past spiralling around, catching up, her father forever appearing and disappearing. *Where are you going? Over the hills and far away.*

The delay in Hastings meant they arrived in Dungeness at dusk. They attempted to light a campfire on the beach, but the mist was rolling in from the Channel and the flames spluttered and died. They decided to drive back to London across the marsh. Bad call. The mist followed them inland; curling wraiths in the weak halogen headlights becoming dense and impenetrable. They took a wrong turning, ended up in a breaker's yard full of rusting double-deckers and guarded by a couple of snarling ridgebacks. Luke reversed the van, the dogs snapping at the tyres. She searched the map and located the nearest Lookers' Hut that would, at least, provide them with some shelter for the night.

There were no farm buildings around, so they didn't have to worry about being spotted as they humped their gear across the wet grass. They gathered the dropped branches from the overhanging willow, piled them on the soil floor of the hut, wary of using the old fireplace in case the chimney was blocked by birds' nests, managed to ignite the wood by scrunching up the pages of a newspaper and using it as kindling. 'Beltane fire,' she said, without thinking. As she spoke she pictured the green-haired woman and her herbal remedies – the packet of bitter withy – found herself slipping from the melancholia that had dogged her all day to something bleaker – childlike powerless-ness, events she could not control. She rescued a thin willow branch from the campfire, waved it in the air like a wand.

'What are you doing?' Luke asked.

'I'm fighting off the curses with my withy wand.'

'Withy?'

'It's another name for the willow.' She swished the stem above her head, wrote her name in the night with its tip. 'The willow is the only tree to perish from the inside out. Heart first. That's the curse of the bitter withy.'

She pointed the wand at Luke.

'Are you cursing me?'

'No. I'm blessing you, protecting you from the darkness.'

A branch on the campfire flashed green and he jabbed the flames with his boot, sent a puff of burning ash skywards. She watched the smoke mingling with the mist, spotted the shadow of the barn owl as it circled, drawn by the glow of the camp-fire, wings spectral in the night.

'Do you believe in ghosts?' she asked.

He said, 'I believe people can be haunted, have ghosts in their heads. What about you? Do you believe in ghosts?'

She hesitated. 'No, I don't believe in ghosts. But sometimes I think I see my dad. Glimpses. I'm sure he's there and then he's gone.' She found it easy to tell Luke about Jim; he wasn't judgemental. 'Seeing him makes me wonder whether he is dead after all, whether it was his corpse in the morgue.'

'Wasn't it you who identified him?'

'Yes, but I was in total shock, out of my mind. Scared. I felt like I was tripping, I couldn't tell what was going on. When Liz saw the body in the morgue she gave him one look, said he was an imposter and walked off.'

'Really?'

'It was an emotional reaction. I think. But maybe his death was a fix after all and I didn't spot it. A con job, like everything about his life.'

She hadn't realized how much she censored everything she said before she met Luke. How much she had never said, to anybody. When she was with Luke, she could speak and watch her words fly away; bonfire cinders in the night, red sparks fading to grey then vanishing. Being with him was a release. He accepted her for who she was – spikes and all – she didn't have to explain, apologize.

'I suppose it's not impossible that his death was a fix,' Luke said.

He was never dismissive of her fears, never suggested she was a fantasist, which made her less defensive. Hearing some-body else accept her darkest anxieties made it obvious they were improbable.

She said, 'Well, it's hard not to think that anything is possi-ble. He was a spy and the state asked him to fake another life for himself, so why shouldn't the spooks also fake his death and then resurrect him? But, when I think about it rationally, I know it's my anxiety. Not real. It must have been his body in the morgue.' He definitely had been killed by a hitman behind Vauxhall Bridge, she told herself. 'I know it's mad to think he's still around,' she added.

Luke said, 'It's not mad. It's grief. Although, I think grief is a form of madness, an infection.' He should know – he was an orphan; his father had died when he was six and his mother, Monika, had died of cancer when he was twenty. 'It's temporary. It's not who you are, it's something that lands on you, a cloud. Grief smothers everybody at some time or another. Everybody has to deal with death, it's part of being human.'

It was a relief to hear him talk about grief in that way, not a regimented process in five stages, but something that descended and then moved on, lapwings flying to the next field.

'Time doesn't heal,' he said. 'But it makes loss easier to live with. Makes you feel less mad.'

He had more emotional intelligence than she did. Liz had once told her that relationships weren't like the crosswords she so obsessively completed. But as far as Sam was concerned, relationships were like cryptic clues. She had to work them out, stand back, parse the words, twist the letters around. Luke was the opposite; he wasn't a navel gazer, didn't spend hours analysing how he felt, but he had a knack of solving the emotional anagrams churning in her brain. He lay back on the ground and she could see his eyes searching the night sky.

He said, 'Ghosts are like projections of your own feelings. Maybe you see Jim because you are feeling guilty.'

'Guilty?' She turned the idea over in her mind; testing whether his suggestion fitted her emotional space. 'Why would I feel guilty?'

'Because of your father's work. You don't know exactly what he did, but you must worry sometimes that he crossed the boundary, walked on the far side. Anybody with a conscience would worry about that.'

He was right, she did worry about what Jim might have done. 'Sins of the father,' she said.

She skinned up. Lay on the ground next to him, the warmth of his body seeping into hers, and her mind traced the ghost of Jim in the mist and smoke.

'It's not usually the guilty who feel guilt,' he said. 'And it's often the innocent who are accused, by implication or otherwise. But you have to ignore the finger pointers. They're mindless wankers.'

His words reminded her of the man who had approached her on Oxford's Cornmarket, whispered in her ear, *You are Jim Coyle's daughter*, sent her tumbling, left her feeling marked. Accused.

Luke rolled over, his face comfortingly close to hers.

'You know what, though, you should probably be careful.'

'How do you mean?'

'Well, you've got to protect yourself,' he said. 'You're probably on the Force's radar because of your dad. And he isn't around any more to dig you out of trouble if somebody decides to take a shot at you.'

'I hadn't thought of it like that.' She propped herself up on one elbow, the word *shot* rattling around her mind. 'You're right, though. I don't want to attract attention by doing anything too outrageous.'

He wrapped his arm round her. The campfire flames had died down, glowing embers, the lingering remnants of its heat.

'I don't want to land anybody else in trouble either,' she added. 'I would feel terrible if you were targeted because of me.'

'I didn't mean it like that. Nobody's going to target you. Or me. We're not planning anything that's going to attract attention anyway. We'll be fine, you and me, we'll look after each other. If anybody comes after us, we'll hide out here in our safehouse. We'll do a Bonnie and Clyde.'

Bonnie and Clyde sealed it. The Lookers' Hut became their

secret hideaway. They spent most of May in Romney, then June, driving down between their nightclub shifts – a bottle of wine, a spliff, the campfire, the barn owl circling, the only witness to their unguarded moments. Tonight, just before the second anniversary of her father's death, was the first time Luke hadn't done what he had said he would do, hadn't turned up.

She extinguished the torch, eased the photo of him into her back pocket, tried to sleep. She could still hear his voice in her head, smell his sweat, feel his weight on her. Not only the dead that haunted. Desire, she thought then, was as much a madness as grief, like being possessed. She searched for a soft spot on the hard earth, dozed, stars turning around her head, a distant green flame dancing, a will-o-the-wisp tempting her into the marshlands.

The cooing of wood pigeons woke her, coral sky above, ground cold below. She reached over to touch Luke, and then she remembered she was alone and felt a stab in her side, a pain of absence. She sat up. The willow leaves rustled. She held her breath. There it was again – something heavy pushing through the undergrowth. She wrestled with the zip of her sleeping bag, pushed herself to her feet, out of the hut. A muscular badger barrelled past her, almost knocked her sideways as it crashed through the nettles, desperate to return to its sett. She laughed. Scared by a badger. She surveyed the meadow; rabbits scampered and waved their scuts. Rooks mingled with the lambs. And then the early-morning peace was shattered by the noise of an engine revving. Behind her. Luke? She pounded down the mound and heard the vehicle pulling away. The road was hidden by a line of stunted willows and the mist that hung above the sewers at dusk and dawn. She made a beeline for the boundary, feet slipping on dewy grass, came to a halt at the channel's bank, stood on her toes among the reeds. Too late.

She couldn't see anything. Diesel engine, though, she could tell from the sound it made. She walked along the field's border, searching for footprints or other giveaways that might reveal the presence of an intruder. Nothing. She was on edge. Just a farmer doing his rounds, checking his flocks. A colony of pipistrelles swept through the morning mist, swarming before they returned to their roost. She was letting her mind wander too far; time to drive home.

She traipsed back to the Lookers' Hut, rolled up her sleeping bag, cast a final glance around the shelter and spotted a rusty horseshoe lying in the disused hearth. She'd not noticed that before. She walked over, kicked the horseshoe with her foot and dislodged a clump of hair that had been trapped beneath one of its ends. Curious, she squatted, prodded the strands with her fingernail. It definitely wasn't Luke's hair, far too straight and dark for that, which was a relief. She poked in the loose earth and dislodged something solid, half buried. She scrabbled and eased out a small black object. Not a stone. She blew the dirt from its surface – a bone. She examined it, rolling it in her hand. Sheep bone. No, there was something improbably human about it. She panicked, dug. Searching. Her fingers touched hard surfaces. Pebbles. Old brick. Broken glass. She gouged out fragments, dirt behind her nails, fingers scraped and oozing blood. Gripped by a sudden, irrational fear that Luke's body was lying under the soil. She dug and dug until she was satisfied there was nothing there. No more bones. And then she sat back on her heels, wiped her forehead with the back of her arm, licked her lips, tasted the salt. Laughed at herself. Of course Luke wasn't dead and buried here in the Lookers' Hut. She was becoming a crazy woman, love sick.

She picked up the small bone she had found, examined it again and tried to assess what was in her hand. New? Ancient?

Charred, possibly. An animal – if not a sheep then a cat. What was it doing there? Was the bone connected to the hair? The horseshoe? Impossible to tell. She thought about Alastair's crate-top mortuary – bird skulls, toad's carcass – and speculated that the objects could be some kind of spell or charm left by a superstitious Looker. Smuggling, dissent, witchcraft, Alastair had said they all went hand in hand out here on the marsh, the contested ground. She laughed at herself. Too much hanging out with ageing dope-smoking hippies who collected toads' bones. They were random objects, finds of an archaeological field walk, a surface hodgepodge; a stray lock of hair caught under an abandoned horseshoe, the bone the remains of somebody's dinner. Still it amused her – calmed her – to have a story, no matter how irrational, to explain her findings. Shepherd's charms. She decided to leave them in the hearth. Then a chink of doubt made her scoop up the bone and hair again, wrap them in a tissue and place them in her pocket. Next time she saw Dave, she would show them to him. Ask for his expert opinion on the bone. Sheep? Cat? Human even? It was the kind of thing he found interesting anyway – body parts, decomposition. She could entertain him with her theories.

She whistled the familiar zither tune to herself as she crossed the bridge and clambered into the van. She couldn't keep the notes out of her head. *The Third Man*. The film's shadows and tunnels played in her mind, and she wished she could banish them, these persistent reminders of the dark places inhabited by her father. She focused on Luke. He had driven back to London because she hadn't turned up at the Lookers' Hut at six. She would find a message from him on her answering machine when she returned to Vauxhall, and it would explain exactly what had happened. She was sure of that. She released the handbrake, glanced over her shoulder; Saturn gleamed on the horizon.

CHAPTER 4

SHE WIGGLED THE key in the lock. She felt at home here in south London. Dave had been part of the comfort. They met at a party the previous year: she was leaning against a wall canoodling a cigarette when Dave gravitated to her side, and they discovered their common experience – the recent death of a parent. He had studied biochemistry at Oxford and was completing a PhD at Imperial. He told her, with his Brummie accent and a wry smile, that he was researching marine biota anthropogenic radionuclide concentration in the immediate environment of a nuclear power station. You what, she replied. He was measuring the amount of human-produced radioactive shit that ended up in the flora and fauna around Dungeness. Caesium 137 was his speciality. Was there a lot of radioactive shit in the fish from Dungeness then, she asked. Not so much as there was around Sellafield, he said, where all the waste products from the nuclear industry were processed; the Irish Sea had much higher concentrations of anthropogenic radionuclides than the English Channel. Phew, big relief for us southerners then, she said. Cod generally contained the highest levels of radionuclides, he explained, because of its position in the food chain. She made the requisite joke about fission chips. He said eating the cod wouldn't do anybody any long-term damage anyway; you needed a ton of the stuff for that. How do you know it won't do any long-term damage, she spluttered. It's been tested, by scientists, like him, he added, at Dungeness, in the experimental research station where he analysed the concentration of caesium 137 in samples of marine life collected from the beach and exposed other samples of marine life to caesium 137 to monitor the impact of different levels of radiation.

He was exactly as she would like her older brother to be if she had one, she decided – quirky, dead-pan, clever. She had turned to him when she was disintegrating and he had invited her to share his house in Vauxhall. Well, it wasn't exactly his house. A short-term lease from a housing co-operative on the far edge of a square of once grand and now run-down houses inhabited by a rebel alliance of Birk-wearing tofu-eaters, ageing anarcho-syndicalists, Spanish punks and militant earth mothers. The tide of London's redevelopment had not yet reached Vauxhall. The square was a rubber dinghy of alternative living in a sea of mouldering council estates, drug dealers and MPs who mistakenly thought they were purchasing a second home in the more salubrious enclave of Kennington down the road.

'I think he's got a thing about you,' Jess had said after she had helped Sam to move in and Dave had skulked around, joining in with their banter.

'Just because we get on. You always think everybody has a thing about everybody else.'

She was irritated with her sister for bringing sex into the equation with Dave, tainting her comfort.

She had been unsettled when Dave had decamped to Norfolk for six months, left her living alone temporarily. Although Luke was around a lot, of course, filled the space. Still, she missed Dave's company. Dave had been awarded his PhD just before reactor number four at the Chernobyl nuclear power plant exploded, 26 April 1986. He had watched the news reports coming in from the Ukraine with fanatical interest. The explosion had sent a plume of radioactive isotopes high up into the atmosphere. Caesium 137. Iodine 131. Strontium 90. The cloud headed east on the prevailing wind.

'The most volatile isotopes take the longest to return to earth,' he said. 'In a few days' time, the plume will be a mass of caesium 137.'

He became obsessed with the weather, constantly phoning a meteorologist friend for news. Dave provided her with a running report; the wind had shifted direction, twirled around. South. West. North-west. Heading their way. Then he was outside the front door, in the middle of the street, craning his neck and eyeballing the clouds, heavy with foreboding.

'If the plume hits this lot, we're fucked.' He sounded grimly satisfied with the prospect.

'Why?'

'Because we'll be drenched in radioactive rain.'

The storm clouds swept across England and burst on the northern uplands. Dave observed that every cloud had a silver lining and, in his case, it was a surge in demand for experts on the environmental impacts of anthropogenic radionuclides. The phone started ringing. His head, bespectacled and prematurely balding, appeared on late-night news programmes, spouting stories about the half-life of caesium 137, radionuclides rained into the ground, sucked up by grass roots, eaten by sheep and cows. Radioactive roasts and glowing milk bottles. Although, of course, he added as an almost disappointed afterthought, the scientific evidence so far suggested it was unlikely the levels of contamination in Britain would be high enough to have any major impact on human health. His performance earned him a six-month research post at Imperial's field centre in Skell: baseline mapping of caesium 137 in the biota of Norfolk's saltmarshes.

'I'm going to miss you,' she said.

'Come on. You've got Luke. He's practically moved in here. I'm beginning to feel like a gooseberry in my own home.'

'Don't be silly. You know Luke always wants you to join in.'

'Yeah. Exactly.' Sam ignored his tone. In early May, as she was planning the protest in Dungeness with Luke, he had hired a van and transported half his gear to some academic's second home in Skell. Left her feeling guilty in Vauxhall.

She shoved the door with her shoulder. The dampness made it stick. The door gave, she stumbled into the hall, the answering machine flashing in the dim light. She leaped over and pressed the message button, watched the spools on the small cassette rewind, stop and play. A crackle on the line, then Luke's voice cut in and prompted an instantaneous surge of relief.

'Sam. Are you there? Will you pick up? It's me. Luke.' Pause. 'Oh god, I hope you haven't set off already. Oh shit. Look, Sam. I'm so sorry about this mess. I have to go. Something has come up. I can't hang around here. Listen, there's something else... Dave... Don't worry, OK. Everything will be fine. Really. I'll call.'

She replayed the message. Her immediate relief was replaced with acute anxiety. The message was so strange, the tension oozed from the answering machine. *I have to go. Something has come up.* What was that about? And why did he mention Dave? She dialled Luke's home number, twisted the skin on her forearm between her finger and thumb while the phone rang and rang. No answer. She made some coffee, called Luke's number again. Still no answer. She replayed the message he had left. The tension was palpable, but now she heard sounds and intonations she had missed the first time. Fear. Real fear that made her skin prickle. And at the end of his message there was a sudden crackle of background noise, as if he had opened the door of the telephone box and the white noise of the external world had intruded. Was that a voice? She couldn't quite make it out, the quality of the recording wasn't clear enough. What time had he called? Her first conversation with him, the one where he had called to tell her he was already in Dungeness, had been at nine. She left the house at ten, so she reckoned he must have left the message shortly afterwards. Ten thirty perhaps. She replayed the tape again. 'Don't worry, OK. Everything will be fine.' Why did he think it was necessary to say that? Because he was worried that everything wasn't going to be fine? What was going on? She eyeballed the phone, willed it to ring. It did. She leaped for the receiver, jammed it to her ear. A pause filled with electronic twanging.

'Hello. Sam, is that you?'

Liz. Her heart sank.

'Hello, Mum.'

She could hear her own voice bouncing around in electronic space.

'I'm sending you a postcard.'

'Great. Thanks for letting me know.'

'I'm writing a recipe on it. Vegetarian.'

'Recipe?'

'A traditional Greek recipe. We went to a taverna yesterday evening when we arrived.'

We. Sam didn't want to know about we.

'Roger bumped into this man he knew and the man gave him the ingredients for the recipe. You have to try it.'

Typical. Liz hardly ever phoned her and when she finally bothered, it was at the moment that she was hoping somebody else would ring. And she wanted to talk about a recipe.

'Mum. I was at the graveyard yesterday morning for Jim's remembrance ceremony, you know, the one you were supposed to come to but didn't, and then I went down to Dungeness and camped out overnight. I've only just got home and I'm too tired to talk about recipes. But thank you for thinking of me.'

'Try the recipe,' Liz said.

Sam couldn't quite be bothered to contest.

'OK, I will.'

'Good. The really interesting thing about *Paradise Lost*, of course, is that Satan is a sympathetic character.'

'That is really interesting, Mum, but I'm going to have to go now because I'm waiting for another call.'

'Oh.'

An offended oh, Sam realized, but frankly, right then she reckoned she was the one who should be offended by Liz's failure to behave in a normal motherly sort of way.

'Call me back another time,' said Sam.

'Will do.'

'Bye.'

'Bye.'

She replaced the receiver. *Paradise* bloody *Lost*. Jim had kept Liz grounded, in touch with reality. Since Jim's death Liz had cut loose, aided and abetted by Roger, and now she floated around in the stratosphere talking in literary quotes and interesting recipes she had unearthed in Greek tavernas. What kind of family did she grow up in if the parent who kept them grounded was an undercover cop who spent half his life on secret missions pretending to be somebody else?

Thinking about Liz reminded her she had been given Harry's number and an instruction to call him. She could do with a conversation with Harry; he was always unflappable. She dug in her pocket, found the paper. Dialled. The phone rang.

'Hello, Harry here.'

'Harry, it's Sam. You left a message with Liz.'

He didn't bother with niceties. 'You been causing trouble again?' He said it jokingly, but she knew he wasn't.

'No,' she said. 'Why?'

'Somebody thinks you have.'

'Who?'

'I don't want to alarm you, Sam, but word is somebody has opened a file on you.'

'A file?' So what, big deal. 'I thought the Force had files on everybody who'd ever been on a protest.'

'Well, maybe they do, but there are files and there are files. And this is one of the files that belongs to the latter category.'

Harry's voice unnerved her, the softness of his Welsh accent doing nothing to mute the seriousness of his tone.

'So what kind of a file is it?'

'The kind that if you're not careful ends up being transferred to an Intelligence computerized index of possible terrorists.'

He said it matter-of-factly, but his words made her gasp.

'Computerized index of terrorists?'

'R2 it's called. MI5's list of people they think need watching. Subversives. Possible terrorists.'

'But I'm not a possible terrorist.'

'Of course you're not. And you're not actually on the list. You are just on the pile for further investigation, as far as I know.'

She couldn't entirely comprehend what he was saying; it was so ridiculous.

'Why is anybody even considering adding my name to a list of possible terrorists when I'm clearly not one?' Her voice was shrill.

'OK, stay calm. Nothing irreversible has happened yet.'

'Yet? For Christ's sake, what's this about? Am I under surveillance? What have I done? How can I stop it?'

'Look, don't panic. We can work this out. Mistakes happen. False information gets put about.'

'Obviously.'

'Do you think you know anybody who could be classified as a terrorist? An extremist of some sort or another?'

'No.' Don't be ridiculous, she wanted to say, but didn't because she didn't want to sound rude.

'You've not been hanging out with any dubious people then?'

'No. Only my sisters.'

'They don't count. Nobody else?'

She wrestled around in her mind, was about to tell Harry about Luke's disappearance, decided it was better not to. She didn't want to confuse the issue by talking about the planned Dungeness protest, the contact at the power station. Didn't want him to think there was any possibility she might have done anything to warrant a file. Harry interrupted her internal dialogue.

'Does the name Dave Daley mean anything to you?'

She jumped. 'Dave?'

'Yes, Dave Daley.'

'He's my housemate. Or he was. He's gone to Skell for six months. Why?'

'It's probably nothing. Somebody mentioned his name, that's all. He's not a loony leftie like you then?'

'Dave? God no. The only time he ever protests about anything is when the ref gives a yellow card to an Aston Villa player. He's an environmental researcher. He knows people in Greenpeace but, to be honest, he tends to be a bit sniffy about campaigners. Amateurs, as far as he's concerned, unless they have a PhD from Imperial.'

'Well, as I said, somebody mentioned him. Nothing more.'

Luke's answerphone message played in her mind. *Listen, there's something else... Dave...*

Harry said, 'I'll see what I can find out.'

She wanted him to say something more reassuring. He didn't.

'I'll contact you one way or another when I've got something. In the meantime keep your head down till I know what's what. Sit tight. I'll sort it.'

'OK.'

'You've got my number. Bye for now. Oh, better to use a phone box next time.'

Harry replaced the receiver abruptly and she realized she'd forgotten to ask him about the whistling, 'The *Third Man* Theme', check whether that was his *call me* signal. She thought about ringing him back, but didn't want to aggravate him. It would have to wait until the next time they spoke. The whistler seemed like a minor worry right at that moment anyway compared to a file marked terrorist. *I'll sort it.* She wasn't sure whether she was relieved or alarmed to hear that phrase. *I'll sort it* when uttered by an agent of the secret state usually meant you were already up to your neck in it. First Luke disappeared and now this, her file waiting to be added to a computerized terrorist list. What was her name doing on that pile? And what was all this about Dave? That had to be a mistake. Sit tight, Harry had said, but it didn't feel like a viable option when she was being dragged sideways by hidden tides and crosscurrents. She lay down on the floor, miserable, limbs trembling with tension and exhaustion.

She opened her eyes; her bones ached, the hallway had already darkened in the afternoon shadows. She must have slept there, on the damp boards, for hours. She gazed up at the cracked ceiling tiles; asbestos, Dave had said, invisible killer. Time bomb, ticking away inside. Not even aware you've inhaled the fibre until you wake up one morning thirty years later to discover your lungs are fucked and you've got six weeks left before you die. Thanks, Dave, for the interesting information. She coughed. Patted her chest. A snail inched past her nose, retracted its horns when she sighed. She pushed herself on to her hands and knees, crawled to the phone, dialled Luke's number. Nobody picked up. She was like the snail, fumbling along the damp wainscot, no idea where she was going. She needed to recover herself, clear her head, walk along the river.

She stood on Vauxhall Bridge, the dusk air thick with city grime. Downstream, the eastern horizon of Docklands was crowded with cranes reaching heavenwards, as if searching for salvation. Behind, a ruddy sun was setting on the derelict cold store and the chimneys of Battersea power station. She fixed her eyes on the water running below and summoned her father. The first time she had seen Jim underneath Vauxhall Bridge was earlier that year. January. She was walking home late from the nightclub where she worked twice a week. A vast perigee moon hung over Westminster, the river little more than a mercury ribbon, sucked dry by the lunar pull. She glanced over the bridge and saw a figure standing among the rotting timbers, the remains of a Bronze Age jetty that marked the muddy foreshore. She knew instantly the figure was Jim, although she couldn't be sure how she knew. She called out his name. He didn't react. Still, she was certain it was him. She wasn't scared, she wasn't even surprised – she had half expected him to reappear. *Where are you going? Over the hills and far away. Will you come back? I've always come back before, haven't I?* When she looked again, he had vanished. Death hadn't changed the pattern.

She watched a solitary waterman rowing with the current, oars dipping, pulling. Traffic growled over the bridge and a helicopter buzzed along the line of the river. Through the white noise she heard a mournful whistle, the familiar tune. She leaned over the railing, couldn't see anything, hurtled down to Albert Embankment. The land below the bridge had been purchased by property developers and fenced, the gate padlocked, but there was a hole in the chainlink under Alembic House. She crawled through, around the scattered bricks, prostrate scaffold poles, down the slipway to the shore. The river flickered from lead to quicksilver as she descended to its level. There was no sign of Jim. She scanned the muddy banks. A trickling caught her attention; water running down a channel from a tunnel entrance in the embankment wall, invisible from the bridge. Sewage? She stumbled across the rocks, clambered on to the grey concrete lip, bilge water seeping into her shoes, waded up past greening timbers. The entrance was blocked by a vast portcullis sluice gate that looked like the mouth of hell, and above it a sign. *River Effra run-off*. She had always imagined the underground Effra to be a wild torrent flowing deep below the streets of south London. Not a crap-filled dribble. She pushed against the iron; it refused to budge. She squinted through the gaps, shadows danced along the tunnel wall, a rat crept through the rubbish. She hollered.

'Jim.'

Her voice echoed around the bricks. Jim… im… im. Then silence apart from the drip, drip, drip of water trickling. The wetness of her shoes made her look down. A line of footprints in the wallow trailed into the tunnel, as if somebody had managed to walk through the sluice gate. Jim was in there somewhere, hiding out in the rivers buried beneath London. She dismissed the idea. She shouldered the iron barricade again.

Definitely locked. And yet, there was the trail of footprints – somebody obviously had walked into the tunnel, somehow. She squatted, poked at the tangle of rotting vegetation, cans, plastic bags, matted hair entwined around the base of the sluice. A smooth grey object caught her attention. She yanked and nagged until it was free, carefully wiped away the slime and found a spiteful face grimacing at her from the belly of a ceramic pot, its neck sealed with a lump of cracked black wax. She shook the bottle gently; it rattled. She tipped it upside down without thinking, stuck her hand under the bottle's mouth as the wax splintered, caught the falling objects. A puff of fetid mist filled her nostrils and a dribble of liquid passed through her fingers. She coughed, almost dropped the lot. What was that smell? Asparagus? Worse than that. Urine. She unfurled her fist and gingerly examined the bottle's contents she had scrunched in her palm. A slither of what looked like bark and a roll of shrivelled brown felt. She spread the material with a finger; it was cut in the shape of a heart and had three dressmaker's pins stuck through it. She reeled; there was something unnerving about the way these strange artefacts – bones, hair, bottles with peculiar contents – kept appearing at her feet; she was a field walker among the darkness. She poked the woody slither and thought of the green-haired woman she had met at the spring fair when she was eleven, the packet of bark shards she had pushed into Sam's hand. Was it willow? The bark of the bitter withy, the tree of death and grief and weeping? She contemplated the bottle's strange contents for a while, then pushed them back into its belly. She was examining the gurning face again when she sensed somebody watching her. She looked up. A man in a parka holding a metal detector waved at her from the river's edge; there were often treasure-seekers here when the tide was low.

'What have you found?' he shouted.

'I'm not sure.' She jumped down from the run-off channel, walked over to him, showed him the pot. His eyes gleamed.

'That's a nice one, very nice.' He had an Indian accent. 'Very well spotted. I've found one myself, but it was cracked.'

'What is it?'

'A bellarmine. A witch's bottle.'

She twitched, nearly dropped the bottle. She had been right, she was an archaeologist of the occult. She tried to remember whether *Daemonologie* mentioned bellarmines; she didn't think it did. King James was more interested in torture methods than the artefacts of magic.

'It's a protection against witchcraft, a counter-curse. People thought the river had mystical powers, so they chucked charms and counter-charms in the water. And then hundreds of years later they surface, appear in the mud.' He eyed it enviously. 'Where did you find it?'

She pointed to the sluice gate.

'The Effra run-off,' he said. 'The Vauxhall sluice, they've just finished building that. It's supposed to provide extra drainage for the Effra, flood control. They'll need that by the end of the summer with all the rain we've been having. They open the gate when the drains are full and let the water out into the river.'

She pictured the footsteps leading along the chute.

'So the sluice gate is usually locked?'

'Yes, that's right.'

'It's not possible to get in?'

'Oh, it's easy to get in. There are hundreds of entrances. You just have to find a manhole. Most of them have access ladders.'

'Seriously?'

'There's a whole other world down there below London, the underground rivers, the drains and sewers. Some people say you can tell which manholes lead to the rivers by the gurgling they make. And the smell they give off. I've never been down there myself.' His brown eyes swivelled back to the bellarmine. 'You should take that to the Museum of London. It could be old. Seventeenth-century even. Although, people didn't stop using them then, so it might be much more recent than that.'

She thought of the green-haired stallholder again, wondered whether she was a user of bellarmines as well as a seller of herbal remedies.

'I could take it if you want,' he said.

'No, it's OK.' She said it too quickly, curled her fingers around the bottle like Gollum clutching his precious. The treasure-seeker didn't take offence.

'As you like. It's a lucky find. Very lucky.' He paused. 'Unless of course you tip the contents out and then you reverse the charm and curse yourself, and that would be very unlucky.'

She giggled nervously, wiped her hand on her coat. 'I wouldn't do anything so stupid.'

'I was only joking anyway, I don't believe in all that witch-craft stuff myself.'

'Me neither.'

He nodded at the bellarmine. 'Although there are plenty of people who do. There's a lot of it about – irrational beliefs, fears and accusations. That's why I come out here, to escape.'

He replaced his headphones over his ears, trudged under the bridge, waving his metal detector in front of him, disappeared from view. She lifted the bottle to her face; the malicious bellarmine face leered back at her. Jesus, what had she done? She'd upended a bloody witch's bottle, tipped its contents out, and reversed the charm. She was so stupid. Maybe if she handed it over to a museum, got rid of it, she could negate the curse, undo any damage. Somewhere deep inside, she knew that wasn't going to work. Whoever had dropped it in her path – the River Effra, the maker of the footprints, a cunning woman – she was the finder, so she was the keeper. She had to deal with it; she couldn't pass it on. She weighed the bottle in her hand as she slithered back across the shore, decided against taking it home because it smelled so rank, and left it at the top of the slipway above high tide mark, well hidden in a gutter. She would come back for it when she had decided how to deal with its peculiar contents.

A trail of wet footprints followed her as she traipsed under the railway arches. She dialled Luke's number as soon as she reached home. It rang. And rang. Then somebody picked up. Elation.

'Hello.'

Deflation. It was Spyder. Luke's scumbag housemate. She met Spyder when she started working in the Soho nightclub the previous September. He worked in a club around the corner. Hate at first sight. Posh boy slumming it, small-time drug dealer, all-round git.

'It's Sam. Is Luke there?'

'No. Ain't he with you?'

Ain't. Seriously, who was he trying to kid with his mockney accent?

'No. He isn't with me.'

'I wonder who he's stayin' with then.'

Piss off, scumbag.

'When did you last see him?'

'Friday night at the club. We both worked the shift.'

'You didn't see him Saturday morning?'

'I told you that. Friday night. I stayed out after the club closed, he said he wanted to get home. I got home about five in the morning, crashed, woke up midday and he wasn't there.'

'Did he say anything to you about where he was going or what he was doing on Saturday?'

'No. What's all this about anyway? Has he left you?'

'No. Thanks for your help.'

'Pleasure, darlin'.'

She jammed the receiver down, sat in the dark hall with her arms wrapped around her knees, listened for the gurgling of the Effra somewhere way below. She pictured the bellarmine, its pierced felt heart, the willow bark. She held her palm to her face – her skin still reeked of piss. She had upended the contents of the witch's bottle, reversed the magic, flipped it from a blessing to a curse. She was turning everything she touched to shit.

CHAPTER 5

SHE WAS WOKEN in the early hours by the call of a vixen. The cries of nocturnal animals – the shriek of an owl, the scream of a fox – had an unnerving human edge. She went to the window, pulled back the curtain. Not one fox, but a pack of fifteen or twenty animals, weaving between parked cars and puddles like trained urban assassins. The creatures halted in unison and lifted their heads. A solitary howl set them running again, hunting unseen prey, some beast deadly enough to warrant a co-ordinated pack attack. The red stream flowed down the road, merged with the shadows. She returned to her bed, lay awake, thinking of Luke. Dave.

She waited for the first pale light, ran down to the phone box – she was wary of using her own phone to call Dave, she didn't want to reveal her plans to anybody who might be tapping her line. Dave was an insomniac, like her. Three a.m. was her witching hour, the time when she gave up on sleep, crept downstairs to make a cup of tea. Dave was often sitting at the kitchen table already, the glare of the bare bulb glinting off his bald patch, squinting through his John Lennon gold-rimmed NHS glasses, usually reading a journal article he had photocopied earlier in the college library. Three a.m. was the time they had found his mother, Astrid, floating face up in the Digbeth Branch Canal, under Love Lane Bridge. She was from Berlin, fourteen years old in 1945 when the Soviets invaded. Astrid had been raped by the Red Army, her mother too. They had survived, ended up in Birmingham. Astrid had met John Daley when he came over from Tipperary to find building work. They fell in love and had four children, the youngest of whom was Dave, and they seemed to be happy for a while, but the past caught up with her in the end.

Early morning was the time Sam missed Dave most, since he had decamped to Skell. He answered the phone after two rings. He attempted to ask her how she was, but she launched straight into the disappearance of Luke, or at least the story she felt it was safe to relate. The plan to meet Luke at Dungeness, Luke's message on the answerphone. She didn't want to tell him about Harry and the file, not on the phone. She wasn't sure how she was going to tell him about that anyway. She wasn't coherent, jabbered on. Dave was dismissive.

'He's probably gone off for a couple of days to see a mate.'

Difficult to convey the seriousness of the situation when she was self-censoring.

'Yes, but what about the Greenpeace stuff?'

She whispered, as if it would make any difference if somebody was eavesdropping.

'The Greenpeace stuff? I wouldn't worry about that. It's not like, you know, you're doing really dodgy stuff.'

Condescending sod. As she had explained to Harry, Dave maintained what he saw as a professional relationship with environmental campaigners; he was happy to provide them with scientific advice, but he was not a protestor.

'I know we're not doing anything really dodgy. But it doesn't mean to say that other people won't interpret it as dodgy, does it?'

Impatient tut from Dave at the other end of the line.

'Listen. Can I drive up to Skell and talk?'

'Of course you can. But Sam...'

'What?'

'Take it easy on the road. You sound like you're getting a bit...'

'A bit what?'

Hysterical. She silently dared him to say it. He didn't.

'Tired and stressed. Drive up here, we can talk everything through calmly and work it out.'

'OK. I'll be there this afternoon.'

'OK.'

'And Dave.'

'What?'

'Thanks for being helpful.'

'Don't mention it. Anytime you want to dump your shit on me, Sam. It's fine.'

She ran home, eager to get on the road, fumbled with her key, pushed the door, the red light of the answering machine flashed. She pressed play. The cassette whirred, paused, a breath, the familiar tune and then somebody spoke. 'Trust nobody.' Was it Harry's voice? Was there the hint of a Welsh accent? She rewound the tape, replayed. She couldn't be sure it was Harry, but the message was unambiguous. *Trust nobody.* A clear warning. About whom?

She walked into the kitchen, Harry's question in her head. *Does the name Dave Daley mean anything to you?* She fiddled with a saucepan, water, coffee. The black sludge glugged, a geyser of erupting volcanic gases. Coffee brewed the Turkish way, as demonstrated by Luke, in memory of his late father. Strange how the bereaved and damaged found one another out, recognized each other in a crowded room. Negative attraction. Her, Dave, Luke. Luke's father was English and Monika, his mother, was German – another reason he and Dave had bonded.

Monika came from Cologne; she had married Ben, an Englishman and a failed academic according to Luke. Ben thought he should have been a Professor of English Literature but didn't quite make the grade. Shortly after Luke was born, Ben had become bitter and critical of everything European, including his wife. He left them to be something big with the British Council in Istanbul where he said he felt at home. Ben admired all things Turkish and claimed that Ottoman culture was far superior to anything Europe had to offer. Luke visited him in the summers and it was during one of these holidays that his father died of a heart attack. Luke had found the body but he couldn't remember the details because he was only six at the time. His mother had filled the blanks in when he was older. All his memories of his father were echoes, he said, not real but retold stories. Luke's Turkish coffee was another of these ripples, a small attempt to connect with his long dead, largely unknown father.

She sipped the coffee and felt his skin touching hers, ached with his absence. She rubbed her damp eyes, walked back to the phone in the hallway, dialled his home number, counted the rings. Five. Nobody picked up. She couldn't put the receiver down, just in case somebody was there. Ten. Fifteen. Twenty. Still, she couldn't let go. Not yet. She would hang on until he answered, until eternity. Twenty-five. Twenty-six. Somebody picked up. Spyder.

'Kinell.' Kinell. The South London alphabet: K is for fucking hell. 'Will you stop ringin' the friggin' phone. Who is it anyway?'

Pause while she wondered whether she should say anything or replace the receiver without speaking.

'It's Sam.'

'Oh, you. Might have guessed. He still ain't here. So you can piss off and stop buggin me.'

He slammed the receiver down.

*

Skell wasn't much more than a hundred miles from Vauxhall, but all roads leaving London were slow. Heavy rain had left pools of standing water that fanned as the camper van ploughed through them. Single lane across East Anglia. She ignored her impatient tail of cars as she crawled through the regimented pines of Thetford Forest, past the RAF base, a black transporter plane coming in to land like a giant hornet. Dogged rain bombarded relentless cabbage fields. She didn't spot the sea until she'd been looking at it for ten minutes because it had merged with the sky in a seamless grey blur. Off the main road, into the hawthorn-hedged lanes, over a humpback bridge, swifts diving for midges in the meadow beyond. Battered Land Rover behind. Skell's dilapidated windmill sails marked the horizon; a reminder that the place had once been a port busy enough to have its own red-light alley, until the river inlet had silted up and left the harbourmaster's house overlooking a salt-marsh. Stone terraced fishermen's cottages, narrow flint passageways once bustling, now abandoned to the cold easter-lies blasting in from the North Sea. Skell had the forlorn air of a cheated wife, unsure how long to hang on before she gave up hope and walked away.

Sam parked her grime-caked van around the back of the village, water pouring down the run-offs at the side of the road. Through the puddled flint-walled lokes between the houses, sharp around a right-angled corner. A wild strawberry glowed like a ruby in the grass edging of the path. She stooped, plucked and dropped the tangy berry in her mouth, then spat it out when she saw a Labrador advancing, leg-cocking and spraying the verge as it moseyed along. The Barbour-wearing dog walker tweaked a stiff smile as she passed.

The foxgloves in the walled garden behind Dave's place drooped with the weight of the day's deluge. She poked her hand through the wrought-iron gate in the wall, tried the latch. Locked. She made her way along the side of the house, peered through the kitchen window, light on. Dave must be home; he always switched the lights off when he left the house. She leaned to one side, trying to see if he was at the far end of the kitchen, but her line of sight was obscured by a palm cross propped against the pane. She rapped the glass with her knuckle. No reply. She walked almost to the end of the loke where the path joined the main street through the village, cut right across the paved front garden with its neat lavender and rosemary beds, and rang the doorbell. No answer. She rang again. Nothing. She stooped, pushed the letterbox open, peered, nothing, nobody. Her eyes watered, breath shallow, throat constricting.

'Dave. Where the fuck are you?'

Eventually his voice.

'OK, OK, I'm coming. Give us a chance.'

She watched him waddling towards her through the rectangle of the letterbox, and before he had a chance to reach the door, she shouted, 'What were you doing?'

He opened the door.

'Having a crap. I didn't realize I needed to clear it with you first.'

'I thought something might have happened to you.'

'God, you're jumpy.'

They retreated to the kitchen; rusty-red flagstone floor, pine dresser displaying hand-thrown thick pottery mugs.

'Look at all this.' He waved his hand around the kitchen dismissively.

'What about it?'

'It's so… so bourgeois.'

'Better than the curling lino and stained Formica we have in Vauxhall.'

'I'd rather be in Vauxhall.'

'I'd rather you were too.' She meant it, although even as she said it she heard Luke's voice in her head – *Listen, there's something else… Dave* – and a slither of something she didn't like crept into her mind. Doubt. She brushed it away.

Dave said, 'It's not like you to be so forthcoming with your affections. What's wrong with you?'

She was about to say, well, Luke's gone missing, but silently reddened instead.

'I know,' Dave said. 'Of course. You need a shoulder to cry on.'

'That's not what I meant.'

'Don't worry. I understand.'

He brewed her a cuppa – a Barry's tea bag dunked in one of his precious Aston Villa mugs. He had two and he had taken them both with him when he moved to Skell. Loyalty to his beloved football team prevented him from drinking tea out of anything else, least of all a hand-thrown pottery cup. The kitchen had an Aga but Dave couldn't quite cope with the extravagance of leaving it on the whole time in order to use it occasionally. He had acquired a range of electrical equipment to supplant its various functions: plug-in kettle, Morphy Richards toaster, Baby Belling cooker, single-bar heater. His collection of cheap domestic appliances and his tacky football mugs made him seem like an unwelcome refugee in this expensively rustic interior.

'So, what's the story?' Dave asked.

'Luke is in some kind of trouble because of the protest at the power station. He went down to meet this power station worker at Dungeness and then he disappeared.'

Dave shook his head, tipped himself backwards on the dining chair, foot resting against a table leg, arms folded, eyeing her through his thick lenses.

'A protest at a power station? Why would he be in trouble because of that? Why would anybody give a toss?'

Dave was dismissive about politics, activism, conspiracy theories. So even if she did tell him about the file and MI5's computer index he would probably scoff. His aversion to politics stemmed, she figured, from his Brummie Irish childhood. He remembered the carnage of the IRA's pub bombings in 1974 and he experienced the backlash against anyone Irish afterwards. The events made him wary, not angry – more interested in physical chain reactions than political agitation for change.

She said, 'Well, you can be cynical about it all, but look what happened to the *Rainbow Warrior.*'

'Yes, but the *Rainbow Warrior* was a bit different from a couple of people waving a banner around in Dungeness. The *Rainbow Warrior* was a highly organized set-up. They were in New Zealand because they were planning to disrupt the French government's nuclear weapons tests. The *Rainbow Warrior* was challenging the French state's security apparatus. Which is why the French secret services blew it up. It was a real threat. You and Luke, I mean you are just asking a few people to come and join you at a bloody roadside and shout a few slogans. It's a symbolic gesture. It wouldn't be a threat to anybody.'

She didn't respond.

'He's probably gone off somewhere for a couple of days. As he said. To see a mate, I would guess.' He dunked a chocolate Hobnob in his tea, swirled, removed the biscuit, sucked the soggy half. 'Luke's really got under your skin, hasn't he. You can't stop obsessing about him.'

She scowled. Dave seemed to enjoy scratching at her relationship.

'I'm just saying, that's all,' he said.

'Just saying what?'

'Just saying that he doesn't have to ask your permission if he decides to head off somewhere by himself for a couple of days.'

'He didn't say he was heading off somewhere. He said something had come up. He sounded scared.'

Dave reached for another biscuit.

'Maybe he made it sound more dramatic because he was worried you would blow your top at him if he said he wanted to go off for a few days with his mates.'

She took a slurp of her tea, examined the mug, beginning to feel she had made a mistake, driving up to Skell.

Dave said, 'OK. Let's see if we can work this out. Was he in Dungeness when he called you on Saturday morning?'

'He phoned me twice. The first phone call, the one I picked up at about nine on Saturday morning, was from Dungeness. He told me he was there early, waiting to meet this contact from the power station. The second phone call, which I think he made at about ten thirty, must have been after the meeting. I had already gone, so he left me a message.' She replayed Luke's words in her head, tried to make sense of them. 'He said he had to go. He must have been about to drive off somewhere. There was background noise on the tape, wind and breakers I think. So I suppose he was still in Dungeness then.'

A flicker of – what – concern, or doubt about her version of events perhaps, registered in Dave's dark eyes darting around behind the lenses. What was he thinking? She's deluded?

Or was he hiding something from her? *Trust nobody.* She dunked her biscuit, watched it disintegrate and sink to the bottom of the mug, tried to block the disquieting voices in her head.

He pushed himself away from the table. 'Let's have some-thing to eat, then go for a walk.'

'You've got something cooking in the Aga then?'

'Nope.' He rummaged in a cupboard, produced a can of baked beans, tipped it in a saucepan, plonked it on the Belling.

The sky was clearing behind them to the west, but it was still leaden overhead and coal-black in the east. Spitting rain hit her cheeks, the back end of the downpour. They crossed the high street – once the main harbour road – ducked under the arch by the old customs house, slithered along the muddy edges of an oily puddle, disturbed a toad, cut around the back of the wind-mill and climbed the steps to the coast path. She balanced on top of the stile, watched the waves of wind-flexed rushes. The mudflats, the saltpans and the tidal lagoons shimmered in the low evening sun, radiated yellow, and she thought of Chernobyl's plume, the nuclear rain falling across the uplands.

She jumped down from the stile, swished her hand through the damp stems.

'What did you say about the dangers of radioactive contam-ination from the Chernobyl fallout?' she asked.

He pushed his glasses up his nose, surveyed the coastal plain.

'Well, obviously there's the immediate direct hit, and the north of Britain got some of that, although nowhere near as much as countries closer to the original source. Ukraine, Belarus, Germany and Sweden. But then there's the secondary contam-ination with long-lived radionuclides like caesium 137. That happens through soil absorption, wash-off, bioaccumulation in plants and animals – the stuff we eat – that sort of thing.'

'Comforting.'

'You know my view. Levels of contamination in Britain are unlikely to be high enough to harm human health.'

'Not even in the long term?'

He shrugged. 'Who cares about the long term? In the long term we're all dead anyway.'

'That's a bit flippant.'

'OK. Sorry. But the thing is, the long-term impacts of Chernobyl are not going to be anywhere near as bad as the long-term health and environmental impacts of straightforward air pollution – car fumes, industrial smog. I'm always amazed by the extent to which people turn a blind eye to the hazards they live with every day, because it's too inconvenient to recognize them.'

He pointed across the headland. 'That's the field centre where I work, beyond the dunes, at the end of Flaxby Point.'

The distant building sat at the furthest edge of a beckoning finger of shingle and sand that curled round to form a bay on its inner side. The ocean was bluer here than the grey Channel at Dungeness, but it was the same longshore waves that coaxed the fringes of the land into these shifting, unreliable spits and marshes. A red-rimmed rainbow arched the sky, bright against the cloudbank, and dropped down on the roof of a solitary house. She pointed. 'Look where the rainbow ends.'

'Bane House.'

'Does anybody live there?'

'It's deserted. I've seen people camping in it occasionally.'

'Let's walk over and see if it's harbouring a crock of gold.'

The drizzle eased, the rainbow evaporated, leaving the dusky sky and sea more amethyst than blue. A grey heron took off from an inlet as they approached, its landing gear still trailing. She felt at home in these ghost lands borrowed from the water, earthsea, inhabited only by smugglers and the fishermen who had travelled this coast for centuries. What was that phrase that Alastair had used? Den and strand. The fishermen from Dungeness had rights to land and dry their nets on these beaches, summer migrants to East Anglia returning south to Dungeness for the winter fishing. Dungeness. Her mind snapped back to Luke, his disappearance. She couldn't stop thinking about him.

'Is it possible Luke might have been given some information from this power station worker he met that's put him in danger?'

'Like what?'

'Safety problem? Maybe Dungeness is another Chernobyl waiting to happen.'

'Well, there have always been questions about why anybody in their right mind would build a nuclear power station on a bed of shifting shingle in an area prone to flooding. But that's hardly secret information.'

'OK then. Could he have found out about some criminal activity?'

'What sort of criminal activity?'

'Dunno. Somebody stealing nuclear material.'

'Why would anybody steal nuclear material?'

'Build a bomb.'

'That's pretty far-fetched, even by your standards.'

'But theoretically, is it possible?'

'Theoretically, anything is possible.'

'Jesus. You know what I mean. Is it possible, for example, that somebody could build a bomb with the waste material being transported from Dungeness to Sellafield?'

He frowned. 'I'm not an expert on nuclear weapons, but I'd say it certainly wouldn't be easy.'

'Yes, but possible?'

She watched his face while she waited for him to answer and she sensed that her question had troubled him in some way she couldn't fathom.

'OK, if you want a sensible answer, let me think it through.'

The wind strengthened as they approached the coast. A vee of geese flew silently overhead. She moved closer to Dave so she could hear him speak.

'So, well, nuclear bombs are usually made from plutonium. The fission process in a power plant produces plutonium. And, of course, the spent fuel rods do contain the products of the fission process.'

'Bomb material?'

He shook his head.

'Not easily. For a start, the plutonium produced by power plants is generally reactor grade, not the purer weapons grade. Which doesn't mean reactor grade plutonium can't be used to make a bomb – but I would imagine it's extremely difficult to do. Those spent fuel rods are not exactly small. Any would-be bomb maker would have to magic away a piece of metal that weighed several tons, perform some kind of extraction process to obtain any fissionable material and then create a device that could set off the chain reaction for an explosion when and where you wanted it to happen. And you have to do all of this while protecting yourself from radiation. Otherwise you're fried. Obviously it's possible. But, personally, I think you would need some sort of state backing to steal nuclear material and turn it into a bomb. It's a bit of an organizational nightmare. It would cost a fortune to put all of that in place.'

She plucked a frond of sea lavender, wound the tough stem round her fingers. Dave revelled in being the rational scientist. He referred to himself as a northern chemist, even though he came from the Midlands. Political divide, not geographical, he maintained – anywhere north of Watford was off the radar as far as Westminster was concerned. Whatever. He wasn't even a proper chemist. He was a biochemist. He twiddled his lip nervously, as if there was something eating him. She attempted to process what he was saying and not saying, winkle out the cause of his edginess. She said, 'I still think the power station worker must have given Luke some information that has made him feel he might be targeted in some way.'

He snapped, 'Why does everybody assume there's always some threat or conspiracy attached to anything to do with nuclear power? Why can't people just look at the science?'

She was taken aback by the fierceness of his response.

'OK, so what's so good about the science?'

'It's amazing. Nuclear scientists are like modern magicians. They worked out how to split atoms, transform metals.'

'Transforming metals?' She asked nervously, wary of provoking another flare of intensity. 'Like alchemists.'

'Yeah. Like alchemists. But instead of the chemical processes the alchemists were searching for, they use physical processes – nuclear fission.' He frowned. 'Where did alchemists spring from anyway?'

'Dungeness. When Luke didn't appear on Saturday, I ended up talking about alchemy with this new age hippy who lives in one of the fishermen's cottages on the beach. Alastair. He came to the meetings we organized down there.'

The marbled wings of a redshank rose from the shingle in front of her feet; the bird fluttered away.

'He told me he had a spirit guide.'

'Oh my god. This is what happens when I move out of the house for a few months. You start consulting spirit guides.'

Dave's tone had returned to its normal level of teasing, clearly relieved the conversation had moved away from Luke and the power station.

'He was interesting.'

'What, the hippy or the spirit guide?'

'Both. One and the same, I suppose. His spirit guide was a real person, a seventeenth-century alchemist called John Allin.'

'Did you meet John Allin?'

'Possibly.'

'And did this John Allin claim to have found the alchemical formula?'

'Well, the way Alastair explained it, alchemy was a spiritual quest as much as a material one so maybe he did find the answer in some way. Perhaps he managed to transform himself.'

They turned north along the shingle headland, white-crested breakers crashing on the shore, and she saw a figure emerging from the foam of the waves and thought for a moment it was Jim, but then she realized it was nothing more than spindrift.

'Or perhaps Allin drove himself to despair because he couldn't find the formula to turn base metal into gold,' she said. 'Perhaps he flipped to the darker side. That's what Alastair was saying about alchemy, dabbling in the occult, people might start off with good intentions, but once the power is unleashed it can be turned around, become a curse. Reverse alchemy. Isn't it the same with nuclear science? Isn't that why people are afraid of it? Einstein despaired when he realized the atomic science he had helped discover could be used to make a bomb.'

'Yeah, I know. Poor bloody Einstein having to live with that on his conscience. Hiroshima. Nagasaki. The thing is, though…' He stalled, adjusted his glasses; picked the conversation up again. 'I mean, you're creating lots of conspiracy theories in your head about the power station, Luke and nuclear bombs, but you don't need to build a nuclear bomb to create terror. You could just release radioactive material in the air. Or into the water supply. It wouldn't be as instantly destructive as a bomb, but it would be easier to do, and it would certainly terrorize people with the fear of radiation – poison pumped through your system and dying from the inside out. There are plenty of sources lying around in places that aren't even half as secure as a power station. Hospitals. Research labs...'

He dried up. Neither of them spoke, heads down into the wind, Sam wondering what Dave was getting at as they scrunched along the shingle. They neared Bane House, with its chimney pot squatting on the slate roof in a one-fingered gesture of defiance to the elements.

'What's a house doing out here in the middle of nowhere anyway?' she asked.

'Nobody really knows. But according to local legend it was built by smugglers.'

'A lookout place, I suppose.'

'More gruesome, I'm afraid. The barman at the Butcher's Arms told me informers were taken here for questioning by the local smuggling gangs to find out what they had told the authorities. Sometimes they would be kept alive for weeks, apparently. Chained up, beaten, forced to confess, reveal the information they had given away. And then they were killed anyway, their bodies returned to their relatives in hacked-up pieces as a warning not to talk...'

'God, that's grim.'

'I don't know why you're sounding shocked. People still torture informers these days, don't they?' His voice was agitated again.

'What people?'

'Oh, you know, Sam. The mafia. The IRA. Drug gangs. The CIA. Anybody carrying out some kind of dodgy activity they're desperate to keep secret. That's how most shadowy activities come to light, isn't it? Informers. And so any dubious outfit is going to be on the lookout for tell-tales and will try to scare everybody shitless so they don't say anything. Possibly by hacking the odd tongue out and sending it to a loved one.'

She poked the tip of her tongue against the back of her teeth and remembered all the times she had been told to say nothing about Jim, his work, anything she might have seen or over-heard, because it was dangerous to talk, pass his secrets into the wrong hands. Loose tongues cost lives. Hers as well as his.

'That's why it's called Bane House,' Dave said. 'Because it's fucking cursed.'

He stuck his hands in his pockets, hunched his shoulders. He was behaving so oddly tonight, not his normal self at all. She had a definite sense that Dave was hiding something. Was he keeping a secret that he was too scared to tell? They were right below Bane House now. She assessed the building's façade: two windows, one edged with jagged glass, the other partially boarded. She glimpsed a movement behind the shattered pane, a fleeting whiteness, a pale face staring through the window, directly at her. No, she must have been mistaken. Scudding clouds reflected in the broken glass. They scrambled up the steep shingle ridge from the shoreline. The house disappeared from view as they climbed and then reappeared when they reached the flat top of beach.

Sam said, 'What if there is somebody inside? If they are doing something illegal and we burst in on them, they might react badly.'

'I shouldn't have mentioned smugglers.'

She slowed her pace, her feet silent on the carpet of bird's-foot trefoil and sea blite underneath.

He said, 'If you don't want to look in, we don't have to. It doesn't bother me.'

'We're here now. We might as well look inside.'

An outside toilet with a red door stood apart from the house at the bottom of a slope. As she passed it, a kee-wick call from the marsh startled her.

'Was that an owl?'

'It could have been.'

She looked across to the far side of the headland and the bay inside the spit's curling finger, but there was no sign of the bird.

'Is there a path that way?'

'Yes. It goes down to a jetty, the water route to the research lab. You can take a boat from the harbour of the next village along the coast road.'

She spotted the dark line of the path threading through the marsh to the bay. Tied alongside the jetty, she could just make out the shape of an inflatable dinghy with an outboard motor. A Zodiac possibly, like the one the French secret agents used to blow up the *Rainbow Warrior*. She wanted to point it out to Dave, but he had already reached the house and was looking through the broken window. She caught up with him.

'I don't think there's anybody at home,' he said.

She must have imagined the face. Ghosts of her mind. She shaded her eye with her hand, searched the corners, spotted an empty crisp packet.

'But I think somebody has been in here.'

'Undoubtedly. It's not locked up.'

She followed him around the side of the house, to the back door, unlocked. Inside, one large brick room, the last of the evening light exposing its emptiness. A broken chair. Long extinguished firewood in the grate. Empty beer bottle. Used condom.

'See,' Dave said. 'There's nothing nefarious going on here.'

He sounded relieved. The low sun shot into a far corner, glinted. She walked over. Not gold, but the silver cover of a book of matches with black letters on the front.

'Matches from Heaven,' she said. 'I've got a friend who's a bouncer at Heaven.'

Dave glanced over, eyebrow raised.

'St Peter?'

'Not that heaven. The gay nightclub underneath the arches behind Charing Cross station.'

She lifted the matchbook – the archaeologist's instinct to examine any artefact – then remembered Jim telling her about pocket litter, the bus tickets, till receipts, sweet wrappers that accumulate in people's pockets and give away secrets about their identity. Jim and his tradecraft tips. She eyed the book in her hand; it had dropped out of somebody's pocket, revealed something about its owner. She flipped the cover open. One match remained, black stem, silver head. She tore it out, swiped against the strike; the match exploded, a blue flame burned, fizzled and died. The matchbook couldn't have been lying there long; it wasn't damp. She slipped the empty silver cover into her overcoat pocket.

'Come on, let's go,' she said.

She walked out the back, glanced right, noticed the red door of the outside toilet flapping open in the wind, and then spotted an indistinct figure striding along the pathway to the jetty and the dinghy. Tall, thin, dark-haired, or was it a hat? She squinted. There was something about the silhouette, the movement, that made her think it was a woman. She stared until the twilight air fizzed and danced and she realized the figure had vanished. Perhaps she hadn't seen anything in the first place. Her fatigued mind was playing tricks on her this evening, the dusk distorting her vision. She fingered the book of matches in her pocket, turned and watched the curling breakers hitting the sea-facing side of the spit, the ranks of waves stretching over the North Sea to the Lowlands. Amsterdam. She loved Amsterdam. She and Luke had made an unplanned trip there in the dreary days of February. He appeared in Vauxhall one Friday evening with tickets for the ferry train. They had a weekend of hash cafés and parties in huge squatted factories. On their return, pie-eyed and happy, they were hauled aside by the customs officers at Dover, made to empty their rucksacks. The customs men found nothing. Who would be stupid enough to carry hash on them when they were returning from Amsterdam?

Dave closed the back door of Bane House behind him, joined her.

She said, 'This part of the coast would be a good landing place if you're coming from Amsterdam.'

'So?'

'Maybe this place is still used by smugglers after all.'

'I've never seen any sign of it.'

'Maybe you've not looked very hard.'

'Maybe I just don't go searching for the dark side. Unlike some people I could mention.' Who was he kidding, she thought, he was definitely in a saturnine mood tonight.

'Do you still have the phone sessions with the therapist?' he asked.

'Yes. Why?'

'I was just wondering.'

Fuck him and his digs. She said nothing. The tide was flooding in as they returned along the headland. They walked on the flat shingle, between the breakers and the saltmarsh, the wind pressing from behind, thankfully, rather than lashing her face. She kept her eyes on the horizon, the silhouette of a small boat breaking the line between sky and sea, thought she saw the black dot of a dinghy nearer to the shore, dipping through the swell. Was that the Zodiac she had seen earlier by the jetty?

'You're quiet,' he said.

'You don't usually mind if nobody says anything.'

She didn't like this tension with Dave, it wasn't how it was supposed to be. Dave was her mate. She balled her hand, shoved it in her overcoat pocket. Her knuckles touched the bone from the Lookers' Hut – she'd forgotten about her finds. She pulled it out, held it on the flat of her palm. Peace offering.

'Look what I unearthed in one of the Lookers' Huts out on Romney. Is it a sheep's bone?'

He took the bone from her hand, held it up to his face, lifted his glasses.

'No. It's not a sheep's bone. I reckon it's human. Metatarsal.'

'Jesus. Really? A finger?'

'Yep. It's quite large so probably male.'

'How old do you think it is?'

'It's impossible to say. You'd have to radiocarbon test it to find out.' He stroked his chin. 'It looks to me as if it has been burned.'

'What, you mean somebody threw a finger in the fire and burned the flesh off it?'

'Possibly.'

'You don't think it could be Luke's finger, do you?' Her voice was tight.

'No. No. For god's sake no. Of course it's not Luke's finger.'

She relaxed, dug in her pocket, removed the folded tissue holding the lock of hair.

'I found this too. Probably nothing to do with the bone. I wondered whether it was some kind of charm. You know, a shepherd placing a lock of hair in the hearth to block out evil spirits.'

He reached for the tissue, unfolded the package she had made and stood dead still, staring at the contents, his face pallid.

'What's the matter?'

'Nothing. Well, it's very black.'

'So? It's not Luke's hair.'

'I can see that. Can I keep it?'

'What, the bone?'

'Yes. And the hair.'

'Sure, I don't want them.'

The way he was behaving made her head swim. *Trust nobody.* Her gut tightened. *Listen, there's something else… Dave.* The tension made her want to spew. She couldn't stand having niggling doubts about her best mate. She couldn't trust nobody, she had to believe in her friends. She didn't want to question him. She didn't want to argue with Dave.

They headed inland in silence, across the saltmarsh, the first stars appearing above. A hawk swooped though the reed beds like a dambuster; hefty, golden brown, endless wingspan.

'Marsh harrier,' he said.

She concentrated, mind on the hawk gliding, hovering low above the reeds, water furrows below. She caught a movement, drab among the green. A bunting, frozen in terror. A wave of sickness ran through her body; she knew she should dive and catch the small bird, but she couldn't face the kill. She left it, the saltmarsh spreading out below her as she gained height, the indigo creeks forming fractals in the green and brown of the spit. The harrier soared away with a shrill shriek and she returned to earth.

CHAPTER 6

SINGLE FILE ALONG the sea wall path. The headlights of a car driving the coast road lit up the grey houses of Skell then disappeared inland. Sam, mind elsewhere, stumbled over a rock, caught herself on a knee and an outstretched hand. She straightened, brushed off the soil, glanced over the steep bank to the reed beds below.

'Any solid ground down there?'

'If there is, it's difficult to find. Saltpans, creeks and irrigation channels. It's not like Romney, there's no sea wall holding the water back here, the tide comes in behind the shingle and fills the creeks and lagoons.'

She scanned the marsh, picked out the white zed of a wading bird and, as she looked beyond to Flaxby Point, a flicker of light flared and died.

'Will-o-the-wisp,' she said.

'Yeah, I saw it too. And I saw the leprechaun carrying it.'

'Seriously. I did see a light. Look. There it is again.' The point of light hovered, lengthened, vanished.

'It's a torch,' Dave said.

'Somebody walking the path from the jetty to Bane House.' The figure she had seen earlier, the person she had thought might be a woman, were they returning now they knew the coast was clear?

'No. Not a torch. Definitely a will-o-the-wisp.' Dave

chuckled. Then he stopped abruptly and said, 'Do you ever see your dad?'

She was still watching Bane House, the headland, but nothing was visible apart from the froth of the breakers crashing against the shore.

She said, 'Sometimes I glimpse him. I see his face in the crowd. And then he disappears.'

She didn't want to tell him about Vauxhall Bridge, the figure on the shore, the Effra run-off. The footprints leading into the tunnel. They were both silent now, listening to the howl of the wind, the terns mewing as they flitted overhead.

Sam asked then, 'Do you ever see your mum?'

He didn't respond immediately and she wondered whether he was crying, although when he spoke his voice was steady.

'I saw her a couple of times after she died. That's quite common, I would imagine.'

'But you don't believe in ghosts. Lost souls hanging around, doing their time in purgatory?'

'No. I'm a scientist. I leave the superstitions to my old Irish rellies and the yokels of Skell.'

'I didn't think there were any yokels left in Skell, it feels so desolate.'

'Well, the London lawyers and academics have snapped up a fair few of the quaint fishermen's cottages and pushed most of the remaining yokels out, but they've just gone down the road to the new-build houses on the outskirts. And now they make a living out of servicing the second-home owners. But I don't think their beliefs have shifted since the witch-hunts of Matthew Hopkins's day. Mind you I'm not sure the beliefs of the lawyers and the academics have shifted that much either.'

She wondered whether he was right. *Daemonologie*. Beliefs

etched indelibly below the surface, written in our sacred texts. *Thou shalt not suffer a witch to live.* King James Bible, Exodus 22:18.

Dave continued. 'There's still nothing the English enjoy better than a witch-hunt, a collective venting of the spleen. A good public hanging and burning on the front pages of the tabloids. Irish. Unemployed. Immigrants. Whoever.'

He was always animated by a chance to have a dig at the English. She didn't blame him. He had told her that when he was an Oxford fresher and had done the obligatory introductory glass of sherry with the Dean of his college, he had mentioned that his father came from Tipperary. Later, he had overheard a tutor repeating the information with a sneer and a reference to the 'Bog Irish'. Dave had been shocked. He couldn't quite marry the small-mindedness of the remark with his expectations of Oxford as an intellectual hothouse.

'Like the woman who comes to clean the house, Marge,' Dave said. 'She had a go at me the other week for leaving my toenail clippings on the floor in the bathroom. Told me I had to be careful in case somebody with a grudge gathered them up and used them against me. She told me, in all seriousness, that there were still some people around here who dabbled in the old ways, casting spells and cursing neighbours when slighted. Maleficent witches.'

Her hand went to her cheek and down again. Dave didn't spot her reflex action, continued talking.

'Although, to be fair, Marge isn't really a yokel. She moved out here from the suburbs of London.'

She swiped at furry reed-heads as she walked, mind going over fragments – her birthmark, witchcraft, conversations with Luke – wondering whether she was on the radar because she was Jim Coyle's daughter, whether it was her who had drawn some kind of negative attention to her boyfriend which had forced him to disappear. Was it all her fault?

Dave said, 'You're worrying about Luke again.'

'It's difficult not to.'

'You're freaking yourself out. There's usually a simple explanation for everything. He's probably...'

He left the sentence hanging.

'He's probably what?'

'He's probably decided he needs a break or something.'

'What, you mean from me?'

'Maybe.'

'Fuck you, Daley.'

'Why are you angry with me?'

'Because you suggested Luke needed a break from me.'

'Everybody needs a break every now and then. And he has said... You can be...'

'What? I can be what? What did he say?'

Dave didn't answer. They passed the windmill in silence, crossed the car park, trod the waterlogged path by the customs house. Disturbed the toad again. Over the road, along the loke, lit only by the bedroom lights of a nearby cottage.

'So what did Luke say about me?'

'Look, he's mentioned he thinks you are having a hard time getting over your dad's death.'

'There's nothing wrong with that.' She was shouting, her voice amplified by the flint walls enclosing them.

'Who said there was anything wrong with it? All I'm saying is that Luke said sometimes it can be a bit...'

'What?'

'Well, it's difficult spending all your time with somebody who is in an emotionally difficult place. So maybe he decided to take a break.'

'Is that what he said? That I'm difficult?'

'No, he didn't say that you are difficult. It's difficult being with somebody who is… What he meant… he was a bit worried about you.'

'When did he tell you this anyway?'

'It was just a conversation.'

A conversation. She could hear how it went, because she'd had it with herself. She was hard work, a pain, she knew it deep inside. She wanted to kick herself for being useless, or Dave for pointing it out. Or Jim for ruining her life by dying.

'Is that what you think? That I'm hard work?'

'Look. I don't mind. I'm the bloke whose mum committed suicide.'

He paused and in the silence she saw an urban Ophelia, face up in the Digbeth Branch Canal, under Love Lane Bridge, caught among the coke cans and beer bottles.

Dave said, 'I'm used to misery. I've been there.'

They stumbled along the unlit alley while she wondered why he was telling her about this conversation with Luke now, whether he was exaggerating, deliberately stirring, trying to stoke a rift between her and Luke. *Trust nobody*. It must have been Harry who left her that message. A follow-up, a reminder of their earlier conversation, a confirmation that somebody, somewhere, who was compiling a computerized index of suspected terrorists had come across the name Dave Daley. A bat flitted and swooped across their path.

'That's a barbastelle,' Dave said. 'You can see the outline of its pug nose. It's amazing how they use echolocation to find their dinner.'

She wasn't paying attention. Any other time she would have been interested, but right then she didn't care.

'I was trying to make you feel better,' Dave said.

'By telling me I'm a pain?'

'No, that's your interpretation of what I said. I meant there are some fairly obvious, mundane explanations for Luke's non-appearance at Dungeness.'

They turned a corner, round the back of Dave's garden, along the side of the house. She sniffed, wiped her nose on her coat sleeve, wondered whether she was a wreck, and had driven Luke mad with her misery. Although, if she had to analyse it, she would say she wasn't miserable when she was with Luke, she was happy. Maybe she was guilty of dumping her miseries on Dave and he was projecting his feelings about her on to Luke. She couldn't fathom it. Best to change the subject, her default tactic when dealing with emotional situations she couldn't handle.

'So, the Professor who owns this place, the one who let you stay here. Does he indulge in irrational beliefs as well? Is he a big Christian?'

'No. What makes you ask that?'

'The Palm Sunday cross.' She pointed at the window as they passed, the palm leaf crucifix pale against the gloom of the unlit kitchen.

'It's there for show I should imagine. He probably goes to one or two services a year to keep in with the second-home owners posh set. You know, Easter. Christmas Eve. That kind of thing. His wife probably makes him do it.' He removed the front door key from his pocket.

She said, 'Another long-suffering man having to put up with the irrational and unreasonable demands of his overemotional wife.'

Dave sighed as he pushed the door open.

'I'm sorry I said anything. Let's drop it.'

*

She locked herself in the bathroom, lowered the toilet lid and sat down, elbows on knees, face on pummelled fists. She wanted to be somewhere happy. She wanted to be with Luke. She needed to talk to him, feel him next to her. Dave knocked on the bathroom door.

'Sam, please.'

She stood up, leaned on the sink and examined her reflection in the mirror. Her eyes were pink and puffy. She splashed cold water on her face, surveyed her image again. If she turned her face away from the light, she could see the fine lines forming around her eyes, unspoken anxieties eating into her skin. She opened the bathroom door. Dave was in the hall, arms crossed, his face tortured.

'I'm sorry,' he said.

'No. I'm sorry. You're right. I'm overreacting to everything.'

'No you're not.'

'I am.'

'Well, actually you are a bit. But it's understandable. You're worried. Come downstairs and have a drink. We could sit in the back garden.'

Dave sat at the wooden table. Sam lay on the ground, ignored the dampness of the grass, watched the Milky Way emerge, a thumb print marking the sky.

'That which is below is like that which is above and that which is above is like that which is below,' she said.

'Don't tell me,' he said. 'More hippy rambling from your friend at Dungeness.'

'Yep. The *Emerald Tablet*, Hermes Tresmegistus. Some ancient alchemical text. Newton had a translation apparently. As above so below.'

'I suppose there is some truth in it in a very general way.'

He opened the wine with the corkscrew attachment of his penknife, poured. She rose from her grass bed, came and sat beside him at the table.

'In what way?'

'Well, the chemical elements that are in us are elements that come from the earth, the plants around us, and those elements come from stellar explosions. We are made from stardust.'

He knocked back his wine, placed the glass on the table, twiddled the thin stem, stared at the puddle of red liquid covering the bottom of the glass, poured some more, knocked that back too.

'Oxygen. Carbon. Hydrogen. Calcium. Iron. All of our elements are listed in the periodic table. And sometimes when I study the periodic table, I reckon it holds the secrets of human behaviour and human history. We are like the chemical elements from which we are made, and we are bound by the same periodic laws.'

His voice was monotone, as if he was in a trance. She wondered whether being out here all by himself on the bleak edge of Norfolk was taking its toll, affecting his stability, pushing him to weird places.

'I could map my life on the periodic table, with all its repetitions, the same actions and reactions in slightly different form – every two years. Or eight years. Or eighteen years.'

He filled his wine glass again. Leaned over and topped hers up too, brushing her arm as he sat back. She pulled away, scared of being pulled down, drowning. She dug in her overcoat pocket, pulled out her puff in its clingfilm wrap, rolled herself a spliff, lit it, inhaled, let the stars swirl around her head, searched for the patterns. The periodicity. The death of her father, then two years later Luke's disappearance, Jim's diary, the whistle on the phone, the reappearance of Harry.

Time loops. She tugged on the roach. Dave was studying his wine glass. He knocked back the dregs, reached for the bottle, and she surveyed the heavy outlines of his face, the marks of his sadness.

'I suppose it's my way of dealing with the difficult stuff. I'm not saying I'm bound to top myself like my mother. But I do think it helps to deal with the past if you can recognize the tendency to repeat the traits of your parents.'

She searched for something comforting to say.

'You can change the patterns. You can be like an alchemist and transform the elements.'

'But you have to work with what you've inherited. Nobody is a blank slate.'

'I don't know about that. Sometimes I think I am a blank slate because I don't really know that much about my father. He was always a mystery.'

Dave straightened, looked at her with a sudden intensity.

'What, you mean because he was a cop? An undercover cop? Like a spy?'

She took a final puff of the spliff, stubbed the dead roach in the soil. The conversation faltered. She wasn't in the mood for talking about Jim – she had only mentioned him to stop Dave dwelling on his mum's suicide. She wished she hadn't bothered. Why was Dave interested anyway? The screech of an owl broke the silence. She listened, waiting for another call; a car passed, wind rustled the oaks. A faint whistle. She stood, stepped over to the flowerbed below the flint wall. She considered climbing the apple tree, but spotted a large terracotta urn upturned on the soil. It looked sturdy enough to hold her weight. She pulled herself up, head and chin above the wall top. Cat's eyes fizzled and disappeared around a corner. Nothing else. She jumped back to the ground and examined the pot she had been standing on.

Dave persisted. 'So was he really a spy? Or was it more mundane than that?'

She should humour him, stop being so prickly. Fight the doubts about her friend.

'He was a kind of spy. He worked for this funny part of the Force that was like a cross between cops and Intelligence.'

'Who did he spy on?'

'I don't know. I blanked it out. Laughed it off. He was always disappearing. We didn't know what he was doing or when he would be back. It scared me so I tried not to think about it.' She heard her parents arguing in her head, Liz cackling, the front door slamming. 'The Home Secretary knew what he was doing, apparently.'

'The Home Secretary?' He gave her his sceptical look.

'It was all very cloak and dagger. They used spy tradecraft – fake identities, secret codes. Drop boxes.'

'Drop boxes?'

'Pre-arranged places where you can leave messages. Secret information.'

She poked the ceramic pot with her foot. 'Like this. This would make a good drop box. You could leave papers in here. And then somebody else could come and collect them.'

She stepped back, examined the pot from a distance. 'Although, it should be somewhere more accessible. And neutral. A place not connected with either the dropper or the collector.'

She was making it up as she went along, the rules of the spying game. So what, she reckoned she was probably right anyway. She'd read Kim Philby's autobiography. Dave glanced at her. She glanced away.

'I'm tired. I need to sleep.'

She walked into the kitchen. He followed behind. She pointed at the palm cross in the window. 'There's something you could use as a signal to say you've left something in the drop box. It's easy to see if you're walking down the loke, even in the dark.'

She moved the cross to the right end of the ledge. 'If it's on the right, that means no message. If it's on the left, it means you've left some information under the urn in the back garden. And look, if you turn it upside down,' she added, 'that means danger. Something bad has happened. Be careful.'

She laughed unnaturally. Dave didn't join in. She tipped the palm cross to see if she could make it balance on its head, stood back to admire her handiwork and something in her head snapped. She righted the cross, and swivelled around to face Dave.

'Why have you been talking to Luke about me? Why have you been stirring?'

She folded her arms, shifted her weight.

'God, Sam, will you stop being so aggressive?'

She flicked her hair. 'I thought you were my friend.'

'I thought you were mine.'

'I need some sleep. It's a long drive and I want to set off early tomorrow.'

'Fine.'

She stalked to the kitchen door.

'Listen,' he said.

She wavered.

'Luke can look after himself. I think you should just forget about Luke for a while.'

'I don't give a shit what you think.' Her hand reached out and found an object on the dresser. Her fingers grasped and hurled it at the far wall. It smashed, splinters raining on to the flagstone floor. She registered the mess but it took her a moment to work out what had happened.

'Sam, that's my Aston Villa mug you've broken.'

She glared at him and she could see he had tears in his eyes. She was too angry and confused to say anything. She turned and marched up the stairs. She sat on the bed, listened to Dave pottering around downstairs. The kettle boiled. She pictured him making a cup of tea in his one remaining Aston Villa mug. She felt like a naughty child; she knew she should go downstairs and apologize for what she had done, but she wanted him to come upstairs and forgive her, put his arm around her and tell her she wasn't bad. He didn't. She could hear him cleaning up the mess she had made, the clink of china being swept and dropped in the bin. He padded out of the kitchen, into the hall. He was phoning somebody. Who would he be ringing at this time of night? Perhaps he had a secret girlfriend. She tiptoed over to the door, pulled it open a fraction. Whoever he was calling, they weren't answering. He left a message.

'Hi, Dave here. Sorry to call so late, mate.' Obviously not a girlfriend then. 'I just wanted a quick chat. Something slightly odd's come up. It's… I wanted to talk it through with you. Call us tomorrow if you are around. Cheers, mate. Ta-ra.'

Something slightly odd. Was he talking about her? Their argument? Or was it something else? He coughed. He climbed the stairs. She closed the door quietly, leaped back into bed. She willed him to stick his head around the door and say good night, so they could make up. He walked past her door, went straight to his room.

CHAPTER 7

SAM ROSE EARLY. Six a.m. Mainly because she didn't want to see Dave. She crept about the kitchen, made herself a mug of instant coffee, fiddled with the palm frond cross leaning against the window while she waited for the black liquid to cool, left the cross in its original place against the right-hand side of the ledge. She scalded her mouth as she drained her coffee, decided not to leave a message for Dave.

The blue flash and eerie snigger of a jay greeted her as she headed out the door, tiptoed across the gravel path, stole down the loke. The clouds had returned in the night, massed on the horizon. She clambered into the van, mildly hung over and strongly pissed off. Dave was supposed to be her friend but he had been talking to Luke about her behind her back, stirring, some kind of petty revenge on her because – because what? He was jealous of her relationship with Luke. Or was there some-thing more going on with Dave? *Does the name Dave Daley mean anything to you? Trust nobody.* Perhaps she had been reckless, visiting him, confirming to anybody watching that she was his friend, a co-conspirator.

She followed the cobweb-festooned lanes back to the main road, grey tarmac ahead, queue of champing cars behind, tailing her through Thetford Forest. The day was still dismal even when she emerged from the shade of the pines. Low on petrol and energy, she turned off the road and pulled into a service station for breakfast. She pumped a few quids' worth of fuel in the tank, enough to see her home, grabbed a watery coffee and a cheese sandwich from the shop and perched on a picnic bench. She munched on the soggy bread in the thin daylight. Traffic droned. The pall of fumes hung heavily. Her eyes swept the forecourt; juggernauts on the far side, greasy-haired Harley rider filling his bike, family saloons parked in front of the shop. Volvo estate. Black Audi. Land Rover with a badly dented left front wing. Still in rich agricultural country then. She absent-mindedly rubbed her lip with her hand, tried to work out which of the figures wandering around might be the Land Rover's owner, watched the glass door, expecting to see a green-wellied farmer emerge or a Barbour-wearing City type pretending to be a rural lord. The Land Rover remained empty. She attempted to calculate her next move. Maybe for once she should do exactly as she had been told, sit tight, follow Harry's instructions and wait for him to sort out what was going on with the file. Steer well clear, as far away as possible from a potential terrorist list. MI5. R2. Let the professional handle it. But she had to find Luke, so she couldn't do nothing. She glanced at the Land Rover again, still waiting for its owner to return. Dawdling along the crisp and chocolate aisle in the shop perhaps. Time to hit the road anyway.

She arrived back in Vauxhall, locked the van, crossed the road. A poster on the boards of a long-empty shopfront caught her eye. Kennington Park funfair, a picture of a big wheel and a stall with a striped awning, coloured lights. She took a sharp breath, tasted sweetness at the back of her throat, conjured up a face, steel eyes, crescent-moon scar. The candy man. Her vision went fuzzy, her head heavy. She screwed her eyes tight, blocked it out, told herself she was fine. Opened her eyes, checked her watch – ten forty-five, pushed the front door, saw the red light blinking. Message. Her stomach knew it wasn't Luke. Was it the whistler? Or Liz again, assuaging her guilt for being a crap mother by phoning her to talk about Milton and Greek cuisine. Well, she could piss off. Sam ignored the light, ambled into the kitchen to make a cup of coffee, proper Turkish coffee this time. Turkish coffee – everything led her back to Luke. She brewed the muddy sludge, knocked it back, walked along the hall, heading for the stairs, intending to retreat to her room and the solace of a good book. The answering machine winked at her aggressively as she passed. She paused. Could it be Harry? She pressed the button. The cassette inside the machine whirred, spinning back to the correct part of the tape. It crackled and sighed, as if somebody were breathing heavily into the phone, and then somebody spoke. Not Harry. Nor Liz. It was Dave.

'Sam.' His voice wavered. There was something ghostly about his tone that startled her, filled her with a sudden dread. He paused. Then his disembodied voice again. 'Sam. Are you there? Are you back yet?' Another heavy pause. 'Listen, call me when you get in, will you? I need a quick word with you.' Heavy breathing. And then a sad, 'Ta-ra.'

What was that about? She dialled his number. She heard it ringing at the other end, waited for him to pick up. Ring. Ring. And then his answering machine cut in. Dave's voice again, asking her to leave a message after the tone. She put the receiver down. He was probably in the toilet. He spent an immeasurable amount of time in the toilet. Men and toilets. Oh fuck, what was happening? She would give him five minutes. She took a deep breath, walked halfway down the hall then stopped; she could hear a noise upstairs, an odd, soft rattle. She climbed the stairs, hugging the wall. A blast of air brushed her cheek, as if somebody had rushed past. She froze. Counted to sixty in her head. Nothing. Continued up the stairs. Stopped, listened. The sound was coming from the back bedroom, Dave's room. She paused, hand on the door, pushed. The room was empty. Periodic table blu-tacked to the wall. Science textbooks neatly lined on the shelf. Silence. Then a buzz, coming from his built-in cupboard. She threw open the door; the familiar smell of mildew radiated from Dave's box of journal articles and a dozy wasp zapped past her face. The top paper was skew-whiff, its corners resting across the edges of the box. *Distribution of caesium 137 between abiotic and biotic components of aquatic ecosystems. By Simon Burns.* She bent down to square it up, then spotted the article underneath. *Microalgae and aquatic plants that can eliminate radioactive caesium from the aquatic environment. By Richard Avery.* Strange. B before A. The top article was out of place. Dave was fairly obsessive about ordering his information, journal articles always alphabetical. Had somebody been rummaging in his papers?

She decided to leave the pile as she had found it, returned downstairs, dialled Dave's number. He didn't pick up. Come on. Come on. The answering machine clicked in again. She put the phone down. What was he doing? She sat on the stairs. Agitated. Flipped her wrist and checked the time, watched the second hand do its round, once, twice – she dialled again, ringing, ringing. She would have to leave him a message. The answering machine clicked in. She put the phone down, on edge, didn't want to leave her voice, her name, on his tape. What if somebody else was there, in the house, listening? She shook, filled with a sudden fear that Dave might have disappeared, like Luke. She was being paranoid, she told herself. Then she went through his strange reactions, his edginess the evening before when she wanted to talk about the power station, his digs about Luke. Harry's question – *Does the name Dave Daley mean anything to you?* Yes, it did mean something to her, Dave Daley meant a lot to her, but now she was beginning to fear that she didn't have quite such a straightforward relationship with him as she thought she had. *Listen, there's something else... Dave...* She had to contain the doubts. It would all turn out to be nothing. Dave had nipped to the shop to buy a pint of milk and he would call her when he got back and start talking about something trivial. The breeding habits of spoonbills. She was being paranoid, as usual.

She retreated to her room, under the bedcovers with a book. Somewhere in the distance a police siren wailed. Traffic hummed. A train clunked across the railway arches en route to Waterloo. A neighbour's radio twittered. She pretended not to be listening for the phone. Who was she trying to kid? She levered herself out of bed, teetered at the top of the stairs. The hairs on her arms bristled, an icy breeze on the back of her neck. She clutched the banister as she traipsed down, crossed the hall, reached for the phone and dialled Dave's number. No reply. Somebody was playing mind-games with her, disappearing the men she cared about, one by one. She shut her eyes briefly, pushed back the dark void.

She forced herself to eat; a half moon of dry pitta wiped around the remains of an out-of-date pot of hummus. The only near-edibles left in the fridge. She called Dave. He failed to pick up. She played the message he had left again. Now the spaces between his words were obvious: breaths, silences, tightness in his voice, panic. He was trying to convey calm control, but she could hear the fear. She had to do something. She had to help him. She walked back into the kitchen, brewed some more muddy coffee in her battered saucepan, poured it into a thermos, located a packet of Garibaldi biscuits in the back of a cupboard, checked the back door was locked, picked up her battered boombox from the front room and a handful of cassettes. She passed the phone and it rang. She jumped for it. Dave. It wasn't. Her hand froze, the whistle playing in her ear and then the voice. 'You are in danger.' Clunk of receiver. It didn't sound like Harry. Perhaps he was muting his Welsh accent in case there was a listener on the line. Or perhaps Harry had instructed somebody else to leave her a warning? *You are in danger.* God, how did a message like that help? It only made her more anxious. She couldn't call Harry right now anyway, she had to go. She double locked the front door, dumped her supplies in the back of the van, rested the boombox on the passenger seat, fiddled with the key in the ignition. The van chugged as the engine revved; usually comforting, now the familiar noise merely reminded her of the miles she had to travel, alone, *you are in danger* rattling around her brain.

Slow going east through the blackened terraces of London. The cruddy, never rebuilt bomb holes between the houses filled with discarded domestic appliances. North through Essex. Decaying factories and empty warehouses. She left the road at the same junction she had taken this morning, pulled into the same service station to top up the tank. This was proving expensive if nothing else. She used the toilet, grabbed a cup of weak coffee and sat at the same bench she had occupied eight hours previously. Her earlier presence was almost visible, a faint glimmer sitting at the bench eating a cheese sandwich. Her eyes wandered the sky, clouds hanging over the flat wheat fields, ratcheting up the humidity of the late afternoon. She ought to keep moving, face whatever was waiting for her in Skell. She drained the last of the coffee, scrunched the polystyrene cup in her hand, tossed it into the litter bin, wasps orbiting like Jupiter's moons around the overflowing debris. She turned and caught sight of an old army Land Rover parked in front of the petrol station shop. Odd, it looked exactly like the one she had seen earlier this morning, bashed front left wing. She strolled across the forecourt, stared into the petrol station shop window at the AA Road Maps of Great Britain display, and observed the Land Rover's reflection in the plate glass. Empty. She read the inverse number plate. C783 LLB. Was that a London registration? She made a mental note of the number, strolled back to the van, turned the ignition and pulled away.

The further into Norfolk she drove, the darker the sky became. She reached Thetford Forest, plunged into the gloom of overreaching trees. She shivered, too cold for June, reached over to the boombox with one hand, pressed play. Joy Division. 'Love Will Tear Us Apart'. The sudden clatter of the raindrops almost drowned the music. She slowed, thirty, twenty-five miles an hour. Better not to go any faster in this weather, the wipers couldn't cope with the deluge, her view was obscured, only the blur of oncoming headlights visible through the sheets of rain. A nutter in a silver Mercedes sped past, sprayed water in its wake, disappeared in the blear. She glanced in the rear-view mirror, hard to see much through the back windscreen. Was that a flash of green? A Land Rover. She almost jammed her foot on the brake, nearly swerved on the wet road, regained control, concentrated on her driving, emerged from the forest, out into the open air. She checked behind her again; the car hogging her bumper was a white Peugeot, no Land Rover in sight. Her paranoia. She put her foot on the accelerator, nearly at Skell.

The final stretch, hemmed in by hawthorn, caught behind a line of horses, steaming flanks, riders swathed in black raingear, heads down, faces shadowed inside their hoods. The riders peeled right at the junction beyond the bridge. She forked left, drove past the village green, the Butcher's Arms, the church. Two panda cars had parked precariously on the verge along the side of the road heading to the sea. Her stomach lurched. The right turn, the one that ran behind the village with access to the lokes, was cordoned off. Three coppers were standing in front of the lane, arms folded, repelling any inquisitive passers-by. Shit. Her brain raced. She drove on, swerved into the old harbour road, past a gaggle of people huddled by the post office, swerved left into the driveway that led down to the old windmill, parked in the gravel forecourt. Handbrake on. Sat back in the seat for a moment, trying to control the anxieties, think clearly. She leaned over to the glove compartment, rummaged inside, pulled out a pakol, an Afghan rebel's hat, the one Luke had bought her as a present from Kensington Market. The rough felt comforted her hand. She pulled the hat on, rolled the brim over her head, its rim scratching her skin, glanced at herself in the mirror. She looked stupid, but it might help keep her dry. Catching her reflection, some instinct made her tuck her sandy hair inside the hat. Disguise herself. She pulled the hat's rim further down over her brow to keep the hair in place. A lump formed in her throat. Her mind was numb, on the verge of tears, the fear in Dave's voice eating into her mind.

She splashed through the puddled path under the arch by the side of the customs house. The toad croaked at her as she passed, as if it recognized her from the previous evening. A familiar. The loke opposite, the entrance to the path that ran along the side of Dave's house, was forlornly draped with dripping yellow incident tape. Two rain-caped cops guarded that one as well. Jesus. She momentarily considered asking them what was going on, telling them she had a friend who lived up there and she wanted to find out if he was all right. Better not, she decided. Best remain invisible until she had a clearer sense of the landscape. Her gut was cramping now. Anxious. Shivery. Tired. Something had happened to Dave. Had he been kidnapped? Killed? She pictured the ghostly face in the window at Bane House, the figure walking away, the flash of the torch in the dark, and she suspected now she hadn't been imagining things, there was somebody there, watching them, tracking them. Whatever had happened to Dave, it was connected to Luke's disappearance, she was sure. And in the pit of her stomach, she knew it was connected to her. Luke was right, she was an undercover cop's daughter, she had been on the radar all along, she was like a flashing beacon of dots and dashes spelling watch me, watch my friends, track us. She had inverted the bellarmine. She had tipped the heart with its three pins and the bitter withy bark. No wonder all the people closest to her were disappearing.

She crossed the road, headed away from the coppers guarding the loke, tagged on to the bedraggled crowd – fifteen people or so, heaving, shifting, people jostling for space on the tiny corner of pavement bordering the road. Something of a mad carnival atmosphere; an incident in Skell, of all places, where nothing ever happened. She searched faces – women in Barbours, cagoules, headscarves, greying men in dark windcheaters, a younger man with a camera, local hack perhaps. Dave was absent. People were gabbling. She clutched at sentences, phrases, words. Who would have thought? Not here. Kept himself to himself. Nice lad. What a shame. Smart too. Field station. Always thought there was something odd about him. Not quite right in the head. What do you expect? Irish.

Sam edged her way into the huddle, searching for solid information, caught the eye of a middle-aged woman, damp peroxide bob falling out from the hood of her tan raincoat and a shoulder plumping stance that suggested she was enjoying the disturbance. Eager to tell everybody how much she knew. The woman smiled at Sam in a commanding way, and elbowed over. Sam found herself bustled into a twosome, apart from the mass.

'I stopped off to pick up some milk from the shop on my way home,' Sam said. She nodded in the direction of the corner shop, which she had fortunately remembered was situated around the bend in the road. 'I usually park up the back there, but it was blocked off.'

The woman nodded, savoured her moment, not ready to impart her information too easily.

'What's going on?' Sam asked.

The woman inclined her head, smiled triumphantly. 'Suicide.'

A surge of relief: Suicide? Phew. Not Dave then. That wasn't what she had been worried about with Dave. Murder. Kidnap, possibly. Suicide, no. Dave wouldn't have committed suicide. Not like his mother. He had told Sam as much himself, last night when they talked about it. Not suicide. Not the periodic repetition. Not Dave.

'Up at the Professor's house,' the woman continued.

Sam tumbled down the bank, into the ditch, free fall, blood throbbing in her ears as she descended, brain misted up, no oxygen, unable to breathe. Drowning. The woman's voice was coming from far, far away, up above her, a gaping circle of coral lipsticked mouth talking, talking, talking as she sank down in the black marshy waters.

'Nasty,' the mouth said. 'Marge found him.'

Marge. The name tugged Sam upwards. A detail. Cling on to it, don't let go. Find the air. Oxygen. Listen to the details, they could save your life. Marge. Her head bobbed up, broke the surface. She gasped.

'Who is Marge?'

'The Professor's cleaner.'

Of course, Dave had mentioned her.

'She cleans my house too,' the coral-rimmed mouth added hastily, in case there was any doubt about the nature of her relationship to the char.

'Marge found him this morning. In the kitchen. There was blood everywhere.'

Sam nodded, her mind screamed no. Not Dave's blood. Please no.

'Of course, Marge had to go to the station and provide a statement.'

Yes of course, Marge would have to do that.

'She called me, though. After she had called the police and before they arrived. She needed somebody to talk to.'

Sam nodded again.

'They can't find any of his relatives,' the woman continued.

No, they wouldn't be able to because Dave's father moved to the States after his mother drowned herself. His family splintered. Shattered. His brothers no longer spoke, no longer communicated with our kid Dave. Sam was one of his closest friends. Was. And now he was dead. She didn't care what he was involved in, what he had done, why he had done it. She wanted to have a laugh with him. She wanted to hear him say something condescending about her tendency to paranoia in his irritating Brummie accent. Above all, above everything else, she wanted him to be alive. Too late.

'The Professor's going to have to come back and identify the body. If he's recognizable.'

'How did he...'

'Gun.'

Gun? She managed to swallow her shriek. Where would Dave have found a gun? She pulled her sodden coat around her, the damp cloth sticking to her already drenched jeans.

'Did the gun belong to the Professor then?'

The woman's eyes narrowed. 'No. The Professor didn't keep a gun.'

'I thought he might have been a hunter.'

'Good god no. Not the Prof. It was the lad's own gun. In the mouth.' The woman pointed two fingers into her gaping coral hole, hooked her thumb into a trigger. Then she smiled, thought she was being funny in some way. Jesus, the woman was mad, a seething Aga owner, fuelled by an ever burning fire of contempt. Sam wanted to kick her, wanted to cry. Poor bloody Dave. It couldn't be true. Even if he did find a gun, why would he do it now?

'Unrequited love,' the blonde bob continued.

'Oh. How do you know that?'

'He left a note. Marge saw it. This girl from London.'

Sam spluttered, raised her hand to her face, wiped away the drips to cover her reaction.

'He shot himself because of a girl from London?'

The woman nodded. Sam turned away, staring mad-eyed down the road for something, somebody, anything that might save her. There was nothing. Salty water rivulets poured down her face, dripped into her mouth. Surely Dave hadn't done himself in because of her. Maybe Jess was right, perhaps he did have a bit of a thing about her, but not that much of a thing. In her head, she replayed the message he had left on her answering machine; the barely suppressed fear. Fear of what? Himself? Fear he couldn't stop the periodic repetition. Like his mother, only shot, not drowned. Or was there something else going on with Dave? Sam turned back to face the woman, arms folded defiantly.

'Long yellow hair according to Marge. She found a couple of them in the bathroom this morning. The hairs.'

Sam's eyes must have bulged.

'Is something the matter?'

Sam shook her head. Christ. Long yellow hairs. She was glad she had tucked her rat tails into the hat.

'Marge thinks she is a witch.'

'A witch?'

She felt an urge to laugh; that would amuse Dave, the superstitious yokels and their peculiar beliefs. It couldn't amuse him now, though. She was struck by a wave of nausea.

'Yes. The girl from London cursed him.'

The conversation was heading off into insanity. Her deepest fears surfacing, becoming real, as below so above, paranoia solidifying. She edged away from the rabble; tears pricked her eyes, lump in her throat. The rain was becoming heavier again, stinging, ditch water rising around her feet. She had to escape. The bobbed woman wasn't about to let her go, determined to continue her account, forced Sam to listen.

'The girl was here last night, Marge reckons. Two wine glasses in the sink.'

Jesus, that would teach her to leave the washing up. Marge had probably given all the details to the police. Would she be hauled in for questioning? Sam pulled away. The woman edged closer, gawped at her face. For a moment Sam thought one of the strands of her hair had wriggled loose.

'What's that on your cheek?'

'It's a birthmark.'

'A birthmark?'

Oh god, spare her.

'You'd better be careful with that around here,' the woman said. 'People will think you're the witch if they see that mark.'

The woman was speaking loudly now, and a couple of others from the crowd sidled over, catching the end of her sentence. Sam backed away, stepped off the pavement, into the road. A car honked and swerved into the ditch. A slosh of gutter bilge engulfed the gathering. People twisted and stared, muttering, sniping. She had a sense of slipping time: witches, shadows, ghosts, death. The periodic repetition, the time loop: history repeating itself, first as tragedy and then as even more tragedy. Sam stepped away, started down the road.

The woman's voice followed her. 'Where did you say you lived?'

'Next village along the coast.'

Sam strode briskly away. She glanced over her shoulder, caught the angry faces glaring at her, heard the malicious laughter. Birthmark; you just have to look at her to know. Hexer. Curser. Sam picked up her pace, defied the spears of rain. Trial by water. King James. *Daemonologie. For a supernatural sign of the monstrous impiety of witches, God hath appointed that the water shall refuse to receive them in her bosom.* If she didn't drown, the water rejected her, then she would be hanged. Her tears mingled with the drops, dribbled, and she stuck her tongue out to taste the salt and she thought of Dave. Bullet in mouth, head blown apart. Her fault; she had cursed him with her presence. She was guilty, she caused the deaths and disappearances, tainted everybody she touched. She was a witch. She passed the cordoned-off loke leading up to Dave's house, came to a bend in the road and saw the blue spiral light reflected in the window pane ahead. She stepped back as the ambulance passed and picked up speed on the road to Norwich. Dave.

'Ta-ra our kid,' she whispered.

A mosquito buzzed around her ear. She swiped, thought she had missed, opened her fist and saw the blood-stained streak across her palm.

CHAPTER 8

THE SUNLESS DAY was fading, rain picked her bones. The water had nowhere to run, collected in the scum-clogged gullies at the side of the road, soaked her feet. She thought of Dave pushing his glasses up his nose, explaining the secondary contamination, wash-off, bioaccumulation of caesium 137. She had to find out what had happened to Dave. Had he committed suicide? She drew up a mental map of the village, identified the rear loop and, after the last of the slate roofs, headed inland, followed a footpath across a fallow field, exposed, boots squelching as she tried to walk faster in the claggy soil, rooks cawing above her head. She reached the village back road, covered by a canopy of oak trees. A bat flitted through the dripping branches, pug nose, a barbastelle, the same creature Dave had spotted and identified the evening before – when she had been too angry with him to talk. She was unforgivable.

She arrived at the far entrance to the loke, no cordon. She paused, breath quick and shallow, glanced over her shoulder, decided she would risk it, walked cautiously along the sodden grass edging. The whiff of fag smoke reached her a moment before the voices. Two of them. Smoking at the bottom of Dave's back garden, talking and guffawing, apparently unaware of the possibility of being overheard. She walked cautiously to the garden boundary and stood in the lee of the flint loke wall. The loudness of her own breath scared her, made her gasp for air. She pictured the Oval gasholder, and it comforted her. Inhale, exhale. The cop's obnoxious banter floated over the wall – a misogynistic dissection of the cleaner's body in lurid anatomical detail. The hierarchy was audible in the bullying and obsequiousness of the statements and responses. The side-kick amplified his boss's nastiness, laughing at his snide digs.

'Time to call it a night.' The top cop had no particular accent, just a hardness of tone. 'Where are the digs then?'

'Cromer.' Not local cops, if they needed somewhere to stay. Down from London, she guessed. What was the Force doing out here, in the sticks?

'The pathologist seems like a pain in the arse to me.'

'He's user-friendly. He said he couldn't see any immediate evidence that pointed to anything other than suicide, so that's that. I'll leave it up to you to tidy any loose ends here. The Prof bloke should turn up at the morgue tomorrow for the identification. Not that there's much of his head left to identify.'

She wanted to retch.

'Ask him about the gun. He'll confirm it doesn't belong to him, no doubt. Dave Daley, Irish as we already knew. And a Catholic, so he fits the profile. Unlawful possession of firearms, confirms our suspicions. I would imagine it's not going to be hard to trace the links.'

Her mind started wandering, grasping for the implications of the cop's words. Possession of firearms. Suspicions. Irish. Links. She poked her fingernails into her arm, made herself pay attention.

'We'll have to see what we can find on the girl.' The way he said *the girl* made her sweat.

'Don't think we can do much more today.'

She listened to their footsteps diminishing; the back door of the house banging shut. She slumped down on the edge of the loke, oblivious to the damp spreading through her coat. A car door slammed, engine revved, tyres slick on wet road. She sat with her head on her knees in the darkness; the shrieks of hunting owls played in her head. She wanted to curl up and howl. Somewhere in the back of her mind she heard Jim telling her to get a grip, quit the self-pity. Think about Dave, poor bloody Dave.

She lifted her head, surveyed the corridor. A movement at the far end, a blind corner, made her freeze. Yellow eyes glowed and vanished. Fox. Or cat. Everything assumed a larger size in the dark. The back of the house was unlit. She stood, breath shallow, edged along the wall until she came to the kitchen window. The upside-down palm cross glowed white against the darkness of the kitchen. Jesus, Dave had left her a message; he had moved the cross to the far edge of the sill and turned it on its head. A warning. Danger. A sign that he had left something in the drop box. Through the open kitchen door she could glimpse the hallway, partly illuminated by the outdoor security lamp on the far side of the house. The blinking light of Dave's answering machine caught her attention. Red flash. Somebody had left a message. There was something not quite right about the silhouette of the machine, though; the lid of the cassette slot was open. Somebody had removed the tape. God, what was going on?

She pressed herself hard against the flints, ignored the spikes in her spine, sidled back along the passage to a spot where the overhanging apple tree branches would give her some purchase. She had to give it a go, she owed it to Dave. She grabbed a branch and a protruding flint, hauled, clambered on to the flat wall top, checked the house again – no signs of life – dropped on to the flowerbed on the far side, bent double as she edged along the garden wall. She reached the ceramic urn, lifted it, slipped her hand under. Her fingertips touched something smooth and miraculously dry. She edged it out carefully, let the urn drop back into place. A slip of paper: a folded page from one of Dave's lined A4 notebooks. She placed it in her back pocket. She looked at the urn, decided she wanted to double-check, squatted, tipped the urn, stuck her hand under, and her fingertips touched something soft. She almost screamed. Dead mouse? Calmed herself, pulled the substance out. Black hair. She blanched, inserted her hand again, fumbled around and touched a small hard object. It was like the party game they used to play where you had to wear a blindfold and somebody stuck your finger in a bowl of jelly and said that's Napoleon's eye. She clutched the object, removed it. A blackened bone. The bone and the hair she had found in the Lookers' Hut and given to Dave to identify; the shepherd's charms. Why had he left them there? She was wondering whether to take them or not when a rustling on the far side of the garden startled her, made her look up. She glimpsed yellow eyes, hastily shoved the bone and hair under the urn, dropped it back into place, clambered back over the wall and jumped down into the loke.

She retraced her muddy trail across the field and walked down to the marsh, located a causeway to the windmill. Her monkey boots slipped around and she was sniffling by the time she arrived back at the van. She almost trod on the toad squatting at the edge of the puddle below the van's door, its warty skin blending with the gravel. She was too tired to drive back to London. The windmill car park was, she reckoned, a relatively safe place to spend the night. Relatively. Was anywhere safe for her right now? She wormed her way into the back of the van, squashed in the narrow gap between the seats where it would be difficult to spot her, unless you peered through the windows. Water must have seeped in, because the floor was damp. She scrabbled in her bag for her torch. She took the folded paper from the back of her pocket and read it in the beam – 55 *pluto*. Was that it? 55 pluto. What was that about? The 55 meant nothing to her. The most obvious meaning of pluto was that it was short for plutonium. Was he communicating something about their protest at Dungeness? What had he told her about plutonium? Only reactor grade in the spent fuel rods, not weapons grade plutonium. Maybe he wasn't trying to communicate anything, maybe it was just a random scrap from his notebook that he'd stuffed in the vase to let her know he had been thinking about her. Their last conversation. The periodic repetitions. Perhaps pluto was a reference to the god of the underworld. Maybe it conveyed his dark descent, beyond reach, not waving but drowning. And 55? Could 55 be something to do with his mother? Her age? She tried to work it out. Fourteen in 1945. Committed suicide in 1980. Fifty-five was the age his mother would be now if she had lived. Oh no. Please no. She cried as she thought of Dave, wondered whether he had quietly planned, acquired a pistol, bullets, kept the gun there, in the house, loaded. Waited for the moment when he could no longer resist the stardust pulsing through his veins, the pull of the stellar cycle, the repetitions of the periodic table. She could have helped, she could have stopped him. It was her fault, whichever way she looked at it. She had cursed him, tainted him. She started to drift, her head lolled.

The cry of an owl roused her. She must have dozed, because she found herself sprawled across the floor, head against the front seat. The back of her hand was wet. Dribble. Snot. Tears. A pain below her ribs – the jabbing heartache, the empty cavity; Luke, Dave. She wiped her face on her sleeve. Three a.m.; her witching hour. Toads and bats for company. She reached for her thermos and her foot cramped, she winced, pulled her toes backwards to stretch the arch. She needed a walk, a breath of fresh air. She crawled into the front seat, peered around the car park. No signs of life. She opened the door carefully and crept out like a fugitive.

Waves of rain drifted as she climbed the steps to the causeway. Faint moonlight oozed through the clouds and burnished the dark surfaces of the irrigation channels. She ambled a short way down the path, slithered around in the crud. Stopped. The sound of a diesel engine made her turn; headlights of a car heading down the coast road, the gravel crunching as it turned into the car park. She scuttled back along the path and hid herself in the shadows of the trees. Battered green Land Rover. She tried to catch her breath, stay calm: late-night Labrador walker surely. She watched transfixed as a figure emerged, khaki jacket, hood up, face invisible. He stood still for a moment, a fox taking its bearings, stalked over to the camper van, switched on a torch, drizzle caught in its arc, directed the beam through the van's front windows, checked the front seats, the dashboard, the back. Jesus Christ. Plain-clothes copper? He walked slowly around the van, the beam moved to and fro, as if he was hunting for something specific. Or someone.

The beam swung round, across the windmill outhouses. A bat disturbed, flitted away. The torchlight swept the steps and illuminated the backside of the customs house, caught the pulses of precipitation in its cone. She breathed a sigh of relief. The beam swung back. Caught her. Shit. Shit. Shit. His feet pounded the gravel. She didn't stop to think, belted down the causeway – head start, draw him away from the car park, circle, return to the van and drive off before he could reach her. She stumbled, foot caught in cord grass, eyes distracted by yellow trefoil runway lights. She heard his boots clatter up the steps. She could get away if she was fast enough. She had to keep running, maintain her pace. She could hear him behind on the path, already gaining ground, faster than her, her monkey boots losing purchase.

'Sam.'

Fuck. He knew her name. Who was he? Why was he after her? *You are in danger.* Her clothes were drenched, battered by the incessant pounding of wind and rain. She was knackered. Petrified. She glanced down to her right, saw the solid ground of the drained lea, started in that direction then spotted the fence. She would lose too much time scrambling over, he would catch her on the wire. She looked to her left, across the salt-marsh in the direction of Bane House. Snap decision. She slithered down the soaking dropwort-covered bank, splashed among the reeds, up to her ankles in the sump. Knew instantly she had made a mistake. Dave had warned her, there was no solid ground in the saltmarsh, only slick mudflats, sucking reed beds, rushes in the tidal flow, no safe path among the creeks and ditches. Mired. She had no choice, she had to keep moving. Trial by water. She glanced back as she pushed on into the darkness; he had reached the point where she slid off the path, square-shouldered on the causeway path, dark against the bloody corona of the moon.

'Sam.'

She had heard that voice before. Where? Her mind whipped around, her feet fumbled along the slimy channel edge, searched for a foothold, slipped into the swampy brine as the wind slashed her face.

'Sam. I want to help you.'

He had to be kidding.

'Stop. For fuck's sake. Stop. I want to fucking help you.'

The accent. South African? Then she remembered. Shit. He had tracked her down, after all this time. She instinctively ducked lower among the reeds, as if she was dodging a bullet, as if she could escape if he chose to aim at her. He was a total nutter. The misted light of the shrouded moon came and went, cast gleams then smothered them. She was wading through black pools, inlets, drains, not bothering to find the firmer ground, hoping the head-height reeds would provide her with some cover. She glanced behind again, spotted her pursuer tumbling down the bank, hitting the reeds, splashing, arms hacking at stems as he tracked her. In the distance ahead she perceived a white flicker. Barn owl? No, a figure over to the right, further along the headland, silver in the haze. Jim. He was there, her father. Jim would know what to do, he always did. She shouted his name into the wind. He didn't stop. He was striding away across the saltmarsh, following the path from Bane House to the jetty, leaving her behind. Why had he abandoned her? Left her alone to face a madman? Did he really think she would be safer by herself?

'Wait. Jim. Wait.'

She stumbled, didn't watch where she stuck her feet, determined to reach her father, certain he was her salvation, unaware she was at an angle until the spikes brushed her face and she sensed that she was tripping. Past the midway point of no return. She lurched forwards to catch herself, grabbed at blades. Her ankle twisted the wrong way. She was down, winded, face in brackish water, mud, bogland; a mouthful of infected earth and radionuclides. Up. Up. She had to get up. She pushed herself on to her knees. Deep breath, brine inhaled. She wheezed, spluttered salt. Collected herself, ready to run again. She sensed a presence behind her and she looked back over her shoulder. Too late. His face loomed over her, haggard, unshaven, mud-smeared, brain-fried, pointing a pistol at her. Christ all fucking mighty. She thought that was it. Over. He was talking, rambling insanely.

'Please, Sam, to every thing there is a season...'

Psychotic Bible quoter. She caught the glint of the gold chain and cross at his neck and some instinct overrode the paralysis of fear that gripped her stomach. She heard Jim's voice in her head, and she remembered all those times he had nearly flipped but not quite, more mad than bad, and she knew then that she could talk her way out of this if only she kept calm. Her mouth spoke the first words that landed there.

'And a time to every purpose under the heaven.'

Her voice was breathless, tightly wound, near hysterical. Even so, her words seemed to calm him, brought him to his senses. And as she spoke the line it soothed her too, a litany that drew her mind back to her body and gave her courage.

'Ecclesiastes,' he said.

'The Book of the Preacher.'

'You read the Bible.'

'Yes.'

The lie came easily. *To every thing there is a season*: she'd learned the verse from Jim. She pushed herself up so she was facing him and saw he was much as she remembered, black flickering eyes, cropped dark hair as if he couldn't let go of the military habits, thick-lipped volatile mouth. Trip-wired to explode. Not much older than her – maybe late twenties – although he had aged, time lines, scars on his skin like tribal tattoos. She cast her eyes down to his hand, the pistol. He clocked he was pointing a gun at her, let his arm relax, pushed the weapon into his jacket casually, as if it was a packet of fags. She thanked Jim then, for being so edgy she was able to deal with psychopaths.

'I wasn't going to shoot,' he said. 'I was trying to make you stop.'

She opened her mouth to make some sarky comment about

how she certainly would have stopped if he'd pulled the trigger. She closed it, reminded herself that he was a hitman, a contract killer who, she had discovered two years previously, had shot her father.

'What do you want?' she asked.

'Can't you see? I'm fucking trying to help you.'

The words sounded more desperate than angry and he was crying, rivulets, tracks in the grime of his cheeks. He was crazy and she couldn't find a sane response. He sniffed.

'Your hand is bleeding,' he said.

She tried not to react – suspected a trick – if she cast her eyes down he could fire without having to look into her face. She held his gaze, let the warm blood trickle across her palm. She must have slashed it on a reed blade as she fell. He stuck a hand in his jacket pocket. She froze – he was reaching for his gun again. He smiled and he pulled out a cotton handkerchief.

'Here. Use this.'

She didn't move.

'Take it. I want to help.'

He raised his hand and the wind jerked at the white square.

'Why on earth should I believe you? You're a hitman.'

'I never shoot civilians.'

Perhaps he wasn't lying: two years ago he'd killed her father, she assumed, but he had helped her to escape. Yet he was still a madman who pointed his gun at her when he claimed he was trying to assist. She felt the blood running down her forearm, under her sleeve, reached for the handkerchief, wrapped it around her palm. She looked up, tears still streaming down his cheeks.

'Why are you crying?'

'I cry for the dead.'

No way. He created the dead. He was a corpse maker.

Crocodile tears. If he cried for anything it was for his own guilt and redemption.

'Why are you here?' she asked.

'I keep telling you, I came because I want to help you. I want to protect you.'

His eyes flicked to the spot she had seen Jim's shadow when she was cutting across the marsh.

'Your father sent me,' he said.

'But you know my father is dead.'

'His spirit is still here.'

He must have heard her calling Jim's name, worked his way into the wounds of her mind, psyched her.

'I don't believe in ghosts,' she said.

'I've seen him. I've seen his shadow. I hear him talking.'

'What does he say?'

'He tells me that I have to help you.'

'That's not Jim talking.' The guilty conscience of a deranged killer. 'I think somebody sent you after me.'

'Look, please, I came to help you. If I wanted to shoot, I would have done it by now.'

He reached into his jacket and pulled out the small black revolver he had pointed at her, threw it on the ground in front of her feet, on top of a clump of scarlet pimpernels.

'Browning.'

He reached into the other side of his jacket, removed a pistol with a longer barrel. Threw that one down too. 'Firebird.' Casually acquainted with deadly weapons, but then she knew that already. She stared at him and waited for the next move. Uncertain.

'Take them,' he said.

She bent down slowly, eyes steady on him. He didn't move. She picked up the Firebird, heavy in her hand, the grip pushed against the handkerchief-wrapped palm as she pointed the gun at him and straightened herself.

'Tell me what you know.'

He nodded his head at the Firebird. 'The safety catch is still on.'

He flashed her a smile; he was good-looking when he smiled. Well, he was good-looking when he didn't smile, but the smile made him more attractive. She tried not to return the gesture but she couldn't stop her mouth twitching and she heard Jim laughing in her head. There she was, calling out the hired hitman with a gun she had no idea how to use. Eejit. She relaxed her arm, Firebird pointing at the ground, grip still pressing into the red sticky handkerchief. She had a sudden thought.

'What about Dave?'

'Dave?' His face showed no sign of recognition.

'My friend, environmental researcher. He died yesterday morning. Shot in the mouth. Suicide, according to the cops. But now I'm wondering whether it was you who pulled the trigger.'

He shook his head.

'Not me. I told you, I don't shoot civilians. And anyway, I was following you yesterday morning. I was behind you on the road. Land Rover.'

'What's the number plate?'

'C783 LLB.'

So it was his Land Rover she'd spotted at the service station.

'Do you have any idea what happened to Dave?'

He shook his head, but she spotted a sideways flick of his eyes that made her wonder exactly how much he was hiding.

'I don't know anything about your friend, but if he has been killed, then you are in trouble.'

She didn't need him to tell her that.

'I can understand why you might not trust me,' he said.

Understatement.

He frowned. 'I've come here to help you.'

She shut her eyes, wished everything away and opened them again. He was still there. She was still slowly sinking in an oozing reed bed in the middle of a saltmarsh with her father's killer who quoted Ecclesiastes.

'I need to make up for your father,' he said.

He didn't use the word *killing*. An unexpected crack of anger made her grip the Firebird, her thumb searching for the safety catch; he couldn't make up for killing her father, she wanted to make him pay. She was surprised by her own reaction, an alien creature lurking in her stomach, snarling and leaping when her mind was elsewhere. She felt uncomfortable, momentarily ashamed by her vengeful instinct. She thought she was above an eye for an eye. Thought she had the inner demons under control.

'Look…' She started and she faltered.

'You need somebody on your side who knows how to use a gun. You need protection.'

You are in danger. She fingered the shaft of the Firebird.

'You have to believe me.' He was on the verge of tears again. 'You have no other choice.'

How had she ended up in this mess? She took a deep breath.

'Are you still going round…' She paused, uncertain how to phrase it. 'Doing contracts?'

'No. No.' He put his hands in his pockets.

She wiped her forehead with the back of her hand, tipped her head skywards; the wind had swept away the clouds to reveal the craters and seas of the waning moon. She looked back at her hunter.

'What have you been doing then, for the last couple of years?'

'I've been working as a courier. I've done some other stuff as well, mechanic, repairing motorbikes, cars. Whatever pays – a bit of guitar playing. Not that I get much money for that, although it's always welcome, a few quid for a pub gig. And the music's good for the soul. Mine at least, if not anybody else's.' He flashed a smile. She ignored it.

'Why are you walking around with two guns in your jacket?'

'I kept one for self-defence. The Browning. And I picked the Firebird up the other day, in case I needed it.'

'How long have you been trailing me?'

'Only a couple of days. I followed you down to Dungeness and I guarded you while you were out on the marsh.'

She had a recollection, a glimmer of green in the dark.

'How did you find me in the first place?'

He hesitated, a split second too long.

'I was on a night out with a friend in Soho a few weeks ago, we walked into a club and I saw you behind the bar. I recognized you, and I was overwhelmed with a sense that you needed help, so I followed you.'

He didn't sound even slightly convinced by his own story, and neither was she, but this wasn't a great time to push him. What was it Jim used to tell her – don't latch on to the lies, let them pass. Especially if you are knee-deep in sludge water facing a hitman. Come back to them later. If there was a later.

'What's your real name anyway?'

He scratched his head, as if he wasn't sure, as if the answer didn't matter. 'Steve. But most people call me Sonny.'

'OK. I'll call you Sonny.'

He half smiled, pleased at the first offering of friendliness. He reached in his jacket. Marlboro carton. He removed a fag. Offered her one. She shook her head. He lit his with a Zippo, took a drag, cracked his jaw, sent a smoke ring drifting. The circle broke, dispersed in the weak dawn, and she felt the tension release and realized she was crying now. A couple of wrecks brought together by some cosmic joker, out there on the saltmarsh. She couldn't deal with it.

She said, 'Sonny. Please leave me alone.'

'But don't you understand, I want to help you.'

'If you want to help me then go away. Please.'

She thought he would argue again, but he didn't.

'If that's what you want,' he said.

'It is.'

His eyes were still wet.

'I wish you would stop crying.' She didn't want to be touched by his tears, wanted to maintain the distrust. He wiped his eyes on the back of his sleeve.

He said, 'Keep the Firebird.'

'I wouldn't know what to do with it.'

'You need to know.'

'I don't want to know. I don't shoot people. The Firebird belongs to my father's world. Not mine.'

'You're in his world.'

'I don't want to be.'

'You have no choice.'

'There's always a choice. And I'm choosing to stay out.'

'It's too late.'

She shook her head, denied it.

'You know too much,' he said.

'I don't know anything.'

'Maybe you don't know what you know. But perhaps other people do.'

His answer caught her unawares, reminded her of a conversation with Jim, something he had mumbled once, all those years ago. *You don't always know what you know.* What was Sonny talking about? How could she not know what she knew? How could anybody else know what she knew, if she didn't know herself? Her tired mind was tying itself in knots. She searched for answers in his face, but found none. She sighed, exhausted with the chase, the sadness of Dave, the effort of assessing risks and motives.

'I want you to leave me alone. And take the Firebird with you.'

'OK.'

He picked up his weapons, turned without another word. She watched him slog through the reeds, clamber back up to the causeway, a silhouette against the pallid sunrise, blown along the path by the gusts. She waited until the Land Rover pulled out of the windmill forecourt and found the road inland. Maybe she'd made a stupid call, sending him away, but there was no call that made any sense. What could she do? A hitman who claimed he wanted to help, wouldn't shoot her, but kept a loaded Browning in his jacket and had hair-trigger reactions to situations he couldn't control. She reckoned he would follow her anyway, watch out for her perhaps if he felt guilty enough about her father. And if he wasn't up close then perhaps she would have a chance to run if he flipped his lid. Right now, she felt that was the best she could hope for – a head start, a moment's grace to find her footing and flee from unknown hunters.

She searched the marsh; the strip of light growing in the east, terns flocking overhead, but there was no movement out on the headland. She must have imagined the figure heading from Bane House, the ghost of Jim. She couldn't let it go, wanted to check even though she knew her father wouldn't be there, waiting for her. She retraced her steps, too tired to care whether she was sloshing through water or not, scrambled up the bank, along the causeway, to the sea. The fresh wind dried her coat until it was stiff with salt and silt.

She reached Bane House, walked round the back, pushed the door, entered. The brown tape was obvious, lying in the middle of the floor, pulled from its spool, chopped and left in a pile, glinting in the first light. She retrieved a curl, let it dangle over her finger, located the cassette flung in another corner. She thought of the open lid of Dave's answering machine, the red light blinking. One message. Who had removed the cassette and dumped it here? Why? What was on the tape? She pictured the dark-haired figure she had glimpsed crossing the headland when she walked to Bane House with Dave, the person who had dropped the matchbook from Heaven. The same person, she suspected now, who had taken the cassette from Dave's answering machine and dumped it here. Somebody who was connected, in some way, to Dave's death, she was sure. *Listen, there's something else... Dave...* And Dave's death was connected in some way to Luke's disappearance. She had to find Luke before they got to him, whoever they were. She had to make sure he was safe. She squidged the tape between her fingers, wished she could rewind time, reverse the repetitions. She gave the floor one last sweep, cast her field-walker's eye around for objects – and spotted the silver underside of a badge lying near the cassette tape. She stepped over, bent down and examined its topside. White background, black clenched fist in the circle and cross of Venus feminist symbol. She attached the badge to her coat, above Jim's Che Guevara and her nuclear power no thanks sun. Perhaps she had been right, the figure she had spotted walking the path between Bane House and the jetty was a woman. A militant feminist? *Anybody can pick up a badge and wear it.* That's what Jim had said that day – the man at the fair, the CND badge, the steely eyes, the scar. She felt a wave of faintness, black dots dancing, covered her face with her hands, breathed in the saltiness on her skin, pushed the memories away.

She traipsed the beach. The rays of the rising sun were mirrored on the ocean, a golden explosion across sea and sky. As above so below. She thought of Dave, their last conversation; we are nothing more than stardust, elements passing through an endless stellar cycle, and she cried.

CHAPTER 9

SHE DOZED ON the floor of the camper van. The sun woke her, shining pink and womblike through the red nylon of her sleeping bag. She lay there for ten minutes or more, the sleeping bag over her head. Reluctant to move. Eventually she decided she had to face the world, drive back to Vauxhall, past the RAF base, through the pine echelons of Thetford Forest one more time. Joy Division playing on her boombox. She kept checking for the green Land Rover in her rearview mirror as she drove, but there was no sign of Sonny – an absence which left her with an unexpected twinge of disappointment.

The house whiffed of damp and mould. The red light flashed. She was developing a phobia of the answering machine, afraid to listen in case there was a message from somebody who was dead or disappeared. Or the whistler. She pressed the play button.

'Sam, are you there?'

The therapist.

'Give me a call when you get a chance. I know it's a difficult time of year for you – the anniversary of your father's death – so I wanted to check how things are going.'

She took a deep breath; maybe it would help to talk to somebody. She had a bath, a cup of coffee. She called the number, the therapist picked up.

'Hello.'

'Oh, hi Sam, are you OK?'

'Yes.'

'Shall we have a chat?'

She stalled, nervous again about talking on the phone.

'Maybe we could arrange another time.'

'Sam, is there something wrong?'

Sam considered the angles, and then said, 'It's difficult for me to say exactly what I feel like saying on the phone because I think my line is bugged.'

Silence on the other end for a minute. 'That's unlikely, isn't it?'

'No.'

'Why would anybody bug your phone?'

'Because that's what the secret state does and I know about that because my father was part of the secret state.'

'You know, Sam, sometimes we transfer personal feelings from an individual to abstract entities, like the state, or the police. It's projection. A way of avoiding how our reactions and emotions relate to ourselves and traumatic events, like your father's death.'

The phone call was pointless; she shouldn't have bothered. She took a deep breath. 'I have to go now.'

'OK. Well, let's talk about this at our usual time. I think we can make some progress here, start to unpack some of the issues around the first stages of grieving.'

Sam wanted to throw the phone at the wall.

'Right. Bye.'

She replaced the receiver, considered the possibility that her mother had set her up with the therapist in order to drive her mad, or to trap her into revealing something about Jim that Liz could use to justify her relationship with Roger. She traced a silver snail trail across the lino with the tip of her shoe and decided that even her mother wouldn't go quite that far.

She wandered into the kitchen to search for food. The fridge was empty. Dave's biscuit barrel was in the cupboard and inside there were three Hobnobs. He had bought the biscuit barrel after he had asked her to buy a packet of plain chocolate Hobnobs and she said she preferred milk. He came home with the barrel from Brixton market and said they could buy a packet of each and store them. She stared at the biscuit barrel. She couldn't for the life of her work out what had been going on with Dave, whether he'd killed himself or been killed, whether he knew something about the power station he hadn't wanted to tell her, why he had been so edgy the last time they saw each other. What she did know was that she and Dave and Luke were friends, and that was what mattered. In her head she said sorry about the Aston Villa mug she had smashed and he said not to fret, he had another one anyway. She promised him she would support Aston Villa from now on even though they were crap. He laughed and said her therapist would be pleased that she'd managed to go straight to the bargaining stage of grief with his death and she laughed too.

She cried for Dave and she slept. She woke and she cried and she whispered the words of Ecclesiastes to herself for comfort. *To every thing there is a season, and a time to every purpose under the heaven: A time to be born, and a time to die; a time to plant, and a time to pluck up that which is planted.* The only biblical verse she could remember Jim reciting. He didn't believe in God, but he was taught by the Jesuits and he knew the Bible. Ecclesiastes, he had said, was the one book that contained meaning he could grasp as well as beauty in its words. The Book of the Preacher. Perhaps it was a coincidence that Sonny had quoted those lines from Ecclesiastes when he was pointing the gun at her. Perhaps it was the inevitable periodic repetition. To every thing there is a season.

She went downstairs, called Luke's number. Nobody picked up. Dusk already, its arrival accompanied by the drumbeat of rain on glass. She had spent the whole day doing nothing. She had a choice to make, she could stay at home and wallow in misery or she could take the bus to Soho and do her shift behind the nightclub bar. If she didn't turn up, nobody would call to ask her where she was or reprimand her for not showing. Although, she wouldn't be able to work there again. She watched the rainwater sluicing the window and considered her options. She couldn't care less if she lost her job. But there was a good reason to do the shift; at the end of it she could walk round the corner to the club where Luke worked, and talk to Spyder. Ask him face to face what he knew about Luke, watch his reactions. Check whether he had been lying to her on the phone and knew more than he was saying. So that was her choice. She could sit tight, as Harry had instructed, wait for him to sort it, deal with her file. Or she could try and find Luke. She pushed herself off the bed, rummaged in her cupboard for her club gear.

There was no dress code for the nightclub staff apart from black. The other women working there wore skimpy dresses. She went the other way and covered herself in a forties trouser suit she had found in Portobello Market. Armour against the evils of the capital's night-time economy. Helen had found her the job through a mate; Helen knew all the clubbers and club owners in Soho – she was part of that whole fashion student and photography *i-D*, *Face* scene with its shifting tribes. New Romantics, Goths, Buffalo, wild camp. The Ballroom was an outlier, the tepid edge of cool in a basement on the fringe of Soho. Easy to miss if you didn't know it was there; the inconspicuous entrance gave no clue to the crumbling beauty below the pavement. Bombed in the Blitz, left to rot, rediscovered at the turn of the eighties by a fast-footed entrepreneur who varnished the dance floor, swagged the red velvet curtains, hung a few disco balls and opened the doors for business. Sam found it easy to carve herself a niche among the Ballroom's subterranean enchantments. She was a quirky fixture with her disinterested gaze, puritanical garb and the book she kept open on the bar to read in quiet moments. Other girls came and went, usually because they were caught with their hand in the till. She persisted. She put her hand in the till too – you would have to be crazy to spend six hours serving drinks in a smoky basement for nothing but the pittance they called a wage, but she made sure she wasn't caught. On a busy night, trendy Wednesday when they flew a DJ in from Paris, she could make a fortune. Another good reason not to wear a skimpy dress: trouser pockets were essential for storing the takings.

She watched the clubbers with a cynical eye – all that hustling for recording contracts, modelling jobs, bit parts in naff TV soaps. And yet she couldn't entirely deny the draw of the Ballroom's wish-fulfilment magic, because it was where she had met Luke. He was working behind the bar in a club around the corner. The Wag was much trendier than the Ballroom. Larry, the huge bouncer with the shaved head and tattooed neck, patrolled the queue and ritually humiliated anybody who didn't register on his scale of cool by telling them to fuck off. But there were unspoken arrangements among the bouncers and the bar staff of Soho; they let each other in and poured free drinks to their fellow workers from around the corner. A rough and ready extended family. Although, Sam rarely made full use of the reciprocal club-workers' hospitality – she usually picked up the early-morning edition from the newspaper sellers in Leicester Square and walked straight home over Vauxhall Bridge.

Luke had turned up at the Ballroom one Monday night, which was the night the swing band played the standards.

Old-time jazz for old-timers: wartime brides with their GI husbands, ancient Cockney ladies with sugar-spun hair, gold t-bar shoes and balding partners. The wrinkly couples swayed so gracefully around the floor and always touched her with the melancholy of lasting love and fading beauty. The glamorous trannies and leather-dressed madams who hung around the club's shadier corners with the Lords and ex-cabinet ministers touched her too, for reasons she couldn't fully explain.

She hadn't noticed him at first, watching her across the bar. She was sitting on a stool at the back, reading Angela Carter. *The Magic Toyshop*.

'*Nights at the Circus* is better.'

She glanced up. Ugly good looks: big nose, generous skewed mouth smiling, chestnut curls. The kind of face you think nobody else would find attractive and then, later, you realize everybody is drooling over him. There was a sadness about his sea-green eyes, though, which was probably what hooked her.

'I work at the Wag,' he said.

She automatically reached for a glass, offered a free drink.

'No, it's OK. I just wanted to have a look. One of my mates told me the Ballroom was worth seeing. So I thought I'd take a break and come over.'

She smiled, tongue-tied. He smiled back.

'I haven't seen you at the Wag. You don't go there after work, do you?'

She shook her head.

'Why not?'

'I like to walk home.'

'You should come over some time. The music on Monday nights is brilliant.'

She couldn't think of anything to say. She felt like a numskull. She reddened.

He said, 'I like the music here better in some ways, though, the old-fashioned jazz band. Do you ever dance?'

'No. You need a partner.'

'Come and dance with me.'

Her cheeks burned. 'I'm not very good at dancing. I don't know how to do all that ballroom stuff.'

'Me neither. Let's go and be left-footed together...'

'I can't leave the bar.'

'Don't you get breaks?'

'Yes.'

'There are two other people behind the bar and nobody asking for a drink.'

'OK. I'll take ten minutes now.'

'Luke.'

She joined him round the other side of the bar. 'Sam.'

He grabbed her hand, navigated the swaying couples, pulled her close, carried away by the music. Laughing. Tripping. Larking around. Uncomplicated enjoyment that made her happy in a way she couldn't remember feeling for a long time. Perhaps she'd never felt quite so happy. A kind of chemistry she'd not experienced before. Everything glowed and shimmered and all the ancient couples smiled at them, thinking – we were like that once.

Something shifted in her then and, after that night, she couldn't stop obsessing about him. She tried to keep a lid on it, but it didn't work. Her brain flipped around, returned to the things he had said, going over every word, the nuance of each syllable, his breath on her face. He must already have a girlfriend and even if he didn't, he wouldn't fancy her. But that Wednesday when she had finished the shift, shut the bar, tallied her till, climbed the stairs, blinked in the sleazy light, Luke was there. Waiting for her. Standing, one foot against the wall, outside the entrance, hands in the pockets of his leather jacket, chatting to Tony the Ballroom bouncer.

'I fancied a walk,' he said.

Tony winked at her and said good night. She shrugged, tried to look more casual than she felt. They walked across St James's Park, past the fairytale cupolas of the Foreign Office rear end, and she told him about the curlew she had spotted poking its long curved beak in the soil just by Buckingham Palace. He was interested. They stopped on Vauxhall Bridge, had a spliff as the sun was rising over Docklands. It became their routine. Monday nights, she finished first, went over to the Wag, waited outside and they walked back to her place together. Wednesdays, it was his turn to wait outside the Ballroom.

That was January. And now it was June and it was raining so she decided to catch the bus to Leicester Square. She was too jittery to enjoy the swing band or take a cut of the money handed over the bar in exchange for spirits. Time was dragging in this dingy corner of the basement. The ageing men squirming around on the red velvet banquettes with the over-made-up hookers made her queasy. She departed the club promptly at three, charged up the stairs, out into the neon-lit dregs of the night, made her way north past the gambling dens and the high-heeled ladies lounging in Soho's peep-show doorways. The rain had become warm mizzle. A man with a comb-over, fifty odd, respectable in his buttoned trench coat, stepped in front of her, waved a tenner in her face. She pushed him aside with a fuck off you wanker. You stuck-up whore, he shouted after her. She couldn't be bothered to answer back.

Larry was leaning against the wall outside the Wag, smoking, wearing his leather jacket despite the sultriness of the urban night. She often chatted to him when she was waiting for Luke to emerge after his shift. She had found him intimidating at first, but he had a soft spot for Luke, and Larry knew she was Luke's girlfriend.

'Luke's not here tonight,' he said as she approached. 'Spyder said he's sick.'

'Oh?' Christ, perhaps he was in hospital. Emergency treatment. She hadn't thought of that possibility.

'Didn't you know?' Larry asked.

She could hear the assumption in his voice. Luke hadn't told her – she'd been dumped. An instant nobody in the absence of Luke. She managed to say, 'Yes, I knew he wasn't here. I just wanted to check with Spyder and find out how he was doing.'

Larry let her in with an indifferent nod. She tried to reply with a charming smile of gratitude, but he wasn't looking – too busy eyeing up some girl in pvc staggering drug glazed on to the pavement.

The narrow staircase was draped with near comatose bodies. Zombies. Girls with eyes unfocused, slipping out of fifties dresses, men sporting silver earrings and leery smiles. Hands up skirts. She stepped over the casualties, up the stairs, into the dim back room, walls dripping, sticky underfoot, rent boys in the corner, toilet queue for hard drug taking. The bass hit her. An irresistible rush that pulsed and transformed the seediness into some mystical high. Low blue lights shaded the clubbers swaying, hypnotized by the rhythm, mesmerized by the twirling sharp-suited black dancers. Through the pall of smoke, she spotted Spyder dancing behind the bar. He was doing tragic jerky arm thrusts, thrashing the air like a man being electrocuted; enough to bring anybody back down from their transcendent cloud. She had loathed Spyder from the moment she met him. He looked like a rat with his Brylcreemed hair and his narrow-lapelled grey suit hanging off his twitchy thin shoulders. His attempt at fifties cool. He didn't fool her. She knew he was a posh boy, slumming it, playing hard. Small-time drugs dealer, supplier to all the nightclub workers including her when she was desperate, served behind the bar at the Wag most nights of the week, which he thought made him mister big. Luke had laughed when she said Spyder was a creep and she thought he was mad to share a house with him. That was part of Luke's charisma; he didn't let anybody get to him. Well, apart from the occasional new age hippy. Luke said the rent was cheap and Spyder was the ideal housemate because he was out of the house most of the time. Crawling through the sewers, searching for shit, Sam reckoned. She had to keep a lid on it, her venom, until she had extracted some answers from him.

He turned away as she approached, pretended he hadn't seen her. Reached up, glass in hand, released a shot of amber whisky from the upside-down bottle behind the bar.

'Spyder,' she shouted above the thump of the bossa-nova bass. He ignored her. Deliberately of course. Git.

'Spyder.'

He swivelled round slowly.

'What can I do for you, darlin'?'

She suppressed the urge to tell him he could stop calling her darlin' for a start. Quit pretending he had been dragged up in the mean streets of east London.

'I'm looking for Luke. Larry said you told him he was sick.'

He ran his tongue around his thin lips. 'I was covering for him. Told the gaffer he had flu and he'd be back next week. He's done it for me before when I've not made it in. That's what we do. Cover for each other. Cos we're good mates.' He leered at her. 'Don't you know where he is then?'

'No.'

'Blown you out, has he?'

She ignored him.

'Has he been home since Saturday?'

'I told you already on the blower. I haven't seen him since Friday night when I left the club. I've no idea whether he was in when I got home. He wasn't there when I got up on Saturday morning. But, you know, that's nothing unusual.' He gave her a snide look. 'Cos he's often away.'

'He often stays with me.'

'Spose so.'

She willed herself not to let him wind her up, gritted her teeth. 'Do you have any idea where he might be?'

'Am I my brother's keeper?' He hunched his cadaverous shoulders in an exaggerated shrug. 'It's none of my business what he does. Where he goes.' He licked his lips again. 'And if he didn't tell you, then maybe it's none of your business either, my little friend.'

Fuck the slimy wanker. She wanted to turn and walk, but she made herself stay. She had to see this through.

'I'm a bit worried about him. Seriously, do you have any idea where he might be?'

He lifted the tumbler from the bar, knocked back the whisky shot he had poured, wiped his mouth on the back of his sleeve. He was eyeing her up, over his forearm. Arsehole.

'What's it worth?'

'Not much.' She swung away. He leaned over the bar, grabbed her arm, pulled her back.

'Hang on a minute.'

She yanked her arm free; his ferret eyes darted around her face, calculating lecherously.

'He told me last week he'd been to see that mate of yours.'

Her muscles tightened.

'Dave?'

'Yeah. Him.'

'I knew about that.' Her heart was thumping. Had he been

to see Dave without telling her? Is that when he told Dave he was worried about her?

'Oh really?' Spyder said. 'He told me not to mention where he was if you phoned.'

She could see his jagged teeth as he pulled his lips back into something resembling a smile.

'Thought maybe he'd gone to sort 'im out.'

'What do you mean?'

'Luke told me you and Dave were very close.' He raised an eyebrow. She found it hard not to react.

'We are close.' No, we were close. 'But not in that way.'

'What other way is there?' He smirked, grabbed her arm again. She felt her lip curling with disgust.

'You owe me one,' he said.

He jerked her arm up to his mouth, attempted to bite her flesh. She pulled her limb upwards, out of his grip, wiped it on the bar, unable to keep the repulsion from her face.

'I owe you fuck all.'

She shoved her way through the punters crowding around the bar, and as she left she heard Spyder shouting, 'Maybe he's got a new bird.'

She barged across the dance floor, down the stairs, out into the dirty street, the pavement littered with bottles, fag ends, needles. Larry had disappeared. Overhead a wave of starlings flocked and spiralled. She tripped over the kerb, righted herself, spotted something scurrying among the black rubbish bags piled in the gutter. Rodent. Never more than six feet away.

She gathered speed as she headed south. She was a mad woman. Crazy. Off her head with love sickness, an infected heart pumping poison round her system. What a waste of time that had been, letting Spyder wind her up for nothing. Now she was worried that Luke had thought there was something going on between her and Dave, that it might have pushed him away. Jesus. Why hadn't he just mentioned it to her? She could have told him straight up there was nothing going on. She had to block out Spyder's insinuations. She knew deep down that wasn't the reason Luke had disappeared; he'd gone because he was scared. He was hiding from something. Someone. She had to find him, sort it out. She charged along the alley to Trafalgar Square. Her neck bristled. She recognized the sensation – somebody was following her. Spyder. It must be Spyder. He was after her. Coming to claim his dues. Fucking, fucking jerk. She sheltered against the wall, below the fig tree, in the shadow of the National Portrait Gallery. A nightbus pulled up. She checked the window as the double-decker slowed, searched for Spyder's ratty reflection, spotted a figure hanging back in the passage. She waited for the bus to pull away, then darted, made a leap for the back platform, clung on to the pole. Along Whitehall, past the Treasury, around Parliament Square, into Millbank. She jumped off as the bus reached the north end of Vauxhall Bridge. The first rays of the rising sun should have been visible in the east, but a ridge of ragged clouds behind St Paul's was muffling the light, the river swathed in early-morning mist. She breathed in the cool air coming off the Thames. The Tate's translucent glass dome glowed in the amber phosphorescence of the street lights. As she stepped on to the bridge, she felt a presence and glanced over to the other side of the road. A man bending down to tie his shoelace. He didn't look up. Couldn't be Spyder, too broad – and anyway she'd lost him at Trafalgar Square. She breathed a sigh of relief and headed south, reached the far end of the bridge, leaned over the railings, searched for Jim along the foreshore as she always did. No sign of him this time, the gentle water ripples and the twisting vapours the only movements by the river. She turned to walk on and gasped; somebody was standing right behind her.

CHAPTER 10

THEY SAT AT either end of her favourite embankment bench; the Houses of Parliament ahead, the verandas of the old St Thomas' Hospital behind. She came here so often to sort stuff out, deal with the phantoms, she considered it her outdoor office. The silver disc of the sun gleamed through the clearing mist. She wrestled silently with the situation, attempting to dissect her feelings rather than reveal them. She needed somebody to help her, she was running out of friends. He had been following her around anyway, and he was unlikely to go away if she ignored him, so she might as well acknowledge he was there. But he was her father's killer. There had been no investigation, accusation, trial or judgment, there had only been a cover-up and speculation. She couldn't claim injustice, demand the truth, because her father had chosen to inhabit the shadowlands of the spooks where everything was shrouded in deceits. Although, that didn't stop her feeling angry. Or scared. And here she was sitting next to the guilty hitman who walked around with loaded guns and was prepared to kill anybody, if the price was right. But he hadn't killed her, not yet anyway. Maybe he was waiting for a better deal. She briefly wondered what her therapist would make of it, where she would place this meeting on a riverside bench with Jim's assassin in the five stages of grieving. Still stuck in denial. Yes, but denial was sometimes a good survival mechanism, and she was in survival mode. She shuffled along the bench.

Sonny searched in his pocket for a fag, cupped one hand around its end and flicked his Zippo with the other. Cracked his jaw and blew a smoke ring. She studied the circle as it wobbled and dispersed, and racked her brain for a neutral subject to talk about.

'South London,' she indicated behind her, 'used to be marshland. The big sink. And then by the seventeenth century it was filling up with small industries. Leather tanning. Prostitutes. And of course it's full of plague pits.'

Sonny puffed a second smoke ring, sent it chasing through the first. 'Plague?'

'1665. Thousands of people died in London.' A black-beaked plague doctor's mask floated into her head. 'The graveyards were overflowing so they dug vast pits. Collected the bodies in carts at night and chucked them in, unnamed. London is one large necropolis. Never more than six feet away from a rat and a skeleton.'

A pigeon hopped along the embankment wall. A cormorant perched on a barge railing, spread its black wings to dry.

'Vauxhall.' She inclined her head to the left. 'That was Jim's favourite bridge.'

Vauxhall. Talking for thirty seconds and she had slipped Jim and the location of his assassination into her supposedly neutral conversation. She couldn't control herself, the compulsion to return to her dad's death, even when her rational self knew it was a bad idea to needle. What was she playing at? Perhaps she needed to cross the shadowlands if she was going to escape the darkness hanging over her. Maybe it was inevitable that her travelling companion should be her father's killer. The repeat patterns. The cormorant took off, flew downstream, searching for breakfast. Sonny stared straight at her and she wondered about his parents because his watery eyes were so dark; she had always thought white South Africans were either sandy Dutchmen or red-necked Germans.

'Are both your parents South African?'

He wiped his nose on the sleeve of his jacket, like a schoolboy, shook his head.

'My father is Afrikaner. My mother is Italian. I don't remember her clearly. She left my father when I was young.'

Perhaps he was inventing a sob story to make her feel sorry for him.

'You haven't tried to find her?'

'I'm always looking for her. She ran away with an Englishman and came to London, but I don't know his name.'

'Why did she leave your father?'

'She couldn't put up with his drinking and the life.'

'Why didn't she take you with her?'

'I don't know.'

He hunched his shoulders.

'So your father brought you up in South Africa?'

'Yes. In the Transvaal. He's a stoer boer, a farmer. He kept cattle; there's not a lot else to do in that part of the Transvaal. He taught me how to hunt. You have to know how to survive out there, you need bushcraft.'

She twitched as she remembered how he'd tracked her down across the marsh, a weasel chasing the petrified rabbit.

'That's why I ended up in the Recces, because of the bushcraft. I had to do my national service and the sergeant put me forward for the Special Forces.'

She sighed. He wanted to explain how he had arrived here, next to her, a South African hitman in London. She folded her arms, decided she might as well let him get on with it, justify himself.

He said, 'We were in Angola 1982, busting SWAPO. My

commanding officer was a madman. I suppose they all were. We did so much drinking, even in the coffee there was always some whisky – Renoster koffie. It was a mark of pride, being able to hold your drink.'

The detail struck a chord, although not an easy one – she was familiar with the macho drinking culture of men in uniform.

'We were on patrol, the two of us alone, my commanding officer and me. He liked going out on patrol with me. He called me his fundi – his apprentice. We looked for animal tracks, hunted game. We shot duiker and took them back for the braai. And then one day we came across some boys playing football in the bush, they were using dirty shirts for goal posts. They were teenagers, about ten of them, wearing rags, barefoot, kicking a ball around in the sand. They didn't see us coming, they carried on playing.'

He puffed another smoke ring.

'I remember the sand whirling and the laughter. I was struck by their happiness. Maybe it was their happiness that annoyed the CO. He said take them out, straight like that, as if they were nothing more than antelope. I said you're kidding, but he repeated the order. In a year's time they will be fighting for SWAPO or some other commie-backed militia, he said, so take them out now and save somebody else the bother later. It would be doing everybody a favour – including them, because they could die quickly, painlessly, here, and then they wouldn't have to crawl through the bush with flies swarming around their blood and guts. Get on with it, he said. But something in me flipped. I told him no way. He got mad, said it was an order. I said fuck you, man. I don't have to take orders from every draadtrekker who gives me shit. And I turned on him. One shot.'

He pulled on his fag. She watched the Thames swirling, the tide indecisive, on the turn.

Eventually she said, 'That was brave.'

'It wasn't brave. It was a reaction.'

Hair trigger, she thought.

'I wasn't able to obey him. So it was one jerk for the lives of ten boys. Well, one jerk and me because then I had to run.'

He strained the filter of his fag, removed another from the carton, lit the second from the first and dropped the dead one on the ground.

'I headed back into South Africa because that's where I had friends. But it was a mistake. I knew I couldn't stay there long. I found a bike and I set off north. In my head I was going to England. I thought I would find my mother and everything would be OK, she would help me. I got as far as Zaire and I met this man in a bar in Kinshasa. He was a security expert, he told me. He guessed I was on the run, he offered me work. I thought I could trust him and I made the mistake of telling him I'd shot my commanding officer. He promised me a new identity, a British passport. A fresh start. But he used the story I'd told him to twist my arm. He threatened to hand me back to South Africa whenever I refused to do his shit.'

Sonny's expression was pleading, his eyes damp. 'I would have been court martialled if I went back. Executed. I had no choice.'

She kept her sight fixed on the Thames, the eddies and the whirls.

'There's always a choice.' If she said it often enough, perhaps it would be true.

He gave his filter one last tug, dropped the butt; it fizzed in a puddle – raining again and she hadn't even noticed.

'I want to make up for what I've done,' he said. 'I want to help you.'

His story had a ring of truth, but she didn't trust him. Why would she? On the other hand, at least he didn't treat her as if she was a paranoid wreck. He acknowledged there was something to be worried about, it wasn't all in her head.

'You are in trouble,' he persisted. 'Your friend Dave has been killed.'

She nodded.

'Tell me,' he said.

She sucked her top lip, the sharpness of her teeth cutting her skin. It would be a relief to talk. She had to be careful, though, not to reveal too much. She said, 'I arranged to meet my boyfriend Luke in Dungeness and he didn't turn up.'

'You were looking for him that evening when you camped out on Romney Marsh alone?'

He had been following her then, of course; it must have been his Land Rover she heard driving away in the morning.

'Yes. We were planning a protest against the transportation of nuclear waste, he went to meet a contact from the power station, then he disappeared, left me a message saying he had to go away. He sounded scared. I haven't heard from him since.'

He fiddled with his stubble – glints of silver in among the black. She was going to tell him about the note from Dave – 55 pluto – but decided that was too much. Too raw.

She said, 'I have a friend – Harry – he's an ex-cop. And now he works for some part of Intelligence, but I don't know which and he wouldn't tell me if I asked. So I don't. But he told me he's seen a file with my name on it.'

'Is it a serious file?'

'Apparently it's on a pile for further investigation and inputting into some list of possible terrorists that Intelligence keeps on a computer. R2 it's called, the list.'

'R2? That is serious.'

'I know.'

She rubbed her neck, her muscles aching, and then she yawned; too tired to think straight, too drained to fight her instinct that he was not bad, just lost, fumbling for a safe path through dangerous territory. Not unlike her. She made a decision.

'We are going to get wet if we stay out here and I need some sleep. You might as well come back and hang out at my place for a while.'

Sonny nodded. 'OK. Ja.'

Funny, the way that South Africans sounded like posh Englishmen from the thirties, the yahs and clipped tone. They walked back along the embankment, under the railway bridge, past the Royal Vauxhall Tavern. A huddle of men in biker jackets and ripped jeans leaned against the railings, talking, laughing, sharing a last smoke before they split. One of them wolf-whistled as they walked past. Sonny turned, smiled at his admirers, and she thought there were some things about him she found appealing too.

She had to rest. She offered Sonny the use of Dave's room. She woke in the late afternoon, surprised to find how easily and for how long she had slept. She had no food in the house so they walked over to South Lambeth Road and ate in the Portuguese café where they always had football on the television. He had clams and squid. She ate potato croquettes and mushrooms with garlic and flirted with the waiters.

'I'm a vegetarian. Well, I do eat fish occasionally,' she said. 'I've found it difficult to eat meat since…' She couldn't finish the sentence. He knew what she was going to say anyway, she could tell by the way he looked at her with his doleful brown eyes.

'Two years ago,' she added. When she had identified her father's waxy corpse in the morgue.

'About the same time I...' His hand went to the crucifix. She wanted to disapprove of his Christianity, see it as fake, but she could see he needed the faith to help him deal with his demons, and she wondered what it said about her that she warmed to his tortured soul.

'You didn't believe in God before?'

'I was brought up a Christian. We went to church and I listened to the pastor. We said prayers at home and read the scriptures. But I didn't believe.'

She pushed the half-empty bowl away, reached for her espresso. 'What made you see the light?'

He lit a Marlboro, puffed a stream of grey smoke through his nostrils.

'It was when...' He tapped the fag against the ashtray, gave her an earnest look. Or perhaps it was more psychotic than earnest. 'I wanted to start afresh. Leave all of that behind – the contracts, the agents. But I couldn't sleep. Every day, I was getting closer to the edge, thinking I didn't deserve to live, that I should just end it all quickly.'

He was gazing at her with his wet eyes and she tried to shake off the sense that they had some deep connection, both grappling with the same bleak legacy. She needed to keep her distance.

He asked, 'What did you do after your father's death?'

'I went to university. And then I...' She didn't want to confess that she had a crisis too that had precipitated a year off, hanging around in Vauxhall. Dungeness.

'Is that where you met Luke? At uni?'

She shook her head. She hadn't clicked with any of the men at Oxford; the rugger buggers and the Hooray Henries were non-starters, and when you had dismissed them the pool was considerably diminished. Even among the potential kindred spirits, she hadn't met anybody who had bowled her over.

Nice men. Interesting men. Clever men. Yet they all seemed…
were lacking a certain – what – recklessness? Edginess? No
chemistry. Nobody clicked. Maybe she hadn't been in the right
frame of mind.

'I met Luke when I was working at the nightclub.' She
nodded her head in the vague direction of Soho.

'What does he do?'

'He's a photographer. He got a scholarship to do a photography course in an American college. LA. And then he ended
up working with this NGO that gives cameras to people living
in war zones, or in Third World slums, so they can record
their lives.'

'I met some people doing that kind of thing when I was in
Angola with the army. He is older than you?'

'He's twenty-six. I'm twenty.'

'Good-looking?'

Sam nodded. 'But that's not why I like him.' She reddened.
'I want to find him.'

'Do you think it's wise to go looking?'

'Wise?' She tipped her coffee cup, surveyed the swirl of
muddy grounds, wondered whether the patterns could be read
like tea leaves.

'I'm not sure wise comes into it. I have to find Luke before
anybody else gets to him. I have to make sure he's safe.'

'Ek verstaan,' Sonny said. 'I understand.'

She tipped the espresso cup a different way and watched the
brown sludge slip across the china; she didn't have much to go
on in her search for Luke. Dave's note – 55 pluto. The match-
box from Heaven and the clenched fist sign of Venus feminist
badge left by the slender dark-haired figure in Bane House.
Perhaps she should start somewhere more obvious, go to Luke's
place, look around his room, see if she could find anything that

might indicate where he had gone, or exactly what had made him run.

She said, 'Luke's housemate Spyder will be out working tonight. Maybe we should go and have a look around, see what we can find.'

'Have you got a key?'

'No. But I know how to get in round the back without too much difficulty. We'll have to wait a few hours. Spyder won't leave until eight or so.'

Sonny shrugged. 'If it's what you wish to do, I'll help you.'

God, it was like having a gun-toting genie in a bottle for a companion.

They set off at ten. Spyder's house was on the edge of Rotherhithe, east along the river. The property developers had taken over and they had to negotiate the blocked roads and diversions that accompanied the building mania. In the seventies, Jim had worked in Tilbury docks downstream in Essex and he always said the deep water container port would put the London docklands out of business. He was right. But then the city started booming and there was cash everywhere and loads of it was pouring into the vast industrial wasteland sitting on the money market's doorstep. Docklands was one vast building site now – wet docks, dry docks, wharves and warehouses ripe for conversion into luxury flats. Anybody who had lived there before – boatmen, dockers, packers – had been shunted elsewhere. Although, in among the chaos of bulldozers, cranes, dug-up roads, gas pipes waiting to be buried, there were untouched streets; warehouses, cobbles and back to backs. Bastions of resistance. Spyder had managed to grab a slice of the real-estate action – purchased a small house squeezed on to a corner beside a disused pub on Rotherhithe

Street before prices started rocketing. Riverside view, in estate agent's terms; the grey waters of the Thames visible through a gap in the houses opposite if you craned your neck out of the top-floor window.

Sam parked the van by the river. The construction workers had departed for the day and the drills and bulldozers were sleeping. The eerie silence of the empty streets was broken only by the scurrying of rodents and the creak of a pub sign swinging in the breeze. Spyder's place was the last in a row of condemned houses. Apart from his, they were all boarded up, front doors marked with red crosses like the houses of plague victims, families locked inside with their already dead relatives, waiting for their turn, the sweet scent of rotting flesh in the air.

The clang of a bell startled her and she thought for a moment it was the corpse collector calling for the dead.

'Church bells,' she said. 'Eleven.'

Spyder's house was a wreck even though it wasn't condemned. A squalid drug dealers' den; peeling wallpaper, broken panes replaced with hardboard, missing floorboards that meant you could see the room below when you used the toilet. And anybody in the room below could look up and see you peeing. When Luke discovered that *Oliver Twist* was set in nearby Jacob's Island, he had painted a sign saying Fagin's Lair, nailed it to the frame above the front door. Luke rented a room from Spyder at the back of the house, which he had painted black. Sam had stayed overnight once, but that was enough. Spyder's presence, the squalor, the lack of a toilet floor had been too much for her and, after the one-night trial, Luke always came back to Vauxhall with her.

The house was dark. No movement. No sounds of life.

'I'll knock,' Sonny said.

'Spyder's not the kind of person who would answer, even if he was in. I'm certain he's not there anyway. He's working at the Wag.'

'Do you know this Spyder guy quite well then?'

'No. Thankfully.'

'Did you meet him through Luke?'

'I met Spyder first, before I knew Luke. Last September when I started working at the Ballroom. He turned up one evening and introduced himself. He's a dope dealer as well as a barman. He tends to get everywhere, like a virus.'

She wasn't sure Sonny was paying attention, too busy assessing the house, searching for an entrance.

He said, 'Over the wall round the back?'

She nodded.

'Why don't you stay here, and I'll go inside and look around.'

She tutted. 'I'm coming with you.'

They clambered over the brick wall into the small courtyard behind the house, littered with upturned tables, broken wardrobes, smashed crockery and three-legged chairs. Spyder had chucked the unwanted rotting furniture out the back when he moved in. Something scuttled.

'Rat.'

They picked their way across the yard to the back of the house. Sam took the credit card that Barclays had sent her the first term she was at Oxford and slipped it between the bottom and top frame of the sash window. She jiggled the catch free and then wiggled the bottom frame upwards.

'Where did you learn that trick?'

'Jim.'

He had demonstrated on their back window – emergency measures in case she was ever locked out. She edged over the windowsill. The kitchen was scuzzy; the orange street light

176

cast a sickly glow on the sink full of dirty plates and the tin foil takeaways stacked on the table. She suspected this was more evidence that Luke hadn't been here for days. He knew how to use a rubbish bin.

'I'm going to look in his room first,' she said.

'Use a torch,' he said. 'Here, take mine.'

'I've got my own.'

She stuck her hand in her pocket; touched her Swiss Army knife and found her torch. The thin beam picked out dirty underpants, dirty mags; Spyder's scum. She picked her way through the debris, up the stairs, into Luke's room, sat on the bed and put her face in her hands, overwhelmed.

'Are you OK?' Sonny was standing in the doorway.

'I'll be fine.'

'We'll work it out. Don't worry. I'll go and check the other rooms.'

She wiped her nose, stood, opened the door of Luke's cupboard, ran the torch over its contents, spotted his donkey jacket, his prize shirt from Johnsons with the skulls and roses print. His leather jacket wasn't there; he would have taken it with him to Dungeness. She pictured him, tried to imagine what he would be wearing – biker jacket with the badges on the lapel – nuclear-free zone, Anti-Nazi League, his anarchy and peace Crass badge – black jeans and eighteen-hole DMs. She closed the cupboard, went over to Luke's desk; nothing there apart from some pencils, a couple of empty film canisters and the shoebox he used to store his favourite photos. She opened the lid. She was top of the picture pile – a black-and-white photo of her sitting by the campfire at the Lookers' Hut. She hated having her photo taken, she always pulled a stupid face at the wrong moment, but Luke had managed to capture her smiling. She riffled through the pile; a couple of power station shots, close up of a starfish, the Lookers' Hut, and then a photo that caught her by surprise – a shot of the article she had found lying on the top of Dave's academic papers in his bedroom cupboard. *Distribution of caesium 137 between abiotic and biotic components of aquatic ecosystems. By Simon Burns.* The photograph disconcerted her – she had no idea what to make of it. She couldn't remember him taking it or mentioning anything about it. She stared at the photo for a moment before replacing it in the box with all the others.

She backed away, lost in thought, swept the beam around the room. The bookshelf held a selection of his favourite authors – Herman Hesse. Camus. Sartre. Orwell. The walls were bare. He didn't have many possessions, didn't like to hold on to stuff. Was he the same with people? Spyder's voice intruded. *Maybe he's got a new bird.* She shook her head, she was letting his venom infect her.

She shone the torch along the bedding, unruffled apart from the dent she had made when she had flopped in despair on the duvet. She squatted down, peered under the bed. A dirty sock gathering dust and hair. An A4 notebook. She stretched, hooked the wire spiral with a finger, pulled. Unused, but half the first page had been ripped off. She directed the beam at the paper, the torch caught the indentations of a pen on the page behind the missing half. Bingo. She almost shrieked with glee. Somebody had written what looked like a telephone number with a degree of pressure on the top page, as if they were writing under stress, determined to get the number right, and then had torn it out, leaving the indentation underneath. She leaped over to the desk, grabbed a pencil and scribbled over the lines to reveal them, held the paper at an angle to the torch beam. *P. Grogan 01797 66364.* Grogan. The name sounded familiar, but maybe she was mistaken. She certainly recognized the area code – Romney. She bubbled – a breakthrough, a clear lead to Luke.

'Where are you?'

'In here.'

He was in Spyder's room, studying a small black notebook. She said, 'Look at this.'

He glanced up, moved as if to put the notebook in his pocket, changed his mind, and left it by the side of Spyder's grotty bed.

'He's a junkie,' Sonny said. 'I found his works.' He pointed to the bedside table and an open case cradling a syringe.

'Well, he's a dealer, so it's hardly surprising. But look what I've discovered.' She waved her efforts with the pencil triumphantly under his nose.

'It's a name and a Romney phone number. I found the notebook under Luke's bed. I bet you anything it's the number of the person who works at the power station. The man he arranged to see on Saturday.'

'Great. We're...'

His sentence was interrupted by a crash from below. Furniture banging. Plates smashing on the floor. Sonny's hand went straight for the inside pocket of his jacket. A scream cut into the air. He drew the Browning.

'Wait,' she said. Jesus, he really was trigger happy.

The scream was answered by another. And another.

'Cats,' she said.

'Is it?'

A hiss, a scuffle. Sonny's arm relaxed, he replaced the gun in his jacket.

She said, 'I left the window open. They're probably fighting over the remains of Spyder's chicken tikka masala.'

A mangy specimen ran off as they entered the kitchen. Sonny scooped the surly beast sitting on the kitchen counter into his arms and cradled it like a baby. He tickled its head and it purred contentedly.

'I love cats,' he said.

'Me too.'

She heard the distant chimes of St Paul's striking midnight as she clambered into the van. Too late to call the Romney number; that would have to wait until the morning.

'I'm turning into a nocturnal creature,' she said. 'I only sleep during the day. What about you? Don't you sleep?'

'I don't need much sleep.'

She gave him a sceptical look.

'Military training,' he said.

'Really?'

'And a little bit of poor man's toot as well.'

That didn't bode well, she didn't fancy having to deal with him when he was having an amphetamine-induced psychotic attack with his hand on his Browning.

'Might be better if you gave it a break. The speed. Rots your brain cells. Makes you paranoid.'

'OK. You're right.' He was so submissive. It could go to her head, the power. She'd never experienced it before, never wanted to order anybody about, bend them to her will. She could be an irritating smartarse, she knew, but it was a product of her determination to avoid doing what anybody else told her rather than a desire to dominate.

'Why don't you give me the toot so I can look after it and make sure you don't stuff any up your nose without thinking.'

He nodded, handed her a fold of paper. She wound the window down and emptied the packet outside; the crystal grains whirled and glittered in the street light, a decaying city snowglobe.

'Oh man,' Sonny said. 'What did you do that for?'

'If the Old Bill stop us and find a packet of speed, they won't even have to bother planting something on us to haul us down the cop shop.'

He curled up in the front seat like an admonished child and she felt mean. She glanced at him and smiled, he caught her eye and smiled back. She looked down and caught sight of his forearm, bare, sinewy below his rolled-up sleeves, a band of pen and ink crosses like an incomplete bracelet near his elbow. Or were they gravestones? One cross for each of his victims? She blinked, her stomach tightened. He sat up, pulled the shirt cuff down. But not before she had spotted the last cross in the line, more recent than the others because the skin was raised and bruised around the lines, like a grave that had not been filled long enough for the earth to settle. She shivered. Roger was right, she could be quite naïve sometimes. She'd bought the soft, submissive guy under the hard nut exterior act; it was just as likely that he was leading her on, and she was the one who was following meekly.

CHAPTER 11

THE SNAIL WAS sitting on the doormat. She lifted it gently, carried it outside, noticed the dextral spiral of its shell as she placed it gently in the gutter, returned inside. The answering machine flashed – two blinks. Sonny tactfully removed himself to Dave's room. She took a deep breath, pressed play. First message from Liz.

'Sam, are you there? You're never there these days when I want to talk to you. I'll try again later.'

Seriously, Liz was accusing her of being unavailable. She pressed erase. Played the second message.

'Sam, it's Jess. I don't suppose you could come over tomorrow, could you? I've got something for you.'

She watched the moon through her bedroom window as it edged behind the rusty struts of the Oval gasometer. She gave up the search for rest. Sonny was sprawled across Dave's bed, slumbering peacefully. She tiptoed down the stairs, dialled the Romney number she had found in Luke's room. Grogan. Where had she heard that name before? Nobody picked up. Not reassuring. She crept to the kitchen, brewed a saucepan of thick coffee as the grey morning light slipped in.

Eight a.m. The phone rang. She ran and grabbed it so Sonny didn't wake.

'Hello, Sam. Sorry to call early. I wanted to make sure I caught you in.'

The therapist.

'I'm on my way out,' Sam whispered.

'Sam, I wanted to go over something with you quickly.'

'Oh?'

'I'm worried about you and I'm trying to help you see what's going on here.'

'Look, maybe...'

'Do you remember we had a conversation about the event that precipitated your crisis at university?'

'Yes.'

'You told me that a man walked up to you on Cornmarket and he said he knew you were Jim Coyle's daughter.'

'Yes.'

'I wanted to go back over this ground very quickly, because what I want you to see, Sam, is...'

She flipped her mind back to that event in the spring of the previous year; the strange man on Cornmarket who had left her feeling marked, caused a crisis. But then she hadn't heard or seen any further signs of anybody on her tail, shadowing her. Piece by piece she had rebuilt herself: the house in Vauxhall, Dave, archaeology in Dungeness, the Lookers' Huts, Luke. A wall against the strangers whispering in her ear, the spooks and counter-spooks; knicker sniffers. It had worked, she thought; kept them all at bay. Then she had heard the whistle on the phone and Luke had disappeared. And now, as the therapist encouraged her to recall the Cornmarket event again – *I know you. You are Jim Coyle's daughter* – she wondered whether she had been under surveillance all along, ever since that day. She dismissed the idea, it didn't make sense. Not entirely anyway. The therapist was still yabbering in her ear; Sam wasn't sure how much of the conversation she had missed.

'... I'm trying to help you understand these anxieties, your fears about people watching you, eavesdropping on the phone – these are ways of holding on to your father. His life. It's a denial of his death.'

'Yeah, I see what you mean.' She needed to wrap up this pointless conversation, get on the road, find out why Jess wanted to see her.

'I'm glad you've found it helpful. You'll need to process what I've been saying.'

'Yes. Thanks. I'll think about it. I have to go now.'

'OK. We'll talk more at our usual time.'

'Right. OK. Bye.'

She replaced the receiver, mind elsewhere, arguing with herself about leaving a front door key for Sonny, concluded it was no greater risk than letting him sleep in Dave's bed, dropped the spares on the kitchen table, left the house, headed for the South Circular in the van.

The silver chopper parked on the verge in front of the house meant Jess was at home. Sam examined the panes of glass in the front door as she fiddled with the key; the tiny etched schooners that once all sailed the same way were now sailing in opposite directions. Ships that had passed in the night. She pushed the door. Jess ran down the stairs to greet her.

'I got your message,' Sam said. 'So I came over. The ships...'

'Is it obvious?'

'Oh. You did it. What happened?'

'I had a party. It got slightly out of control. I wasn't paying much attention when the glazier came round to repair the damage. I doubt whether Liz will notice. Interior decoration has never been one of her preoccupations.'

'Well, if somebody had spray-painted "Shakespeare is shit" across the front room she might have been annoyed. But mainly because of the sentiment rather than the deed.'

'Liz just phoned, anyway,' Jess said. 'She wanted to know if I'd seen you, in fact. She's worried you're not eating properly. She says she sent you a postcard with a recipe on it.'

'What's that all about? She never cares what I eat when she's here, so why is she worrying about it now that she's in Greece?'

'I don't know. Maybe she's afraid you'll go off your rocker again and won't go back to university in October.'

'I didn't go off my rocker.'

'So what if you did anyway. There's nothing wrong with going off your rocker. I mean, why wouldn't you go off your rocker? We had a mad dad doing a fruitcake job and he dies suddenly just as you're about to go to university. Of course you go off your rocker. We've all gone off our rockers a bit since he died. We'd be mad if we didn't.'

Jess was shouting. She didn't usually shout. Jess was the easy-going one of the family.

'Shall I skin up?' Sam asked.

'Yes. No don't. That's been playing on my mind too.'

'What?'

'Smoking a reefer on Jim's grave the other day.'

'What was wrong with that?'

'I didn't want to be disrespectful to Jim.'

'I doubt whether Jim would mind you smoking on his grave. He didn't object to you doing it when he was alive.'

Jess was rubbing her hands, face distressed. Sam couldn't think of anything to say to make her sister feel better. She licked and joined a couple of Rizlas.

Jess said, 'You're right, though, Jim didn't object. He only ever gave me one lecture about smoking. Did I tell you what he said?'

'No.'

'He said he was hardly in a position to pontificate about the risks of smoking, given the amount he drank. But what he wanted me to know was that half the dope dealers in London are touts.'

'Touts?'

'Yeah.' She inhaled, blew out. 'Narks. Grassers. The cops are letting them deal in exchange for information.'

'What sort of information?'

'Anything they can squeeze out of them.'

'I didn't know that.'

'Seriously? I did. But it was useful to hear Jim confirm it, and remind me to be careful around dealers, especially small-timers, because they are the ones most desperate for cash.'

'Right.'

In her head she compiled a list of dope dealers she had said too much to recently. Dungeness Alastair was top of the list.

Jess said, 'Jim was always fairly pragmatic; he knew he couldn't stop us smoking, or you and your protests. He never tried to intervene, so long as we didn't get ourselves into too much shit.'

Sam inhaled, tried to crack her jaw, blow a smoke ring. Failed. 'Why did you want me to come over anyway?'

'Oh yes, of course.' She dug in her pocket. 'Harry dropped a note round for you yesterday morning. He knocked on the door and asked whether I could make sure you got it early today. I said I'd give it a go. He told me not to mention his name if I spoke to you on the phone.'

Sam unfolded the paper: '*Meet me at the allotment Friday afternoon.*'

Perhaps Harry had sorted the file – the thought cheered her.

'Whistle-stop visit, I'm afraid. I'd better be moving, I'm supposed to meet Harry this afternoon.'

'Is something going on or shouldn't I ask?'

'No. Don't ask.'

'I won't then.' She paused. 'But if there is anything you want to talk about, you'd better tell me now. I'm going down to Cornwall with a couple of mates tomorrow. We're riding the bikes down, doing a camping tour of the coastline, so I'm not going to be around for a week or so.'

Sam opened her mouth, let the smoke drift and curl in the window's light.

'Sam.'

She jolted. 'Sorry, what did you say?'

'I said, is there anything you want to talk about?'

'No. No, I'm fine. I'd better go now anyway.'

'Oh, OK. I give up. But hang on a moment, I've got something else for you. A letter turned up in the post for you the other day. I left it up in my room. I'll go and find it.'

Sam walked to the front door, eager to leave, eyed the cupboard under the stairs and remembered she had left Jim's bag of discarded rubble there. She grabbed it, might be worth a closer look. Jess reappeared, envelope in hand. Sam recognized the writing on the front. Her friend Tom. Journo. She stuffed it in her pocket, for later reading.

The Great North Wood covered the hills of Sydenham and Dulwich. Harry's allotment was on the far side. She had been there many times when she was a child because Harry asked Jim to tend the plot when he went away on his extended trips to undisclosed locations, and Jim delegated the task to his daughters. Sam followed the familiar claggy path through the hornbeams, reached the crest of the hill, tipped her head back and opened her mouth to catch the rainwater from the morning's downpour as it dripped from the leaves. Wash-off, she heard Dave's voice say in her head. Secondary contamination. She let the tepid water dribble down her gullet anyway.

The allotments covered the southern downslope; beanpoles, dog roses, chrysanthemums and cucumber frames. Harry's bulky windcheater-swathed form was hunched over a spade. She wound her way around the patchwork of plots and when she was within speaking distance he acknowledged her presence with a nod of his head and a concerned smile, his fleshy face hanging more heavily than the last time she'd seen him, nearly two years ago now.

'OK?' He asked in a way that made her feel she might not be when he had finished talking to her.

'I'm fine. The rain hasn't spoiled your veggies.'

He gestured across the flourishing allotment. 'South-facing slope. Well drained. London clay. Quite claggy up there,' he pointed to the top of the hill, 'where the water collects. And down there, where the clay meets the chalk, that's a different story again. Chalk, tricky stuff. But then I suppose it would be, all those crushed skeletons.'

Listening to Harry reminded her of Jim – they had both been in the army and the Force, and she could detect the same speech patterns, the clipped sentences, the authoritative yet evasive words of the spook. She had inherited some of those tics too – the evasiveness rather than the authority – echoes of her father.

He stood back from the spade, glanced around the allotments. Blackbird perched on the broken arm of a scarecrow. Hum of bees and cars. Drip, drip, drip of rain trickling off a shed roof into a metal bucket.

'I've heard something interesting on the grapevine,' he said.

'Interesting?'

'Well, interesting if you are interested in cops and their doings. The Force has set up this new unit, it deals with the overlap between terrorism and organized crime. The Sewer Squad, as it's unaffectionately known.'

She parked herself against a water butt; she could tell this conversation was going to be neither quick nor easy. 'Why the Sewer Squad?'

'Because they spend most of their time wading through the shit.' He chuckled, and then stopped laughing abruptly. 'It's important work – difficult work – trying to untangle the flow of money and weapons to terrorist groups. Terrorists acquiring weapons from criminal gangs. Drugs and weapons trafficked along the same routes. No clear boundaries out there in the shadows.'

A heavy weight was forming in her stomach, a sense she was being sucked down, trapped in the sticky London clay.

Harry said, 'Crawford, Superintendent Crawford, he's the officer in charge of the unit.'

'But what's Crawford and the Sewer Squad got to do with me?'

'He's been investigating the death of your friend Dave Daley.'

She stifled her shock with some effort. Crawford must have been the obnoxious top cop she overheard talking the night of Dave's death.

'And Crawford's the officer who is dealing with your file.'

Her lungs tightened, trachea constricted.

'I don't understand,' she said. 'I really don't get it.'

'According to Crawford, your mate's death was suicide.'

He narrowed his eyes when he said that, gave her the old gimlet stare. She said nothing, tried to maintain a blank face.

He continued. 'Crawford is interested in the weapon he used to shoot himself. He's working on the theory that Daley was planning some sort of attack on a nuclear waste transport vehicle at Dungeness. Using firearms.'

Sweat dribbled down her chest. She flapped the neck of her tee shirt to circulate some fresh air around her torso.

'Firearms?'

'Well, singular. One gun, supposedly for holding up this container vehicle, but then used, unfortunately, by Daley to shoot himself. You don't have any guns in your possession, I assume?'

She shook her head vigorously. She hadn't taken up Sonny's offer of the Firebird, so she wasn't lying. Christ, how did she get into this mess?

'Daley's suicide was something to do with a girl in London, apparently, according to the note he left. Crawford believes the girl is you.'

'That doesn't make sense to me.'

Harry shrugged. 'So there's a gun. And then, apparently, they found a note in the house in Skell, a rough plan of the event.'

'What was the plan?'

'Use the gun to hold up the lorry carrying the spent fuel rods container and force the driver to a different location.'

Sam screwed her face up. 'Why would anybody in their right mind do that?'

'According to this note, to demonstrate how easy it would be for terrorists to hijack one of the spent fuel rod transport carriers.'

'That's nuts.'

'You might think it's nuts. And I might think it's nuts. But Crawford has to go on what he's got.'

Harry leaned on the spade, looked her in the eye.

'You don't know anything about this gun or a plot to hijack a nuclear waste transporter then?'

'No. Of course not. I'd never get involved in anything as ridiculous and as dangerous as that.'

'But were you planning anything?'

She sighed, realized she was going to have to say something. 'Yes. A protest about the transport of nuclear waste at Dungeness. But with banners and placards, nothing more. There was no gun involved.' She wanted to cry.

'And what about this Dave Daley? Could he have been planning to do this hijack malarkey without you knowing about it?'

She hesitated too long, she knew. She was getting in a muddle, didn't know what to say and what not to say, didn't want to mention Luke, because she didn't want to bring him into it if his name wasn't on Crawford's list. She didn't want to air any doubts about Dave, didn't want to consider the possibility that her best mate had been involved in something totally stupid.

'No, not Dave,' she said. 'He wasn't even involved in planning the demo. He has an academic interest in the effects of radiation, not a political one. Had,' she added.

'Word is, he had connections with the Provos, which explains how he got his hands on a gun.'

Her brain was scrabbling, perceptions slipping around like quicksilver.

'No. No. Maybe some of his relatives are connected to the Provos, I really don't know, but he wasn't in contact with his relatives anyway. He didn't speak to his brothers. His father is in the States.'

She rewound the conversation between Crawford and his sidekick she had overheard from the far side of the flint wall. It wasn't the details that stuck in her mind, but his tone, his bullying, his bigotry.

'Is Crawford good at his job?' She asked the question cautiously, feeling her way – didn't want to reveal she'd been earwigging on a cop.

'Crawford? He's tough, make no mistake. He has to be. But he's dedicated to the work. He's built up quite a reputation. He has contacts all over the place – Intelligence, CIA, you name it.'

'You don't think he might be...' She fumbled for the right words. 'Jumping to conclusions about Dave because he's got an Irish father?'

Harry took a deep breath. 'Crawford's not exactly known for his liberal views. But the thing is, from what I've heard, the information is there, on the record.'

He examined the clouds when he spoke, didn't look straight at her face.

'Apparently you've been involved in the planning of this Dungeness...' he flicked his hand, 'fireworks fiasco for months, according to their informer.'

'Informer?'

'Reliable unnamed source. Somebody's been dripping information about you.'

An alarm bell rang in her head. Dungeness. Informer. Small-time dope dealer. Alastair. She paled, tried to recall exactly how much she had told him about what and when.

'I think I know who the informer might be.'

Harry folded his arms, frowned.

'This hippy bloke I met. He came along to these environmental meetings we organized in Dungeness, when we talked about a protest. I think he's a dope dealer as well. Maybe he's been making things up, handing over stories to the cops in exchange for cash, or to keep them off his back.'

'Possibly. It does sound as if somebody has been feeding Crawford false information about you. It's the most obvious explanation for all this. But, look, I don't want you doing any detective work yourself, thank you very much. No going round exposing informers, please. That wouldn't be clever. Best thing to do with Crawford on your tail is sit tight, keep your nose clean. He'll certainly want to pull you in for questioning at some point, to clear up any outstanding issues around Dave's suicide if for no other reason. But I suspect he won't contact you for a couple of days because he's prioritizing the weapon, tracing it back to its source. And anyway he's got a lot on his plate at the moment. He's been dragged back into another difficult case. Hangover from his last unit.'

'Anything interesting?' She only asked to take the focus away from herself for a moment; she needed a breather.

'Murder. Ex-detective. He left the Force and set up his own private investigations agency. Apparently it was a professional job, couple of bullets in the back of his head. Two days ago.' He wiped his hands on his trousers. 'It happened quite near here in fact. Over by Crystal Palace.'

'So where's the connection to Crawford?'

'Well, Crawford was his boss before he left the Force. They were both working on this bullion case – you know that airport robbery – the haul was worth millions, but it was all in gold bars, so it required a vast laundering job, dragged the whole of the south London criminal fraternity into the operation – smelting, mixing, layering, converting it into dirtier currencies. Drugs mainly.'

'Turning gold into shit. Reverse alchemy.'

'If you say so.' He raised a pale eyebrow. 'Is that relevant? Alchemy?'

Her eyes glazed for a moment. 'I don't know. It's a pattern, like a Fibonacci sequence, a spiral, a periodic repetition, that's all.'

'You've been smoking too many funny cigarettes.' He huffed. 'But yes, there's been a lot of gold smelting going on in garages all over the sticks.'

He paused then, as if something had occurred to him. 'You're familiar with that edge of town, aren't you?'

'You mean the periphery, where we used to take the dog for a walk – where Jim is buried? The criminal belt?'

'Yes, that's right. That's what Jim called it – the criminal belt.' He sounded sad, or possibly more reflective than sad. He snapped out of it, returned to Crawford.

'Unfortunately for Crawford, he can't entirely shake this case. This ex-cop, the one Crawford was managing, had to leave the Force because there were corruption allegations flying, stories that he was taking cuts from the gold launderers he was supposed to be investigating. Nothing proved, but he had to go. And it's almost certain he's been done in by his criminal contacts because his fingers got too sticky. Of course Crawford is familiar with all the ins and outs, so he's had to go over the old ground.'

She spotted a brown flash at the edge of the allotment, a fox patrolling a row of raspberry canes.

Harry continued. 'The only lead they've got so far is this old lady who was taking her dog for an evening walk. Westie, I believe – the dog. She insists she passed a man with a funny halo walking along the road where it happened, shortly after the time the murder took place.'

'A funny halo?'

He nodded. 'It's what she said. The man had a funny halo floating above his head. But the witness is eighty-six and somewhat short-sighted, so I'm not sure anybody is taking the description too seriously. Wanted, pistol-carrying member of the angelic horde. Doesn't quite stack up.'

'No, I suppose not.'

He stuck his hand in his back pocket, produced a newspaper cutting.

'I spotted the report in the local paper this morning. Made me laugh – the haloed hitman – so I tore it out. Have a look if you want a bit of light entertainment.'

'Thanks.'

He handed her the folded article. She put it in her coat pocket.

'Anyway, hopefully Crawford will be kept busy by old ladies and their Westies for a couple of days and by the time he gets round to contacting you, I'll have worked out what's what. Sorted out where all this dodgy information is coming from. So don't do anything stupid, please, and certainly steer clear of protests around nuclear power stations, thank you very much.'

She dug her toe into the soil, prodded around, sent an earthworm wriggling. 'We've got a right to protest. We weren't planning anything illegal.'

'I'm not saying you were, but you've got to be careful if you want to stay out of trouble. Watch it. Stay below the radar. We need to contain this, we're trying to keep you off a bloody MI5 computer index, not issue a minute with your name underlined three times in red. Be circumspect about who you choose to hang out with. Trust nobody.'

She was about to bite back, an instant reaction, when she registered his words. *Trust nobody.*

'Harry, I meant to ask, somebody has been leaving messages on my answerphone, whistling that *Third Man* tune.'

'*The Third Man*?' He hummed. 'The one Jim always used to whistle?'

She nodded. He frowned.

'No, not me. I can't whistle. One of your mates messing about?'

'Don't think so.'

'Well, I suppose it's a reminder, in case you needed one, that you can never be sure who is on the other end of a line. Never trust a spy you cannot see.' She remembered Jim using that line when she'd told him she had heard a click on their home phone – spooks, he said, different parts of the secret state monitoring each other. Never trust a spy you cannot see, he added, and then he laughed and disappeared. Harry continued. 'Use a phone box when you call me. And don't keep using the same one.'

He walked over to a pile of carrier bags at the edge of the potato patch. 'Here, take these, some tomatoes I picked this morning.'

'Thanks.'

'My pleasure. And Sam.'

'Yes?'

'Stay out of it, will you? Go camping for a couple of days.'

'OK.'

'And go easy on the whacky-baccy.'

Raindrops splashed her face as she pushed her way along the side of the allotment. She looked over her shoulder; Harry back at his digging, the fox slipping along the hedgerow behind. Harry glanced up and she caught the concern on his face, the furrowed forehead, before he had a chance to smile. She waved, trudged up the slope to the Great North Wood, under the shadow of the dripping trees. She pulled out the cutting he had given her, the case of the haloed hitman, read as she strolled, ignored the wet splodges on the newspaper. The name of the ex-cop turned private investigator then killed by a haloed hitman almost made her trip. Flint. The same name she had seen scribbled in Jim's diary, 6 June 1984, the stick of candy-floss doodled underneath. A gagging sweetness filled her mouth, her throat, her nose. She retched. Her legs buckled.

She slumped on the path, stuck her head between her knees, blood beating in her ears, fragments flying around her brain. Flint. The candy man – cold steel eyes, scythe-shaped scar. The man she had seen at a May Day fair in 1978. The man Jim had been desperate to avoid. She had assumed he was a murderer, or a terrorist. But now it looked like the candy man was a cop. A bloody cop. A bent cop taking a cut from the criminal belt bullion launderers. And, if that was the case, why had Jim met up with him in 1984, two weeks before he was killed? Maybe it was all irrelevant, because this was 1986 and if Flint was the candy man, then he was dead. Killed by a haloed hitman. Perhaps it was good news, of sorts. Yet it felt more like bad news, uncomfortable news, news that made her feel small, vulnerable, exposed to danger, but unable to identify its source. She stood, stuffed the newspaper cutting in a pocket, brushed her trousers, listened to the oak leaves rustling, jays laughing. A fat droplet ran off an overhanging branch, plopped on the back of her neck, and for a moment she thought it was a bullet.

CHAPTER 12

SHE WANDERED INTO the kitchen, bag of Jim's belongings picked up from her parents' house in one hand, bag of tomatoes from Harry in the other. Sonny was cooking. Head bent over hob, stirring whatever was in the saucepan, steam billowing hellishly round his dark head. The sight of him being domestic in her kitchen flipped her momentarily. He stood back from the oven and smiled at her coyly. Or was he being sly? She took a deep breath.

'What's on the menu?'

'Spanakopita.'

'Is that a South African recipe?'

'Greek.'

She must have grimaced, although she wasn't conscious of any facial movement.

'Sorry,' he said. 'I found a postcard on the mat this morning.'

He handed her the card lying on the counter top.

'I couldn't help reading it. There was nothing personal on it.'

There wouldn't be, if Liz had written it.

'It said you must try this recipe, so I thought I would. It's vegetarian, spinach is the main ingredient. I walked over to the Sainsbury's on Wandsworth Road, bought the ingredients and some other food. You don't have anything to eat in the house.'

'You cook a lot?'

'I had to do the cooking when I was a kid. In fact I had to

look after the house. I was a surrogate wife, I suppose, for my father.' He looked ashamed when he said that.

'Cooking is a useful skill to have.' She said it quickly, avoided his eye, didn't want to show him too much empathy, examined the postcard. The front was an idyllic scene – topaz sea, turquoise sky, whitewashed villas. The message on the back was typical Liz. Lots of randomly underlined words that she undoubtedly thought were incredibly important but the significance of which left everybody else completely mystifed. *You must try this recipe. We think it's <u>lovely</u>.* We. Bloody we. She didn't want to know about any we. Liz and Roger. *Spanakopita.* Ingredients. <u>*Unsalted*</u> *butter. Flour.* Instructions with more random underlinings. *Love from Mum.* Not underlined.

'I'm sure it would please my mother to know that somebody bothered to use one of her recipes.' She said it tersely.

'I'm sorry. Have I upset you?'

'No. Not even slightly.' She handed the postcard back to Sonny, wondered whether he was chipping away at her psyche, searching for the vulnerable spots before he struck. Bushcraft: the hunter had to know his prey. He was back at the stove, tilted the frying pan, allowed the flame to lick its sides, peered at the postcard, reached for a lemon squeezer. The absurdity of it hit her then, her father's killer preparing a meal for her using a recipe posted from her mother. She cracked. Caught herself off guard with her bottled-up mania. Started laughing and couldn't stop. Hysterical. Had to lie on the floor. She rolled around wheezing, her sides hurt, she couldn't breathe. Foetal position. Cheek on lino. Down among the dead matter; hair balls, toenail clippings, sloughed-off skin. Dave's remains, his last traces. She was slipping, below the earth's crust, among all the dead people, a danse macabre with her favourite corpses. Everybody was dead. Jim was dead. Dave was dead. Luke was dead too.

He must be dead; she could see his bones, his hair down here in the catacombs. She had to get a grip. She turned and lay on her back, breathed deeply, let her eyes travel the cracks in the ceiling, traced the drab edges of the bat-shaped water stain. Bath leak. Normal. She had surfaced, back in the realm of the living. Luke wasn't dead. There was a lot of muck under the kitchen table, but it was just normal household grime. And yes, she had found a bone and some hair in the Lookers' Hut, and she had shown them to Dave and he had left them under the urn in his back garden. But they weren't Luke's remains. They were a shepherd's charm left in the hearth to ward off evil. She became conscious of Sonny watching her warily.

'Are you OK?'

She levered herself upright. 'I'm fine, thanks.'

'I thought you were having a fit.'

'I was. But it was a fit of laughter and I'm over it now.'

'You looked as if you were crying.'

'I wasn't.' She licked her lips, tasted the salt.

'Ek verstaan.'

'I don't think you do understand.' Prudish schoolteacher voice. Her head was fuzzy; she rubbed it. 'Did I bring some bags in with me?' She was asking herself, still dazed.

'You put them over there.' He pointed to the small table in the corner of the room.

She said, 'Jim's relics. Nothing very interesting. Couple of old police issue diaries.'

He nodded.

'And some tomatoes.'

'Tomatoes? I could make a salad.'

She handed him the bag.

'From Harry.'

'The ex-cop who now works for some part of Intelligence?'

'Yes.' Sonny didn't forget details, she noted. 'I went to see him at his allotment.'

'Did he have any more useful information for you?'

She detected an edge of nervousness to his voice, she was sure.

'Yes. The cop who has the file on me is called Crawford. He's in charge of the investigation into Dave's death.'

She watched Sonny concentrating on the frying pan, checking the recipe, reaching for the spinach.

'Do you have a colander?' he asked.

'What for?'

'So I can rinse the spinach.'

'I don't normally bother doing that.'

'You should. You don't know what it's been sprayed with.'

She rummaged in a cupboard, located a colander, tipped the dead spider on the floor.

'You should look after yourself better,' he said.

She passed him the colander. He walked to the sink, turned the tap, washed the spinach.

She said, 'Crawford works for the Sewer Squad, this strange unit that investigates the links between terrorism and crime.'

'Why do you think Crawford is interested in Dave? And you?' he added.

She stared at his back, bent over the sink, uncertain how much she should tell him. He smiled at her as he crossed to the oven.

She said, 'Because they think the gun he had came from the Provos.' She rubbed her neck, blurted, 'And for some fucking reason I can't fathom, he thinks I was plotting with Dave to use this gun to hijack one of the nuclear waste lorries from Dungeness as a protest to show how easily it could be done.' She could hear her voice cracking as she spoke.

'There's an informer who has been feeding crap about me

to the cops for months, apparently. Reliable unnamed source. What kind of a jerk makes up information and sells it to the police?' She answered her own question. 'Drug dealer, I reckon.'

'Any idea who the informer might be?'

She paused, considered whether she should share her suspicions about Alastair. Better not.

'No. No idea.' She changed the subject. 'I'm going to try the Romney number again, the one for the power station contact. See if anybody is at home yet.'

'Good idea.'

She picked up the bag of Jim's leftovers, walked out of the kitchen, closed the door behind her and deposited it in the damp cupboard under the stairs. She dug in her back pocket, removed the scrap with the number she had found in Luke's bedroom. P. Grogan, Romney. Dialled. The phone rang. And rang. No answer. Not good. She put the receiver down. Took a deep breath. Dialled Directory Enquiries and asked whether they had any telephone numbers listed for the fishermen's cottages on Dungeness. She knew it wouldn't work, but she thought she'd give it a go anyway.

'Sorry, love, you need a surname.'

'OK, thanks.'

She wasn't sure what she would have done with the number even if Directory Enquiries had given it to her. She could hardly phone Alastair, demand to know whether he was a police informer and expect a straight answer. She returned to the kitchen. The windows were steamed up. She walked over to a pane, wrote her name in the condensation as she had always done when she was a child. Sam Coyle. She stood back, examined her handiwork, the letters already smudged and dripping. Her father yelled, *You shouldn't have done that, you'll leave greasy fingerprints on the glass.* Why was he always shouting at her, telling her off? It wasn't her fingerprints that were the problem, it was Jim's; the traces he had left that could only be seen from certain angles or when the sun was low in the sky. In the pit of her stomach she sensed this mess was Jim's fault, although she couldn't trace exactly why or how.

'Dinner is ready.'

Two plates on the table. She took slow mouthfuls of food, enjoying the taste, perused Tom's article while she was eating.

'I was told it was rude to read at the table,' Sonny said.

'So was I.' She carried on reading.

'What is it anyway?'

'It's an article by Tom Spiller.'

'Who?'

'Friend of mine. Journalist. Haven't heard from him for ages. I pissed him off.'

'I can't imagine you pissing anybody off.' He must have been picking up tips on sarcasm from her.

'He was offered a job with *The Times* but he turned it down because of Wapping.'

'Wapping?'

'Some of their journalists went on strike last year and they were sacked. Murdoch moved the newspaper offices to a building in Wapping, introduced electronic printing processes and made a lot of the printers redundant.'

'Where is Wapping?'

'Docklands. On the north side of the river, opposite Rotherhithe in fact, near where we were the other night. Spyder's house.'

Sonny nodded.

'So anyway, Tom turned down a job in Wapping. Although, I suspect it couldn't have been a particularly good job – he's not that noble. He ended up working as a stringer for Reuters and he's been in Afghanistan, reporting on the war with the Soviets.

Hanging out with the Mujahedeen, the Afghan rebels. And he's written me this note, which, typical Tom, doesn't say much other than he's had this piece published in some newspaper and he thought I might like to read it.'

She finished the article, folded the cutting. She missed Tom every now and then. She would contact him again. At some point.

'I've got to hand it to him,' she said. 'It's quite well written. He can be a bit of a tosser, though.'

'You don't believe in stroking men's egos, do you?'

'No.'

She glared at him, attacked the spanakopita with her knife. 'The food is good.'

'Thanks.'

'You're welcome.'

He finished his food, lit a fag. Something twinged in Sam's gut. She rummaged in her pocket again. 'Here's a newspaper cutting that might interest you.'

She handed him the folded report about Flint's murder that Harry had given her.

'What's it about?'

'A dodgy ex-cop, an old woman, a Westie and a haloed killer.'

He stubbed the not even half-smoked fag out on the ashtray.

'Why are you giving it to me?'

'Dunno.' She wasn't lying, she didn't know. Instinct. 'Thought you might find it entertaining.'

She was woken by a noise. She sat up, urban semi-darkness, the street lamp shining through the curtains. The house was heavy with an empty silence and the whiff of mildew. She heard the noise again, outside. Car engine starting – the camper van. She leaped out of bed, ran to the window, yanked the curtain, headlights fuzzy in the streaked pane as the van performed a nifty three-point turn. She banged on the glass. The van's orange behind trundled along the street, heading east. Keys. The spare van key was on the ring with the one from the front door she'd handed him that morning. She stormed down the stairs, out the front door, shouted. Too late. The van turned north on the main road, to Vauxhall Bridge. Sonny had pulled a fast one on her. A warm prickliness made her look down, she was standing in a puddle, sludge lapping around her bare feet. She kicked the oily water, stubbed her toe on the pavement, yowled with pain. She had been duped by his bloody spanakopita. What an idiot. Trust nobody, least of all a hitman. She knew next to nothing about Sonny, except for the fact that he had killed her father and god knows how many other people too. He was a monster. A psycho. Yet she had let him into her life. Her home. How stupid was she? She ran back into the house, slammed the door, up the stairs, into Dave's bedroom. The duvet had been straightened in an anal military way. She spotted his bag, tidied away in a corner. Green canvas rucksack with leather straps, like the one Jim used to carry. She rummaged, removed its contents. Thick grey socks, rolled in a pair. Couple of white tee shirts. Boxer shorts. Cassette with *LOVER'S ROCK* written in red felt-tip capitals on one side. Two books: the King James Bible and *Linda Goodman's Love Signs*. *Linda Goodman's Love Signs*? What was he doing with that? She rummaged in the bag again. The Firebird was at the bottom, wrapped in a rag. She unwrapped and examined it. Loaded. She laid it on the bed, tipped the bag, shook. Nothing left. The Browning was missing. Wherever he was going, he had taken the Browning with him. She ran back to her room, pulled on her jeans, moth-eaten jumper, overcoat, was about to run down the stairs when she changed direction, swerved into

Dave's room, grabbed the Firebird, double-checked the safety catch, stuffed it down the waistband of her trousers.

She caught the scent of damp again as she ran through the hall, realized the door to the cupboard under the stairs was open and Sonny had removed the bag of Jim's belongings. She flicked the kitchen light switch; Jim's broken aviator glasses lay on the floor, the rest of his remains emptied on the table. The soft black police diaries unbundled and fanned out as if Sonny had picked them up, one by one, examined them. She selected one, pressed its soft cover in her hand, retraced her steps back to the day at Jim's graveside, the remembrance ceremony, her failed attempt to draw the line. The diary left by his tombstone. She had neglected to ask Sonny whether he had tailed her to the church but, of course, it had to be him who had moved the diary, replaced it open at the pages for the week at the beginning of June. An image flashed into her brain. Sonny holding another small black notebook in his hand, identical to Jim's police diaries. That evening they had broken into Luke's place; while she was in her boyfriend's room, Sonny had rummaged around in Spyder's. He had found a black diary alongside Spyder's needles. Spyder the junkie dope dealer. She screeched with frustration, rapped her knuckles against her head. Sonny had worked out the obvious and she had missed it: Spyder was the tout. Spyder was a small-time jerk of a drug dealer who had been selling any old information to the Force about her and Dave. Spyder had set her up, probably for some petty cash. She should have guessed, it was so fucking, fucking obvious. And now Sonny had taken her van and driven over to Rotherhithe to deal with Spyder, the informer.

Shit. She had to find Sonny, stop him before he annihilated Spyder. She hated the jerk, but she could do without another gruesome death haunting her. And anyway, she wanted to talk to him, make him confess, torture him, extract any information he had about Luke. She jammed her plimsolls on, pelted out into the steamy night, down the street and hailed a black cab trawling the main road.

Through the backstreets of Southwark, beyond London Bridge, roads disembowelled for gas pipes and sewers, red no entry signs looming in the dark. Sam clambered out of the cab, its rear lights dissolving in the steam as it pulled away. The odour of rotting river vegetation hung in the air. She heard a whistle, the familiar tune, caught sight of a figure melting into the darkness of the embankment, started down the road to investigate, stopped halfway. Stupid. No time for chasing shadows. She inhaled, wiped her face, retraced her steps, walked to the front door of Spyder's house, knelt down, lifted the flap of the letterbox, peered inside. Murky, silent hallway. Empty. She walked around the side of the house. The back door leading to the fire escape was open. She called Sonny's name softly. No response. She backed away and stepped along the cobbled road running parallel to the river. Three pigeons tiptoed along the kerb. Why weren't they roosting? Disturbed by something, or somebody. Sonny had chased Spyder down this road waving his Browning. She paced a few feet, spotted a black rectangle lying in the gutter. Police issue diary. Spyder's. She scooped it up, stood under the nearest street lamp, drizzle drifting through its haze, and turned to the latest entries in the diary. *S called to ask about L's whereabouts. S came to nightclub to ask about L's whereabouts. Said she knew about D. Agitated. Said he hadn't turned up at Dungeness. Seemed to think it was something to do with planned Dungeness protest.*

She flicked back, January was full of Ss, Ds and Ls too. She remembered now how he had sauntered up and chatted to her last September, when she started working at the Ballroom, told her he could supply her with dope, good stuff, cheap, asked her what she did in her spare time, where she lived, with whom. Casual chat. Innocuous pieces of information, she thought. The fucking bastard. Reliable unnamed source. He was about as reliable as a… as a junkie who needed a fix. She stuffed the diary into her pocket. In the distance she heard a shout – Sonny's voice – quickened her pace, the grey high tide waters of the river visible through a break in the derelict wharves and houses. The rain slashed harder as she paced the street. Through the downpour she could discern the rusting metal supports of an old pier, jutting out into the water, a perilous platform high above the river. Two figures danced along the jetty. A rubbish barge slid past, the backwash slapping the river walls. As she neared, she could hear Sonny ranting. 'To every thing there is a season…' His words were drowned by the barge horn sounding as it approached London Bridge. Through the long note she heard a splash. A click, then two cracks. Seagulls squawked.

She sprinted, arrived breathless – the pier gate padlocked, a sign warning *Danger. Keep out.* Sonny was standing alone on the far point of the jetty. A cormorant came in to land on the upstream end, then pulled skywards at the last possible moment when it caught sight of the gun-pointing man standing there, staring into the water.

'Sonny, what the fuck have you done?'

He turned to face her, hesitated, replaced the Browning in his jacket pocket, picked his way back along the rickety jetty, feet sliding in the wet, vaulted across the gate. He was soaked. He put his hands up, palms outfacing.

'He jumped.'

'Jesus. Don't lie.'

She craned over the embankment wall, studied the choppy Thames. A disco boat appeared around the bend, ploughed a middle furrow, 'Stayin' Alive' blaring from its speakers, tipsy deck-top dancers doing John Travolta moves oblivious to the river's dramas. Flashing lights – red, green, blue – illuminated a dark hump in the water. The river boiled, glugged and swallowed the body. Sonny came and stood by her, steam rising from his torso.

'That's some big fucking rat,' he said.

'Spyder. He's dead.'

'He's a fucking tout. He's a – what do you call it – a nark. A copper's nark.'

'You shot him.'

'I didn't. He jumped. He was off his face.'

'You're lying.' The anger was making her cry. 'You shot him. He's not a cop or a spook. He's a civilian and you killed him. You're a psycho. You can pen another bloody cross on your arm and go to fucking hell.'

'He ran when he saw me coming. He was tripping. High.'

'I heard two shots.'

'That was the splash when he hit the water.'

'And the quote from Ecclesiastes?'

'He didn't stand a chance once he was in the water. It was all I could think to say. Last rites. Ja. A blessing.'

'A fucking blessing.' She didn't believe a word of it. 'We could have found out who asked him to spy on me, whether he knew who else is involved in all of this.' Her voice rose in a crescendo. 'We could have asked him about Luke.'

Sonny gazed across the river, spoke into the middle distance. 'He wasn't about to talk. His brain was so frazzled.'

'I would have made him talk. I would have stuck pins down his fingernails 'til he told me what I wanted to know. Don't you get it? I have to find Luke. I owe it to him.'

She checked herself; remembered it was a bad idea to shout at a hitman, especially when he was carrying a loaded gun. Although, Sonny seemed calm, emollient even.

'You should think about yourself. I wanted to protect you.'

'I don't see how you're protecting me by shooting somebody. The river always gives up its bodies. Somebody will find him washed up on a sandbank down by bloody Gravesend. And then they'll start doing enquiries, follow a trail back to you. Me.'

'Nobody's going to give a shit about him. There's so much gear in his place, they will know he was a junkie snout.'

She gazed along the river, the distant beat of 'Staying Alive' pulsing and the coloured lights bleary on the rain-pocked water as the disco boat limped home to Chelsea Harbour Pier. She couldn't take it – the deaths, the lies – she had to escape. She strode off in the direction of London Bridge. She didn't care what Harry said, she wasn't going to sit around and wait until some poxy cop showed up and told her that Luke was dead, like Dave, and dragged her off to the station because a fucking junkie had sold them a load of bullshit about firearms and they'd decided to believe him and stick it in a file marked terrorist. She was going to find Luke, make sure he was safe. And then she would extract them – her and Luke – exit this shadowy world that she wanted nothing to do with. Hitmen. Junkies. Cops. Spooks. Arseholes. They could all go take a flying fuck at the moon.

Sonny caught up with her. 'It's stopped raining.'

She tried to outpace him. It didn't work.

'You know, Sam,' Sonny said. 'Spyder, he might be a civilian, but he wouldn't have cared if you were killed. You've got to understand, these guys mean business.'

She caught her breath, tried to think clearly.

'Which guys?'

'I don't know. But we have to stay one step ahead of the hunters.'

'How do we do that if we're not sure who the hunters are?'

'I can protect you.'

She searched the contours of his face. Helen had once told her that everybody's face had a devilish side and a more angelic side. She had checked her face in the mirror. The left side had a cherubic softness to it. The right profile, the side with the birthmark, had a sharper edge. She could see the same contrast in Sonny's face: angel and devil, light and dark. He was a liar, a murderer. And yet, he had a kinder, caring, good side that she couldn't help liking even if she still wasn't entirely prepared to believe that it was genuine.

'I can look after myself,' she said.

The damp cobbles were slippery underfoot. A sleek black cat trotted past with a luscious dead pigeon in its mouth.

'It's dangerous being a pigeon in this city,' he said. 'Deadly enemies round every corner.'

She ignored him.

'You have to be sharp if you're a pigeon. You can't afford to give anybody the benefit of the doubt in this town. You might as well hand them a loaded gun.'

He was the one with the loaded gun. She shuddered, became conscious of the Firebird pressing her stomach. She touched it through her tee shirt, felt the shape of the grip. She stopped walking, thought for a moment, and then she said, 'I took the Firebird.'

He nodded. 'That's fine. I want you to have it.'

'I want you to show me how to use it.'

The sky cleared as they drove east along the river through Rotherhithe to Deptford's borders. They found a derelict warehouse on the waterfront; a disoriented seagull flitting between the ceiling pipes, moonlight falling through missing roof panels. She removed the Firebird from the belt of her trousers, tested it in her hand, the feel of the grip, the tension of the safety catch.

'Speed is the most important thing,' Sonny said. 'Don't hesitate. Hold the grip in both hands. Extend your arms out front. Like this.' He moved behind her, wrapped his arms round hers, held her hands in his, warm breath on her neck; the smell of sweat engulfed her. She twisted round to say something, found herself pulled right in to him, face to face.

He said, 'It helps to keep an eye on what you're trying to shoot.'

She turned away again, unnerved by how easily he had drawn her in, how vulnerable she would be if he turned on her. She concentrated on the Firebird, determined to learn how to use it well.

CHAPTER 13

THE FAMILIAR WHISTLE floated on the air outside her bedroom window. She pulled on her clothes, careered down the stairs, through the front door and sprinted to the main road. The early-morning street was empty apart from a bin truck and a solitary figure, striding away under the railway arches, his swagger instantly recognizable.

She shouted after him. 'Jim.'

He didn't react. She pelted along the pavement, past the Vauxhall Tavern, under the railway, across the Albert Embankment, to the Thames. A trail of dark footprints marked the foreshore. She followed the tracks, across the mud, along the concrete channel of the Effra run-off to the sluice gate, pulled the torch from her pocket and directed its beam through the chink between iron and brick. A shadow grew and slid along the tunnel wall.

'Jim.'

No answer. She stared at the footprints in the sludge, heading under the sluice and into the tunnel – as if the gate had magically lifted for the trail-maker. She bent and traced the shoe marks with her finger, felt the indentations, uncertain whether she could trust her perceptions. Waking dream. She squatted there for a while, arms wrapped around her knees, seat of trousers hovering above the outflow, and stared at the sluice gate. Eventually the Effra's bilge forced her to stand.

She jumped down from the chute, traipsed across the grey sand to the embankment. At the top of the ramp she stooped, eased the bellarmine from its hiding place, tipped the bottle and allowed the felt heart to fall into her cupped palm. Rainwater had dribbled inside. The dressmaker's pins were leaching rust into the fabric heart. The bark was soft. She squished the woody slither between her fingers; it disintegrated. If she wasn't sure before, she knew it now: she had broken the bottle's seal, upended its contents, flipped the counter-curse and reversed its power through her own stupidity. The dark forces were against her. She replaced the fetishes in the vase and stored it neatly in its hiding place, stood back and surveyed the river. The ancient jetty posts were visible above the low water, blackened and eroded by time and the tides. She didn't care who or what was against her, she was going to find Luke anyway.

She crossed the well-trodden ground of the old Vauxhall plea-sure gardens and examined the leads in her head. Spyder was dead. That left the cryptic note from Dave – 55 pluto – P. Grogan's number that nobody was answering and the objects she had collected from Bane House – the clenched fist feminist badge and the matchbook from Heaven. The nightclub was a long shot, but worth a try. Nothing to lose, although she wasn't sure how she would sell the idea to Sonny. She reached her front door, rummaged in her coat pocket, fingers touching scraps of paper, penknife, torch, Rizlas, everything but the bloody key, and as she fumbled she heard Sonny's voice coming from the hall; a phone conversation.

'I keep telling you, you've got to give me a chance. It's not easy, ja. You've got to hold off. I need more time.'

She stood hand in pocket, mind on red alert. Who was he talking to? He needed more time to do what exactly? She located the key, gripped and twisted it in the lock, heart pounding, slammed the door open. Sonny had retreated to the kitchen.

'Do you want some scrambled egg?' he asked as she entered, unperturbed by her frosty glare. He cracked and whisked the eggs with a fork, tipped the yellow gloop into a saucepan.

'You were talking to somebody on my phone.'

He glanced up from the pan. 'Sorry. I should have asked. I'll give you some coins for the call. I had some unfinished business I needed to sort.'

'What business was that then?'

He reached for the salt pot. 'Nothing. The usual.'

'The usual?'

He tipped the pot, shook it. 'You know.'

'No, I don't know. Tell me.'

'Drugs. The toot you threw out the van window, I bought it on tick, and I was just calling the dealer to let him know I'm going to give him the cash in a couple of days. The thing is, he lives at the far end of north London, and I can't be bothered to make the trip up there right now.'

He went to the oven, ignited the gas. She wanted to give him the benefit of the doubt. Why was she prepared to believe him? Was it because she, the undercover cop's daughter, was so used to turning a blind eye to what her father was doing she had lost the faculty of clear-sightedness or was it because she needed him on her side? He stirred the eggs, concentrated on the curds forming in the bottom of the pan.

She asked, 'Will you help me with something?'

'Sure.'

'I want to find the person I saw the night before Dave died, hanging around Bane House, that old smuggler's place out on the saltmarsh.'

'Why do you want to do that?' He lifted the pan from the flame, continued beating.

'I haven't got much else to go on. There has to be some connection between this person at Bane House and Dave's death. And there's obviously a connection between Dave's death and Luke's disappearance. If I can trace the person from Bane House, maybe I can find a lead to Luke.'

'Sure, but even if those connections exist, how are you going to find this person?'

'Well, I think it's a woman. I saw the figure in the distance so maybe I was mistaken. But they dropped this feminist badge.' She pointed to the clenched fist pinned to her coat.

'It doesn't prove anything.'

'I realize that. It's a hunch.'

'And knowing this person is a woman hardly helps you locate her.'

'I also found a book of matches from Heaven.'

'You mean the gay nightclub?'

'Yes.'

He opened a cupboard, grabbed two plates.

'Look, it's a long shot. But there's only one mixed night a week, and I've been to it a couple of times – I know one of the bouncers – and not many women go. I reckon, if we went along, I could pick her out in the crowd if she was there.'

'Do you want some scrambled egg?'

She nodded. 'We could go tonight.'

He dolloped the egg on the plates, butter-yellow. 'That really is a long shot.'

'I know. We could have a dance if she doesn't appear.'

They bought sandwiches from a deli on Old Compton Street and sat on the patchy grass of Soho Square. Sonny examined the Dictaphone she had purchased from Tottenham Court Road; it held a micro-cassette, exactly the same size as the one in her answering machine. The Dictaphone was small enough to carry in a jacket and powerful enough, according to the shop assistant, to pick up muffled voices against nightclub noise so long as you kept it in an outside pocket, microphone uppermost. The whistler's messages on her answering machine had sparked the idea of taking a Dictaphone along to Heaven. If they did locate the woman from Bane House, she reckoned one of them could try talking to her and record the conversation.

Sonny's scepticism was irritating her but, despite his doubts, he practised switching the machine on and off surreptitiously – a quick hand dip into his pocket as if he was searching for his Zippo – attracted by the mechanics of subterfuge. She watched the passers-by. Soho was changing. She had been on a Reclaim the Night march through Soho's backstreets a few years previously. Then the straggle of hard-core feminists protesting against porn and sexual violence had been met with dirty looks from the punters and bemused cat-calls from the strippers hanging out in the peep-show doors. Now the same peep-show joints were boarded and the kerb crawlers were young and attractive. Old Compton Street was cleaning up its act. Not the result of their protest, she suspected. The trendy cafés with their aluminium chairs and steaming Gaggias were pushing the sex industry out – along with all the bent cops who were getting backhanders from the porn business.

'Wonder where the dirty money is these days,' she mused. She thought she was talking to herself.

Sonny replied, 'Drugs.'

'Drugs?'

He shrugged. She was sure he knew more than he was telling her.

Heaven was underneath the railway arches behind Charing Cross station at the end of a dingy street lined with overflowing rubbish bins, cardboard box homes and their bedraggled owners. The bouncer opened the doors and they were in a different world; a vast, strobe-lit, Jocelyn Brown throbbing space full of leather, dirty denim and sweating bodies. AIDS had taken the edge off the hedonism, but the club still had an air of contagious abandon. Sam relaxed in Heaven's atmosphere. Sonny moved awkwardly, shrinking into himself, trying to separate himself from his surroundings, unnerved by the come-on looks he was attracting perhaps. Or agitated by Sam's plans. They wandered smoky passages, past dancers in podium cages, across beer-sticky floors and found Frannie near the VIP bar, kitted out in black leather. She assessed Sonny through kohl-rimmed eyes. He glanced down at the floor.

Frannie's job was to patrol the bars and keep a check on excesses. She had a sharp eye and a sharper tongue, which was why Max the club manager employed her. He didn't give a toss that she was a woman working in a gay men's club. Neither did she. Sam knew Frannie through the West End nightclub worker fraternity. They had hit it off over a cryptic crossword puzzle.

'Have you come for a dance?' Frannie shouted. It was difficult to make yourself heard over the thumping hi-energy beat.

Sam cupped her hand, yelled into Frannie's ear. 'I'm looking for a woman.'

'You've come to the wrong place.'

'No. I'm looking for a particular woman and I think she's been here.'

'What does she look like? I know most of the women who are regulars.'

'Tall, thin, blackish hair, sort of spiky.'

Frannie narrowed her eyes, lit a fag, sucked hard, made its tip burn red.

'I worry about you. You can be so bloody green sometimes. You're the kind of girl drug dealers pick up to use as a mule.'

'I'm not that stupid.'

'I hope not.'

'Does that mean you think you've seen this woman?'

'You didn't give me much to go on.' She blasted smoke jets from her nostrils. 'Why don't you just go off and have a dance?' She glanced at Sonny. 'With your new boyfriend.'

Sam reddened. 'He's not my boyfriend.'

Frannie edged closer, whispered in her ear, 'He looks all right to me.' She grabbed Sam's hand, slipped something into her palm, crushed her fingers around it.

'Enjoy.' She gave Sonny another once-over, winked as she walked away. Sam opened her fist, found a brown glass bottle lying there, *Sniff Me* on its label.

'Poppers. Amyl,' she said. 'It's not illegal. You inhale. Like this.'

She unscrewed the lid, thumb over bottle top, up to her nose. Breathed deep. Her head exploded with the rush and intense, uncontrollable desire, her insides pouring out and taking over. Donna Summer 'I Feel Love'. She yanked Sonny. She wanted to dance. He resisted. For a moment, she was struggling with him, tugging him closer, lost in the high, heart pounding with the music. And then she came crashing down, two-minute hit over. She realized what she was doing, let her arms flop to her side. His eyes were wet.

'I don't like dancing,' he said.

'Sorry.'

'It doesn't matter.' He wiped his forehead with his sleeve. 'I sometimes wish my life could be different. I'd like to erase the past and start again.'

'There's always time to change. The past doesn't have to shape your future.'

He shook his head. 'That's hippy bullshit. Some things can't be erased. Some events set the course for everything that comes afterwards.'

'No. Not true.' She wasn't sure she meant it. She suspected he was right. She was still plummeting, hadn't bottomed out yet, didn't know what she was doing there dancing in this club because everything was pointless. She might as well give up, hand herself over to Crawford, confess her sins, whatever they were – make some up if necessary – she was probably too late to help Luke anyway. She had cursed Dave and Luke and everybody around her. She tugged on Sonny's sleeve, intending to pull him to the entrance, then through the strobe flash she saw a figure leaning against the wall – skinny, black crimped hair, pale powdered skin, ripped biker jacket and dull, dark eyes, vacant, purple-ringed. She could have been dead, a zombie. The woman lifted her arm to her face, dragged on a cigarette, her movements jerky in the white blasts of light, an actor in a silent horror movie.

Sam pulled Sonny's arm again, tugged him into a darker corner of the club.

'Did you see her?'

He nodded.

'I want to speak to Frannie again. She obviously knew who I was talking about and didn't want to say anything.'

They pushed through sweaty bodies, searching for Frannie, found her leaning against a wall, watching a caged man writhing. She scowled when she saw them approaching, tipped her head at the far end of a bar. They followed her to a passageway filled with swirling dry ice that clogged Sam's lungs, made her choke, but at least it was marginally quieter here.

'Find her then, did you?' Frannie asked.

Sam nodded. 'She's a scruffy Siouxsie Sioux.'

'Yeah, all Goth and no glamour. I have seen her around. But seriously, Sam, you should leave well alone.'

'I need to find out about her. A friend has gone missing and I think she might know something about his disappearance.'

'A friend? You mean some bloke?'

Sam nodded.

'Let me guess – you're chasing this Luke you're so moony-eyed about.'

'He's vanished. And he is my boyfriend.'

Frannie shook her head. 'You are stupid. You should know better. What are you doing – chasing after a bloody man? If he comes back, fine. But if he doesn't, he wasn't worth the effort in the first place.'

'You don't understand.'

'Sam, I don't know anything about Luke. But I do know that woman because she's been here a few times in the last couple of months, and every time she's here, she meets up with this squat, ugly geezer who Max asked me to keep an eye on. So if Luke's disappearance has anything to do with them, then you really do need to steer clear.'

Sam rubbed her eyes; the dry ice was making them sting.

'Why has Max asked you to watch this bloke then?'

Frannie sighed with irritation. 'All I know is he's American and he's got an expensive club membership pass, which gives him access to the VIP bar. Max thinks he's using it as his office. He's always meeting up with odd men, not clubbers, not men anybody here knows – and this woman. Max says he's pushing his luck and the cash he's splashing isn't worth the potential trouble he might be attracting.'

'Is he here tonight?'

'Actually, he hasn't been here for a week or so, but if that dead-eyed woman has turned up then I would guess he's quite likely to put in an appearance at some point too. Stavros. That's what I call him.'

'Stavros? I thought you said he was American.'

'He's got an American accent. But I bummed a fag off him once, and he gave me a packet of Assos.'

'Assos? I've never heard of them.'

'Aristotle Onassis's favourite brand.'

'Oh. I see. Stavros. Dodgy man with Greek connections. So what do you think he's doing then?'

'Come on, Sam. We are in a London nightclub. This bloke is loaded and he's got all these weird contacts. The woman looks like a ghoulish junkie. There's obviously dealing of some sort going on. Take a tip from me – don't touch him with a barge pole.'

Sam rubbed her eyes again, they were really streaming now. What was dry ice made from? Carbon dioxide. Poisonous? 'OK, thanks for the tip, Frannie. I'll leave it.'

Frannie grabbed her arm. 'Listen, I can see you're not going to leave it. So here's another piece of advice – why don't you let him deal with it?' She nodded at Sonny. 'He's bigger than you and, anyway, he's not going to stand out in this crowd. Unlike you. If you go anywhere near this Stavros and his vampire friend, they're going to spot you a mile off. You're female, and you're the only person here who looks like they've just walked out of a fucking library.'

She stalked off before Sam could answer back, jabbed Sonny with her elbow as she passed him, vanished in the smoke.

'Sorry,' Sam said.

'For what?'

'For Frannie. She can be…'

'She's right, though. Why don't you leave it to me? Nobody will notice me if I hang around. I can watch this woman, see if she meets up with the American Frannie was talking about. And if she does, perhaps I could get close enough to listen.' He patted the top pocket of his jacket. 'I've got the Dictaphone here.'

Sam folded her arms. 'I want to find out what she knows.'

'Ja, but the best way of finding out is to let me try. I know how to do this stuff.'

She didn't like the idea, she wanted to be the one who found out what was going on, but she could see it made sense for Sonny to trail her.

'OK. I'll leave you to it. I'll wait for you back at the house.'

One a.m. The sky sulphured by light pollution. She walked down Whitehall, across Westminster Bridge, along Albert Embankment. She had trodden this path so many times she could see her own footprints in the paving slabs. She wondered whether anybody else could sense her here, whether her shadow would linger after she was dead, whether her ghost would be any different from her living self. Perhaps she was a ghost already. She stopped at her favourite bench, sat down, noticed a movement in her peripheral vision, turned – at the far end of the seat she spotted something orange flip-flopping about. She sidled over: a goldfish in a plastic bag. Somebody must have won it at Kennington funfair, ping-pong ball in the bowl, couldn't be bothered to take it home, left it on an embankment bench. She grabbed the bag, almost devoid of water, rushed to the wall, held it upside down and shook. The tide was high. The gold-fish somersaulted into the river. She doubted whether it would survive long, but it had to be a better end than suffocating on dry land. She swished the last drops of water from the plastic bag, stared at the now empty goldfish container and retched, retreated to the bench, sat with her head in her hands feeling nauseous. The funfair. Jim abandoning her. The candy man. The crescent-moon scar and the steely eyes. Flint. A bent cop. Too much. She didn't want to think about it. Push it all away.

The Oval gasholder was empty, unlit windows of the house watching her as she opened the door. The answering machine flashed. She couldn't ignore it, pressed play, heard the familiar tune, the breath and then the words: 'Time is running out.' She glanced over her shoulder, rubbed the back of her neck. Her teeth chattered. She clamped her jaw but her arms started shaking. She needed to calm down.

She walked through to the kitchen, rummaged for her coffee-brewing saucepan, cast her eye over the postcard Liz had sent her, covered with oil stains from Sonny's cooking efforts. Liz and her recipe cheered her – it was so… irrelevant. Pointless. Spanakopita. *Brush with _oil_. Bake at gas mark 4 for 30 minutes _only_. _Keep_ an eye on the oven.* She laughed, dropped the postcard on the kitchen surface. In the witching hours, the bottomless dips, it was good to remind herself that she was doing quite well for somebody who came from such a dysfunctional family.

Two a.m. She sat on the back step, smoked a spliff, listened to the regular clink of a moth throwing itself against the bare kitchen bulb. She couldn't sit still, couldn't stop thinking about Sonny, his tainted past, his strange relationship with her, the swings between empathy and distrust. She needed to get a fix on him. She compared Sonny to Luke. Sonny didn't like dancing. He didn't talk about politics, didn't seem to have any burning opinions. Luke was always ready for a dance, music, but he was serious as well. He had principles. Only the other week – only last week – they'd both dressed up to go to some new club in Soho and Luke said he couldn't face the West End, it wasn't really his place. Sam had agreed, it wasn't really her place either – she just fancied a dance. And then he remembered a dive bar in Brixton he'd heard about. They thought they'd give it a go; it sounded more like their thing: a club in a squatted anarchist bookshop on Railton Road, door takings going to help the bloke next door who had been busted after the riots for no reason other than being black. He fought back when the cops kicked him in, according to the rockabilly who took their money and let them in, so the Filth flipped it, charged their victim with assault. The club was a pit – in the basement, electrical wires dangling, paint peeling off the walls, no ventilation, hardly any light; a shadow Soho Ballroom. The music was brilliant – Northern soul, reggae, rap. Afterwards, when they left, Luke was on a high. That's where it's at, he said, pleasure but with a purpose. Not lining the pockets of some get-rich-quick git of a club owner, but supporting a community, a bunch of people trying to do something positive. She had wondered then how many men she would meet in her life who were so neatly aligned with her beliefs, the things she enjoyed doing, the way she wanted to live and, on top of that, she actually fancied him. Not many, she suspected. And now he had vanished. Frannie was wrong; she wasn't moony-eyed. She was being realistic. She knew the scarcity value of what she had lost; the elusive chemistry, the elixir.

Three a.m. Sonny was taking his time. What was he doing? Had something happened? She needed a distraction. She dug out a newspaper, searched for the cryptic crossword, concentrated.

Four a.m. Sonny returned, sweaty, smoky, forehead wrinkled.

Sam demanded, 'Did you lose her?'

'No.'

'Did she meet the American?'

'Yes.'

'Did you manage to get close enough to hear what they were talking about?'

'Yes.' He stuck his hand in his jacket, produced the Dictaphone. 'I don't know how much this picked up, but I overheard quite a bit anyway. Your friend Frannie was right. This Stavros, he's really not good news. This is really deep shit.'

'Oh?'

'I mean it. Deep shit.'

'OK. Well. I'm in the shit already, as far as I can see, so I need to know how much further I could sink.'

'A lot further.'

'I need to know.'

'Fine. Don't say I didn't warn you.'

They retreated to the kitchen. He fumbled with the machine – it produced crackling noises, a throbbing bass line – 'It's Raining Men'. Rewind, stop, fast forward, stop.

'Here. This is the beginning.'

At the table, heads bowed over the Dictaphone. He pressed play. The tape hissed before a north London accent cut in.

'Skuse me, mate, you got the time?' Sonny's voice answered. 'One fifteen.'

Sonny pressed stop. 'Wrong place. Sorry. I'll try again.' Forward. Stop. Play. American accent this time – New Yorker, if she had to guess.

'Yeah, good holiday.' Rustling in the background. 'Fucking pen pushers.' The thump, thump bass line made it difficult to make out the snatches of conversation. 'Hey Regan, need a light?' So that was her name – Regan. American accent again. Sylvester playing now – you make me feel. Somebody who must have been standing next to Sonny was singing along, badly out of tune, his voice cutting the American's conversation into disjointed snippets. '... office boys... make me feel, mighty real... jerk off lawyers... make me feel... blowback.'

Sam pressed pause. 'Lawyers – what was he talking about?'

'He was whinging about the back office boys, worrying too much about the small print, the liabilities and blowback.'

'Blowback – isn't that spook talk?'

'Yes.' He pressed play.

'These guys... real deal... Old Testament prophets... bunch of tribesmen on donkeys... risk their fucking lives...' She leaned closer to the Dictaphone, struggling to make out the words. 'I can relate to... more than I can... fucking assholes running our fucking station...' Glasses clinked, music throbbed, somebody had a hacking cough... '... I'm a fucking Janis...'

Sam jammed her finger on the pause button. 'Janis what?'

'Janissary. The Janissaries were an elite military force, part of the Ottoman empire, used by the Turks when they conquered Greece. They took on the missions that were too dirty for everybody else.'

He knew his military history. But she wasn't sure how much it helped her pull the pieces together. American spook, Old Testament prophets. Janissaries.

'So he's saying he's doing something off the record?'

'Exactly. Totally off the record. I had to move in closer to pick up the next bit. I was lucky to catch it. This is where it gets really wild.'

He pressed play.

'If we can kick... it's gonna hurt.' The American's voice was almost drowned out by the background beat now; Sylvester ramping up to his finale. 'One time KO to the commies... dose of...' Something indecipherable.

Sonny pressed pause. 'He was talking about giving the Soviets a taste of their own medicine.'

Play again. '...facilitate... make them glow... half a cup of water and they'll be radiating.' Laughter. Wild cackling. And then Regan's voice, her words slurred. 'One more run... your guy down on the coast...' Her sentence was broken by crackling. The American's voice cut in. 'Yeah... made it safe.'

The recording stopped abruptly.

Sonny said, 'I didn't hear much more of that last bit. I had to switch the machine off and leave. Regan – the woman – she was beginning to act edgy.'

Sam nodded, but she wasn't listening to Sonny; snatches of conversation floated through her brain.

'Sam, are you OK?'

'I'm thinking.'

The moth circled the dangling bulb, unable to pull away from the light. Sonny reached for a fag, clicked the wheel of his Zippo, dragged and puffed.

She said, 'What do you think it was all about?'

'The American – Stavros – he was obviously talking about Afghanistan.' He grimaced and she could see that he was working out which of his own thoughts he should share with her. 'I assume he was talking about some operation to support the Mujahedeen. He's trying to facilitate an attack on the Soviets.'

'Afghanistan.' She mulled it over; an American discussing the Mujahedeen in a gay nightclub to the accompaniment of Sylvester, half a cup of water, a dose to make them glow. It sounded nutty, unbelievable, and yet the elements were familiar. She churned the pieces round in her mind, tried to work out where they overlapped with things she knew already, words, places, people she recognized.

Sonny said, 'What do you...'

She didn't wait to hear the end of his question; something had fallen into place. She scraped her chair back, ran out the kitchen, upstairs, rummaged in the drawer of her bedside table, grabbed Tom's piece about Afghanistan, ran into Dave's bedroom, flung open the cupboard door, grabbed the top article from his pile of photocopied journal papers, flew back down the stairs to the kitchen. She placed the papers triumphantly on the table. She pointed at the journal article. 'Look, this article is about the distribution of caesium 137 between abiotic and biotic components of aquatic ecosystems.'

Sonny's face was blank.

'What about it?'

'What did the American say? "Something to make them glow. Half a cup of water and they'll be radiating." This article is about the effects of caesium 137 when it is dispersed through water.'

Sonny was still looking perplexed.

She said, 'He's talking about contaminating the water supply with a radioactive substance. Caesium 137, possibly.'

Sonny screwed his eyes.

'Would that be fatal? Drinking water contaminated with caesium 137?'

She spluttered, 'Well, if anybody ingested a glassful of water contaminated with caesium 137 it would do more than make them glow; it would frazzle them from the inside out. The question is how quickly and how many people, and I suppose that's about the amount and concentration of the dose. Maybe there's an antidote, I'm not sure. Presumably you'd have to get to it quite quickly to stop the damage.'

'But if the Mujahedeen contaminated the local water supply, wouldn't they frazzle their own insides too?'

'Not necessarily.' She jabbed Tom's article on Afghanistan. 'Tom, this hack mate of mine who has been hanging out with the Mujahedeen, he says the Soviet military is stretched by the logistics. Afghanistan is impenetrable. Mountainous. Arid. The Russian military bases near the frontline are vulnerable because they need to maintain access to basic supplies. The frontline bases don't have piped water.'

'I suppose they wouldn't.'

'According to Tom, the Mujahedeen can't outgun the Soviets because they don't have the fire power, so they are looking for ways to disrupt the army's supplies. And Stavros has dreamed up a way of doing it, a "one-time KO to the commies", by supplying the Afghan rebels with caesium 137 to dump in the Soviets' water storage tanks.'

'Neat.'

She screeched, 'Neat? It's nuts.'

'Well, you've got to admire his inventiveness. It wouldn't take much of a dose to completely terrorize everybody. It sounds like something the KGB might dream up. Maybe that's what he meant when he said give them a taste of their own medicine. Perhaps he got the idea from a Soviet informer.'

'But do you think Stavros is working for the CIA? Everybody knows they are helping the Mujahedeen, supplying them with weapons. Well, that's what Tom says anyway.'

'I'm sure he has worked for the CIA. The question is whether or not they've cut the rope. Maybe he's gone rogue, decided to take the battle into his own hands because he doesn't think his side is doing enough. You heard all that complaining about the backroom boys.' He reached for his fags. 'So I told you it was deep shit. See what we've dug up? A psychotic CIA agent and a fucking commie frying radiation plot. Your friend Frannie was so right. We should steer clear.'

'Frannie was wrong about the drugs though. There's obviously no drugs involved in this.'

'You don't think so? I think drug smuggling is Regan's day job.'

He sounded so certain; she wondered whether it was a guess or something more.

Sonny continued, 'But you know, when you hear this Stavros talking about those rebels in Afghanistan, the Mujahedeen, it's hard not to have some sympathy. They've been invaded by the commies. They are fighting back with nothing but some donkeys and faith in their god. It's a holy war against godless, ruthless bastards. I can buy into that.'

She nodded. She and Luke had sympathized with them too, the mountain tribesmen fighting the Soviet regime. David and Goliath. That was why he'd bought her a pakol from Kensington Market – a show of solidarity. But she wasn't sure how much beyond wearing a hat she would be prepared to go. Not least because Tom's article had also said the Mujahedeen were a bunch of women-hating fundamentalists. She put her head in her hands. Something was niggling her, but she didn't want to think about it. Sonny touched her arm. She jumped.

'Are you OK?'

'Not really, no. I was just thinking about this conversation I had with Dave the night before... I asked him about stealing radioactive waste, spent fuel rods, from a power station to make a bomb and he said that was far-fetched.' She heard Dave's voice in her head. *Ludicrous even by your standards.*

'But he said something else.'

'What?'

'He said it would be much easier to pick up radioactive

material from a source like a hospital or a research lab. Release it into the air. Water. Contamination.'

Sonny didn't say anything.

'They're stealing caesium from the research lab at Dungeness. They must be.'

'Maybe.'

She knotted her brow. 'Why would this Stavros swipe caesium from a lab in England to take to Afghanistan? Couldn't he find a closer supply?'

'It's an easy source, I suppose,' Sonny said. 'And indirect. The old CIA rule – never leave a trace of American involvement. Especially if you're not official – because then you've got a million more reasons to make sure whatever you do is untraceable.'

Her limbs trembled; she couldn't stop her mind churning. The patterns formed in ways she didn't like. Dave's edginess. His evasiveness. The late-night phone call. The gun. *Your guy down on the coast*, that was what Regan said. *Listen, there's something else… Dave.* She nagged at the fragments while she watched Sonny from the corner of her eye. Dave. What the fuck had he been up to? Could he possibly have been helping some mad American smuggle caesium 137 out of the Dungeness research lab, around the coast, across the Channel, through Europe to Afghanistan? At first glance, the idea seemed preposterous. She tried to see Dave in a different light. You could never be sure what other people were doing, what was going on inside their head. Everybody had secrets. Although, she liked to think that because of her dad's work, she was more alert to the signs than most. But Dave? Crawford had his suspicions about Dave and Crawford knew what he was doing, according to Harry. No smoke without fire. Spyder needed something to feed off; he didn't have the imagination to make it all up himself. Perhaps Crawford was half right. Dave was involved in something nefarious, but it wasn't an armed hijack of a nuclear waste container.

'This might sound mad, but I'm beginning to wonder whether Dave was involved in some way. Do you think he could have been Stavros's guy on the coast, the one Regan mentioned?'

Sonny tapped his fingers on the table. 'I don't see it. Nee.'

His reactions annoyed her. He sounded so certain, as if he knew exactly what was going on, had some vital piece of information she didn't have.

'OK. I'm going to sleep on it,' she said. 'Think about what we do next.'

'Next? Isn't this enough?' He gestured at the Dictaphone. 'This Stavros is a lunatic. Doesn't that make you want to back off? Run in the opposite direction? Why can't you let your friend Harry sort out your file and leave it at that?'

'I can't be bothered to go through this again. I've got to find Luke. I don't have any choice.'

'There's always a choice. That's what you told me. I'm with your friend Frannie. It's stupid running after blokes who have disappeared.' He pushed the chair back. 'I'm going to bed. Goeie nag.'

He left the kitchen, the moth still thrashing against the lightbulb.

'Gooey bloody nag to you too.'

She needed a cup of tea, filled the kettle, turned the tap harder than she intended, water gushed violently, flushed a silverfish from its cranny. It slithered across the Formica. Silverfish, Dave had told her one evening when she had suggested that bleach might be the answer, perform an elaborate courtship ritual. The male and female stand head to head, antennae touching, then they break apart and reunite in a strangely moving dance before the male runs away and the female has to chase him so they can mate. Dave had almost succeeded in making her like silverfish. He didn't love nature in a sentimental or spiritual way, he was fascinated by the science, the principles and forces that made the earth spin, and that was his salvation from the repeat patterns of his family, the suicide of his mother. He studied the periodic table in order to conquer it. He was an empiricist, a modern Charles Darwin, not interested in politics and the battles of competing ideologies. Or so she had thought. Perhaps she had missed something. She squashed the silverfish with the back of the coffee spoon, pressed hard to make sure it was dead. It occurred to her then that it could be personal. His mother was raped by the Red Army, she killed herself because she couldn't live with the pain. His life was blighted by her death, his family destroyed. He had no reason to care about the Soviet soldiers. Perhaps he saw himself as saving the Afghan women from the same fate his mother had suffered. She could see it was reason enough – the deep, deep burning pain and resentment. He probably rationalized it, told himself the contamination would be contained. She had always thought he was blasé about the effects of radiation anyway. Jesus. Dave. And she hadn't spotted it.

But then, if he was working with the American, why had he ended up dead? Suicide? She didn't think so. Not Dave. The note – 55 pluto – what did it tell her? Pluto. The god of the underworld. The bleak descent. He was falling, wanted out, had tried to tell her when they were walking along the beach but she hadn't understood. And what about 55? She had a momentary image of Dave sitting on his bed, dunking a Hobnob in his Aston Villa mug, the periodic table blu-tacked on the wall above his head. She concentrated, conjured up the chart in her mind, the numbers, the symbols. Of course.

Element number 55 was caesium. Obvious. The note was Dave's confession. 55 pluto told her exactly what he had been doing, his involvement. Maybe he'd started off by providing advice to Stavros, nothing more, and then he'd found himself dragged further in, pushed to provide access to the research lab, his arm twisted, bullied. Tripping over the abyss. He wanted to extract himself, but by the time he tried to tell her, left the note, it was too late. She had missed all the signals. Regan hadn't. What had Stavros said when Regan mentioned the guy on the coast? *Made it safe*. She pictured Regan walking away from Bane House the night before Dave died. Regan was there, watching, sensing he was cracking up, wobbling, about to spill the beans. And so he had been killed.

CHAPTER 14

IT WASN'T THE drumming rain that was depriving her of sleep. The taped conversation between the American and Regan was playing in her head. Something needled her, a disconnect between tape and events, Sonny's reactions, his evasions. She couldn't put her finger on the problem. Fast forward. Pause. Rewind, back to the beginning of the conversation. The very beginning. 'Skuse me, mate, you got the time?' Then Sonny's voice. 'One fifteen.' 'Cheers.' Stop. Rewind. Play again. 'One fifteen.' She sat up. One fifteen was the time Sonny had started recording the conversation at Heaven. How long had he been standing there eavesdropping? It couldn't have been more than twenty minutes. Which meant he finished taping about one thirty-five, give or take a few minutes. The walk back from Charing Cross took forty minutes max. He should have returned by two fifteen, say two thirty at the outside. Yet he didn't knock on the front door until gone four a.m.

She twisted the questions, doubts around in her stomach, knotted her gut, tighter and tighter. She reached into the drawer of the bedside cabinet, touched the cold metal of the Firebird, gripped it, stalked down the hall, entered Dave's bedroom. Sonny's body half covered by the duvet, half uncovered; a slight shift in his breathing. Bushcraft – never taken by surprise.

'Sam.'

'Yes.'

'Did you want something?'

Both hands on the Firebird, she pointed at his head, clicked the safety catch with her thumb.

'Tell me what it is that you're not telling me,' she said. 'Or I'll shoot.'

He smiled, condescension at the corners of his mouth. 'You've got to sound as if you mean it.'

'I do. Fucking tell me.'

He reached over, as if he was about to take the weapon from her hand.

'Don't,' she said. 'Don't move.'

He assessed her face.

'Tell me,' she said.

'Tell you what?'

'What you did between one thirty and four last night.'

He stretched his eyes, wide and brown – innocent.

'It's on the tape,' she said. 'The time that you started recording the conversation.'

He blinked.

'Tell me.'

'Look, it's no big deal.'

'So tell me then.'

'OK. OK. I followed Regan out the club. That's all. She took a taxi and I took another and I followed her back to her place. Or at least, I assume it's her place. Maybe it belongs to a friend or whatever, I don't know. I didn't hang around to find out.'

Her arms were trembling; she couldn't hold the gun steady. 'Why did you lie to me?'

'Sam, sometimes it's easier not to know. The truth can be a burden. I'm trying to protect you.'

She thought then about Spyder, Sonny's insistence he hadn't

shot him, wondered whether he had lied about that so she wouldn't be complicit in the killing.

'I'm not a child. I can deal with it. You should have told me about Regan.'

'I was afraid you would do something stupid, like go and spy on her.'

She flicked the safety catch on, let her arm relax. He locked his hands behind his head, sunk back into the pillow.

'Where is this place she went to anyway?'

'It's near the river, past Waterloo Bridge. It looked like some kind of warehouse conversion. If it's hers, she's obviously not short of money.'

'So?'

'So, as I said last night, your friend Frannie is right. Regan is involved in drug dealing. Money out, smack back.'

'And this Stavros – you think he's involved in the drug smuggling as well?'

'No. I think he's plugged into her network to get the caesium delivered – makes life easier for him. It's the same route, the Silk Road, to Afghanistan and back. Just add the caesium to the outward-bound packages.'

'Oh,' she said.

'Oh what?'

'Reminds me of something Harry said about organized crime and terrorism, the overlaps.'

Sonny shrugged. 'Well, the links are obvious, ja nee?'

'I suppose so. It's what Crawford's lot deal with – the Sewer Squad.'

She returned to her room, replaced the Firebird in her bedside cabinet, hand on drawer, lost in thought, trying to understand the patterns. The phone rang. She ran downstairs, grabbed it.

'Hello.'

Liz. She almost replaced the receiver. Thought better of it. How to explain her mother's knack for always phoning at precisely the wrong moment? Psychic. Occult tendencies ran in the family, the witchcraft gene, this dark power to needle. Perhaps she had inherited it from her mother after all, not Jim.

'Mum, if you're going to ask about the postcard, then yes, it has arrived and yes, I have tried the recipe.'

'Was it helpful?'

'What, the recipe?'

'Yes.'

Helpful? How could a recipe be helpful?

'Yes, the recipe was helpful. Thanks. How is Milton?'

'Heavy going.'

She could have told Liz that.

'Actually, Roger and I decided we would forget the research and enjoy ourselves.'

Sam didn't want to know. 'When are you coming back?'

'Tomorrow.'

'See you then. Bye.'

Sam was replacing the receiver as her mother said, 'Take care.'

Too late to reply. Line dead already. She tried to swallow, there was a lump in her throat. She missed Liz. Shame about Roger. She'd just have to learn how to put up with him. The wanker.

Sonny was sitting at the kitchen table. He ferreted for his fag packet, produced his Zippo, flipped the lid, flicked the wheel, puffed. She watched him, stretching back on the chair so casually, doing his smoke ring thing, like a magician's trick or a skylark's song – a distraction. Look at the ring, not his face.

'We can walk along the river to Waterloo,' she said. 'Check out the place you saw this woman Regan go to last night. See what we can find out.'

239

'What's the point?'

'You know the point. The point is it could help me find Luke. What if Luke discovered something about this caesium stealing from his contact, the power station worker he met at Dungeness? What if the contact gave him Regan's name? What if he bumped into her, caught her in the act? That's probably the reason he's gone into hiding.'

'I thought you'd decided that Stavros and Regan are stealing caesium from the research lab, not the power station. So what would a power station worker have to do with all that?'

He was irritating her again with his sceptical tone. He was right, though, the power station worker was a link that didn't quite join. She sighed, stuck her hands in her trouser pockets, dug out the piece of paper with the number of the contact she had found in Luke's bedroom. P. Grogan. What was it about the name? She ogled the scrap until her vision blurred, and she called up all the places she might have seen it before, had an idea, hurtled upstairs to Dave's room, flung open the cupboard door, pulled out his box of journal articles, dug down, yanked out the one she was looking for – an article Dave had written and had published in a refereed journal. He had been pleased with this one; she remembered him telling her how many hours of hard labour at the lab it had taken to produce the results. She went straight to the list of acknowledgements.

'I would like to thank all the staff at the Dungeness experimental research station, including Patrick Grogan...'

That was where she had heard the name before. She ran back down the stairs to the kitchen.

'The man Luke met the Saturday he disappeared. Grogan.'

'What about him?'

'He didn't work at the power station. He worked at the

research lab with Dave. I met him there once when Dave showed me around. He's called Patrick. It's beginning to make sense now.'

The sky was overcast – rain pending, but at least not precipitating. The low tide was on the turn, sludge water wheedling. She wanted to walk in silence. Sonny was edging to talk.

'How long have you been seeing this guy Luke anyway?' he asked.

'About five months.'

'Five months? Is that all?'

'Longest I've ever managed.'

'Really?'

'Yes.'

'I bet you're a dumper. I bet you're always doing a runner. Leaving men standing.'

'No. Well. Maybe.' The truth was she hadn't cared about boyfriends one way or the other before she met Luke, couldn't be bothered with the game playing of relationships. Had a tendency to tell men to get lost if she felt they were intruding too much on her life, the things she enjoyed doing – hanging out with her friends, reading, archaeology, mooching around.

'But Luke is different. You fell for him straight away. Love at first sight. Ja nee?'

'It wasn't like that.'

She wasn't sure why she was denying it. Habit. She didn't like talking about her feelings, thought it was almost a weakness to acknowledge emotions. She must have inherited that attitude from Jim; maintain the cover, don't give away anything that matters.

'What's so great about Luke then?'

She conjured up an image of Luke in her head, his skin close to hers, his mouth on her neck, his weight on her. The aching absence.

'We share interests,' she said. 'History. Nature. Bird watching.'

Sonny chortled. 'Come on. You're this worked up for somebody you like watching birds with?'

'He makes me laugh. He's fun. And we share the same political views.'

'That's romantic.'

'It's important to me.'

'What are the political views you share then?'

'Leftie. Don't think much of political parties.' She nodded her head in the direction of Westminster. 'You know. Whoever you vote for, it's always the government that gets in. And in Britain, the government is usually composed of a bunch of public school boys. Thatcher and her bully boys. They're probably in there scheming away at this very minute, identifying some more heads to kick in now they've trampled all over the miners. So yeah – Westminster? Forget it. We are more interested in direct action. Protesting, campaigning. Anti-Thatcher. Against nuclear power and nuclear weapons. For nuclear disarmament. Luke's more militant than me, though.'

'In what way?'

She thought of Luke's reaction to Alastair. He definitely had a thing about hippies.

'Well, this protest we are organizing.' Are. She realized as soon as she said it that the protest was unlikely ever to happen. 'This protest we were organizing. I enjoyed meeting people, hanging out in the pub, having a laugh. For me it's half the point. But Luke, he's more focused on getting things done.' Her hand went to the badges on her coat lapel: the feminist fist, Che Guevara, smiling sun nuclear power no thanks. She had bought the smiling sun when she was with Luke and they stopped to talk to a woman selling badges to raise money for the Friends of the Earth. Luke had rejected the smiling sun, said it was too wet, bought a badge with a radiation warning symbol – the three rays – and a red line through it. Nuclear-free zone. More his style.

Sonny said, 'It's strange, isn't it, the things that draw people together and the things that keep them apart.'

She nodded, and thought of all the small, surprising things she had found she had in common with Luke. John Donne. February, a frosty, star-spangled night and they were walking home from their Soho shifts. 'You remind me of John Donne,' she told him as they crossed Vauxhall Bridge. 'The way you look.'

'That's a compliment,' Luke said. 'He's my favourite poet.'

Donne was her favourite poet too; she had a copy of his collected poems on the bookshelf in her room, between Blake and T.S. Eliot. Not only did Luke like poetry, they both liked the same poet. These little things confirmed the bond. Even their birthdays were close. She smiled to herself – they had a funny conversation about birthdays and star signs early on in their relationship. They were lounging around, reading the Sunday newspapers together. She found the horoscope page of the colour supplement. 'What's your star sign?' she asked.

'Capricorn,' he said.

'The goat.' And then she said, 'No, hang on. You must be Gemini. You told me your birthday was two days before mine – 7 June.'

He laughed. 'Yes. You're right. I'm a Gemini. I've never taken much notice of horoscopes and all that stuff.'

'Me neither.'

'So what are Gemini people supposed to be like then?'

'Quick-witted, imaginative, enchanting.'

'Well, there we go – that's you.'

She laughed. 'And you too.'

'I meant it,' he said. She found herself tongue-tied, too touched to reply. That was another difference between Sonny and Luke, now she came to think about it – you wouldn't catch Luke with a copy of *Linda Goodman's Love Signs* in his bag.

The first gobbets of rain darkened the embankment paving stones, gave them a reddish gleam. They passed the squat concrete ziggurat of the South Bank, skateboard wheels reverberating around the concrete cavern below Queen Elizabeth Hall. Heading east – disused garages, rubble-filled skips, around the OXO building.

'This way,' Sonny said.

South, leaving the river, threading through the backstreets; derelict warehouses, decomposing pigeons caught between shattered windows and iron grilles.

Sonny stopped at a corner. 'It's at the bottom of this street.'

She spotted a row of shopfronts further along the road, boarded apart from a greasy spoon at the far end.

'Let's go to the caff and have a coffee, take stock from there.'

The café was empty and stank of burned oil and greasy bacon. They sat at a corner table with a slanted view of Regan's building. A five-storey warehouse; the gibbet winding winch still had a rope dangling and the windows had horizontal wooden shutters below the frames for resting sacks before they were pulled inside. But you could tell it had been converted because it was the only building in the street that didn't have smashed panes and the entryphone by the door was visible.

'Bet it's nice inside,' she said.

'I'm in the wrong business,' he said.

'I'm sure they'd employ you if you asked. I should imagine you've got a lot of the skills they're looking for.'

'Thanks.' He wiped his mouth with the back of his hand, flipped the lid of his fag carton, flicked a fag in the air, caught it in his mouth, lit it and puffed tersely. She wished she hadn't said anything, felt mean. She watched the road as they ordered from a waitress in a grubby apron. They waited. Nothing happened, the street deserted. The waitress plonked a full English in front of Sonny and a slice of buttered toast in front of Sam. He squirted HP sauce on his sausage, silently mouthed grace before tucking in. She picked at the toast, sipped her black coffee, imagined herself living in a converted warehouse with Luke. He would have a photography studio. She would be... what would she be doing? Writing up the finds from her latest archaeological dig? Teaching a history course in some part of London University? She gazed through the window, visualized the interior of the apartment, her future life with Luke, jumped. A crew-cut heavy was standing outside the warehouse; feet apart, shoulders squared, hoodie under leather jacket. He looked hard. Somebody must have buzzed him in, because he pushed the door and disappeared.

'Did you see him?'

'Yes.'

'Do you think Regan's in there?'

'How would I know?'

'Let's see if he comes out, and then we can follow him.'

'Why?'

'Why not?'

'He's obviously a heavy. An enforcer. Almost certainly armed.'

'So are you.'

She paid for the food, sat down. The door of the warehouse opened, the heavy emerged, head jutting, neck bulging below the bristles, rolling hoodlum swagger down the street. He rocked off north, then right, east, heading deep into the docklands. They followed, kept their distance, under the criss-crossing viaducts, the grind and spark of steel on steel as trains passed overhead. He took a right, a left, across a main road, double-decker splashing dirty gutter water, into the maze of cobbled streets behind London Bridge. She wasn't about to let go. Past the straggle of market stalls underneath the arches, and then right again, doubling back. Under a low, dingy tunnel. They followed, then stalled. Their quarry had vanished. The street was empty apart from a black Audi Quattro pulled up against a warehouse door. They hesitated, then retreated around the corner.

'He must have gone into one of the wharves,' Sonny said. 'Meeting whoever was in the Audi, I suppose.'

'There's a skip just inside the tunnel. We could wait behind that, see what happens.'

'OK.' He didn't agree with any enthusiasm.

The skip was overflowing with bricks, rubbish bags oozing dirty nappies, chicken bones, squashed baked bean cans. A seagull patrolled the contents proprietorially. They squished themselves into the gap between its dirty metal sides and the sooty bricks of the tunnel wall; the smell of rotting flesh and excrement made her gag. Clink Street, a road sign above their heads proclaimed, site of the old prison. A pigeon flapped, dissolved in the tunnel's darkness, solidified in the daylight at the far end. A car roared up behind them, swerved the corner, sped past the skip, low and black, braked suddenly, pulled up behind the Audi, left the engine idling.

'Porsche,' she said. 'I bet it's the one I saw in Dungeness the day Luke disappeared.'

A car door slammed, the Porsche revved away, left a tall skinny figure standing on the cobbles.

'It's Regan,' Sam whispered. She was sweating, adrenalin

pumping, fired by the sense that she was finally homing in on Luke. 'What do you think she's doing? Collecting something?'

Sonny shrugged in a couldn't-care-less way. Regan disappeared into the warehouse. The Porsche had sealed it as far as Sam was concerned; she was certain Luke must have discovered something about Regan's involvement in the caesium smuggling from Patrick, and had probably seen her that day in Dungeness, maybe with her enforcers; which was why he had vanished. He had been scared by Regan.

'We should go now,' Sonny said, 'while we have a chance. I think we've seen enough to confirm that she's a dealer.'

'I'm not going now. No way.'

She was jittering; stress, the cold dampness of her coat.

'Sam, it's time to leave. There's nothing we can do here.'

She didn't even bother to reply, eyes trained on the warehouse door through which Regan had disappeared. Waited. Unmoving. Willed the door to open. It did. Regan reappeared, trod the street in their direction. For a moment she thought they had been spotted, but she passed through the tunnel, pale face ghostly in the dimness, and turned north in the direction of the river. Sam shuffled sideways along the wall, waited a few moments before she stuck her head around the skip to see what was going on. She had to pursue Regan, find out what she knew about Luke. She inched out from behind the cover of the skip. Sonny yanked her back.

'Don't be stupid.'

'Let go.' She pulled her arm away, broke free, sprinted along the road, not caring about the risks, possessed by anger, fear for Luke, a determination to protect him whatever the cost. Regan had disappeared. The road angled sharply right along the river wall. Sam peered over. A flight of rickety, wooden stairs fell down from the embankment to the river. A black dinghy was easing away from the bottom step, two figures on board, one hoodie-covered, the other Regan, fiddling with the outboard motor.

The prospect of losing her lead filled Sam with desperation. She bellowed, 'Regan, where's Luke?'

Regan looked up, her eye sockets dark circles in her anaemic face, thin mouth twisted in a knowing leer.

'You fucking what?'

'My boyfriend. Luke.'

'I don't know what the fuck you're talking about.' She smirked, fired the motor, turned away as the Zodiac headed downstream.

Sam leaned over the wall, wondering whether there was any way she could still reach Regan. If she climbed down the stairs, waded out into the water. She heard footsteps running up behind. Sonny.

'She's getting away,' Sam said, pointing wildly. 'She said she—'

Sonny interrupted. 'We've got to move. Four of them have piled out of that warehouse. One of them was swinging an iron bar around. God knows what weapons the others have got.'

'I don't care.'

'I do,' he said. 'You'll get us killed.'

A voice yelled, 'They must have gone this way.'

The shout brought her to her senses, aware of the imminent danger.

'The backstreets,' she said. 'We can lose them in the old Mint.'

CHAPTER 15

THEY DARTED BETWEEN a viaduct and a wall of derelict warehouses. The shield of anger that had made her immune to danger when she thought she was on Luke's trail had evaporated. She was scared. She could hear shouts. Boots on cobbles. They cut across a no-man's wasteland by the railway arches; acrid smoke from an oil drum fire drifted around the yard, caught the back of her throat with its toxicity, made her eyes sting. She glimpsed a black-clad figure stirring the brazier flames. He looked up from the oil drum and she saw icy eyes, a crescent scar. He shouted – stop. She ran on, but she couldn't help turning. There was nothing to see. Everything veiled in smoke. She gagged, memories taunting her. Then she found her feet, pounded. Left, right, right again.

They headed into the Mint – a lowland festering sink which once provided shelter for London's fleeing debtors. Rubbish, blocked drains and persistent summer rain had returned the Mint to near swampland once again. Glimmers of the setting sun crept like intruders over the roofs of boarded warehouses but failed to penetrate the narrow streets below. An old man slumped in a doorway flashed a smile as they passed; or maybe he wasn't so old. His teeth looked suspiciously good. A watcher?

She had to slow down, she couldn't keep this pace, she had a stitch. They turned a corner. She was uncertain of her bearings. A shuffling bag lady appeared from nowhere, tan blanket pinned around her shoulders, crutch in one hand, dragging a wheeled Black Watch shopping bag with the other. Sam tried to sidestep, but the woman pushed her trolley out as Sam passed and she half stumbled over one of its wheels. Sam righted herself and was about to say something. The bag lady spoke first.

'It's the smell I can't stand.' She spoke as if they were old friends, her voice warmer than her appearance. She tapped a manhole cover with the peeling rubber tip of her crutch. 'You hear that gurgle? The Neckinger. It gets its name from the gibbet at its mouth – used to hang smugglers by the neck.' She cackled, then stopped abruptly. 'Listen again,' she said.

Sam heard footsteps pounding.

The bag lady said, 'You're dead if they catch you. Better find somewhere dark to hide till they've passed.'

She waddled off, the wheels of her shopping trolley squeaking as she went. The footsteps were getting louder, heavier, but in the mazelike streets of the Mint, it was hard to relate noise and distance. Sam heard a shout. 'That old man's seen them.'

They must be right behind. She looked down at the manhole cover, nudged it with her foot.

He followed the line of her gaze. 'Down there?'

She nodded. 'We could see if there's an access ladder. I've got a torch.' Even as she suggested it, she wished she hadn't because she knew she didn't want to do it.

Sonny didn't hesitate. He gripped the manhole cover with his fingers, shifted it to one side.

'Give me the torch, I'll go first.'

He crouched and disappeared backwards through the hole. She followed, moved without thinking because she knew that if she stopped to consider what she was doing, she wouldn't budge. Over the edge, easing the manhole cover back into place above her head, shutting out the light. For a five-second eternity they were in complete darkness, suspended in space, nothing but the roughness of rusty metal on her hands and a deep gurgling noise rumbling up from way down below. Sonny lit the torch, swept the walls with its beam. A vertical chute, once red Victorian bricks fading to grey, a ladder clamped to the wall and running off into oblivion.

'Are you OK?' His voice reverberated.

'Not sure. How far is it to the bottom?'

'I don't know.'

They descended the vertiginous ladder into the darkness, feet searching for rungs, fingers gripping metal. Eventually her shoe hit a flat surface. Sonny swung the torch, yellow eyes reflected, scattered. Rats. The tunnel ran on into nothingness, the air was stale; a heavy muskiness cut by the tang of piss. She listened for the scrape of metal, the giveaway sounds of pursuers, but there was nothing except for the distant rumbling she had heard as they descended. They stood without talking for a while, taking in their situation, drawn below the streets by some strange force of gravity. She felt the tears in her eyes and realized then how scared she was; how stupid she had been.

'I'm sorry,' she said. 'I shouldn't have chased Regan. I couldn't stop myself.'

'It was reckless. But I can understand why you did it. It's hard to think straight when emotions kick in.'

She wiped her nose on her sleeve. 'We could wait here for half an hour or so and then climb back up,' she said. 'I don't want to get lost. A treasure-seeker I met by the Thames told me about the tunnels, the underground rivers. It's a labyrinth.'

'I'm not sure I can stand still.' His voice had an edginess she hadn't heard before and she realized he was afraid too. 'If we keep to one tunnel, we'll be OK. Let's walk, see if we can find another exit.'

'OK.' It wasn't OK, but then nothing was particularly OK at that moment.

He directed the beam along the tunnel; the floor tilted at a slight angle, a black ribbon running slowly along its centre. She stooped, examined the viscous trickle. 'God, what is this black stuff?' The sludge had a phosphorescent glow, a radioactive luminescence. She dabbed her finger in the tarry mire, held it to her nose. It didn't have the overpowering whiff of straight sewage, though it undoubtedly had some crap in it.

'Residue,' she said.

She thought of Crawford's Sewer Squad, wading knee-deep in shit, according to Harry. And she wondered whether the trickle contained the wash-off from London's grubby deals, the dark arts, reverse alchemy, the dirty laundering as stolen gold was passed from hand to hand and transformed from something pure into degraded substances; smack, tabs, dope, firearms. The torchlight glinted on the endless stream. 'Whatever it is, there's a hell of a lot of it.'

They kept to the slope of the wall, leaving footprints in the wallow. The intermittent chains slung across the tunnel's bottom were clogged with the discard of a million lives above: grey rags, abandoned toys, dentures, bones, gaudy trinkets glinting in the torchlight. Hair. Lots of bloody hair. Cavernous arches marked intersections where red brick drains joined the sewer, the vaulted ceilings gilded with snail trails and lurid fungal growths. The dark matter meandered down each tunnel, bad blood infecting every vein. The distant rumble grew louder.

'What is that noise? Do you think the heavies could have followed us?'

'They don't know we are down here.'

'Nobody knows we are down here,' she said. 'You could kill me and nobody would ever find my body.'

She shook as she spoke, wished she hadn't voiced her fear to Sonny.

'You could murder me and nobody would find my corpse,' he said.

'You're right,' she said. 'I could.' She wanted him to think she had the Firebird with her. She was regretting leaving it in her bedside cabinet.

'And even if they did find my corpse,' Sonny said, 'they wouldn't know who I was, because all I've got is fake ID.'

Jim used to say the same when he disappeared undercover; if he didn't come back, they might never find out what had happened to him, because nobody would be able to find out his real identity; a nameless body in the gutter, two bullets in the back of his head. Spooks, undercover agents, they were ghosts even when they were alive. She had a sudden urge to scream, scrabble her way back to the surface. She stifled it, swallowed it. Her mind wandered back to Jim, the footprints in the Effra run-off, his shadow sliding along the tunnel walls. And here she was, trapped in the sewers with her father's phantom and his killer. She held her breath and heard a splash, an echo, the familiar tune whistled in a melancholic key.

'Can you hear the music?'

'Yes.'

The notes faded away. She wanted to cry again, with fear, the loss, regrets, she wasn't sure. The torch beam caught a side tunnel. Sonny said, 'Let's rest in there a while. Switch the torch off, save the battery, and make sure we're not being followed.'

His voice sounded fractured too. They perched on the sloping, damp wall of the drain. Torch extinguished. The blackness engulfed her, odour overwhelming, noises hard to identify.

Inside, outside, far, near, dead or alive, it was all the same in the blackness. She couldn't take it. Her hand reached out, searched for Sonny's hand.

'I'm scared,' she said.

'It's OK,' he said. 'We'll be OK.'

His voice trembled.

'You don't have to pretend to be brave for me.'

'OK. I'm scared too.'

'What's your deepest fear?' she asked.

'Dying alone.'

She linked her arm around his.

'What's yours?' he asked.

She didn't answer for a while. Then she said, 'I'm afraid I'm dead already. That I can't feel. I've perished from the heart, hollow inside. A replicant. A ghost.'

'Don't worry,' he said. 'You're alive. You're human.'

She wasn't sure how long they sat in the darkness, arm in arm, without talking, because the only things worth saying were too difficult to be spoken. She didn't stop herself from crying, though, and tasted the saltwater on her lips.

After a while, she said, 'Maybe it's safe to go now.'

'I'm beginning to like it down here. There's a certain security in being hidden from the world.'

'I know. But I think we should face the light.'

He switched the torch back on. They blinked. His face was smeared with grime and tear tracks. He directed the beam at the intersection. 'There's a ladder up there.'

She went first, climbed the long ladder, pushed her hand against the manhole cover. For a moment she thought it wouldn't budge and they would have to return to their underworld. Then it shifted and the last dregs of the evening light fell on her head. She cautiously lifted her face above ground level – surveyed her surroundings. A derelict yard of nettles, lilac bushes and rubble, separated from the street by a bindweed-curtained railing. She hauled herself out. Sonny followed, shoved the manhole cover back into place. She lay on the damp ground, her body shaking.

'Let's rest for a bit,' she said. 'Get our bearings. If anybody comes down the road, they're not going to see us here.'

A fat black cat sauntered out from the jungle grass, gave her a nonchalant amber-eyed stare, sashayed away. Sonny took out his fags. They stayed silent for a while, recovering, glad to be back on the surface.

Eventually Sonny asked, 'So did Regan say anything about Luke?'

'No. Fucking cow. But I'm sure she knew something. I could tell by her smirk.'

She plucked a dandelion, wound it round her wrist to form a bracelet. Sonny lay back, head in the long grass, smoking. Another cat appeared. Ginger street fighter with a torn ear that reminded her of Harry. It yowled at her expectantly, as if they had some sort of arrangement. An unspoken deal.

'What about your friend Dave?' Sonny asked.

'What about him?' she replied aggressively.

'I still don't see how he fits into this.'

She didn't want to talk about Dave, didn't even want to think about him, because it was painful, whichever angle she took.

Sonny persisted. 'Do you really think Dave was the kind of person who would get himself involved in a plot to steal caesium?'

Her mate Dave; his sardonic attitude, the Aston Villa mug and Hobnob biscuit barrel.

'I find it difficult to see him doing it, but scientists can be weird. Naïve. It was a bunch of American scientists who gave the Russians the information they needed to build atomic weapons. They thought everybody should have access to the information.' She paused. 'Dave had a personal reason to hate the Soviets – his mother was raped by the Red Army. She committed suicide a few years ago. Which, as you can imagine, really affected him.'

'You never suspected him before?'

'No, but unlikely people turn out to be the spies. I assumed I was good at recognizing them because I grew up with one. Perhaps I'm blinded by what I know. I'm always on the lookout for middle-aged men who drink too much. Perhaps Dave fooled me.' She pictured the displaced papers in Dave's room, the photo she had found in Luke's bedroom of the article about caesium 137. *Listen, there's something else... Dave.* Perhaps Spyder's assertion that Luke had visited Dave without telling her the week before he disappeared was true. Perhaps Luke had secretly visited Dave, confronted him with his suspicions. That would explain Dave's edginess when she asked him about Luke, told him about the contact in Dungeness. She vocalized the thought crystallizing in her mind. 'Although I suspect Dave might not have fooled Luke.'

Sonny raised an eyebrow. 'Were they mates?'

'Yeah. They had lots in common – dead German mothers for a start, which was a pretty large chunk of shared ground. They chatted a lot. Luke's more perceptive about people than me.'

She wondered now whether Luke had been worried about Dave from the start, picked up on his darker side, locked into his psyche in a way that Sam had been afraid to do.

'I reckon Dave didn't know the dimensions of what he was getting involved with, he was sucked in, couldn't back out and then when Regan realized he was having second thoughts, clocked he was about to talk, she killed him.'

Sonny didn't comment. She cast her eye around the yard, searching for anything to lighten her mood. A magpie bouncing on a buddleia branch. Wheelbarrow. Cement mixer and spade. Signs of construction work stirring. She spotted the top of a worn grey stone protruding through the weeds. She pulled herself up, wandered over, cleared the nettles, oblivious to the stings, and revealed what looked like a rough-hewn tombstone set at an angle in the ground. No name or date. Only a skull and crossbones chalked on its rough surface. Nearby, a small mound of grey stones piled like a shrine, and the faded purple glaze of a chipped vase. A graveyard?

A gate in the railing creaked, swung inwards; the bag lady they had passed earlier shuffled into the yard. She was greeted by a river of cats springing from all corners, flowing and yowling around her. The woman muttered endearments to the animals, produced a bag of nibbles from her shopping trolley, emptied it into a couple of saucers, tickled their heads as they ate. Having dealt with the cats, she looked directly at Sam, without any real surprise.

'So you found your way in,' she said. 'Not too much water? The Neckinger behaving itself?'

'Sticky trickle.'

'I'm surprised. It's been raining so much. Although, the water collects in one part of the system, then they release it.' She remembered the treasure-seeker she'd met at Vauxhall had said something similar about about the Effra run-off; flood control. 'You can hear the wave coming from miles off. The rumbling.'

'Oh god, I think I heard it.'

'You were lucky then – you just missed it, got out before the water hit you.' She tapped her crutch on the ground. 'You must have friends in low places, keeping you safe.' She winked.

'Where are we, anyway?' Sam asked.

'Crossbones, a graveyard for single women. Hookers mainly.'

The click of Sonny's Zippo caught the bag lady's attention. She glared at him, her eyes following the movements of his fag. 'Flash your ash.'

He obliged. She took two; stuck one in her pocket. 'One for now, one for 'ron,' she said. Sonny offered her a light. She puffed, studied the cats as they polished off their food.

'Cats and hookers,' she said, 'have a lot in common.'

'Why is that?'

'Won't hang around if there's no reward.' She tapped her fag. 'I inherited the cat-feeding duties from an old pro who'd been coming here for decades. Pearl. She ended up in Guy's.' She nodded her head at the ugly tower block, looming over the far side of a viaduct. 'Asked me to look after the cats while she was laid up in hospital. When she died, I had her cremated and brought her ashes here. That's Pearl over there.' She pointed her fag at the ceramic purple vase.

'How long has this been a graveyard then?'

'For ever. Southwark, it's the wrong side of the river, outside the jurisdiction of the City. The land was owned by the Church – the Bishop of Winchester controlled everything, he had the liberty of the clink. He charged the stew houses rent, taxed their profits, fined the whores when they failed to obey the Church's rules, but refused to allow them a proper burial. So this is the patch of unconsecrated ground they got dumped in when they flaked out.'

She inhaled deeply, one hand on her blanket to stop it from slipping, coughed. 'This is the home for the unforgiven. The shunned.' She jabbed her fag at Sam.

'Wouldn't worry about it,' she said.

'Worry about what?'

'Ending up in not quite the best circles. Sometimes the best place to be is beyond the pale.'

She prodded Sam in the arm. 'Don't let anybody make you feel bad for being what you are. If they don't like it, fuck 'em. That's what I say. Tell 'em to piss orf. But whatever you do, don't feel sorry for yourself. I've no bloody time for self-pitiers.'

The bag lady straightened, surveyed the graveyard, drained now of all light. 'Those arseholes that were after you have gone anyway.'

'Did you see them?'

'Four of them came down the street, cornered me after I'd passed you. They seemed a bit clueless. Asked me if I'd seen a girl. So I said no I hadn't. I don't see much very clearly these days.' She squinted at Sam.

'Thanks.'

The bag lady collected up the saucers, fumbled with the zip of her shopping trolley, the ginger tom weaving around her legs between the skirt layers. She bent, scooped the cat, caressed its head, made it purr. Then she glared at Sam, beckoned her nearer. Sam obeyed, stood close enough to smell the woman's fag-kippered clothes, the dankness of the blanket pinned around her shoulders. The bag lady peered at her through milky cataracts and whispered, 'Do you have a gun?'

Sam started, went red with surprise and guilt. 'A gun?'

'Don't repeat. It's bloody annoying.' She tutted. 'I hope you know how to use it.'

The bag lady released the ginger tom and shuffled away, without another word.

The moon was covered in a flimsy shroud that reminded Sam of the bag lady's cataracts. They made their way through the creaking graveyard gate, past the Boot and Flogger, through the backstreets of Borough to the river. They walked back along the embankment, the river flowing in now, pushing upstream urgently. She stopped at a phone box at the bottom of Lambeth Bridge, dialled Harry's number. No answer. She tried Patrick Grogan's number. No answer. She dialled Directory Enquiries, asked for the number of the Dungeness research lab, noted it and dialled; there was always some egghead working there, somebody who could tell her how to get hold of Patrick. Except this evening, nobody was bothering to pick up the phone. She replaced the receiver, her gut a knot of frustration. Where was everybody when she needed them?

The searchlight of a police helicopter swept past, tracked across Vauxhall, down South Lambeth Road. The churring of its blades diminished. They turned into her home street. All quiet, the skeleton of the gasholder silver in the moonlight. She breathed a sigh of relief, reached into her pocket for a key. The floppy-fringed head of the anarcho-syndicalist next-door neighbour appeared above her through an open window, his face hanging in the air like the Cheshire cat.

'The Filth were here this afternoon, banging on your door.'

'Oh god. Uniformed?'

'No. Plain-clothes. There were two of them, blokes. I came out when I heard all the noise, asked them what they wanted. They showed me their ID and said they were looking for you. Crawford was the name I remember.'

Her legs went numb. 'Oh shit.'

'He asked me if I knew where you were. I said I had no idea, but as I was shutting my door I heard them talking to each other and saying they would come back tomorrow.'

His face disappeared before she had time to thank him. She fumbled with her key, pushed the front door, stood in the hallway.

'Well, that's it,' she said. 'I've had it. Crawford is going to come back tomorrow and haul me off to the cop shop, ask me what I know about Dave, see if he can charge me with some firearms conspiracy story. I probably won't even be allowed out on bail.'

She twiddled her lip with her fingers, her mind fogged, panicked by the prospect of being locked up, alone in a tiny police cell. Prodded. Tortured. The more she claimed her innocence, the guiltier she would seem. *Daemonologie*. God, James the First declared, would not permit the innocent to be slandered with witchcraft accusations, which meant the accused were always guilty.

'Maybe I should dig out the number of a good solicitor. That's what people usually do, isn't it? Call a solicitor. Unfortunately the only solicitor I know is an old mate of Jim's who's just been sent down for fraud.' She sighed. 'Harry's obviously not managed to talk to Crawford and sort the file out yet.'

Sonny grimaced. 'Perhaps Harry needs a little more time.'

'I don't have any more time.'

'We'll evade Crawford. We can make a plan.'

She said, 'We could have a shootout. I'll use the Firebird. You use the Browning. We'll hammer him as he comes down the road, then leg it out the back and go on the run in the kombi.'

'That was my plan.'

'I wasn't serious.'

'I'm not sure I can think of anything better.'

Tomorrow. Crawford was coming to get her tomorrow. She tried to work out how much she knew, how much she didn't, whether she was any closer to finding Luke, whether he was safe, how she could reach him before Crawford caught up with her. She spotted the red light of the answering machine blinking in the gloom. She pressed play. The whistle, the breath and then the man's voice. 'Time to run.'

She pressed delete.

Sonny said, 'Well, I didn't recognize his voice, but I think it's sound advice.'

'Yes. Maybe he's right. Time to run.'

Go camping, she heard Harry say. The Lookers' Hut, her safehouse. Romney Marsh.

CHAPTER 16

Sonny had left his Land Rover and camping gear in a lock-up behind Cold Harbour Lane. Her kombi was a non-starter, he said. They would be hunting for the number plate and anyway it was tangerine. They. She stood in the hall waiting for Sonny, listed the 'they' in her head and saw the figures surrounding her: Crawford and the Sewer Squad. Regan and her enforcers. The whistler? Whose side was he on? She glanced at the answering machine, reached over, removed the micro-cassette and dropped it in her pocket. She wanted to have Luke's voice at her fingertips. She couldn't bear the thought of finding any more messages from the dead and disappeared waiting for her when she returned.

It was a relief to leave the house and walk in the first light of day to Brixton, birds twittering. Sonny had insisted on going at four a.m. because, he said, they couldn't rule out the possibility that Crawford would turn up at the crack of dawn. She had done the drive so often she didn't need a map. She sat in the passenger seat and directed Sonny, headlights on in the murk, the Land Rover merging with the muddy fields beyond the outer reaches of London. Occasional glimmers of sun pierced the low ceiling of cloud. Irregular shards of conversation filtered through the fug of Sonny's fag smoke.

Hastings was morose – nothing worse than a seaside town on a wet summer's day, trying to be jolly in the rain. The

Channel lay still and lifeless there, a foam caul covering the shore. Beyond Rye, the mudflats of the Rother and the melancholy of the marshes came as a relief. Silver grass and grey lakes gleamed in the dim light, sheep drifted across the leas. A kestrel hung overhead, haunting the leaden clouds. She followed the falcon with her eye, found a thermal, soared, and observed the land from on high; the brown nose of Dungeness edging into the blue channel, shingle fringe, white line of rolling breakers.

Sonny's voice startled her. 'Sam, I said which way.'

'Sorry. Take the right.'

She spotted a telephone box at the end of a straggle of bungalows in Camber. She wanted to check Patrick Grogan's address and she asked Sonny to pull over. She hit lucky with the telephone directories; the local one had not been ripped out. Two P. Grogans listed, one living in Rye, the other in Lydd. The telephone number she had matched the address in Lydd. She memorized the house number and road, then dialled the number again, although she felt Patrick was unlikely to pick up. She was right; there was no answer.

'Lydd's not far from here. We should go to Patrick's house, see if we can work out what has happened to him.' Sonny said nothing. They drove on. Beyond Camber, the lakes spread larger, spiked with reed beds and clotted with greylag geese. She spotted a crow hitching a ride on a sheep's back, a bad omen she thought, a sign of black magic being worked, and she stuck her hand in her pocket, touched her torch and penknife for comfort. Past the army shooting range with its painted targets of dead men standing, under the scar of wires and pylons.

They reached Lydd, an old garrison town, parked the Land Rover and headed in the direction of the sandy square tower of the church. Patrick's house was on a street leading away from the east side of the graveyard. They sat among the tombs and observed the terrace through the clutter of crosses and the angels. A man in overalls balanced on a stepladder snipped the top of a privet hedge, the clack of his shears mingling with the rooks' caws.

'You stay here,' she said to Sonny. 'I'll see if he's at home.'

She followed the path through the graveyard, headed along the row of old workers' cottages, reached Patrick's house, rang the doorbell and waited. No answer. She peered through the letterbox, spotted a pile of envelopes on the doormat. She rang the doorbell again, held her breath, stomach sinking. No answer. She checked right and left along the street – nobody in sight apart from the hedge cutter – peered through the dirty net-covered window. Nothing to see except for a line of dead flies adorning the gap between curtain and pane. She walked back the way she had come; the shears stopped clacking as she passed the stepladder and she felt the eyes of the privet trimmer on her neck.

Back in the Land Rover, they were about to pull away when a black car appeared in the rearview mirror, advancing slowly down the road, two men in the front, the passenger wearing wraparound shades.

'Don't look,' she whispered. 'It's an Audi. It must be Regan's heavies.'

The Quattro slid past, continued down the road, disappeared in the distance.

'Let's go,' Sonny said. 'Before they come back.'

She said, 'Patrick's place has the smell of a deserted house.' She tried to catch her breath, but couldn't, realized she was panicking. 'Do you think we arrived too late?'

Sonny shrugged. 'Maybe he's at work.'

'Let's get out of Lydd then find a phone box. I want to try something.'

They drove to the coast, a straggle of bungalows lining the shore, spotted a telephone kiosk. She jumped out. In luck again, the directory was still intact, the phone in working order. She found the Grogans and this time dialled the number in Rye. She counted the rings. Eight. Nine. Ten. She willed somebody to pick up. They did. She jammed her coins in the slot.

'Hello. Pete Grogan speaking.' Trace of a southern Irish accent. She took a punt. 'Hello, Mr Grogan, I was calling to see if I could speak to Patrick.'

'Oh yes, hang on a moment, I think he's here.' She had guessed correctly; he had retreated to his parents' home.

'Sorry, can I ask who is calling?'

'Yes. It's Sam. I'm a friend of Dave Daley's. I used to share a house with him in Vauxhall.'

'Oh dear. Poor Dave. So very sad. Patrick has been upset by the news, he's taken it very badly. Hang on, I'll find him.'

She fiddled with the loose change in her pocket while Pete went to fetch his son. Somebody picked up the receiver at the other end.

'Hello.'

His voice sounded timid. Scared.

'Hello, Patrick?'

Short silence. 'Who is it speaking again?'

'Sam Coyle. I live with Dave in Vauxhall... I lived with Dave in Vauxhall. I think we might have met once. Dave showed me around the research lab last year.'

'Yes. I remember.'

'I wondered whether we could meet up. I wanted to talk about Dave.'

'How did you know I was here?'

She had to lie, she didn't want to spook him, let him know she had been chasing him for days, found his number in the bedroom of her disappeared boyfriend. 'I spoke to somebody at the research station and they said you were staying with your parents in Rye and gave me your number.'

'Why do you want to talk to me about Dave?'

'It's just…' She stammered, taken aback by his defensiveness. 'I've been really upset about his death and I wanted to talk to somebody else who knew him well.' She stuck her finger in the nine hole on the dial, waggled it around.

'Why do you want to talk to me rather than anybody else who works at the lab?'

She could hear the agitation in his tone. As he spoke her mind was digging, analysing his reactions, picking over the possibility that Patrick was complicit in whatever Dave had been doing. She tried to keep the wariness from her voice.

'I was going through some of Dave's old papers. Sorting out his room. I found one of his articles and saw you were first on his list of acknowledgements.' Dave had told her they were both born in Birmingham, she recalled, both of Irish descent, both Aston Villa fans. 'I thought I would try and talk to you because I remembered you and he were good mates. I've found it so difficult to make sense of Dave's death.'

Heavy sigh at the far end. 'Me too.'

'I'm in Dungeness now with a friend. I wanted to show him the beach. We could drive over to Rye. Meet up at a pub. The Mermaid perhaps.'

'No. Not Rye. Romney. The marsh. There's a pub called the Owler, out beyond Hope.'

'I know it.' Beyond Hope, that sounded ominous.

'OK. Six?'

'Six is fine.'

He replaced the receiver abruptly.

*

She clambered back into the Land Rover. 'Well, at least he's still alive,' she said. Then she wondered whether she had tempted fate by speaking her fear. 'I've arranged to meet him at six in a pub out on the marsh.'

An afternoon to kill. She sat with her head in her hands and tried to work out whether there were any other leads she could find that might guide her to Luke.

'I'd like to visit Alastair.'

'Alastair?'

'He lives in one of the fishermen's cottages down on Dungeness. He turned up at the meetings we organized.'

'We?'

'Luke and me.'

'Of course. Luke.'

'I met him the evening Luke disappeared. I thought at first he was the informer feeding information about me to Crawford, but that was before you worked out that Spyder was the grass. There's something odd about Alastair, though,' she said. 'He's an old hippy. Drug dealer, I reckon.'

'Could he be part of Regan's smuggling network?'

'Maybe, but I suspect he's too small-time to be involved with Regan. Perhaps he's seen something going on along the beach. He's sharper than he seems. He's observant. And he's...' She was going to say *clairvoyant*, changed her mind. 'He's perceptive. He's something of a Magus. A shaman.'

'Sangoma.'

'What?'

'Witch doctor.'

'Yes, one of those.'

'I don't want to visit him then.' He folded his arms.

'Are you serious?'

'I don't mess with that stuff. Witch doctors.'

'Why not?'

'There was one who lived in a nearby village back home. I had a friend who wanted to visit and ask about a stomach pain, so I went with him to the sangoma's hut for a laugh, to see what all the fuss was about. He was wearing this feather headdress and did some drumming, went into a trance, called up the ancestors, did a question and answer routine and gave my friend a diagnosis and some medicine. Pretty much as I had expected.'

'So what's the problem?'

'We were about to leave, but the sangoma told me to wait, and he touched my arm, closed his eyes, went into a trance again. When he opened his eyes again, he said he could see I had a shadow. A ghost. I asked him what the ghost looked like and he described a young woman with long brown hair. I tried to laugh it off, but he said I should have a charm, some magic, to prevent the ghost from stealing my soul. I said no, but my friend was scared and said I had to do it. So I agreed and he asked me to hold my arm out.'

Sonny lifted his forearm, rolled up his sleeve, revealed the crosses in a band around his elbow.

'He made two cuts,' Sonny continued. 'Just here. He rubbed them with sand.'

He pointed to the first cross – different from the others, less pen and ink, more like a scar.

'I offered to pay for the charm but he refused, and it made me nervous, so I asked him more about my ghost, whether she had a name, an identity. Foreign name, he said, one he hadn't heard before. Flavia.'

Sonny's eyes were welling.

'Your mother?' she asked. 'I thought you said she'd run away to England.'

'Ja. It's what I hoped, it's what I thought. I still search for her, but the sangoma made me doubt she is still alive.'

'I'm sorry.'

'That was the week before I left home for my military service,' he added.

First in his line of crosses, she thought. She glanced at the band, and saw there were two pen and ink crosses that looked as if they had been recently added, sore and raised. Two crosses. The last one Spyder, she was sure. Who was the other one, the one she had first noticed when they were sitting in the Portuguese café on South Lambeth Road? He rolled his sleeve down hastily. A crow alighted on the Land Rover's bonnet, preened and strutted from left to right, flew away.

'So I am wary of sangomas or people who have supernatural powers of any kind,' he said. 'I'm afraid they can do more harm than good. Tell you things you were better off not knowing. But I'll come with you, if you like. Don't expect me to join in the conversation.'

'No problem.' She felt uneasy, a nagging fear that Alastair might say something she didn't want to hear.

They parked the Land Rover at the end of the beach track. The concrete mass of the power station loomed, radiated an unnerving stillness, a hobby tumbled around the reactor tower. A weak sun shone through the low cloud, but whatever warmth it brought was whipped away by the onshore wind. They walked heads down against the buffeting, past storm-battered fishermen's cabins, clumps of fading poppies. Further along the shore, a solitary fisherman sat motionless with a rod and line in front of his military green windbreak like some lone survivor of the apocalypse. They reached Alastair's cabin; the funt was outside the front door indicating he was in – although the

270

blankness of the windows made her suspect nobody was at home. She knocked on the door, wind chimes clanking above her head, peered through the glass when there was no answer, spotted a movement inside. She waited. The door creaked, Alastair peeped through the crack.

'Sam,' she said.

'Oh, hello. Good to see you again.' He pulled the door open, smiled – warily, she thought – then frowned when he saw Sonny standing behind her.

'This is my friend Sonny,' she said.

He nodded, surveyed the beach over her shoulder, as if he were searching for somebody.

'Come in for a moment, out of the wind.'

Inside it was gloomy, the intermittent sunlight failing to reach the interior through the grimy panes. The gusts buffeted the walls, calling down the chimney, whispering through the floorboards, and Sam was reminded again of a ship's cabin, lurching in a gale. Alastair retreated to the kitchen.

'No tea for me, thank you,' Sonny said. He stood by Alastair's crate-top mortuary of bird wings and skulls, looked down at the collection with obvious disgust. Or perhaps it was dread. She was drawn to the desk. The test tube rack contained three glass vials filled with a mouldering greenish semi-liquid substance.

Alastair emerged, holding mugs of tea, glanced at Sonny. He retreated into a corner of the room. Alastair tipped his head to one side as he handed Sam her cup. 'Did your boyfriend turn up in the end then?'

'He went to stay with friends,' she said. She tried to sound offhand, not too concerned, didn't want to give too much away. 'It was a misunderstanding after all.'

'Oh right,' Alastair said. His features dropped, puzzled,

realigned themselves. There was an awkward silence that Sam could not decipher. She searched for a safe topic of conversation, a route to the information she wanted, and pointed at the test tube rack on his desk. 'Is that some sort of alchemical experiment?'

He nodded, produced a packet of Rizlas, rolled as he talked. 'One of the letters from John Allin in the archive had some details of his research lab. He had these...'

'Test tubes?' Sam suggested.

'Flasks.'

'Are you hoping to make some gold?'

He snorted. 'I don't think it's likely. Although, gold would come in handy right now. No. I'm just...' He stared out the window. 'I suppose sometimes your life starts... going into negative, a downward descent.'

'When the gold turns to shit,' she said.

'Exactly. What was it you said? Reverse alchemy. Yeah, that's it. When you reach a low point, feel like you're cursed and you have to try and turn your life around, one way or another. Twelve steps. God. Drugs. Whatever it takes.' He waved his hand at the test tube rack. 'This is my therapy. I thought I'd give it a go, see if I can get myself out of the slough by concentrating on Allin's experiments. It gives me something to think about, a ladder, a way of reaching a better place.' His voice was maudlin. She wondered what had happened to make him so depressed.

'What is in the test tubes anyway?' She wanted to sound upbeat. It seemed to do the trick.

'Different kinds of plant life. One of Allin's letters has all the instructions – how to set up your own alchemical laboratory, notes on ingredients and methods. Collect the plants, heat them up, and leave them to brew.'

He handed her the spliff he'd rolled, lifted a cork-stoppered tube from the rack, swished it in the air. More yellow than green, fizzing, sparkling.

She toked and said, 'You can see why Allin might have thought he could make gold out of that. What is it?'

'Nostoc commune. A cyanobacterium. It used to be called witch's butter, or star jelly because it's only visible when it swells up after rain, so people thought it came down from the skies when it poured. It's a strange plant, a survivalist organism. Radiation doesn't kill it – which makes it a very suitable inhabitant of Dungeness.'

He shook the test tube again; the yellow matter swirled and she glimpsed Luke's face in the phosphorescent fronds. She narrowed her eyes and his image disappeared, replaced with her own reflection, coloured golden by the test tube's contents, distorted by the curve of the glass – a deviant angel.

'Where did you find the star jelly?' she asked.

He nodded at the floorboards in the far corner, behind the desk. 'There's a trapdoor and a space underneath.'

'Oh. A space under the floorboards.' She sensed she'd found a thread to pull. She pulled on the spliff, exhaled a cloud of smoke. 'Can I look?'

'Yeah. Sure. Why not.'

She followed him across the room, peered over his shoulder as he levered up the boards to reveal an empty cavity, a shallow grave.

'Do you think it's an old smuggler's store?' She wasn't sure she'd managed to make the question sound innocent.

'Possibly. I don't keep anything down there, though.'

He lowered the trapdoor.

She said, 'I suppose everybody in this area was involved in smuggling once, one way or another.'

Alastair walked over to the window. Sonny stepped back when he neared him, watched him from a safer distance.

'Smuggling...' Alastair stalled, eyes on a container ship drifting along the far horizon. 'This place is a law unto itself.'

He twisted his ponytail around a bony finger; the weak sunlight glinted on the steel strands among the black and deepened the lines in his olive skin.

'People romanticize the smuggling now – the Hawkhurst Gang, Doctor Syn – but I would imagine the smugglers were terrifying thugs and most of the inhabitants around these parts were shit scared of them. People didn't always have much choice in the matter,' he said. 'You find yourself in a situation you can't escape. You don't necessarily want to be part of it, but what can you do?'

He swung round, hand groping for a spliff. She passed it to him and asked, 'Do you think there is much smuggling along this coastline nowadays?'

The question unnerved him. He tugged on the roach, inhaled, exhaled, obscured his face with a cloud of smoke and then he coughed, wheezed, spluttered, reddened. 'Oh god, I need my aspirator.' He scrabbled in his pocket for the blue lifesaver, sucked, pressed and inhaled deeply. Removed the aspirator, toked on the roach again, coughed, switched back to the aspirator. Sam watched him with alarm, and was relieved when he stubbed the spliff and his breathing became less laboured. She assumed his asthma attack had closed down the conversation, but then he pointed out the window in the direction of the lighthouse, and the research station.

'I saw a boat pulled up on the shingle the other day.' He frowned. 'It might have been the day you were down here on the beach.'

'You mean that Saturday?'

'Yeah.' He hesitated. Backtracked. 'I'm not very good on time. But I do tend to notice the boats around here. This one was small. Room for a couple of people in the cabin. Strange thing... the boat.'

The boat. She dimly recalled he had mentioned a boat before, although she couldn't remember exactly what he had said; she hadn't registered it as an important detail at the time.

She asked, 'What was the strange thing about the boat?'

The room was silent, a break in the wind's nagging.

'It was a ghost boat.'

'A ghost boat?'

'A smuggler's boat. When you know what to look for, you can spot them. Sometimes it's the vibe they give off, the air of secrecy, but I recognized the lines of this one because I've seen similar boats before. I reckon it was purpose-built with a double hull and a large void between the two skins for storage.'

She scratched her neck. 'Did you see anybody on board?'

Alastair shook his head, wheezed alarmingly again, pulled on the aspirator, eyes wide, face sucked in like Munch's scream, lined and petrified. He inhaled, exhaled. 'I wouldn't ask too many questions around here. People mind their own business.' He dragged his foot along a faint chalk mark on the floorboards – the line of a pentagram. 'There's a story they tell here about an informer who was captured by the smugglers,' he said. 'They hacked his body to bits and distributed the pieces across the marsh. On nights lit by the full moon, his ghost can be seen wandering the ditches searching for his limbs.' He glared at her. 'You've got to be careful. You know what happens to witches if they are caught.'

She twitched. Death by fire, King James decreed, and none should be exempted from the flames. She didn't say anything, a sickness gurgling in her gut, wondered what he was getting at.

'You have to control your powers, if you want to stay out of trouble.'

Was that a warning or a threat? She sensed Sonny fidgeting behind her. He coughed, and Alastair looked his way, suddenly conscious of his presence. His eyes locked on Sonny's face.

Sonny said, 'What is it?' His voice had a timid edge – a child not wanting to ask their parent when they would be back in case the answer was never. He didn't want to die alone. She moved closer to him.

'Can you see something?' Sonny asked.

Alastair nodded. 'I can see the shadows chasing you.' His voice was flat.

Sonny didn't react, petrified, unable to move, pinned on Alastair's gaze. She had to rescue him, she couldn't stand to see him so disturbed.

'We'd better go now.' She checked her watch with an exaggerated arm movement. 'It's later than I thought. Thank you for the tea.' She paused, reluctant to let any lead slip. 'If we are passing this way tomorrow, perhaps we could drop in and see you again.'

Alastair shrugged. 'Perhaps.' He held the door open for them. 'Channel it,' he said as she passed. 'Focus on the barn owl.'

She headed up the shingle, aiming for the Land Rover, trampling through parched clumps of valerian. The beach was devoid of life. A couple of Arctic skuas circled overhead, scavenging for dead matter. The wind hustled, carrying grit and discarded greasy chip wrappers. Sonny kicked at the pebbles as he walked. 'He freaked me out.'

'Don't take any notice of all his stuff about shadows catching up. It's all an act with him.' She didn't sound very convincing.

'And what about the things he said about you and your powers?'

'Do you really think I'm a witch?'

'No,' he said. 'Well...'

'Well what?'

'You seem to be quite good at putting spells on people.' He put his hands in his pockets. 'Or perhaps you are the one who has been enchanted.'

They passed a dilapidated fisherman's cottage, reflections of a thousand clouds scudding across its shattered window panes. A crow crossed their path, flying backwards in the strengthening wind. They reached the Land Rover.

Sonny said, 'I need a smoke.'

He searched his jacket for his fags and his lighter, cupped his hands to shield the flame from the gusts. He cracked his jaw, created a ring which held for a second before it was blown away. Sam watched it disperse while she attempted to make sense of what Alastair had told her – what he hadn't told her. The strange boat he'd seen on the Saturday that Luke went missing. The warnings about the gruesome fate of informers. He had seen something he wished he hadn't seen, a smuggler's boat dragged up on the shingle, a person with the boat doing something dodgy. And he was worried that whoever he spotted on board had seen him watching, and would come after him if anything was said. Had Alastair seen Regan? Had she sent the heavies round to see him?

The clouds scudded across the sky, covered the sun, cast the beach in shadow. She leaned against the Land Rover's door, slid down, gave in to her sense of despondency, crouched on the shingle, arms around her legs, face against her knees. She didn't want Sonny to see her cry. She lost herself for she wasn't quite sure how long. He sat beside her.

'My father's dead. Dave's dead. I worry I'll never find Luke,' she said. 'I can't deal with all this loss.'

'Loss. It's part of life. Nothing lasts for ever. A rainbow. Shooting stars. Some kinds of love.' He paused. 'Sometimes the most beautiful things are fleeting.'

'I don't see beauty. I only see dead men.'

He put his hand on her arm gently. 'Time blunts the edges.'

In the distance along the shore, the lone fisherman stood and waded into the waves. She wondered how far he would go.

'I want Luke back,' she said.

She kept her eyes on the Channel.

'I think you'll find Luke,' Sonny said. There was an unspoken *but* to his sentence. She decided not to ask. The fisherman was waist-deep in the water as the Land Rover pulled away.

CHAPTER 17

THEY LEFT THE shingle ridges of Denge, the silver lakes of Wallands, and headed into the green sea of Romney Marsh. No sign of the black Audi. He pulled up on the verge by the bridge.

Sonny said, 'I'm going to find somewhere less obvious to park the Land Rover.'

She dug out the gear from the back – sleeping bags, camping stove, saucepan, bag of coffee, biscuits – and crossed the bridge to the meadow. Pools of brown water shimmered among the grass, black clouds of midges hanging above. A heron stood guard over the ditch, its stick legs mirrored in the water, undisturbed by her efforts to drag the camping gear across the sodden field. The rain had given the vegetation a virulent potency; she had to beat back the brambles and deadly nightshade as she tramped across the mound. Nobody, she decided as a stinging nettle whiplashed her arm, had followed this path since the last time she was here. She glanced up at the hut, saw a shadow through the glassless window. She froze, skin prickling. Luke? Jim? A blackbird twittered. She unlocked her limbs, flung herself through the doorway, eyes flicking around the cramped interior of the ruin, as if anybody could possibly hide in one of its four corners. Empty. The willow leaves rustled. Her hand went to her penknife – though she knew it was only the breeze – and found the comfort of its smooth surface. She had mislaid her penknife a few weeks previously and had been distraught. Luke had bought her a replacement, a belated birthday present, and had given it to her the last time they had slept in the Lookers' Hut. The weekend before he had gone missing – the first proper summer weekend of the year. Hot and sunny, Dungeness a riot of yellow and purple, broom and bugloss, the shingle radiating the heat, the power station twinkling like a fairytale castle. Luke had cast a line, caught a sea bass. They had grilled it over the flames of a makeshift beach fire, then retired to the Lookers' Hut, lay on the blackthorn mound and watched the sky fade from coral to crimson and indigo. That was when he had given her the knife. She had been touched by the present – a reminder, he said, of the times they camped in the Lookers' Hut together. A knife to slay the bitter withies. She had only discovered the message engraved on the blade later, when she had returned to London and was alone. *Sam – love you. Luke*. She had been too coy to mention it to Luke when she saw him again. Didn't want to say thank you, make a big deal of it. Love you. Accepted it silently, mulled it over in her head, allowed the words to fill her with warmth.

She cradled the penknife in her palm and thought about the message Luke had left her on her answerphone. *Listen, there's something else… Dave*. Luke had been careful to shield her from his suspicions about Dave, she concluded. He wanted to protect her from danger, so he had followed up with Patrick Grogan by himself, driven down early to Dungeness, tried to keep her out of it. She gripped the penknife tightly.

Sonny appeared in the doorway, made her jump.

'I didn't hear you coming,' she said. 'How did you manage to creep up on me?'

'You've got to think like an animal, Sam, imagine you are being stalked and behave as if you are the prey. Your life depends on remaining hidden, not being heard or smelled.'

Now they were out in the open, exposed, he snapped into a different gear – bushcraft, military training. Jim had been the same, dealing with difficult situations with what could seem like curt authority when he was merely following the drill, concentrating on what needed to be done. Emotional disengagement in order to survive. She had rebelled against it, of course, yet she found it reassuring to see the same reflexes in Sonny. He assessed the interior of the hut.

'Do you think it's safe?' she asked.

'It's well camouflaged by the shrubs. You wouldn't spot it from the road. Does anybody else know about it?'

'I don't think so. I mean, nobody apart from Luke.'

Sonny gave her a questioning glance, filled her with unease and, for the first time in a while, she thought about the bone and the hair she had found in the Lookers' Hut the night Luke had disappeared. Dave had been curious about the odd objects, and she had thought he was just being Dave – with his idiosyncratic interests. All she had cared about anyway was that they weren't the remains of Luke. But Alastair's story about the informer, dismembered and his parts thrown across the marsh, had unsettled her. She shook her head, dislodged her concerns. The bone and the hair were irrelevant, field-walker's finds to be bagged, noted, labelled, examined then left in the bottom of a cupboard for decades.

'Let's find this pub,' she said. 'I could do with a drink.'

Hands feeding the wheel, right turn on to the main road, he nearly failed to clock the speeding bike and almost pulled out in front of it. The bike swerved around the Land Rover; the leather-clad biker leaning close to the handlebars glanced back over his shoulder as he passed, clocked her through the black visor of his helmet.

'Moto Guzzi,' Sonny said. 'Nice bike. It's fast but low – built for Italian shorties.'

An endless stretch of straight and narrow tarmac, boxed in by a dark green wall of maize spears, head height, blocking the view on either side. There weren't many places on the marsh where the far horizon was occluded. The Owler was invisible until they were right on top of it. One of those in the middle of nowhere pubs with a garden that attracted bikers and a police car with a breathalyser on the last Saturday night of the month when officers were trying to boost their charge stats. Start of the week though, the car park was more or less empty. Apart from a Moto Guzzi bike. And, in the far corner, a knot of men with grotesque blackened faces, eyes blinking white, lipless mouth holes, black ragged capes draped around their shoulders and top hats with pheasant feathers in the band. Sam blanched at the sight.

'What are those men?' Sonny asked. He swung the Land Rover into a parking space under a willow.

'Crow-men. Morris dancers from the dark side. I saw them at a May Day celebration in Hastings this year. Although, the first time I saw them was at a May Day fair with Jim when I was a kid.'

She shook as she spoke, the violence of the reaction surprising her; the memory filled her with dread and anger. She picked a fallen withy stem, slashed and sliced the midges clouding her vision.

The wind had dropped to nothing, allowed the sun's rays to penetrate, heated the warm afternoon into a muggy evening, purple clouds gathering above the Weald. In the still air, she could hear the creaking of the crow-men's leather boots as they moved into position – a rehearsal, she presumed. They were a hefty crew, intimidating with their blacked-up faces. She walked over to watch. The musicians started playing – the drum and bone, the squeezebox, the banjo and a leather-jacketed man hitting the spoons against his thigh. The crow-men didn't dance. They stomped, whacked the ground with their wooden staves, then clashed the clubs together in the air over their heads. As the beat of the music quickened, their movements became more manic, violent. She stood mesmerized, unable to shift, flinching each time the wooden clubs were thwacked in the air, jolting with the thud of their boots on the ground. The music stopped.

'That's it, boys,' the banjo-man shouted.

The dancers put their truncheon-wielding arms down, formed a line and, without another word or smile, marched out the car park and down the road. Left the spoon-man standing. He collected the crash helmet that had been placed on one side of the car park, and entered the pub.

'The English do some strange things,' Sonny said.

Inside the pub was dead. The spoon-beating Moto Guzzi owner was playing the slot machine. An old-fashioned one-armed bandit. He pulled the handle and set the dials spinning, lights flashing, music twanging, then pulled the handle again. And again. The noise put her on edge, made her nerves jangle with the Chinese water torture of its repetitiveness. She checked the bar's gloomier recesses for Patrick, but he wasn't there. They sat in a corner and waited. They had arranged to meet at six, and he was already ten minutes late. She fidgeted.

'We shouldn't have agreed to meet him here,' she said. 'We should have insisted on meeting him at his parents' place.'

'I doubt if it would have made much difference. If he wants to show up, he will.'

'What if something has happened to him? The men in that Audi obviously knew his address.'

Sonny shrugged, eyes fixed on the biker playing the slot machine. She checked her watch again. Six fifteen. The bar door creaked. A bespectacled, dun-haired, mid-height man walked in. Patrick. Except he looked thinner than she remembered, frailer, as if some process of osmosis had blurred his boundaries, colour leached, left him diminished. She caught sight of his yellow-striped Adidas trainers and a lump formed in her throat. They reminded her of Dave. Football buddies, fellow Aston Villa supporters, five-a-side mates. He caught her eye and walked over to their table without a smile.

'I can't stay long.'

God, he was jumpy. He sat on the chair nearest the door, didn't bother to think about a drink, fished in his jacket, pulled out a packet of fags, fumbled, flicked his Bic, flame dancing with the trembles of his hand, fingernails bitten ragged. He gave Sonny a nervous glance. Sonny smiled, but he clearly failed to reassure. She wished she had told Sonny to stay in the Land Rover. She'd become used to him, learned to block out the hard man exterior.

'Sonny is a friend of mine.'

Patrick nodded, puffed on his cigarette. Sonny had the sense to shrink into his seat, reduce his presence.

'Are you OK?' she asked Patrick. Stupid question.

He shook his head. 'Dave's death has done my head in.'

'It's done mine in too.' Better to start with Dave, try to build up a connection, rather than rushing straight in to questions about Luke. She had to be cautious; she didn't know the details of Dave's involvement and there was a possibility that Patrick had been dragged into the caesium smuggling craziness.

Patrick said, 'He called me the night before he died.'

'Did he?'

She recalled the conversation she had overheard at Dave's house. *Hi, Dave here. Sorry to call so late, mate. I just wanted a quick chat.* So he was calling Patrick.

'He called me late. I was in bed and I couldn't be bothered

to get up. I should have done, I realize now. But I didn't. He left a message.'

'Right.'

'It was one of a series. We kept missing each other on the phone.'

She knew the feeling. Her life was being driven by a series of missed phone calls. Messages picked up too late. Phantom voices on an answering machine.

'I listened to the message in the morning. It said something odd had turned up.' He glanced over his shoulder, then stared at her hard, as if she should know what he was getting at. 'And it made me edgy.' He squeezed the filter of his fag between his finger and thumb, sucked the nicotine out, stubbed the butt in the ashtray.

'I know Dave likes you,' he said. 'Liked you,' he added.

'I always got on well with Dave. He was like a brother.'

Patrick smiled for the first time since entering the pub. 'Yes, that's what Dave said. You treated him like your brother.' She imagined Dave complaining about her to Patrick. Her cheeks burned, but her embarrassment seemed to put Patrick more at ease.

'Why did his message make you edgy?' she asked.

'It's a long story, goes back a few months.'

He reached for another fag.

She risked a prompt. 'Was it something to do with the lab?'

'The lab's security.'

She attempted to sound surprised. 'Is there a problem with security there then?'

He glanced over his shoulder, fiddled with his lighter. 'Yes. Well, there isn't a lot of security at the lab – why would there be? It's only a research lab; just a load of geeky environmental scientists, that's all.'

'So what's the problem?'

'Well, there's always one person on the site to protect the equipment and also to oversee the security of the hazardous materials. A security guard-cum-caretaker. The guards are provided by this security firm. There's a roster. So they come and go. You might see one guy a few times and then never again, it's that sort of work. Some of them are OK, some of them sit in the office smoking and reading *The Sun* and I don't really notice them.' His words were gushing out now, as if he had turned the tap and couldn't stop the flow. 'There was this one bloke, though, lovely he was. Colombian. Miguel. He was working at the lab until about six months ago. We were friendly. I speak Spanish. We had a bond. Then one day, sometime around the beginning of the year, he told me there was a new security guard on the roster, and he suspected he was doing some kind of fiddle. Vince, this guard is called.'

The slot machine kerchinged. Patrick jumped, lowered his voice.

'Miguel had noticed that Vince always worked the day there's a delivery from Amersham – on the first Tuesday of every month. Tomorrow, in fact.'

'What do they deliver?'

'Radioactive materials for research purposes.'

She screwed up her face. 'You mean like caesium 137?'

'Exactly.' He scowled.

'I know about caesium because of Dave's research,' she explained.

'Of course. Dave always said you were a closet egghead.'

She laughed and then she said, 'So you have caesium 137 delivered regularly?'

'Yes. By van.'

'Jesus. That sounds a bit mad, having radioactive materials being driven up and down the motorway in a van.'

'We are licensed. So is the delivery company. And the amounts they deliver aren't particularly large. Just the vials we need for the kind of experiments that Dave carries out. Used to carry out.'

'Right.' Dave's special subject, she reminded herself, caesium 137 contamination of water and its impact on marine environments.

'Anyway, this guard Vince always did the long late shift on the Amersham delivery day. So he would be there in the afternoon when the delivery was made and stay there for the evening until somebody came to relieve him around one a.m. And one night Miguel was on the shift after Vince. Miguel turned up for work early, mainly because he lived in a shitty place so he might as well be at the research station as hanging around in a cramped room. And when he arrived, he saw somebody he didn't know in the loading bay. He went over to investigate. Then suddenly Vince appeared, looking menacing, told him to fuck off and come back later when his shift started. Miguel questioned him, and Vince told him everything was under control and if Miguel knew what was good for him he'd better keep his mouth shut.'

'Did Miguel say what the stranger in the loading bay looked like?'

She could guess the answer.

'Actually he did. It was a woman.'

'A woman?'

'Yes. Tall, black hair.'

Regan, of course. In some ways it was almost a relief to find the pieces fitted.

'Miguel asked me what he should do about it. Because the

intruder was a woman, I think I was less concerned than I would have been if he'd seen a man. I thought maybe it was Vince's girlfriend, something like that. I was more worried for Miguel's sake. I was never entirely sure of his immigration status to be honest – he'd hinted a couple of times he'd come in on a student visa and never left, so I knew he had to be careful about drawing attention to himself. I told him I'd do a bit of digging around, but I didn't really bother.'

Patrick fiddled with his B&H packet.

'I spoke to Miguel again a couple of days later. He told me then that the manager of the security company had pulled him aside for a chat, said Vince had reported him for stealing lab equipment. So then Miguel had reacted and spilled the story to the manager about seeing Vince in the loading bay with this woman. I thought holy shit, it didn't sound good. In fact it sounded as if, whatever was going on, the manager and Vince were in it together. But I didn't want to scare Miguel. He was already nervous, and he had an accident with a vial of caesium, not being careful enough, forgetting to follow the proper procedures. Shortly after that, he went missing.'

Sam's gut lurched, knotted in anticipation of the inevitable ending of the story.

'Yeah. He didn't come into work. He'd been absent for about three days. We were wondering what we should do about it, because we didn't have any names or numbers of families or friends, when the police turned up. They said he was involved in a smack smuggling gang, and implied he had probably had a bust-up with some dealer or another, gone back to Colombia. On the run.'

Her mind raced, going through the connections.

'Well, it's possible, isn't it? Maybe he was involved in drug smuggling.'

Patrick tutted. 'Come on. Not all Colombians are drug dealers. Miguel was a country boy, trying to earn a bit of money to send back to his family. But the copper in charge of the investigation was insistent that it was all down to Miguel's drugs links, so I began to assume that he must have some information on him.'

'What was the cop's name?'

'Superintendent Crawford. Are you OK?'

She must have paled. 'Yes, I'm fine.' She wanted to retch. 'And did you do any more digging around after Miguel went missing?'

Patrick agitated the wheel of his lighter with his thumb.

'I decided to have a quick look at the accounts. I knew a bloke in Amersham and I was able to get him to look at the delivery log and check it against our log. And nearly every time a delivery has been made over the last six months, one vial of caesium 137 that has left Amersham in the lab consignment hasn't been recorded in the research lab log.'

'So some vials have gone missing?'

He nodded.

'I've been sitting on this information for a while. Wondering what to do with it. Not sure who to tell. But of course I discussed it with Dave a while back.'

'What did he say?'

'Well, you know what Dave's like. He's a bit dismissive. Gave me the you're a paranoid fantasist sort of response. I'm a scientist. I don't believe in all that conspiracy theory stuff.'

'I've had that kind of response from him before as well.'

'Good old Dave.' He sniffed, wiped his nose on the back of his hand. 'So I was beginning to think I was overinterpreting, misread the figures. Or misunderstood them. And then this bloke Luke contacted me and I agreed to meet him.'

She willed herself not to react.

'Do you know him?' Patrick asked.

She hesitated, perturbed. She could understand why Dave wouldn't have bothered to point out that Luke was her boyfriend, but she assumed Luke would have mentioned her in his conversation with Patrick; his girlfriend Sam, their joint protest project. Although, not if he was trying to protect her. She needed to protect herself too, elicit information without giving anything away.

'I knew him vaguely,' she said.

Patrick said, 'I met him on Saturday morning. The Saturday before Dave died.'

She nodded, reluctant to ask too many questions and sound desperate for information.

'He told me he had asked Dave for contacts who could give him a bit of background about the nuclear industry. I used to be a technician up at Amersham, running the research reactor.'

She smiled, hoping her expression covered her edginess.

'I liked him, this Luke, he was easy-going. Charismatic. Not in an intimidating way, more in a way that made you want to be his friend. I told him what I've just told you, I don't know why, it was good to have somebody I could talk it through with, I suppose, and, like I said, he seemed decent.'

Exactly. Luke was that kind of a person – decent. But not a pushover.

'I told him I'd discussed it all with Dave, and we had a bit of a laugh about him and his dismissive ways.' His face fell. 'It was only afterwards, when Luke had gone, that I started to worry about how much I'd told him.'

'Oh.' She couldn't think how else to respond without giving away her suspicion that Dave was involved in all this somehow and Luke had been on his case.

'I sat on it, though, told myself I was being paranoid. Then when I went to work on Monday, I had this feeling I was being followed. Nothing definite, just this sense there was a car behind me. And in the evening, the same car I had seen in the rearview mirror was parked across the road from my house. It was intimidating.'

'What kind of car?'

'An Audi. Black.'

She picked up a beer mat, twiddled it between her fingers, caught a glimpse of the oppressive thunderclouds through the bar-room window.

'So when I listened to Dave's message on Tuesday morning, saying something odd had come up, it really put the wind up me.' He kneaded his fist against his palm. 'I was sure it was something to do with the research lab. I called him back after I'd listened to the message. But he wasn't in. So I left him a message on his answering machine. I told him I'd met Luke and I'd mentioned the security guards.'

She pictured the red light flashing on Dave's empty answering machine, the shredded cassette tape she had found in Bane House.

'And then Dave called me back later. But I wasn't there. So he left me another message. And I didn't get that one…' She could see the tears in his eyes. 'Until after somebody had phoned the lab and told us Dave was dead.'

She wanted to cry too. She told herself to focus.

'What did Dave's second message say?'

His eyes danced, landed on Sonny, returned to her face.

'I don't want to hang around here. Maybe you can come over to Rye tomorrow and we can talk some more then.' She understood – he wanted to speak to her alone. Sonny was staring straight ahead, his head outlined against the window, and behind, the black dots of crows chasing a raven across the clouds. She wondered whether she should ask Sonny to go and walk around the car park.

'Miguel,' Patrick said. 'Lovely bloke. So was Dave.' 'I know.'

Patrick glanced over his shoulder, rummaged in his pocket, shuffled along the pub bench until their legs were touching, pushed something under the table, into her hand, fear marking his face.

He whispered, 'Here, have it. I want rid of it.'

She felt the hard edges in her palm.

He said, 'I've taken a couple of weeks' sick leave from the lab, and I'm going to stay with a friend in Shropshire. Maybe I'll see if there's any work going while I'm there. It's not difficult for me to find work. I'll sell the house in Lydd. It's dead round here anyway.'

He stood before she had a chance to reply.

'See you tomorrow then. Call me in the morning and we can talk some more.'

He zipped his windcheater. She didn't want to let him go without getting the full story, searched for a way of extracting more information about Luke, but she couldn't find the right words to reassure, make him stay.

'Only one good bit of news,' he said. 'I got a postcard from Miguel a few days ago, saying he's back in Colombia with his family. So at least I know he's alive.' His mouth pulled into a sad smile. 'Bye.' He walked away.

'Bye,' she said.

Storm light cut across the bar-room floor as he opened the door. And then he was gone. She heard the engine revving, checked through the window, watched the red hatchback leaving the car park. She glanced down at her hand. She was holding a micro-cassette – the tape from Patrick's answering machine. She slipped it into her pocket.

'Let's go back to the Lookers' Hut,' she said.

Sonny stuck a fag in his mouth, flicked his Zippo, the flint sparked blue, puffed. 'Crawford's a tough cop,' he said.

It sounded like the beginning of a conversation and she waited for him to elaborate. He took another drag, cracked his jaw, puffed a ring. She watched it rise and disperse. And it was only then that she realized the fruit machine was no longer jangling.

CHAPTER 18

PAST THE RUINED church at Hope, right along the fast road, the maize stalks closing in around them, the sky storm-bruised purple. Her eye wandered into the field, drawn into the darkness between the green, the eyes of unknown creatures staring out at her. A peripheral lightning flash, the shriek of a magpie, drew her attention back to the road.

'Shit.'

Sonny jammed his foot, brakes squealed, narrowly avoided a crunch. Further along – a quarter of a mile or so – a mushroom smoke cloud billowed. Her gut tightened.

'Must have been an accident.'

Sonny said, 'Look at the map, see if we can turn around and find a different route.'

'No. I want to see what's happened.'

The siren cut across the end of her sentence. The spinning blue light of a police car approached from behind, overtook, screeched down the wrong side of the road. Sonny reached for his fags. The maize shadows crept across the stationary traffic, the air heavy with petrol fumes. She leaned out the window. Open car doors, ratty people standing on the verge, arms folded, necks craned. A stream of cars travelling in the opposite direction passed by. Dried up. Drivers leaped back into cars, inched forwards. The police seemed to have the situation under control now, the alternating flow of traffic lanes smoother. They reached a panda car blocking their half of the road. The policeman directed them on to the other side, beckoned them forwards.

'Fuck,' she said.

'What?'

'A car's overturned. On its back, wheels in the air.' Like a beetle, unable to right itself, helpless.

'Colour?'

'Red.'

'Bodies?'

The ambulance had partially blocked the view, but she could see the splayed feet against the roadside. One trainer on. Adidas, yellow stripes. One trainer missing. How did he lose the trainer? It was the details that hit, made her want to cry. Had he forgotten to tie the laces? If she had spotted an undone lace as he was leaving the pub, pointed it out to him, delayed him a few minutes while he tied his shoe, could she have stopped the chain reaction, produced a different outcome? Or perhaps his fate had been decided days, months, years ago, written in the stars. She averted her eyes from the crash, concentrated on the road ahead; a single black tyre skid mark slashed across the tarmac.

'Motorbike,' Sonny said. He put his foot on the accelerator. 'Travelling in the opposite direction, came round the corner, swerved in front of him, forced him off the road at speed, I would guess.'

'Shit.' It was all she could think to say. Shit. Shit. Shit.

They drove on in silence. Her limbs were shaking. Tension. Shock. Her sight was blurred, fugue state, slipping, floating free, up above, a magpie looking down on the maize, emerald green sliced by the grey road, black rectangle of Patrick's upside-down car, yellow Adidas stripes on red stretcher sticking out from under brown blanket, white oblong of ambulance leaving, blue light flashing.

'Sam, I said let's go.'

She jolted, looked around, had one of those where am I moments, then managed to find her bearings – realized Sonny had parked the Land Rover off the road, in a small copse, a couple of fields away from the Lookers' Hut. They walked back along the lane, silent except for the warning calls of blackbirds, the rooks cawing, Sonny on alert for signs. A swan came into land on the ditch as they crossed the bridge into the meadow; a doomed DC10 with its long neck and bulky rear, flap, flap, splash as its undercarriage scraped the water, skidded to a halt. She was relieved to reach the shelter of the safehouse, she squatted, fiddled with the camping stove, saucepan, water bottle, in need of caffeine, hands trembling.

She couldn't think about Patrick's death. She had to block it out. Too late to do anything for Patrick. She had to focus on what could be done. *Stayin' alive*. Finding Luke. She said, 'Patrick gave me the cassette from his answering machine. It's a shame we can't listen to it.'

Sonny patted his jacket pocket. 'We can,' he said. 'I brought the Dictaphone with me.'

He fumbled with the tape recorder, removed and handed her the tape from Heaven, the one of the American, Stavros, revealing his nutty Afghanistan plan. She dropped it in her bag. He inserted the cassette that Patrick had bequeathed her, pressed play. The tape crackled. A couple of messages from mates. Meet you in the pub at eight. Wanna play a match tonight? We're one man down. And then the first message from Dave; the conversation Sam had overheard from the bedroom in Skell.

'Hi, Dave here. Sorry to call so late, mate. I just wanted a quick chat. Something slightly odd's come up. It's... I wanted to talk it through with you. Call us tomorrow if you are around. Cheers, mate. Ta-ra.'

She leaned over, pressed pause. It was hard to hold back the tears. She wanted to rewind the tape, loop around, make it come out differently this time, make it better. She pressed play. The tape crackled again. Second message from Dave.

'Yeah, Patrick. Sorry I wasn't in when you called me back, mate. Just taken an early-morning stroll up to Flaxby Point. You remember Sam. Yeah, yeah, that Sam. My housemate Sam who thinks of me as her big brother.'

She pressed pause, closed her eyes, didn't want to look at Sonny. Recovered herself. Pressed play.

'Well, anyway I was calling you because Sam found this bone and a clump of black hair out on Romney Marsh.'

Pause button. 'Christ. I don't believe it. That was what he thought was odd – the bone and the black hair I found.' She pressed play again.

'Yeah, it made me think about the lab security guard, the Colombian who disappeared. The thing is – I dug the old Geiger counter out and the hair registered. I don't know whether it's possible. It's probably me being paranoid, but...' His voice tailed off.

She pressed pause again. 'Patrick said Miguel was so nervous he started having accidents in the lab. He could have contaminated himself somehow, wiped his hand on his hair.'

Sonny asked, 'How is the caesium stored anyway? Would it have been possible for Miguel to have contaminated himself?'

She racked her brain, her conversations with Dave, his papers she had read.

'It's stored in glass vials. Test tubes. And then those are placed inside lead casings to block the radiation. Presumably they have to handle the vials at some point. They must take precautions, but if he was anxious, maybe he got it wrong.'

Sonny nodded, pensively, absorbing the details. 'What does the caesium look like anyway?'

'It's liquid. I remember Dave telling me they put hydrochloric acid in it to stop the caesium particles sticking to the glass. So it has a yellow colour. Like piss.'

'Oh really? Golden?'

'Yes, yes, I think so.'

Caesium, contamination, Miguel, Patrick – thoughts piling in, making her hyperventilate. She took a deep breath, composed herself, lifted her head, pressed play, heard Dave's voice again.

'Yeah, funny you should mention Luke. The thing is... this morning, when I was walking up to the Point, I saw this boat passing close to the shore. I could have sworn... anyway, let's talk about it later. I'm seeing ghosts. Ha-ha. I'd better go. Speak later. Ta-ra.'

The tape hissed. End of message. No more Dave. Sonny lit a cigarette. She hadn't realized how dark it was until his Zippo cast a light, sent shadows leaping across the brick walls. She lay back on the ground, stared through the open roof to the indigo infinity above, eyes tracing the handle of the Plough while her brain tried to process Dave's message.

'Where did you find the bone and hair?' Sonny asked.

'There.' She flicked her hand towards the old hearth.

'You didn't mention finding them,' Sonny said.

'I thought they were some kind of shepherd's charm to stop the witches flying down the chimney.'

'Really?'

'Yes, really. Is that any less plausible than thinking they belong to a security guard who has had his finger hacked off because he's been unfortunate enough to catch somebody in the act of stealing radioactive caesium from a research lab?'

'You don't have to shout.'

Steam was rising from the saucepan on the camping stove. She pushed herself on to her hands and knees, crawled over to the stove, made herself a cup of coffee, stared into the steaming liquid, scryed for answers. There were none. Alastair's story about the informer hacked to pieces plagued her; the ghost searching the marsh for his dismembered limbs. The safehouse she had thought offered her protection now seemed like a trap, a charnel house, not only used by her and Luke but by the people who were threatening them – the drug and caesium smugglers.

She said, 'So they hacked off Miguel's finger as a warning shot. A punishment for blabbing. Sent him back to Colombia.'

Sonny said, 'They seem to be going beyond warning shots now.'

She pictured Patrick's feet, one trainer on, one trainer off.

Sonny continued, 'What I don't get is that your mate Dave doesn't sound like somebody who might hang out with a bunch of mad caesium smugglers. He sounds like a sensible bloke who is scared because he's no idea what's going on.'

Sam didn't reply, mulling over Dave's message in her head. Sonny was right, Dave sounded scared; the voice of somebody who sensed they were in danger, but had no clear grasp of its source. Poor bloody Dave. She stared at the ground, pictured the bone and the hair as Dave had left them, under the urn in his back garden with a note – 55 pluto. What had Dave been trying to tell her? She had assumed the 55 was a confession, an indication he had been drawn into the caesium smuggling. She'd got it wrong. Now it looked like he was simply trying to let her know what he had discovered when he ran a Geiger counter over the clump of black hair. Caesium. Or caesium 137 to be precise, a radioactive isotope. Gamma emitter.

'OK, I'm going out for a breather,' Sonny said. 'I'm going to look for some wood to burn before it gets too dark.'

She waited until she was sure Sonny was out of earshot, grabbed the Dictaphone, removed Patrick's cassette, placed it in her bag, rummaged in her pocket, dug out the micro-cassette that she had taken from her own answering machine, inserted it in the Dictaphone. Pressed play. Listened to the first message, the one from Luke she had carefully preserved. The last time she heard his voice.

'Sam. Are you there? Will you pick up? It's me. Luke.' Pause. 'Oh god, I hope you haven't set off already. Oh shit. Look, Sam. I'm so sorry about this mess. I have to go. Something has come up. I can't hang around here. Listen, there's something else... Dave...'

She pressed pause. She had assumed Luke was implying that he knew Dave was up to something dodgy, but now she had realized Dave was not involved in the smuggling, she had to think again. *Listen there's something else...* What was Luke hinting at? Perhaps the *something else* was the fact that it was Dave who had alerted Luke to the suspicions about the security guards at the lab in the first place. Perhaps Luke was about to tell her that Dave had given him Patrick's name, and Patrick was the contact he had met in Dungeness that morning. And then Luke had decided it was better not to give too much information away on the phone.

She pressed play again, listened to the end of the message. 'Don't worry, OK. Everything will be fine. Really. I'll call.' On the Dictaphone, the recording was clearer, Luke's voice sharper, every crackle more obvious. Higher-quality tape heads. She rewound. 'Everything will be fine. Really. I'll call.' She wasn't listening to the words this time, the background noises had caught her attention. The sudden interjection of wave and winds, the voice in the background. Not just a voice, but a word. *Come*. Then Luke replaced the receiver. 'Come.' Somebody talking to Luke. Had somebody opened the door and said *come on*? Was it a woman's voice? Rewind. Play. 'Come.' She bit her lip. Her stomach flipped, her eyes watered. Get a grip. Think. Work it out. She fondled the penknife in her pocket. *Sam – love you. Luke.* She attempted to reconstruct the events of that Saturday morning in Dungeness. Luke had spoken to Patrick. Patrick had given him the details about Vince the security guard, the caesium smuggling. Patrick had also told Luke about the woman with dark hair that Miguel had seen – and Luke had followed the lead to Regan. Perhaps Regan was hanging around in Dungeness that Saturday morning and Luke had chatted to her, tried to squeeze some information out of her, had more success than Sam had done in engaging her, but then he'd bumped into an Audi, seen her enforcers, realized the full extent of what was going on, the danger he was in, and gone into hiding.

That all made sense. But what didn't make sense now was *your guy down on the coast* – the man Regan mentioned in Heaven. Sam had supposed Regan was talking about Dave, and now she knew it couldn't be him. So who was it? Alastair with his asthma attacks didn't fit the bill. He had seen something, but he wasn't part of it. She cast her eye around the Lookers' Hut, searching for anything that gave her a lead. Her eyes alighted on Sonny's packet of Marlboro and his Zippo. Sonny – what was he really up to? She conjured up an image of Sonny's forearm, the crosses marking his hits. Two new pen and ink crosses – the most recent for Spyder, she was certain.

And the one before that? The cross she had first seen when they sat in the Portuguese café? Flint, the bent ex-cop. Sonny had killed Flint, the candy man; the man she'd seen at the fair, the man Jim had met in 1984, two weeks before his death, according to his diary. She'd half known it as soon as Harry had told her about the hitman with the halo, sussed it in her stomach. The distraction, the magician's trick; look above my head, don't remember my face: the haloed hitman was Sonny blowing his smoke rings. What had Harry said about Flint? He'd had to leave the Force because he'd been caught doing deals with the gang who stole a load of gold bullion and were trying to convert it into drugs. Flint obviously knew all about the southern drug smuggling networks. Perhaps he had also found out about the caesium, and Stavros had despatched a hitman to sort him out. She remembered the phone call she'd overheard; Sonny talking to some unseen person while she stood outside her house on the pavement. *You've got to hold off. I need more time.* Was Sonny working for Stavros; was he one of Regan's enforcers, targeting anybody who got too close to the truth about the lab in Dungeness? Did that include her? Was she on Sonny's hit list?

The rustling of nettles made her jump. Sonny returned with a bundle of willow stems, stacked them wigwam style.

'I thought we could make a small fire now to cheer ourselves up.'

He ignited the kindling, poked, sent sparks flying. The magic of the fire, shared here with Luke so many times. The flames engulfed the wood, Sonny's face glowed red and gold.

'Do you think,' Sonny said, 'your boyfriend would go for a woman like Regan?'

She was startled by his question, the provocative tone.

'I don't understand what you are going on about.'

He stared at her and she could see the unnerving psychotic edge to his brown eyes, the potential for explosion. He cried a lot, especially after he had killed. He said, 'I mean, do you think she is Luke's type?'

She couldn't believe he was asking her that, what kind of a question was it? Why was he winding her up? She mustn't rise to the bait. Make light of it.

'You mean would Linda Goodman think they were astrologically compatible?'

Sonny didn't smile. 'No. I meant do *you* think she is his type.' He really was needling her. Sam's hand touched the feminist clenched fist badge she had pinned to her coat. The badge bothered her, prevented her from dismissing Regan as a total junkie loser.

'I would have thought Regan was more your type.'

'What do you know about me and my type?'

'I bet you go for reckless women. Women who remind you of your mother.'

Jesus, that was designed to hurt. Just about the most stupid thing she could have said, if she wanted to stay alive. She had to keep her fears to herself, hold on to her paranoia, her resurfacing doubts about Sonny.

He shouted, 'You know what I think? I think that hippy Alastair was right about you, you do have malicious powers. I think you are a bloody witch.'

She'd overstepped, pushed him too far. Now she had stirred him up, she had to calm him down. 'Sorry. That was a stupid thing to say.'

He wasn't about to be soothed. 'And what about your type? What's your type?'

'I go for men I can share ideas and interests with.' Stay cool, sound reasonable.

'What about Dave? Didn't you have a lot in common with him?'

Payback for making a dig about his mother. 'Dave was different.'

She didn't want to catch his eye, watched the embers mingle with the stars, the shadow of the barn owl circling. She had to block him, disengage, avoid a shootout she was bound to lose. She focused on the barn owl's shadow, let her mind travel upwards, and now everything was clear below; the receding flames of the campfire, Sonny's head, the sleeping bags, the rectangle of the safehouse walls, the oval of the shrub-covered mound. A movement caught her eye; she homed in on a tiny vole twitching, head twisted, fearful of her shadow. It pleased her, seeing the vole cower like that, scared, made her feel stronger, powerful. She could dive down and snatch it in her talons. She sat up, caught sight of the petrified vole as it scampered away, its tail disappearing through a crack in the red bricks. She rubbed her forehead; her brain felt fuzzy.

'Sam are you OK?'

'Yes I'm fine. So tomorrow night,' she said. 'We go to the research lab, talk to Vince the security guard. Find out what he knows about Luke.'

He sighed, as if he thought she was a trying child.

'You know, I really think it's better to wait for your mate Harry to sort something out, let him deal with Crawford and find out what's been going on with this file. Stay below the radar. Look what these guys did to Patrick. Dave. They are obviously psychos.'

'I thought you were a hunter,' she said. Testing him.

He poked the fire with a stick. 'I am.'

'Well, shouldn't we turn the hunt around? Go after them?'

'You're not even certain who "them" is.'

She didn't like the way he said that; the implication he knew something she didn't, but he wasn't going to tell her what it was. It drove her mad, frightened her.

'I'm going for a walk.'

'Where?'

None of his bloody business.

'Around the meadow.'

'Be careful, you don't want anybody to see you. If you hear a car or a bike, stay still, don't move until they've gone. Blend in. Make your body look like part of the landscape.'

She raised her hands above her head, palms together, balanced on one leg; the yoga pose. 'I'm a tree.'

'It's not a joke. You always joke at the wrong moments.'

'You'd better extinguish the fire,' she said. 'If anybody saw the smoke, it would be a giveaway.'

She made her way through the nettles; it was a relief to be on her own, in the fresh air. The grass squelched beneath her feet. The thunderclouds hanging over the Weald were edging closer, cut by blue flashes that strobe-lit the field. She walked north to the willow-lined ditch, the road beyond. The grey heron was night-fishing in the drain, waiting for a toad to make a false move. She walked along the edge of the channel until she came to a dip in the bank, slithered down the mud, and stood at the water's edge. Bulrushes towered above her head. Marsh frogs croaked. A lightning flash revealed the water boatmen paddling the pondweed. She dipped her index finger, swirled and licked the brackish water. A fat drop of rain hit the stream, dimpled the surface.

She scrambled back up the bank, heard a rumble; the rush of storm air barrelling down the ridge of the Weald. She could see it advancing – tugging at willows and brambles, blasting across the marshes. The gust hit the northern boundary of the meadow. The blackthorns and willows flapped, a mini tornado scudded across her path, a swirl of white elderflower and pink dog rose petals whisked around in the gusts, filling the air with an ominous sweetness. Behind the wind came the rain. Time to run. She started to trot, found herself caught in the headlights of a car crawling along the lane, beams illuminating the weeping willows, long shadows arcing. She squinted. Was the car black? Blue? Something inside danced, could it be Luke, searching for her? She changed direction, ran back to the field's border, hid herself behind a trunk, drooping withies brushing her face. The car decelerated, crept past her hiding place. Without thinking, she darted across the gap between her trunk and the next in line so she could get a better view. The vehicle braked, as if the driver had seen her movement in his rearview mirror. The possibility brought her to her senses. What was she doing? Of course it wasn't Luke – the car was a posh saloon not a hatchback. A Rover. At least it wasn't an Audi. The driver pulled on to the verge. For a moment she stood, paralysed, and then she dropped, slid from squatting to lying flat on the saturated ground, hardly daring to breathe, the rain pounding her back. She heard Sonny's voice in her head – blend in with the landscape. She pressed her body into the grass; she was a log, a willow, a bitter withy, hollow, dead. She heard the car door open, a pause, a cough, the faint patter of a man pissing at the side of the road, almost drowned out by the rain. Another door opened, then a voice. She recognized it instantly.

'Shit, it's a fucking sewer out here tonight.'

Crawford. She couldn't move.

'Coyle,' he said.

Her heart thumped. Had he spotted her?

'Bloody Coyle,' he continued. 'She must have realized we

were on to her and done a runner from the Vauxhall address. I'm sure she's in the vicinity.'

'What makes you say that?'

'Instinct. I can almost smell her. They were always coming down here, her and her Irish buddy. Hanging around the power station. As we know.'

He laughed and his sidekick snickered too.

'So she'll be around somewhere. We could flush her out.' He paused. 'Or we could leave her to her own devices, see if she manages to do something really stupid.'

There was silence then, apart from the beat of the rain, the rumble of the thunder and the palpitations of her heart. She wanted to vomit. She was too close to the cops, separated by a thin screen of withy stems, one of them only had to look in the right place at the right moment.

'Fucking Coyle. Like father like daughter, a pain in the sodding arse.'

The words winded her, caught her unawares. Crawford knew Jim. Was that unusual? Maybe all the cops in the Force knew each other, talked about each other. But Crawford not only knew Jim, his voice revealed he hated him. A lightning bolt hit the marsh and forced a wood pigeon out from between the willow trunks, cooing in distress.

'What was that noise?' Crawford asked. 'I saw something move out there in the field.'

'I can't see anything.'

'Pheasant, I think. Stupid bird. Bred to be killed. Should have brought my rifle. I could have done a spot of shooting.' There was a long pause. 'I could always use my pistol.'

The hairs on the back of her neck bristled, her insides dropped. She held her breath.

'I need a beer,' Crawford said.

She heard retreating footsteps, exhaled and dared to lift her head. Crawford looked round as he lowered himself into the passenger seat. Lightning flashed. She caught a freeze-frame glimpse of his face, a crescent-moon scar. She gasped and inhaled the scent of elderflower, dog rose, the sugary sweetness of candyfloss. She retched. He looked in her direction. Colourless eyes. She dropped her head, rammed her face into the grass, soil, petals, willed herself invisible. She felt his gaze searching, locked in a moment for eternity, watching, waiting. The car door slammed, the engine revved, the car dawdled along the road, its tyres sloshing on the surface water. She rolled over and lay on her back, oblivious to the drenching of the passing storm. All she could think about was the candy man, the face that had scared her all those years ago, the face that Jim had told her she should never forget. He was still alive. He was still chasing her. And he was a cop, but he wasn't Flint. The candy man was Crawford.

Ten minutes, twenty; she wasn't sure how long she lay there winded. The stars spiralled in the clearing indigo sky. A nightingale sang. She levered herself up, trudged through the meadow back to the Lookers' Hut.

'I was worried,' Sonny said. 'The storm passed right overhead.'

'It wasn't the storm that got me. There was a car.'

'And?'

She shook her head. 'Give me a minute. I need to get my breath back.'

She sat on the sodden ground.

'Who was in the car?' Sonny asked.

'Crawford.'

He removed a fag from his packet, lit it, inhaled, let the

smoke drift aimlessly from his mouth. His eyes were damp. She sighed, pulled her hand through her hair. 'Crawford's out to get me,' she said.

Sonny didn't reply.

'I mean, he's not just after me because he wants to talk to me about Dave's death and the gun and this supposed plot to hijack a bloody transporter of nuclear waste. He's not a straight cop trying to get to grips with a load of dodgy evidence supplied to him by Spyder. He's a psycho. He's after me. He wants me out the way.'

Sonny stubbed his fag on the ground. He stood. She wanted to pummel him with questions; she paused, trying to work out where to start.

'I'll go and check the field, patrol the borders,' he said. 'In case Crawford comes back.'

She nodded, sat there in the mud and cinders, rocking, trying to stay calm, stop her jaw from chattering. She hugged her shins, rested her cheek on her knee. She didn't care if Harry thought Crawford was a good cop doing a difficult job, tough but fair. Jim had told her that he was an evil bastard, that she should never forget his face. She hadn't, even though she had tried. Pushed it down, along with all those other memories of Jim's shadow life it was safer to forget. And now she'd seen his face again, and she was scared. He had chased her out on to the marshes, cornered her. He was after her. Why? Was she marked because she was Jim Coyle's daughter? Was it revenge, pursued beyond the grave, for some slight of Jim's she could do nothing about? The half-life of the dead undercover cop, contaminating his daughter. It had to be more than that. What was it Sonny had said when he had caught her out on the salt-marsh? *You don't always know what you know, but other people might.* Perhaps he was right; perhaps she was holding some piece of information about Crawford she didn't even know she had. But Crawford did. What could she possibly know about Crawford? She had only seen him once before, at a fair, holding a stick of candyfloss. It didn't make sense. There had to be some connection she was missing. Sam. Jim. Crawford. Flint. Patterns danced in front of her eyes – particles, petals, fractals, spirals – she could see them clearly, but she didn't know what they meant. All she knew was that she was running out of time; Crawford was after her. Perhaps the American and Regan were after her too. So many enemies closing in, was there anybody she could trust? She stuffed her cold hands into her pockets, touched the penknife, her token of love from Luke, and it gave her comfort.

CHAPTER 19

SHE WOKE WITH the sun on her face, hand still on her penknife, and Sonny sitting by her side. She had intended to stay up all night, but she must have dozed despite the intensity of her fears, her lingering doubts about Sonny. Perhaps she had been able to sleep because her mind had resolved to keep looking for Luke, whatever the risks. The dangers of doing nothing were now greater. She was no longer certain that Harry knew what or whom she was up against. She needed to find Luke, make sure he was safe from Regan and her heavy mob, and then they could deal with Crawford together. She took a deep breath, held it; in the stillness of the air she could hear the flap, flap of the rooks flying overhead.

Sonny had been busy while she slumbered. He had found a fallen willow tree, chopped off two slices for stools. He was perched on one drinking coffee. She sat up, eyed the short axe at Sonny's feet.

He said, 'You know, I think on the inside, people are like the trunk of a tree; the core is your heart, and every year you grow another ring. But where there is a childhood trauma, it marks the core. And then the scar tissue grows to cover it, and ever afterwards the rings of the trunk follow the lines of the scar.'

He pointed at the cut surface of the vacant trunk; the bark, the cortex, the sapwood, the heartwood. 'Look, you can see, the wood is scarred, but it's still growing; it's not rotten. The scarring makes it stronger.'

'That's a good way of putting it,' she said.

The problem she had with Sonny was that whatever her doubts, she couldn't help liking him. He had stuck by her, helped her. He passed her a mug of coffee. She felt the warmth in her hand, blew the steam across the surface of the black liquid, watched it evaporate and wondered whether she had the power to conjure a mist with her mind, draw the vapours from the water. She became conscious of Sonny observing her. He lifted the fag to his mouth, inhaled, cracked his jaw. A smoke ring wobbled and floated above his head, luminous in the morning sunlight, a burnished ring. And then it dissipated – his halo slipped. She wasn't so sure now, in the morning light, that he was working with the American and Regan, but she was certain he had killed Flint. She didn't care whether he confessed or not, she wasn't a witch-hunter. She wanted him on her side – pissing out, as Jim would have said, not pissing in. She wanted information that could save her life, and Luke's, so she had to take him for what he was rather than condemn him. Jim. Flint. Crawford. Sam. She needed to understand the connections.

She took a deep breath. 'Do you remember that newspaper cutting Harry gave me, the one about the ex-cop, the Westie, the old lady and the hitman with a halo?'

He rolled his eyes heavenwards.

She said, 'Flint. That was the name of the ex-cop who was shot.'

Sonny nodded to the sky.

'Harry told me Flint left the Force because there were rumours he'd been taking cuts from these bullion launderers who were trying to convert their stolen gold into drugs money.'

Sonny played with his Zippo, turning it in his hand, chucking it in the air and catching it.

She continued. 'Flint was working with Crawford at the time. Crawford was in charge of the laundering case. So he must have dealt with the corruption allegations against Flint.'

Sonny was still playing with his lighter; there was something irritating about his obsessive fidgeting, something niggled as she watched the Zippo spinning. Harry said Crawford was a good cop, but Jim had told her he was an evil bastard. Flint had been done for corruption, yet Jim had a meeting with him about something. It didn't add up. The Zippo glinted in the sunlight as it twirled through the air, pitched over and fell – like Alastair's alchemy vial, the bellarmine tipped upside down. Curse and counter-curse. Then it clicked. 'Oh god,' she said, 'I see it. He flipped it. Crawford flipped the accusation. That's what coppers always do. Flint was saying Crawford was bent, so Crawford turned the accusation on its head and accused Flint, discredited him, stirred up allegations of corruption, and he had to leave the Force. But then perhaps Flint wouldn't shut up, said he had some evidence.'

Sonny stood, pocketed his Zippo, stepped across to the doorway of the Lookers' Hut, scanned the surrounding meadow, returned, sat down on his willow trunk stool.

She formulated her question carefully, searching for the solid ground. 'Could it have been Crawford who ordered Flint's hit?'

'Crawford?' He dragged deeply on his fag butt, squeezed the filter between finger and thumb. 'A senior cop commissioning a hit? A superintendent the trigger man? He wouldn't be so stupid.' He exhaled smoke jets through his nostrils. 'And anyway, he doesn't have to commission, because he can engineer.'

'How would he do that?'

'He could use information.'

'What kind of information?'

'Names. Who is on the case. What they know. Who they are about to collar.'

She opened her mouth, furrowed her brow, then she said, 'Crawford is a mole. An informer. He leaks information that could provoke somebody else, one of his criminal contacts, to commission a contract on another cop or ex-cop. He issues a death warrant.'

'If they are about to expose him, then yes.'

'Like Flint?'

'Maybe.' Sonny nodded. 'But like I said, he wouldn't ever do anything directly. Leaks here and there. He nudges. He drops a name, twists an arm, pulls in a favour, prods a raw nerve, a fear, a debt – and then a deal is set in motion.'

'That's appalling.' Shafting your colleagues, lining them up for a hit, was about as low as you could go, she reckoned.

Sonny snorted, rocked. She gave him a quizzical stare. 'What's so funny?'

He stopped laughing. 'I'm surprised you are surprised. Your father was part of it, after all.'

He was right. Jim was part of it. She pictured the entry in Jim's diary. *Meet Flint 9 p.m.* The image of a candyfloss stick doodled underneath. And then she saw it, the point of the doodle. The meeting wasn't with the candy man – it was about the candy man. She was sweating, her hands clammy. 'Do you think Flint passed some information on to Jim about Crawford, and Crawford found out?'

Sonny closed his eyes, shook his head. 'I don't know.'

She said, 'But it's possible. And it's possible Crawford leaked some information about Jim, which he knew was almost certainly a death warrant.'

'It's possible.'

'Why didn't you tell me about Crawford?' she asked. 'Why didn't you warn me that he was a hit-engineering psycho?'

He locked his fingers together, twisted his hands, revealed his palms. 'I didn't know. Not for sure anyway. The hitman is at the bottom of the command chain, and doesn't always know who is at the top, especially if it's an indirect order. Somebody contacts you in a dingy bar, gives you the details. So I didn't know, I could only guess. I thought your guess was as good as mine. And anyway,' he said, 'sometimes it's safer not to know. Not knowing is protection. It's better to keep the walls in place.'

She remembered how he had lied about shooting Spyder, trying to keep her out of it.

He shrugged. 'Too much knowledge can be dangerous. As you've discovered.'

'Yes, but I don't know anything about Crawford. So why is he after me?'

Sonny said, 'You don't always know what you know.'

She rubbed her birthmark. 'Do you know what I know?'

'No. I don't.'

She wanted to cry – frustration, anger.

'I've only ever seen Crawford once before, when I was eleven.' Her voice quavered. 'It was ages ago. 1978. I was with Jim at a fair out beyond the burbs, in the criminal belt. You know, near the place where Jim was buried. Jim disappeared and I realized this man was staring at me. He tried to stop me leaving. Jim told me he was evil. That's all I know. It's nothing.'

'There must be some detail there that you don't realize is significant. But Crawford does.' Sonny shrugged. 'It's enough.'

Enough for Crawford to try to fit her up with a record on an MI5 terrorist index, discredit her even if he couldn't make the charges stick, have her permanently on a surveillance list?

Enough for him to engineer a contract on her? A crow landed on the broken wall of the Lookers' Hut, hopped along, wiped its beak against the red brick, cawed and flew away. Crow, bird of death. There were lots of them out here on the marsh. She thought about Sonny's phone conversation she had overheard in Vauxhall. *You've got to hold off. I need more time.*

She said, 'Sonny, do you always complete your contracts?'

He shook his head, reached for his Marlboro carton, flicked a fag in the air, caught it in his mouth, lit it and puffed. 'Sometimes I take a contract to stop anybody else from carrying out the hit.'

She took a slurp of coffee – tepid, but still comforting. She decided she would have to take his word for it; she didn't have much choice. She cradled the tin cup in her hands, concentrated, made it boil, steam rising, the particles swirling, forming a mist, spectral barn owl wings outstretched, soft feathers floating, filling the air.

Sonny's voice brought her back to her senses. 'Is there a church near here?'

'A church?' Churches weren't her thing, but she could do with a distraction, a reason to move; escape this Lookers' Hut that no longer felt safehouse with its bones and hair, ghosts and crows, the menaces of the smugglers. 'There's one not far from here. Thomas à Becket. We could get there without much danger of being seen if we cut around the fields.'

The sun warmed her back as she walked around the fields, picking their way across the ditches, the grass still wet beneath their feet. The hedgerows kept them hidden from any cars passing in the lanes.

'When you were back home, growing up in the Transvaal,' she asked, 'did you confess your sins to the pastor?'

'No. My sins have always been between my God and me.'
He plucked a dog rose from the brambles, twiddled it between
his fingers, let it drop. 'Confession to another person usually
ends in betrayal of one sort or another, I've found.'

The three-stepped brick church rose out of the grass and
mist; its humble appearance was touching – a lowly snail
looking up to its creator. The door was unlocked. The interior
was intimate yet open: white wooden boxed pews along the
walls of the short nave, a timbered roof that resembled the hull
of an upturned boat.

He walked to the chancel and knelt in front of the altar, the
Lord's Prayer and the eye of God looking down on him from a
painted screen. She opened a box pew, sat on a wooden bench
and contemplated the simple beauty of the church, the text
boards attached to the roof.

*'Be ye doers of the word, and not be hearers only, deceiv-
ing your own selves. James ch. 1 v 12.'*

The verse played on her mind and she wondered whether
she was a hearer only, guided by the voices in her head, the
recorded messages on tapes, deceiving herself. She reached into
her pocket, touched her penknife and torch for comfort.

'Will you come and pray with me?' Sonny asked.

Why not, she thought, even though she didn't believe in
God. At least, not the God of this church. She went and knelt
beside him.

'I don't know any prayers,' she said.

'We could recite a passage from the Bible.'

'To be honest, I don't know many Bible passages.'

'Ecclesiastes.'

'Yes, I know Ecclesiastes.'

They said the words together. 'To every thing there is a
season, and a time to every purpose under the heaven: A time

to be born, and a time to die; a time to plant, and a time to pluck up that which is planted; A time to kill and a time to heal; a time to break down and a time to build up; A time to weep, and a time to laugh; a time to mourn and a time to dance.'

He kept his head bowed and his eyes closed, and the low morning light through the church window shone on the tears rolling down his cheeks. He was right, she suspected, it was safer to know nothing than to live with difficult truths. She sensed he had an urge to obliterate himself, return to dust, unable to live with the things he had seen and done, and he wanted to find a church, recite the Ecclesiastes verses, not because he needed forgiveness or reassurance that there was a time to kill if God ordained it, but because he was preparing to die, the dark shadows engulfing him.

Early evening, they decided to approach the research station from the north, avoiding the roads and the coastline where, they agreed, Crawford was most likely to be watching for them. They found a disused track leading into the shingle wilderness between the beach and the marsh and left the Land Rover hidden in a clump of blackthorn.

Sonny tried one more time to dissuade her. 'I still think it's safer to sit tight, wait for Harry to deal with the file and sort Crawford out.'

'Yes, but Harry thinks Crawford is OK. A good cop.'

The thought made her shudder. How come nobody, not even Harry, could see through Crawford? He was like a plague-carrying rat that crept from house to house spreading infection; the bodies piling up around him, everybody blind to the culprit in their midst.

She said, 'Well, whatever Harry manages to do, I still have to find Luke and make sure he is safe.'

'OK. OK. I get it. But take the Firebird.' He rummaged in his rucksack, produced the pistol.

'I don't know what to do with it,' she said.

'Put it in the inside pocket of your overcoat.'

'No. I mean, I don't know what to do with it.'

'You do. I showed you.' He raised an eyebrow. 'I thought you were a natural.' He smiled and added, 'You just need to remember to take the safety catch off, that's all.'

She took the Firebird, even though she felt stupid with it, placed it in the pocket of her coat.

'Let's get moving,' Sonny said.

'Hang on. I want something else.'

She scrabbled around in the back of the Land Rover, located the Dictaphone with her answering machine cassette inside. She wanted the comfort of the recorded voices with her. Luke. Dave. Liz. She fumbled with the machine, flustered fingers unable to remove the tape.

'Come on.' Sonny was edging to go.

She gave up fiddling, closed the Dictaphone lid, jammed the machine into her coat pocket.

The stony desert stretched away before them; the sun beating down and the power station shimmering like a mirage in the glare. They didn't speak for a while; it was an effort to trudge across the pebbles. Cormorants squatted on their untidy nests, balanced on the topmost branches of willow trees that had been submerged in rain-filled gravel pits. They rested in a dip shaded by a stunted hawthorn. The hollow was littered with rusty sheets of corrugated iron, which might once have been somebody's makeshift shelter. A grass snake slithered away as she nudged the debris with her foot. They shared a bottle of water, some bread and cheddar.

'What's the plan then?' Sonny asked.

'Well, from what Patrick said, it sounds as if Regan comes just before midnight to pick up the caesium they've creamed off from the Amersham delivery. I think we should try and get into the research station before Regan shows up. Confront the security guard, Vince. Tease some information out of him. See if he knows anything about Luke.'

She sounded more confident than she felt.

'Let's call in on Alastair first though, and find out whether he's noticed anything going on, seen any more strange boats on the beach.'

The hot airlessness of the day brought mist at dusk. The humidity dispersed the light from the setting sun and filled the eastern horizon with a bloody haze. They neared the outlying fishermen's cabins and she focused on the mist, drew it closer with her mind, let its softness curl and wrap around them. By the time they were directly behind Alastair's cottage, the fog had obliterated the sea and was turning the shingle dark with its moisture. They walked along the stack of crates marking the boundary of the cabin's backyard.

'He's moved the funt,' she said.

'The what?'

'The funt. The lamp he had outside his front door.' She pointed. 'He said he used it as a sign to show whether he was at home or away. I wonder whether he's done a bunk. Let's take a look.'

An untidy pile of not quite clean bones had been left on the doorstep: the toad, the carcass he proposed to throw in a river to strengthen his magic powers. She knocked on the door. No answer. A mildewed curtain pulled across the kitchen window blocked the view of the interior. She called his name. Silence.

She remembered what he had said about the back door, the buggered lock. She placed her shoulder against the peeling painted wood, shoved, the door gave way and she marched through the kitchen – noted the cooker and its gas cylinder still standing below the window. The front room had been cleared of nearly all his belongings – boxes, papers, bird skulls, wings, decrepit armchair – all gone. The walnut desk was the only piece of furniture remaining and, sitting on top of it, the school chemistry rack holding three corked test tubes with Alastair's alchemical experiments still fizzing away inside the glass. The door of the cellar was more obvious, she noticed, now the room was empty. She spotted something new – a pentagram chalked on the wall, a folded piece of paper pinned to the top point. She niggled the pin free with her nails, removed the paper, unfolded it; a hastily scrawled doodle of a boat with two stick figures on the deck. She held it up and recalled her last, stilted conversation with Alastair about the smugglers' ghost boat. The one he thought he might have seen the day Luke went missing. He had stalled when she asked him whether he had seen anybody on board. She examined the stick figures; next to one of the single-stroke torsos he had drawn a small circle around a three-pronged symbol, like a badge. Was it a peace symbol? A CND badge? Or perhaps its was a smiling sun nuclear power no thanks badge. Maybe it was an irrelevant detail, a mystical sign from the Magus. She relegated the badge to the back of her mind, focused on the boat. There was a name written in tiny letters along the hull. She squinted. Pluto. She twitched, half gasped, folded and deftly stuffed the paper in her pocket. Pluto, the name on Dave's note. Pluto, the god of the underworld, she had assumed, a bleak reference to Dave's own downward descent. Wrong again. Pluto was the name of a boat.

Sonny appeared.

'He's vanished,' she said.

'I told you. He's a sangoma. Has he left anything useful behind?'

'Only his alchemical experiments.' She waved at the desk.

He selected a tube, examined its golden substance in the last light of the day. She'd had enough, walked out the back door, stooped and examined the toad bones as she waited for Sonny to emerge. They were nearly devoid of flesh, not quite stripped clean; half-worked magic was better than no magic at all, she decided. She slipped the toad bones into her coat pocket.

'He's gone back to live with the dead,' Sonny said. He pulled the kitchen door shut behind him.

The mist was thick enough to hide them as they walked along the shore; the regular beam of the lighthouse diffracted in the vapour, the rays accompanied now by three blasts of the foghorn. The dense veil hung a fraction above the shingle, revealing the lines and colours of the pebbles, the lichen, the spiky sea cabbage – hyper-real below the blanket. They trailed the high tide tangle of seaweed and plastic bottles until they reached a flat finger of land that ran on below the mist, stretching into the sea. Good landing place for a boat, she noted. Up above, the blurred lights of the research lab were visible. Her whole body was cold and aching; a wave of tiredness and inertia descending as they turned inland. The plan had seemed clear and simple in the daylight, but now out here in the near darkness, it felt like a bad idea. Too simple – the research lab was so easy to enter. What had Crawford said? *Leave her to her own devices, see if she manages to do something really stupid.* Was she doing exactly what Crawford wanted her to do? Was she walking into a trap? She looked up, caught a shadow passing overhead, outstretched wings, circling, the gull's shape distorted, elongated in the haze, large enough to be a vulture.

'What if Crawford is waiting for us inside the lab?' she asked.

'Run. Lose him. Leave the rest to me.'

She glanced over her shoulder, caught sight of a glint in the mist beyond the shoreline. A signal? The fog closed in again, smothered the sea.

'And what if he shoots?'

'He won't be able to aim accurately in this.' He slashed his hand through the white air. 'Not if there is some distance between you and him.'

Hardly comforting. They climbed the last ridge, reached the flat ground and the head-height chainlink fence surrounding the research station. The white prefab labs were clustered at the far end of the compound, hovering like phantoms in the mist. The fifth building, the one nearest to the sea, was brick-built; its outline loomed then vanished behind a wave of thick dampness.

She tried to remember the layout from her visits with Dave. 'The red brick building is where they keep all the equipment and supplies.' She stalled, trawling for details. 'The store room is through a doorway. They lock the caesium 137 and any other radioactive materials in the chest at the back.'

'What did you say the caesium looks like? Some sort of yellow liquid?'

'Yeah – yellow liquid in glass tubes. The vials are kept in a lead casing, like a hockey puck. And they put the pucks in the chest. That's lead-lined too. I remember Dave telling me he needed permission from the lab tech to remove a vial.'

Dave. Alastair's sketch of a boat called *Pluto* had jogged something, knocked a piece out of place. Her mind kept tracking back to Dave's message on Patrick's cassette. He'd seen a boat close to the shore. And he'd seen a ghost, he joked. That was in the morning, just before he was killed. She couldn't reorganize the fragments in any way that made sense.

'It must be very easy,' she said.

'What?'

'Smuggling the caesium. The guard creams off a vial of caesium, somebody fiddles the paperwork.' She pointed behind her at the finger of land. 'A boat lands down there, on the flat part of the beach.' A boat called *Pluto*. 'Regan walks up from the beach, collects the vial from the security guard and saunters back to the boat, sails round, I suppose, to Norfolk, another deserted shingle beach, lands, drops the caesium vial for pick-up and shipping across the North Sea to Amsterdam. Then it's handed over to the Silk Road carriers. There's something quite old-fashioned about it. Timeless. Smuggling, carriers, boats, mules.'

She paused, tried to work out what the *Pluto* was doing on Dungeness beach the day Alastair had seen it. The Saturday Luke had gone missing. If it was Regan that Alastair had spotted on board, she couldn't have been picking up caesium because there was only one delivery a month, on the first Tuesday. The lighthouse beam swept through the dancing particles, the foghorn sounded.

'And yet look at the body count. Dave. Patrick,' she said. 'Stavros and Regan – they don't seem too worried about knocking people off, do they?'

'Well, they are fanatics. You know, they think they are on a mission to save the world from the dirty commies. Righteous men are more dangerous than criminals. So they will do anything, kill anyone, because they have a fanatical belief in their principles.'

'Regan isn't a fanatic. She's a drug-dealing crim.'

'Ja, but the American guy is a fanatic. And possibly the

other people he is working with.' He gave her a sideways glance when he said that. She looked away, listened to the drip, drip, drip of water running off a gutter.

'There's only one security guard,' she said.

'No alarms or security lights?'

'No.'

He pointed at what looked like a speaker on a pole fixed to a concrete fence post. 'What's that?'

She walked over. A dead gull lay at the bottom of the pole, white wings spread as if it was in flight. The spindly legs of a spider straddled its unblinking eye. She peered up at the silent speaker; everything seemed sinister, inexplicable, in the fog.

'This used to be a maritime research centre, they developed and tested ship warning systems. I would imagine it's the remains of some prototype.'

A light spilled from a lab window, illuminated the mizzle pulsing across the courtyard.

Sonny checked his watch. 'Ten thirty. Maybe we should go in now. Confront this guard Vince before anybody else turns up.'

She folded her arms, knocked the hard lump of the Firebird against her wrist. The pistol jabbed her painfully, a reminder of how thin her flesh had become in the last few weeks. Eaten away by anxiety. She felt uncertain, considered doing nothing, stalling, leaving Harry to sort it all out. The fog was sealing them inside its dense white walls, suffocating her body and mind. She had summoned the miasma, but now it was out of control, taking over, spooking her with its ghostliness.

'When we find the guard, Vince, I'm going to ask him about Luke. That's all I want to know. I'm not interested in the rest of it.' She pressed her face against the chainlink; the cold metal burned her skin. 'What if he refuses to tell us anything?'

'We can always apply a little pressure.' Sonny's hand moved to his belt, the grip of his gun. 'Although I doubt whether it'll take much to make him talk. I doubt he has much investment in any of this. It's a wodge of money, a job, nothing more.'

She didn't respond. The silence unnerved her; she couldn't even hear the mews of the terns. The mist that muffled their footsteps could also dampen the tread of anybody tracking them.

'It doesn't feel right,' she said.

'What do you mean?'

'I've got a bad feeling. Barging in. It's too easy.'

'Sure. We could go back to the Lookers' Hut, light a braai, heat up a can of beans. I told you, it doesn't bother me.'

She hesitated, searched the darkness for omens, a sign. There was nothing. She reached into her coat pocket; touched her penknife, thought of Luke. Perhaps he was here, nearby, somewhere, stalking Regan, just as they were. The possibility fired her resolve.

'No. This is our chance. There's only one delivery a month. This is the only evening we can guarantee Vince will be there, so we should go in now and see what information we can get out of him.'

'If that's what you want to do.'

'It is.'

'OK. We can climb over the fence at the side. We need to surprise him. Gain the upper hand. Psychological advantage.'

He dug in the pocket of his jeans, produced the Land Rover keys, his compass. 'Here, you take these.'

'Why?'

'Just in case.' He looked away when he said it.

The foghorn boomed. They edged along the chainlink boundary, the yellow flowers of the prostrate broom glowing like cats' eyes in the mist. 'This is a good place to climb over,' he said. 'There are some crates on the other side to break the drop.'

The store room was sightless on their side. Windows and doors faced inwards, towards the centre of the compound. Easy to cross the gravel around the rear end of the building and reach the door before the guard had any time to spot them. Chances were he wasn't paying much attention anyway. Reading the newspaper. Killing time while he waited for Regan to turn up to collect the siphoned-off, unaccounted-for caesium vial. Sonny hoisted himself up and over, jumped down on to the crates. It was harder than he made it look; she managed to haul herself up, wavered on top, her coat snagging, its contents weighing heavily, swung a leg over, eased down the other side, searching for a toehold among the crates. It would be easier coming back the other way, if she had to leave in a hurry. They huddled together, on the far side of the fence, hidden from view. Too late for second thoughts now they had crossed the border.

'Let me go first,' Sonny said.

She didn't argue. He sidled along the fence. She was behind. He crossed the short space of open ground to reach the wall, edged along. Her too. The rough brick scraped her palm. Sonny was at the corner. Tense. Focused as he ducked below the window. She followed suit, her heart pounding. Adrenalin rush. Sonny flattened himself against the wall by the door. He had his pistol in his hand. Shit. The sight of the gun jolted her, reminded her she wasn't playing games. He opened the door, swung in. Nothing. He leaned back, beckoned her. She inched into the building.

'Stay behind me,' he said.

As if she might think of doing anything else. They stood silently for a moment. A chance to orient herself; match their surroundings to her memory map. Grey five-drawer filing cabinet where the accounting records were kept, locked. Desk with anglepoise lamp, in tray, out tray, ashtray, kettle. Chair. Bare overhead bulb, dangling from a black flex, stark light. And then a door, closed. Not quite. A dark line around the door's edge revealed it was open a fraction.

She nodded at the door. Sonny beckoned with his chin, indicating she should stand behind him against the wall. He took a deep breath, kicked the door, pulled back. No noise. No light. Neither of them moved. Waited. And then a woman's voice.

'I was expecting you.'

Regan. A trap?

'Come in,' she said. 'I'm not armed.'

Sonny eased into the doorway, both hands on his Browning. 'What about the guard?'

'He's not armed either,' said Regan. 'We're doing some business.'

Sonny moved into the room, his back blocking the door-frame, arms still extended in front.

'And what about your friend?' Regan said. 'I presume she's lurking out there. Why doesn't she come in as well, I've got something to tell her.'

'It's OK,' Sonny said. 'Come in, Sam.'

She froze, panicked by the calmness of Sonny's voice. Idiot. What a fool. She shouldn't have trusted him, he was one of Regan's enforcers, working for the American after all; he had lured her into a corner, a dead end. She couldn't believe she had been so stupid. And now she was stuck; she couldn't go back, she had to go forwards. Her hand went to the Firebird in her pocket, clutched the grip, inhaled, walked into the room, found herself behind Sonny. He was facing Regan, Browning aimed, using his body as a shield to protect her.

He hadn't tricked her. He was still on her side. She exhaled. Her eyes adjusted to the darkness, the faces of Regan and the security guard solidifying.

Regan glared past Sonny at Sam's coat. 'I had a badge like that,' she said.

'The feminist badge?'

'Yeah.'

'I found it in Skell. Do you want it back?'

'You can keep it.'

'Thanks.'

'My pleasure.'

Sam returned Regan's poisonous glare and noticed she was holding something in her hand, dull grey metal. Not a gun. Shaped like a hockey puck.

'Is that caesium?' Sam asked.

'Yeah.'

She was so offhand about it. 'Don't you worry about where the caesium might end up?'

'No.'

'You don't care that it might be fuelling a war in Afghanistan?'

Regan's face hung like a pale moon in the near darkness of the room. 'Look, I haven't got time for your sanctimonious questions. I don't care what you think about me. And what's more, I don't think you really care about Afghanistan either, do you? That's not why you are here.'

Sam didn't say anything.

'I think what you are after is outside. Who you are after.'

Her stomach flipped.

Regan checked her watch. 'He should be there by now. Waiting for you. Why don't you go and find him?' She emitted a cackle. It ended abruptly, left a dirty silence lingering.

'What's Luke doing with you?' Sam demanded.

'Why don't you go and ask him yourself?'

Sam couldn't move her feet, desperate to believe that Luke was waiting for her outside, but not ready to take Regan's word for it.

Sonny said, 'Go, Sam. I'll take care of this.'

He glanced over his shoulder. 'Be careful.'

She backed out of the store room.

The air was thick with moisture, the flash of the lighthouse reduced to a smothered gleam, the foghorn disorienting. She clambered over the crate pile, levered herself up on to the fence, swung over. Dropped down. Nobody. Was Regan lying? She peered through the blanket haze, searching for Luke. Nothing. Except the smudgy gleam of lights. Three in a row – a boat on the flat finger of beach below. The *Pluto*? She stalled, swung around, stepped away from the fence, started down the shingle, aiming for the lights. A scrunch of stones made her stop. Muffled footfall. Where? It was difficult to locate the source of the noise in the fog. She twisted her head, trying to work out what was going on. Silence. The foghorn. Silence. Footsteps again, coming from behind. Somebody walking down the slope from the research station entrance. She waited. More steps. And then she saw him, an outline emerging from the mist on the ridge above, solidifying – hands in leather-jacket pockets, the green glint of his eyes visible even in the fog. Luke. She couldn't quite believe it. He was safe. He was OK. He was here. She had guessed right; he had worked out what was going on, followed Regan's trail just as they had. She started to run up the shingle.

'Sam,' he said.

The tone of his voice suggested caution – perhaps he was trying to warn her about something without giving anything away. Self-censorship. Was he afraid somebody was following him in the darkness? She halted. Feet sinking in the stones.

'Luke.' She hesitated. 'Are you OK?'

He nodded. She twiddled her hair, rat-tailed in the mist, rain dripping off the ends, down her coat cuff. This wasn't quite as she had imagined the reunion. Something was wrong.

'What's going on?'

'I can explain.' He sounded cagey.

'I was worried about you,' she said. He didn't reply. She looked at his face, searching for reassurance. He smiled again, but it wasn't his usual smile. Lopsided. She dropped her eyes, focused briefly on his jacket, the badges on his lapel. The red arrow of the Anti-Nazi League. The three fans of the radiation symbol – nuclear-free zone. She blinked, looked back at his face.

'You know Dave's dead?' she said.

'Dave?'

'Yes. Dave. My Dave. Dave in Skell.'

He hardly seemed to react. Shock. That's what it was. Maybe it wasn't wise to mention Dave's death, here, out of the blue, but she thought he ought to know, alert him to the seriousness of the situation.

'Regan...' she started to say.

'Yes. The Saturday we were supposed to be meeting up. I talked to this person from the research station.'

'Patrick.'

'That's right. I realized something was going on. And then I spoke to Regan.'

'How did you find Regan?'

'She was... keeping an eye on the research station. She spotted me hanging around. She explained what she was doing.'

Exactly as Sam had surmised.

Luke looked away, looked back. 'She told me about her

work to support the Afghan rebels. I decided it was a good cause and I wanted to help her.'

Good cause. Sam realized her mouth was drooping, she shut it. Became aware she had a lump in her throat. She couldn't compute what Luke was saying.

'Luke, what are you talking about?'

He didn't answer.

'I'm not sure I'd classify that as a good cause...'

She stalled, her sense of gravity shifting, body slipping, everything inverting, reversing. She was upside down. She needed to reorder the world around her, right it.

'Sam, I can see you don't understand. These people, the Afghan rebels, they haven't got much to lose anyway. They are oppressed. Poor. It's a war of liberation. It's a fight against Soviet colonial imperialism.'

She twiddled her bottom lip with her fingers. This was all wrong. She was talking to somebody she didn't know. Not Luke. A different person, an alien invader of his body. 'Luke, what are you doing, this is ridiculous? Do you really understand what's going on in Afghanistan? It's not even your war.'

'Of course it's our war. It's a war against imperialism. Somebody has to stand up for the rebels. Words and banners won't cut it. Sometimes you have to use force to achieve an objective. And anyway, it's contained.'

'What's contained?'

'The caesium. It's not going to be released everywhere, it's not going to affect innocent people. Limited damage.'

'Contained? That's crazy. How can you be against the transportation of nuclear waste because it's dangerous but for the use of caesium as a weapon?'

He tutted, shook his head as if to indicate she'd completely missed the point.

'And it's already not contained because they're using a bloody drugs network to transport the stuff. Regan isn't a political activist. She's a stupid fucking criminal.'

'Sam, she is an activist. Regan is a feminist.'

She was winded for a moment, mouth open, eyes wide. 'A feminist? Seriously, where do you get that idea? The clenched fist she had pinned to her jacket? Anybody can pick up a badge and wear it. What's wrong with you? Are you going to drop this now, come back with me?'

Any minute now, she knew, he would say yes, let's go. She just had to reach through the haze, the fog, penetrate the outer covering, communicate with the real Luke trapped inside – and then everything would be fine. Normal. Her and him. The Lookers' Hut. The campfire. The nights together.

'It's about principles, Sam.'

'Principles? What principles are involved in stealing caesium? Luke, I think you might have some form of Stockholm syndrome. Have you been spending much time with Regan?'

'Sam, I'm doing this because I want to. I think it's the right thing to do. I thought you had principles too. I thought you'd understand.'

The mist blurred his features, distorted his face, transformed him into a shadow, nothing more than an outline, and she found herself wondering how clearly she had ever seen him.

'Well, if you thought I'd understand, why didn't you call and let me know where you were? Why didn't you just tell me you'd met this Regan woman and you'd decided to help her with all this stuff?'

'Sam. I'm sorry. I was worried that it wasn't safe to tell you about it.'

'What do you mean? Why not?'

'Sam, you know why not, we've discussed it. I was worried

that you would be on the Force's radar because of your dad. I didn't want to get you involved. I thought it would be safer for you.'

She had a niggling sense he had this all prepared, a story he'd worked out in case she confronted him.

'You thought it would be safer for me if you just left me hanging, worrying about what had happened to you?'

'Sam, I left you a message to let you know I was all right, but I couldn't give you the details. Of course I couldn't.'

She lost it. 'Oh right, and what are the details you thought it was better not to give me? I mean, have you been fucking Regan? Is Regan one of the small details you thought it was better not to share with me? You're screwing another woman?'

'It isn't like that, Sam, you have to try and understand.'

'Don't patronize me. Tell me the fucking truth. Are you—'

The muffled air was split by a crack. And then Sonny shouting, 'Fuck you.' Another gunshot. They both froze. Footsteps. A figure running across the courtyard, towards the fence. Difficult to identify in the fog.

'He shot the guard. He's behind me. Get ready to hit him.'

It took Sam a second to clock it was Regan shouting instructions to Luke, telling him to fire at Sonny. Sam fumbled underneath her coat, hand on Firebird, not sure what to do. Regan was clambering over the fence. Sam glanced at Luke. He had produced a small gun, some sort of pistol, and was aiming it at the fence. Where had he got that from? For a moment she thought he was going to shoot Regan. He didn't. Regan flung herself down from the fence, ran up the shingle to Luke. They stood together, side by side, on top of the ridge. Sonny appeared, sprinting across the forecourt of the research station. He was clutching his Browning in one hand and something else in the other. It was glowing yellow. Jesus, he'd picked up a caesium vial from the store room. He'd flipped. He clambered over the crates and perched on top of the fence. Luke pointed the pistol at him. Sonny raised one arm, held the tube in the air; a glowing beacon.

'You shoot me,' he shouted, 'the tube breaks and we've all had it.'

Christ. She was trying to remember what Dave had told her about the toxicity of caesium 137, whether there was enough in one vial to do much instant damage. Whether it was too late anyway because they had all been exposed now the vial had been taken out of its lead casing. At least it still had its cork stopper in place.

Sonny shouted, 'He's been working with Regan all along. I knew it. The security guard confirmed it.'

'Who is working with Regan?'

'Luke. If that's his real name.'

Luke aimed the pistol at Sonny's head. Sam's fingers curled around the grip of the Firebird, pulled it out of her pocket.

Sonny shouted, 'He's working with Regan for the American, Stavros. He's the guy on the coast they were talking about in the nightclub.'

Sam lifted the Firebird in her right hand, pointed it at Regan.

'He's lying,' Regan said.

'Get Luke,' Sonny shouted. She shifted the gun an inch, pointed it at Luke.

'Sam, don't be silly,' Luke said. 'You don't know what you're doing with that gun.'

She didn't reply, placed her left hand on the grip, extended her arms.

'Sam,' Luke said. 'You know I love you.' She'd never heard him say those words before. He might have inscribed *love you* casually on a penknife, but he'd never said it. Not straight out like that. She wanted to believe him, but the phrase rang hollow in her ears. Deep inside, she knew it wasn't true.

Luke said, 'Sam, think what you're doing. How can you trust the man who killed your father?'

'I know he killed my father. But how do you know?'

'Regan told me about him. He's a hitman. There's a contract out on you and he's got it.'

Sonny shouted, 'Sam, you know I only said I'd do it because I wanted to make sure nobody else took it on. If I wanted to do you in, I would have done it by now.'

She was grinding her teeth, trying to stay calm, attempting to work out what was going on. The fog was so dense, all the figures were disappearing, blurring at the edges. Only the golden vial was visible, a luminescent ghost hovering in the air.

Luke shouted, 'He's a hitman, working for Crawford.'

Sonny shouted, 'I'm not working for Crawford. I'm trying to stop Crawford getting to you. Luke's the one who is setting you up. He's working for the bloody American. Stavros. Crawford must know Stavros. Crawford must have given him the contacts with the drug smuggling network – Regan – said he'd turn a blind eye to the caesium. Part of the price must have been setting you up. Crawford wants you out of the picture, however he has to do it. Framing you, contract, whatever.'

'Yes, that's why Crawford commissioned him,' Luke shouted. 'Your father's killer.'

'Sam,' Sonny shouted. 'If you don't shoot him, he'll kill us both.'

'Don't listen to him,' Luke said. 'Come on, Sam. I'm your boyfriend. He's a hitman. He's just waiting for the right moment to do you in. He can hardly gun down a twenty-year-old woman in the middle of London and get away with it.

He's been stalking you, driving you to this point so he can shoot you without it looking too bad. Like you might have done something to merit it. Stealing caesium 137, for example.'

She knocked the Firebird's safety catch with her thumb. Click.

'I'm not here because of Sonny, I'm here because I came looking for you, Luke,' Sam said. 'I followed the trail, your phone message, the photo of the caesium article in your room, Patrick Grogan's number. You wanted me to follow you, didn't you?' She was shouting. 'You wanted to lure me here. You wanted me cornered. Sonny's right, it must have been part of your deal. You don't give a fuck about me. I'm just a daughter of the Filth. I'm dirt. I'm collateral to your fucking principles. Freedom, truth, whatever. You don't give a shit about me.'

'Fire,' Sonny yelled. She wasn't sure she could.

'Think what you are doing, Sam.' Luke said it calmly; personal issues never riled him. He was always good in a crisis. Only politics really got him going. His principles. She tasted saltwater on her lips and something in her head flicked, a connection, what was it Alastair had said the evening she was trying to find Luke? The flatlands, he had said, and she had jumped straight to the marsh, the Lookers' Hut, forgotten he had mentioned a boat, in passing, as if he was too embarrassed to tell her he had seen Luke with Regan, on a boat hauled up on the flatland of the beach below the research lab. He didn't want to break the bad news that her beloved boyfriend, the one she was going moony over, hanging out on the beach alone at night waiting for, was with another woman. Luke must have arranged to meet Regan in Dungeness. She was waiting for him in the *Pluto*, picked him up after he had talked to Patrick.

'Luke, where were you the Saturday evening when you were supposed to meet me here at Dungeness?'

'I was...'

'Were you in a boat with Regan?'

Alastair's hurried doodle had confirmed it, the two stick figures. The badge with the three-pronged symbol. She stared at Luke through the mist, eyed his leather jacket, the nuclear-free zone badge on his lapel, yellow with three black radiation waves. Alastair had seen Luke, and he had been scared. Perhaps somebody, a Porsche- or Audi-driving heavy, had come back and threatened him, told him to keep quiet or else. Or else what? Or else he'd end up with his limbs detached and strewn across the marsh. Patrick's taped message from Dave played in her mind, Dave's voice anxious, *funny you should mention Luke*; he had seen something odd when he walked along Flaxby Point on the Tuesday morning that he was killed. Dave had seen the *Pluto*, he had seen a ghost too – the face of somebody he had been told had disappeared. He had left her a note, given her the clues, but she'd tipped it all upside down, emptied the contents of the bellarmine into her hand, transformed a counter-curse to a curse.

'Luke, were you on the *Pluto*? Did you sail round the coast to Skell that Saturday evening?'

He didn't answer. She had seen a boat on the horizon when she had walked with Dave to Bane House. Had Luke been on board with Regan, shadowing Dave? Planning how to do him in because Luke had found out from Patrick how much Dave knew?

'Would you kill a friend for a principle?'

'That's a… Sam, don't go jumping to the wrong conclusions. Trust your feelings.'

'My feelings? My feelings? My feelings tell me you're a lying, two-timing prick who's been shagging that junky-faced, scrawny, manipulative shit of a…'

'Sam, cool it, you don't want to be a bitter withy…'

She let go of her body and she was up in the air, calmer now that she was above everything up here in the grey, Luke smiling at her through the hazy dark. She didn't have to analyse her feelings. She just had to be. She was whole, mind and body joined, channelling her powers. She fluttered her wings, white in the mist, hovered, took her time, observed the patterns, the whorls and spirals of vapour below, the emerald tablets of his shining eyes. She was in control. She was pure anger and she was focused. She went in for the kill. There was a slight impact as she hit the ground, but that was all. A crack. Perhaps two. A jolt. A scream. The whiff of cordite in the air. And then an eerie silence. The fog had thickened, erased all the edges. She heard somebody sobbing, a woman. Distraught. Regan. What was she crying about? Silly cow. She could see, now, that Regan was covered in blood and Sam thought for a moment she had shot her by mistake, but Regan was upright and she was holding on to a body. It looked like Luke. His tee shirt was a mess. Black and sticky. Regan had her hands under his armpits, she was trying to support him, carry his dead weight down the shingle ridges to the sea, to the *Pluto*, hauled up just above the high tide mark.

Sam lowered her arm, watched Regan drag Luke across the ridge. Had she done that? Had she shot Luke? The conniving, stupid bastard with his fucking bitter withy. She didn't have any choice. She had to shoot him. Sonny was right. Luke was a total fucking liar. She'd flipped it all over in her head, suspected Dave when she should have suspected Luke. It wasn't Luke who was on to Dave, it was Dave who was on to Luke. It wasn't Luke who was worried about her getting caught up with Dave, it was Dave trying to stop her from running after Luke. And Luke had led her on; drawn her along a trail that pointed to Dave, harried her down to Dungeness, the marsh. She'd reversed the whole story, inverted it in her mind. What a blockhead she was. What an eejit for trusting fucking Luke. Well, Regan could have him now, she'd have to deal with his bloody corpse. She didn't give a shit about Luke.

She turned to face Sonny. He had jumped down from the fence and was on the ground, still holding the gleaming vial in front of him with one hand, pistol in the other.

'Sonny, are you...'

He smiled in her direction. There was a shot. She threw herself into a shingle ditch, Sonny leaped backwards, thrown against the fence, still smiling, eyes wide open, even though there was blood dribbling down the side of his face and spreading across his shirt. Another shot. She waited. Silence. Peered over the ridge, spotted Regan retreating into the mist, over the shingle, wading into the water, climbing on board the *Pluto*, waiting and ready to sail away. She crouched and ran low to Sonny, knelt down beside him, watched his grip on the glowing vial loosen. Was he still alive? Conscious? Strange, she couldn't be sure. She had thought the line between life and death was absolute, a border with a clear doorway leading out. And yet she couldn't be certain which side Sonny was on. Perhaps it was wishful thinking. She didn't want him to die, had grown fond of him. Liked him. Loved him, this friend of hers, the strange fallen angel with his smoky halo rings.

'Sonny.' She put her hand on his, felt his warmth. 'Sonny, you're not alone. I'm here. I'm with you. I won't leave you.'

'Thank you. I didn't betray you.'

'I know.' Tears streaming down her cheeks. His eyes damp too. She wiped a drop from his face. But he was gone. She sat there for a moment, numb, reluctant to move from his side. She heard the siren. Blue light swirling through the fog. Cops. She saw the figures advancing. She hesitated, wondering whether she should give herself up, explain. Luke. Self-defence.

No way. She wasn't going to get done for him. Fuck it. She grabbed the vial, lobbed it up as hard as she could, sent it spinning over and over, watched as it twirled higher and higher into the air, shining through the fog, turning and gleaming; a shooting star blazing a gold trail into the night. An alchemical transformation. And she wondered for a moment whether Luke was right and she should have stood by him, what was wrong with the idea anyway? Contained action, CIA involvement, only a little bit of caesium 137 to the Mujahedeen – they were freedom fighters after all – a one-time commie KO, better than a prolonged and bloody war. The vial had reached its zenith. A moment of pure gold. And then it flipped and started falling, twirling, dimming. Reverse alchemy in motion, a dark descent, dropping to the shingle.

A voice shouting, 'What the fuck... stand back, it could be radioactive.'

She turned, skidded down the slope, headed for the sea as the crash of glass splintered the night and the fog closed in around her.

CHAPTER 20

SHE RAN AND let the mist envelop her, screened out the sounds of car doors slamming, men shouting, skied down the shingle ridge, hit the shore, paused for a split second while she gained her bearings. To the west she could see the fuzzy lights of the *Pluto* slipping into the water. She headed east, her feet finding the firmness of the wet sand, forcing her legs to pump, soaked shoes clear in the slither between fog and ground. A shout behind her made her turn. A cone of light, the beam of a torch, swept back and forth carving a path through the darkness. A wave clawing the beach caught her unawares, knocked her stride. She stumbled. Found her balance, regained her breath, ribs aching from the effort, snorted back her tears as she ran on. She reached the line of gnarled sticks marking the pathway to Alastair's cabin, attacked the slope, struggling against the roll of the pebbles, hoping the fog would muffle the sound of her direction inland. Over the dirt track, illuminated by a solitary street lamp, she hobbled the final stretch across the mossy matting, headed for the back door, nudged it with her shoulder. It opened without much resistance. She closed it firmly behind her, searched for a bolt, but there wasn't one. Too bad.

Straight to the front room, its outlines just visible in the sodium glow of the external light. The test tube rack was still on the desk but now holding only two cork-stoppered test tubes. She had guessed correctly, Sonny had taken one of

Alastair's alchemical experiments, stashed it in his jacket. Her eyes swept the floorboards, fixed on the trapdoor. She knelt, scrabbled, lifted, propped the door up with one hand, swung her legs into the void, slipped over the side. Her feet touched solid ground. The small space under the floor was shallower than she had thought. She had to squat to allow the door to move down, and even then it wouldn't close completely, its weight pressed on her back. She squirmed around, feeling for the most comfortable position in the cramped, dark space. An oubliette, a tiny prison cell. Not quite enough room for sitting without bending her neck and squashing her chin against her chest. She shifted her position again, slid her legs forward, lowered herself on to her back, lay flat on the ground below the floorboards, allowing the door to drop into place. Enclosed in darkness and damp, finally able to breathe easily. She couldn't make herself comfortable, the hard edges of objects in her pockets dug into her back. She squirmed around, dipped in her coat, located the Firebird, placed it next to her contorted body. Still she wasn't comfortable. She dug in her other pocket and produced the Dictaphone, rested that on the ground too.

No light, apart from the faint yellow crack where the trapdoor met the floor. She absorbed the distant waves rumbling through the joists, and then another noise: tap tap. Death watch beetles, clicking and calling to one another in the dark, their rhythm hypnotic, inducing drowsiness. Perhaps she should sleep for a few hours, a wounded animal curled up in its burrow. She lifted her arm to wipe a tear, and as she did so she heard the scrape of the back door. She froze, caught a sob mid-breath, half choked, placed her hand over her mouth. Waited. Footsteps, hard on the floorboards. A voice. She knew the speaker, his harsh tone unmistakable.

'Check the other room.'

Crawford. She was sweating, conscious of every breath, every hair standing on end. Scalp prickling as boots trampled above her head. A black block in the crack of light around the trapdoor marked the place where he stood, the line of his soles. She could hear him breathing. The death watch beetle tapped. The boots above her shuffled, reacting to the sound. Then silence, followed by another beetle tap and the footsteps of the sidekick returning.

'She's not here.'

Brief pause. Tap tap tap.

'What's that noise?'

'Don't know.'

Tap tap tap.

'Is it a bird? Trapped somewhere?'

He was right; she was a caged bird, a crow lured into a Larsen trap. A surge of anger hit her, provoked her. She stretched her hand out, conscious of every rustle of her coat, touched the Dictaphone, felt the familiar buttons and pressed record. The button made a click. She hoped it sounded like the tap of a death watch beetle.

'There's that noise again.'

'Yeah. Odd.'

She held her breath. Silence. Then Crawford spoke. 'If we don't find her today, we can catch her later on.'

'Like her father,' the sidekick said. 'I heard he was always worming out of tight corners. He had a reputation for being smart.'

The sidekick's comment must have touched a nerve. Crawford erupted. 'Yeah, she's like her fucking father all right – a total fucking pain.' He ranted, out of control. 'You could see it in her face, her stupid bloody eyes taking everything in. She irritated me even then. And so I made a fucking tactical error, I should have walked away. But I needed to know what he was doing there. And it turns out I was right; she's an evil bitch. She is like her father. I know she's stuck that fucking date, the May Day fair, in her silly fucking memory.'

'May Day fair?' The sidekick sounded perturbed. 'Isn't that what…'

Crawford interrupted with a scoff, as if he was dismissing his own outburst, realized he'd lost it.

'It's nothing. Forget it. It's a fucking boring story anyway.'

A death watch beetle tapped by her ear. She jumped, brushed a joist with her arm, froze, held her breath.

The sidekick said, 'Did you hear that?'

A moment of absolute stillness. Then Crawford said, 'Yes, I heard.'

'Do you think it is a trapped bird?'

Crawford kicked his heel against the floorboards. 'Must be. A trapped fucking bird.'

She couldn't breathe, couldn't move a fraction. Had he worked out where she was hiding?

'Why don't you go and fetch the car? I'll finish up here.'

'Right you are.'

Footsteps as the sidekick departed. Another sound, a dragging noise. Like heavy furniture being moved. Scraping. She couldn't work out what was happening above her head. More silence. Feet on boards, Crawford moving away. Was that fabric being ripped? The back door pulled shut. She breathed a sigh of relief. He hadn't heard her after all. She was safe, for now anyway. She switched the Dictaphone off, replaced it in her coat pocket, lay back, arms languishing at her side, hit by a wave of indifference. She was numb, drained. She didn't care about anything any longer, all she wanted to do was sleep, down here among the dead – Dave, Jim, Sonny. Luke. Friends and enemies. Enemies who turned out to be friends. A friend – a lover – who had betrayed her; an enemy within. And she wondered whether she had killed part of herself when she shot Luke; died a little. Lost her heart. She closed her eyes. In the darkness the death watch beetles called. She could lie there for the night, float away, let bleakness descend. Even as she drifted off, a different noise registered in a far corner of her mind. Crackling. And a familiar smell that was comforting. Campfire. For some reason, her body failed to react as it should. She felt no panic, no sense of urgency. She could add the signs together, and yet she wasn't sure she cared. Perhaps she deserved it. Burned at the stake, a witch's sentence. Fate. The periodic repetitions, as above so below. She inhaled, wood smoke filling her lungs pleasantly, her mind. This girl looks ill, this girl is ill, this girl looks dead, this girl is dead. In the greyness she could see Jim's outline, waiting for her, although there was something sad about him, she could tell. He wanted to say something, his words were in her head. *Don't give up.* Don't worry, it's fine, she said. To everything there is a season, and a time to every purpose under the heaven: a time to be born and a time to die. *No*, Sonny said, *not you. Not yet. A time to heal, to build up, dance.* I'm done with dancing, she said. When did dancing ever do me any good?

She reached up and felt the joists above her head with a sense of detachment, an emotionless assessment of the dimensions of her grave; her fingertips found a gelatinous substance, like an eye attached to the beam. What was it? She prodded. Laughed. Nostoc commune, star jelly, witch's butter; the special ingredient of Allin's alchemical experiments, the golden contents of the test tube she had lobbed in the air. What had Alastair said about nostoc? Survives radiation. She touched the gloop again, stroked its slimy surface and she heard Dave talking, telling her about the dogged plants of Dungeness, how they sent their roots to far places in search of water. *You've got to love the blackened spiky stems of the sea kale*, he said, *its hardiness. Durability. Fight. You owe me one. Do this for me.*

She blinked and now she could sense the acrid smoke around her. Shit. Fucking hell. She roused herself. Crawford had set fire to the cabin. Fight, she had to fight. She reached up with her arms, pushed at the boards above her head. They didn't budge. The scraping noises she had heard earlier fell into place – he had moved the desk on top of the trapdoor. She was locked in. She pushed upward with as much strength as she could muster. No movement at all. Her eyes were watering. She couldn't tell whether they were tears of madness, or thickening smoke. She was going to die here, locked up under the floorboards of some stupid fisherman's cottage on a shingle desert at the end of the bloody world. And she only had herself to blame. Jim's voice said, *Get a grip, for fuck's sake, get a grip.*

'Fuck off,' she shouted. 'You're no bloody help.'

She drew her legs up to her chest, kicked. Pushed and pushed. She heard the desk shifting a little as she managed to tilt the trapdoor. She twisted on to her knees. Placed her shoulders underneath the trapdoor's edge, pushed her back against the planks. Shit. Shit. The desk slid again. Move. Move. She heaved, strained. Finally the trapdoor budged, the desk lurched, she flipped the lid back, pulled herself out of her prison and into the room, momentarily confused by the smoke, flames crackling, dancing red lights. She ducked, thrust her arm over her mouth and nose and caught sight of the dim glow of the power station, through the kitchen window by the back door, pale amber against the rage of the burning curtain, fire licking the walls. She turned, ran the other way, fumbled with the front door lock, shoved her way out into the night air, heavy with water now, not fog but cold rain on her face mingling with the tears of relief.

She traipsed north away from the beach, the research lab, the fishermen's cabins, the commotion, the cops, the smugglers, trudged through the shingle desert, past the refugee cormorants in their willow tree shelters, the blackthorn clumps, and collapsed on the backseat of the Land Rover.

A spider crawled across her face, shimmied along her arm. The sun was climbing the sky, warming her skin through the Land Rover's window. She ached as she had never ached before, her coat was ripped, trousers salt-and-mud caked. She was starving. But she was alive. And that felt good. She scooped the spider on her finger. It rolled round, dived, swung away on its thread. She had to go too. Drive home. She stopped at the first phone box she could find, called Harry. He picked up. She shoved the coins in the slot.

'Harry, it's me, Sam.'

'Are you OK?'

'Not really.'

'Can you meet me at my allotment?'

'When?'

'How long will it take you to get there?'

'I need to stop somewhere for food, otherwise I'm going to starve. Four hours.'

'OK, meet you there at two. Drive carefully.'

'I will.'

'Don't keep checking over your shoulder.'

'It's a habit.'

'I know. That's why I'm telling you not to do it. You don't have to worry. I've sorted it.'

'Do you think so?'

'Yes.'

She replaced the receiver, relieved to hear his voice, even if she wasn't convinced he'd sorted anything.

Through the Great North Wood, gypsies laughing, woodpeckers tapping; the smell of drifting smoke almost made her panic. Gut reaction. She stood at the top of the hill, looked down on Harry's patch, watched him tending his oil drum fire. She wound her way around the neat beanpoles, fluffy carrot tops, blousy pink and orange dahlias.

Harry gaped when he spotted her. 'What have you been doing?'

'I went camping.'

'In a puddle?'

'A marsh.'

'I see.' He poked the fire with a stick. 'I've brought some burgers with me. Fancy one?'

'I'm vegetarian.'

'Me too. I made them from aduki beans.'

'Yes please, then.'

'So, the file. It's in there.' He prodded the oil drum again.

'You're burning my police file?'

'Yep.'

She watched the flames reaching higher. 'Burning awkward police files – is that standard procedure?'

He shot her a sideways glance. 'Very droll.' He reached for a wire grill, placed it across the rim of the oil drum. Perhaps Sonny had been right – her jokes could be irritating.

'How did you get hold of my file anyway?' she asked.

'That would be telling.'

'I'm not sure burning it will make any difference.'

'It was at the bottom of the pile. Nobody got round to entering it on any computer list. There's no record. MI5 have nothing on you.'

'Well, that's a relief. Thank you. But what about Crawford?'

'I've had a word with him early this morning. I said it all sounded like a mistake, unreliable informant getting over-excited, short of cash, concocting bullshit to keep the money flowing. He agreed. In fact, Crawford said he thinks the whole investigation was a wild goose chase. It's all too easy to get your hands on firearms in this day and age, and unfortunately your mate Dave managed it, with very tragic consequences. Sad, but straightforward. Which is almost certainly the conclusion the inquest into his death will come to. It's sorted.'

He gave her a stern look, as if he was daring her to challenge him. She wondered what Crawford was up to. Did he reckon she'd frazzled in the flames at Dungeness? Or had he found another way of getting to her?

'It's not sorted at all, Harry. Crawford is after me.'

'Don't be daft.'

'He engineered a contract on me.'

'Sam. Are you listening? I said don't be daft. He's a senior police officer.'

'Harry. Please. The fact that he's a senior police officer is hardly a guarantee of probity.'

'OK. Fair point. But engineering a contract on a twenty-year-old girl is going it some, even for a senior police officer. It's a wild accusation. Certainly not one that I can see any benefit in you making.'

'He's after me.'

'Why?' He said it with irritation rather than disbelief, as if he already knew there might be some problem but was hoping he wouldn't have to deal with it.

'Because I know something about him I don't know I know, but he does know I know.'

'What are you going on about?'

'Listen. Please.'

He ripped open a Tupperware box, flung a couple of burgers on the grill. 'Go on then, tell me.'

He poked the burgers with a fork.

She hesitated. 'Crawford is corrupt – he's taking a slice from the organized crime he's supposed to be stopping – drugs, robberies, whatever, you name it. And then he has to cover his tracks, so he leaks information about other cops and undercover operations, when he thinks they are on to him.'

Harry flipped a burger. 'Listen. There is a mole somewhere in the Force's senior ranks who has dropped some extremely sensitive information about all sorts of operations, including undercover work, and some officers have been...' – he fished for the right word – 'endangered as a result. But Crawford is not the man.'

'How do you know?'

'Because somebody has tried levelling those charges against him before, and they were proved to be totally baseless. Crawford is clean.'

'Who made the accusations?'

Harry flipped the second burger.

'Flint?' she asked.

'Yes, it was fucking Flint. I knew I shouldn't have given you that bloody article.'

'It wasn't just the article. I found a note of a meeting with Flint in one of Jim's old diaries.'

Harry tutted. 'Fuck it. Fuck that arsehole Flint. He's one of those smart but stupid types. He can suss things out, but then he fucks up when he tries to do anything with the information.'

'What information?'

'Oh Christ, I don't know why we're getting into this. Look, Flint claimed that this contact of his, Holder – specializes in laundering gold – told him Crawford had kept him up to date on the investigations into this bullion robbery. Flint reckoned that Holder had noted down all the dates that Crawford had been to see him, all the things he had said. Flint claimed Crawford, and whatever snivelling sidekick he can drag along, takes a cut of the action. Then Crawford leaks information when anybody starts sniffing around. Names of cops, witnesses, details of investigations into the investigations. Pisses it all over the place. Gangsters. Journos. You name it. According to Flint, he'd been at it since the seventies.'

'Crawford was at it in the seventies?'

'Everybody was at it in the seventies. The relevant point is that it was easy for Crawford to dismiss Flint's claims.'

'Flip them,' she said.

'I have.'

'I meant the accusations, not the burgers. Crawford flipped them back on Flint.'

Harry sighed. 'Crawford's a smarter cop than Flint – that's why he was the boss and Flint was his minion. Flint claimed Crawford was out in the criminal belt doing deals with Holder, but Crawford had an alibi for all the dates he called. Flint was bloody stupid to put it about in the first place without more evidence. More allies. I mean, who is going to believe what some con says about a senior cop?'

'The criminal belt. Is that where Holder lives?'

Harry rolled his lips, as if he was determined not to speak. A blackbird trilled. He wrinkled his nose. And then he said, 'Where Holder lived, you mean. He's dead too. The old two bullets in the back of the head scenario.'

'Like Flint.'

'Like Flint. Dead as a fucking doornail.'

'Did Holder live near where Jim is buried?'

Harry's eyes shot in her direction, slipped back. 'Yes.'

Near the village where she had walked the dog with Jim when she was eleven, the site of the May Day fair. She touched the Dictaphone in her pocket again, replayed Crawford's words in her head. *I know she's stuck that fucking date, the May Day fair, in her silly fucking memory.* That fucking date. 1 May 1978. You don't always know what you know. Unknown known. She knew it, but she didn't know it mattered. Crawford did. She took a deep breath.

She said, 'I saw Crawford on 1 May 1978 in the village on the edge of the criminal belt, where Jim is buried.'

'You didn't,' Harry said.

'I did. I'm telling you. I saw him. Jim disappeared because he didn't want Crawford to see him with me, which was a mistake, because then Crawford tried to talk to me. Crawford was desperate to find out what Jim was doing there. And that was his mistake. He went for me because I was a soft target. But I wouldn't have seen him, let alone remembered him if he hadn't offered me a stupid stick of candyfloss.'

Harry's face was red. He jabbed the burgers.

'Listen to me,' he said. 'You did not see him. You did not talk to him. There was no candyfloss. And let me tell you why.'

He grabbed a bottle of water he had left standing on the ground by his makeshift barbecue, swigged, swished, spat the water on the ground.

'The May Day fair was what Flint was blathering on about before he copped it. Flint started saying it wasn't just Holder's notes, there were other witnesses. No names mentioned. But he did say something about a May Day fair near to Holder's gaff.'

'And then Flint was shot.'

'Yeah. Then Flint was shot.'

She jammed her hand in her coat pocket, shuffled around. 'Harry, I've taped Crawford saying he saw me at a May Day fair.'

She pulled out the Dictaphone.

'What are you doing? Put that bloody thing away. You do not have a tape with Crawford saying anything. Do you understand? We're not playing save the bloody world here, we are trying to make sure you get out of the shit and stay out of the shit.'

She closed her eyes, stomach sinking, too tired to argue. 'Yes. I understand.'

She replaced the Dictaphone in her pocket.

'But Harry.'

'What?'

'He knows I know.'

'Will you stop with the he knows, you know, I know? It's doing my head in.'

'Sorry.'

He gulped another swig of water. 'You're going to have to put Crawford out of your mind. Go back to university, sit in a library and stick your head in a book. All this stuff about Crawford – the accusations, the evidence – it's irrelevant now. Holder is dead. Flint is dead, Jim is dead. You don't have any evidence that nails him. You know nothing, you remember nothing. If anybody is going to accuse him of anything, it's not going to be you. Because now you know what happens when you make accusations about bent cops in the Force.' He examined the underside of the burgers. 'Don't mention Crawford again. Leave it to me. This is in-house. In hand. I'll sort it, OK?'

'OK. Harry, one more thing.'

'What?'

'Crawford dropped the information that led to Jim's death warrant.'

Harry waved at the rows of vegetables as if he hadn't heard a word she had said. 'It's pick your own salad.'

'OK. Great.'

She let her feet sink in the soil, newly moistened by the night's rain. She wandered the plot, stooped to pick some leaves from a row of butter lettuces, glanced back at Harry, watched him wiping his brow with one hand, turning the burgers with the other. The smell of charred beans mingled with the wood smoke. She concentrated on the lettuce again, tugged at leaves, flicked a slug with her finger. Returned to Harry with a handful of green.

'There's some bread in my bag. You can use the lid of that tin as a plate.'

She held out the tin lid. He shovelled a burger on to the white slice. She arranged the lettuce, topped it with a second slice of Sunblest. Took a bite.

'Aduki burgers, great.'

'Made them myself. Secret recipe, before you ask.'

'I wasn't going to, I'm not very good at cooking. I can't be bothered with recipes. The lettuce is fantastic.'

'Organic. No pesticides.'

'How do you keep the slugs and snails at bay?'

'Kill 'em. Red in tooth and claw. Can't be pussy footing around. Don't take any prisoners. It's them or my lettuces.'

She wiped the bean juice from her mouth, caught a movement in the hawthorn hedge running around the bottom of the allotment. 'Look, there's a fox.'

'It's got a den down there. Smart. Knows its territory. Doesn't go straying into unmarked lands.' He nodded at her. 'Good strategy. Stick to the safe paths. Stay on the dry land.'

'The boundaries aren't always clearly marked,' she said. Especially not in the marshes.

CHAPTER 21

THE OVAL GASHOLDER was full. She had a bath, stretched out in bed, listened to the noises of the night: last-order drinkers, foxes overturning bins, car alarms. She waited for the ghosts, the whispering of the dead – but they said nothing. She slept.

The morning arrived in greyness. One of those sullen London summer days that hung around making everybody feel edgy with its presence. Liz rang early. She was back from Greece and wanted Sam to drive over and visit.

Sam parked the camper van by the graveyard where she had agreed to meet her mother – she didn't want to go to the house and find Roger there. Liz was already standing by the tombstone; she had laid some white star wood anemones on Jim's grave.

'I picked them from the field down there,' Liz said. 'They are very late flowering. I suppose it's all the cold and rain. Anyway, I thought he might appreciate them.'

Sam poked the earth with her toe. 'Do you think he really is down there?'

'Why are you asking me? He never told me where he was going when he was alive. Death hasn't made him any more communicative.'

Sam gave her mother a sideways glance. Liz continued. 'He always was a difficult bloody sod, but I did love him, you know. Sometimes.'

Sam nodded. 'Let's go for a walk,' she said.

Out of the churchyard gate, across the field, through the silver birches, heading into the criminal belt.

'Did you have a good holiday?' Sam asked.

'Yes. Fine after I gave up on Milton.'

'What did Milton do wrong?'

'Eve. She falls for the devil. And everybody blames her rather than Satan. It irritated me too much, I'm afraid. A man of his times, I suppose.'

'At least Milton's not as bad as James the First with his *Daemonologie* and his accusations that women are weak-brained devil-worshipping witches who should be condemned to the flames.'

'*Daemonologie*? James the First? You'd hardly expect a king to be anything other than an inbred half-wit. Milton was a poet, a supporter of Cromwell, a radical.'

'Radical men aren't necessarily feminists.'

'No. Nor necessarily to be trusted. Did you get my post-card? The one with the recipe?'

'Yes, Mum. You've asked me that about five million times.'

'Did you understand it?'

'What, the recipe?'

'The code.'

'Code?'

'I wrote you a message in code.'

Sam laughed. Liz frowned. 'I'm serious.'

Sam was still laughing.

'Really, Sam. I'm trying to help you. Roger is trying to help you.'

The mention of Roger's name pulled Sam up short.

'I don't need his help, thanks.'

Liz folded her arms. 'Sam, we were in a Greek taverna the first night of the holiday and Roger spotted somebody he recognized, a man who used to be in the CIA and who has now gone rogue, to use Roger's terminology.'

Sam folded her arms now. 'Does Roger have contacts in the CIA?'

'Of course he does. As you know, Roger was in the Special Boat Service, he attends all the reunions. The SBS are well connected with the security services – abroad as well as at home. Roger had a chat to this man, this rogue officer, and he mentioned the CIA operations in Afghanistan.'

Sam wasn't sure where this conversation was heading, but she didn't like the turning it had just taken.

'He was talking about an aid project the CIA were using to provide support to the Afghan rebels.'

'Oh right.'

'A photography project. Providing cameras to the Afghan rebels so they could record their lives. It was a cover so the CIA could supply the Mujahedeen with weapons. It wasn't aid workers running it, it was agents.'

The path they were following joined a lane, conifers along one side.

'Luke told Roger he had worked on a camera project in Afghanistan,' Liz said.

Luke had never mentioned working in Afghanistan to her. Perhaps he was showing off, playing the hard man in front of Roger, made a tactical mistake and let the truth slip out. Perhaps that was where Stavros found him – working on a CIA-funded fake NGO project in Afghanistan.

'So what if he did mention Afghanistan anyway?'

'Roger thought there was something fishy about Luke and it turns out his suspicions were right. Roger thought you ought to know that Luke might not be exactly what he seems to be.'

'As in?'

'As in he's probably a spook of some kind or another.'

'And you conveyed this information to me in a code embedded in a spanakopita recipe on the back of a postcard?'

'Yes. It was Roger's idea. He was worried your phone line might be bugged. It was quite a straightforward code. The first letter of every underlined word.'

'That's so straightforward it's not a code.'

'You understood it?'

'No, Mum. I didn't.'

'It can't have been so straightforward then.'

'Mum. The not straightforward bit wasn't the code, but the fact that you would think of sending me a message about my boyfriend embedded in a recipe for spanakopita on the back of a fucking postcard.'

'There's no need to swear.'

'Since when have you cared about swearing?'

'Roger thinks swearing shows a limited vocabulary.'

'Fuck Roger.'

'Sam. We are trying to help you.'

'By telling me my boyfriend is a spook?'

'It's quite an important piece of information, don't you think? I mean it could be a problem.'

'Problem? In what way? You married a bloody spook of sorts.'

'Yes, but at least I knew what he was.'

They had come to a gap in the pines.

'Good god, what's that?' Liz asked.

She pointed at a wooden-framed box sitting on the ground, covered with chicken wire, a bedraggled crow cowering inside.

'Larsen trap,' Sam said. 'The crow is a decoy. It's there to attract other crows – they fall through the false roof and then they are trapped.'

'That's terrible. I think we should set the poor bloody crow free.'

'Good idea. I've got my Swiss Army knife on me.' The one that Luke had given her. 'I can prise out the staples.'

She flicked the large blade, tried not to look at the engraving. *Sam – love you. Luke.* Hacked away at the frame, the pathetic bird huddled in a corner. The trap wasn't particularly well constructed so it didn't take her long to loosen enough wire for the bird to escape, but it seemed reluctant to move.

'We're intimidating it,' Liz said. 'It needs space.'

They walked a short distance down the road, watched as the crow found a way through the wire, hopped, tested its wings, flapped off into the wood.

'Good,' Liz said. 'So, Luke.'

'Well, it's irrelevant anyway,' Sam said. 'I dumped him.'

Dumped. She glanced down at the unfolded penknife she was clutching in her hand, couldn't avoid seeing the engraved words – *love you. Luke* – felt a stab in her ribs, like a stitch but worse, much worse, head spinning with the pain. She clenched her fist, felt another sharp stab in her palm, unrolled her hand, saw the line of blood where she had cut herself on the open blade. She folded it, wiped her hand on her trousers, considered dropping Luke's gift on the ground, decided against it, and replaced the penknife in her pocket, vaguely conscious of Liz chuntering away.

'I'm sure it's a good thing that you dumped him,' Liz said. 'I wouldn't have any regrets about that if I were you.'

'I'll try not to let it bother me,' Sam said.

The phone rang as she entered the door. She grabbed it. The therapist.

'Finally. I've been trying to get hold of you for days. Are you OK?'

'Yes.'

'Perhaps we should talk.'

'It might be too late to talk.'

'It's only midday.'

'No, I mean it's too late because I think I'm through with the five stages of grieving. I've definitely done the denial. And I've been very angry.'

'Hang on a moment, Sam. Let's talk about anger.'

'Must we?'

'Well, if you can't talk about it, you're still in denial.'

'Right.'

'What is it about your father that makes you angry?'

She sighed. 'I'm angry with him for dying.' She paused, recalled the day of the fair, Jim's vanishing act, the candy man's stare, his parting shot; *tell your dad he should take more care of you, otherwise something nasty could happen.* Crawford had made good on his threat. 'I'm also angry with Jim for exposing me to the risks of his work.'

'Risks. Let's think about risks. Parents have to enable children to face the risks and dangers of life, they can't cocoon them in cotton wool.'

'Yeah, I know, but there are general risks that everybody has to face, and there are specific risks you have to deal with if your father works for the secret state.'

The therapist sighed. 'Sam, I thought we were moving away from abstract entities, paranoia.'

Sam wasn't paying much attention, she was hearing her parents arguing, Liz cackling, shouting – So if I want to know where you are, I'm supposed to call the fucking Home Secretary, am I? – slamming the door. 'Although, in the end,' Sam said, 'in the final analysis, I don't entirely blame Jim.'

'OK, back on track. So why don't you blame your father?'

'It was the seventies.' 'The Candy Man Can' played in her head. How did that song go? Something about childhood wishes – as if any child would wish for a creep with a bag of sweets. 'Who gave a shit about children in the seventies?' she continued. 'Nobody. Certainly not the Force. But whatever Jim was trying to do, he did it because the Home Secretary wanted somebody to do it.'

'I've lost you. You're blaming government ministers?'

'Yes.'

'For…?'

She hated that patronizing tone of scepticism, the implication that she might be deluded, wrong-thinking. She was telling the therapist what she remembered. Wasn't that the point of these conversations? A dialogue about her childhood, her memories.

'Sam, can we focus on your relationship with your father?'

'Could we continue this session another day? I'm feeling sick.'

'Oh, OK.'

'Bye.'

'Bye for now.'

Bye for ever, Sam decided. She was done with talking.

She found the postcard Liz had sent her lying on the kitchen surface where Sonny had left it, splattered with oil, words partially erased by watermarks. She picked it up, left the house. The sun was heading west to Battersea as she crossed to the green patch in the centre of the square, found a spot in the long grass where she could lie down without being seen. She removed the postcard from her pocket and perused it, noted all the underlined words which she had dismissed as random and could now see, despite the cooking stains, formed a painfully obvious coded message: *lovely, unsalted, knife, eggs, spinach, pepper, oil, only, keep*. Luke spook. Examining it again made her laugh. Who else but Liz would think of telling her daughter that her boyfriend was some kind of secret agent via a spanakopita recipe on the back of a postcard from Greece where she was, supposedly, researching the classical references in *Paradise Lost*? She was laughing so much she started to cry. She couldn't stop. Her life was absurd. She couldn't believe she had been so stupid. Roger had seen through Luke's cover and she had fallen for it. Swept along by the chemistry. He must have had a false identity. Same first name as his real name perhaps, different last name, different date of birth. Were the stories about his parents true? Had he made them up to try to win her sympathy? Maybe there were some half truths there. Perhaps his dad had dismissed his wife in favour of Ottoman culture, and Luke's commitment to the Afghan rebels was a way of proving to his father that he was worthy of his love. But there was obviously a vast tangle of deception holding the truths together. Luke had set her up, used her to build a relationship with Dave so he could keep an eye on what was happening in the research lab. He had fed all sorts of crap about her and Dave to Spyder so he could pass it on to Crawford and Crawford could claim it as legitimate information for a file on her. Not any old stuff it in a cupboard with all the millions of others and forget about it file, but a file marked terrorist.

Dave had suspected Luke. She'd got it all wrong. That evening in Skell, her last evening with Dave, he had tried to warn her about Luke. Tried to persuade her to back off, walk away from danger. She had shouted at him, her mate Dave, smashed one of his favourite mugs. And he'd paid the price for being too smart. She flicked an ant crawling across her arm. How come she was so dumb? She had made the mistake of thinking the only men who did that sort of thing were middle-aged saddos like her father. What an idiot she was. Hadn't she spotted anything? She remembered Luke's slip over his birth sign. She'd pulled him up when he gave the wrong zodiac sign – Capricorn instead of Gemini. But he'd wriggled out of it, turned it into a compliment for her, flipped it smoothly. Give him his due, he was good at his job. Fucking bastard.

She dug around in her pocket, pulled out her pocket knife, stared at the words engraved on the blade. *Sam – love you. Luke.* He had wheedled out her vulnerabilities, encouraged her to confess her guilt, her doubts, her fears and played them all back to her. Bastard. But she'd got him in the end. She really had loved him – she wasn't a bitter withy – and yet she had killed him. She still couldn't quite believe she'd done it. Two shots. How could she deal with that? She pictured Sonny's cross-marked arm, scarred by guilt, the burden etched on his skin. She was distracted from her contemplation by a robin – it alighted near her feet, cocked its head on one side, gave her a cheeky wink then flew away. The robin was right, she decided, she could manage. She stood, brushed the grass seeds from her overcoat. She needed to draw a line. Bury it.

She emptied her duffle bag, the one she had taken from Dungeness to Skell and back to Romney, spread its contents on the floor of her bedroom: dirty knickers, toothpaste tube with white gunk oozing from a crack in its middle, Dictaphone machine containing her answerphone cassette. She rewound, pressed play. The illicit recording of Crawford. She rewound some more. Pressed play again, expecting to hear Dave's voice. There was a crackle, and then, unexpectedly, Sonny.

'Sam. I wanted to leave you a message.'

She pressed stop. He must have taped a message on the Dictaphone that evening at the Lookers' Hut when she went out for a walk in the thunderstorm. She pressed play again.

'I don't know where I will be when you find this message. Wherever it is, please don't worry about me. And I'm not worried about you, because I know your heart is strong. There is something I wanted to tell you. So... I... the last words I heard your father speak were from the Book of the Preacher. I think you know the verse. To every thing there is a season and a time to every purpose under the heaven.'

The message ended. Hearing his voice made her cry. And cry. Sonny's confession. She made herself a coffee and replayed the message again. Only this time it didn't make her cry, it made her think. Perhaps it was nothing more than Sonny's South African phrasing, but there was something ambiguous about his message, a lack of finality – these were the last words I heard your father speak, not these were your father's last words – as if he was telling her that Jim had recited the verse from Ecclesiastes and then walked off some place else. Hinting that he had done the same thing with Jim as he had with her, taken the contract to stop anybody else implementing it. She replayed the message one more time. No, it was all in her mind. Of course. Jim was definitely dead. She removed the cassette, stuck it in her pocket.

The shadows were lengthening as she pushed on the gate to the Crossbones graveyard for the unforgiven. A wave of cats flowed out from the grass, swirled around her ankles.

'I don't have any food for you.'

She walked to a far corner of the graveyard, found a secluded spot, a bare patch of earth among the grass and nettles. She knelt on the ground, started to dig with her hands, soil under her fingernails, dirt in the creases of her palms. A ginger tom nudged her elbow. She rubbed its head, it purred, scampered off in the direction of the gate. The bag lady appeared, the cats cavorted around her in an impatient flurry.

'Oh, it's you again,' the lady said.

She rummaged in her trolley, removed the saucers, the bag of nibbles, dished the food out, the plates a seething mass of multicoloured fur. She placed her hands on her hips, gazed affectionately at her followers.

She turned to Sam. 'What are you doing back here then?'

'I came to bury a few old friends. Outcasts,' she added.

Sam held the micro-cassette in the air. 'Voices, ghosts, whispering in my ear. I don't want to live in the past. I don't want to harbour toxic grudges. I want to let it all go.' Luke, Sonny, Jim. 'I've forgiven them.' She remembered Crawford was on the tape. 'Well, there's one on there I don't forgive.'

'Who's that then?'

'Crawford. Bent cop. More than bent. Evil.'

'I knew a bent cop called Crawford,' the bag lady said.

Sam jumped. 'Really?'

'It was a while back. Soho. In the sixties.'

'Must be somebody different then.'

Sam wrapped the cassette in a plastic bag, dropped it into the hole, sprinkled the loose soil on top, pressed it down, wondered whether she should say something. Anything. A few words. Decided against. She stood, wiped her hands on her trousers.

The bag lady said, 'Sometimes the hardest person to forgive is yourself.'

Sam grimaced. 'But what if you've done something so terrible it shouldn't be forgiven?'

'What would that be? What could you have done that was so terrible you couldn't forgive yourself?' The bag lady was assessing her shrewdly.

'Maybe I've killed a man.' She hoped she sounded vague, casual – the emphasis on the maybe.

The bag lady didn't blink. 'Was it necessary? Would he have killed you if you didn't kill him?'

Sam nodded. 'He was a ghost,' she said. 'He didn't exist in the first place.'

'Oh? You've killed a man who didn't exist. So you can't be caught. Sounds to me like you've committed the perfect crime.'

Sam managed a smile; the perfect crime. She'd killed a ghost.

'Wouldn't make too much of a fucking song and a dance about it if I were you,' the bag lady said. 'You don't want to draw attention to yourself.' She was staring at Sam's face as she spoke, examining her cat-face splodge. Sam's hand rose to cover it.

'Birthmark,' Sam said.

'Marks, scars,' the bag lady said. 'They are reminders that our past is real. Not fake.'

She made a harrumphing noise in her throat that sounded almost like an expression of empathy.

Sam left the bag lady pottering around the Crossbones grave-yard, pulling up ragwort, grubbing for fag ends. She walked beside the river, mud banks merging with water in the dwindling light of the day, headed west. Past the OXO building, the South Bank, St Thomas' hospital. The path joined Albert Embankment at Lambeth Palace. She strolled along, hands in pockets, oblivious to the noise of passing traffic and the wail of distant sirens, reached the wasteland below Vauxhall Bridge. She found the hole in the fence, crawled through, headed to the slipway, crouched and looked for her bellarmine. Still there, the grey pot belly snug in its gutter hiding place. She picked it up, ambled to the bottom of the slipway and was startled by an unfamiliar noise. Gushing water. The Effra sluice gate was open. She walked over to the chute; the summer's rain had been unleashed, washing away the footprint trails in the sludge, carrying off the debris from the sewers – hair, bones, trainers, dead goldfish, caesium particles. Swept out of the drain, down the chute and into the Thames in a manic torrent, past Westminster, Wapping, Tilbury and to the sea. Well, the Effra might have been cleared out and sanitized, she thought, but now all the shit was flowing through the heart of London.

She trailed alongside the chute, down the foreshore to the edge of the river. Beyond the line of rotting timbers of the ancient Bronze Age jetty, she saw the shadow of a man standing. She called his name. He disappeared. She squinted but could see nothing except the water rippling, as if there were land below the surface – undiscovered country. She tasted saltwater, realized she was crying, wiped her eyes on her coat sleeve. She suspected he wouldn't reappear again. Not this time.

She was still holding the bellarmine. She lifted the bottle, the gurning face grinning at her from its pot belly, tipped it upside down and emptied the contents into the Thames. The soggy willow bark and the felt heart with its three rusty pins – Dave, Luke, Sonny – washed away. She watched the grey water swirling for a while, and then she stuck her free hand in her pocket, grasped the penknife from Luke, fondled it in her palm, wondered whether it would fit. She tried it for size, found it slipped quite easily down the bottle's neck into its belly. She rattled the bottle to check the penknife was secure, unable to escape, raised her arm and lobbed the bellarmine into the Thames. A counter-charm to protect herself from future heartbreak and betrayal. The bottle bobbed around for a few seconds, disappeared; she imagined some future riverside walker finding it lodged in the muddy banks of the Thames, and the thought cheered her. She put her hand in her pocket again, touched the toad bones that Alastair had collected to increase his sorcerer's powers. I'll sort it, Harry had said. In-house. She wasn't sure she could afford to take any chances. She needed to be ready for Crawford if he came back at her – ready for any other fucker who wanted to take a swipe. She was hit by a surge of anger, a desire to wreak revenge on her tormentors, the pointing fingers, the unknown threats, the secrets, the lies – throw the curses back with added venom. Fuck the bastards, whoever they were, wherever they were, they weren't going to get her. She'd survived trial by water, punishment by flames – whatever doesn't kill you makes you stronger. She clutched the toad bones tight in her hand and claimed the magic of the Magi and the necromancers, the knowledge of the alchemists, the spells of the cunning folk. She would be mistress of the House of Levitation. She aimed the toad bones high. They twirled in the air, hung for a moment, then spiralled down like apple blossom on to the water and were snatched by the ebbing tide. She touched her birthmark with her finger; if she had to be a witch, she might as well be a powerful one.

EPILOGUE

THE CORONER RELEASED Dave's body. In the absence of anybody else stepping forward, Sam had taken charge of the funeral arrangements. Cremation or burial was a conversation they'd had more than once and Dave was always certain he wanted to be cremated. He liked the idea of the physical transformation by fire. She arranged for a cremation and service at West Norwood. She managed to contact his estranged father in the States, and he asked her to dispose of the ashes in a way she thought that Dave would like. Which was why she ended up taking the box of his remains to Skell when she went to collect his belongings from the Professor's house.

One of those rare English summer days when the sky was cloudless, sapphire blue. She headed off, past the customs house, the windmill still up for sale, along the causeway across the marsh, carrying a rucksack on her back with the ash box and Dave's other Aston Villa mug stowed inside. She swished the rushes as she walked. She was watching a marsh harrier hover above a distant reed bed when she heard a whistle behind. At first she ignored the familiar tune, dismissed it as pure coincidence, but the whistler was persistent, drawing closer. She increased her speed. He was still behind, closing the gap. She felt a tap on her shoulder. She turned, what else could she do? Found herself face to face with an anonymous-looking man in a Harrington. She had seen him before, she was sure, although she couldn't place him immediately; a bank clerk, the manager of the local Tesco? And then it clicked: he was the man who had precipitated her crisis in spring last year when he whispered in her ear. *I know you. You are Jim Coyle's daughter.* Left her feeling marked.

He caught her eye, she twisted away, searched for an escape route, but was trapped by the steep slopes down to the marsh on either side. She turned, he caught her arm.

'Not bad,' he said, 'for a beginner.'

She recognized his voice then, of course, from the telephone messages he'd left. She yanked her arm free. 'What do you want?'

He said, 'Mad plots by rogue CIA agents, bent coppers, psychotic hitmen. Quite a high body count, but nobody that anybody would care about losing.'

She cared, she wanted to shout. She cared about her friends. Dave. Sonny.

'I have no idea what you are talking about,' she said.

'Oh, really? The test tube you chucked into the air at Dungeness was quite a good touch. A little bit of drama. Good thing it wasn't caesium, but I presume you'd worked that out when you lobbed it.'

'You've lost me.'

'The foghorn on the perimeter fence of the research lab. Actually it's a security camera. You don't think they would leave that area unprotected, do you? All those nuclear facilities.'

Her stomach sank.

'It was a foggy night,' he said. 'As you may remember, so not the best picture. As I said, the glowing test tube showed up nicely. Your face not quite so clear. Never mind.'

She hesitated. 'Who are you anyway?'

He smirked, showed his yellowing teeth. 'I'm a man with intelligence.'

He winked. He was a man who made her flesh crawl. Then her mouth opened when she realized what he meant. Intelligence with a capital I.

'You're a man who left me weird messages on my answering machine.' She heard the click, the whistle, the familiar tune playing in her head. 'You tapped my phone, listened to my private conversations.'

'I thought I was being helpful. Checking up on the ins and outs, giving you a couple of prompts. Letting you know what was going on.'

She gasped, almost choked on her sharp intake of air.

'Jesus. You tap my line and then have the nerve to pretend you were helping me.'

'Oh, please spare me the outrage. You know the score. It's your bloody family's business.'

'It's nothing to do with me.'

'Come on. It's in your DNA. It's on your birth certificate. Father's occupation.'

Jesus, he was a loathsome knicker sniffer. 'My father's job has nothing to do with my life, what I choose to do.'

'Are you sure? We thought maybe you might like to do some work for us.'

'You've got to be kidding.'

'It's the dodgy cops we are interested in; we want to find out what they are up to. You're ideally placed.'

'I'm not. I'm a placard-waving leftie.'

'Really? A leftie? There isn't a file on you – I ran a check.'

'That's because…'

He laughed. 'We're not asking for anything difficult. At least not at the moment. Rumour has it you have a tape, a recording with some interesting information on it. Crawford, digging his own grave, we gather.'

She panicked. Had Harry told somebody about the tape? Surely not.

'There is no tape,' she said.

'Strange. A friend of mine told me she'd seen you disposing of it. Wrapped it in a plastic bag she said. I know she's getting on a bit and her eyesight isn't what it used to be, but she's still pretty sharp as old spooks go.'

The bag lady. An old spook. She should have guessed.

'I thought you were a person of principles. Ideals. Here's your chance to do your bit for democracy, the rule of law. Shaft the bent coppers.'

'Oh come on, don't give me that shit. You're not interested in democracy. All you're interested in is your own turf. Making sure nobody invades your patch.'

'So cynical for one so young.'

'Piss off.'

'It's extra money. You could top up your bank account.'

'Not interested.'

He shrugged. 'Suit yourself. What are you going to do with a history degree anyway?'

'Archaeology postgrad.'

'Archaeology? Messing about with skeletons. Sounds like a suitable occupation for the daughter of a dead undercover cop.'

She peered over his shoulder, hoping to see a dog walker or a twitcher, anybody who she could use as a life raft to escape from this creep. The path was empty, the marsh deserted.

'The thing is,' he said, 'the Force has all these strange operations going on, the Sewer Squad. Your father's lot. And nobody knows what any of them are doing.'

She was about to say he wasn't quite right; if her memory

served her correctly, the Home Secretary knew exactly what they were doing. She decided it was probably best to keep shtum.

'And we in Intelligence like to know what our comrades in the Force are up to.'

Of course, as Jim had once explained, their home phone was being tapped by another part of the secret state. The spies and undercover agents, they all monitored each other. Never trust a spy you cannot see.

'Not what you want from the Force in this day and age. Unaccountable cops. It's not good. We're beyond that now. We're a modern democracy. It's all about new technology – the information age. So we had this idea, which we thought you might be interested in.'

'No. I'm not.'

'Hear me out. You're always protesting about something or other. Maybe you could keep an eye open, see if you attract any of these dodgy cops. See if any of them turn up and join one of your groups. Then we can find out what they are up to.'

She almost laughed. 'You're asking me to be a decoy?'

'Yes, I suppose so.'

'No bloody way. I want to be free to do what I want to do. And what I want to do has nothing to do with spooks, undercover agents of any description whatsoever.'

'We're not always quite as free as we like to think we are.'

'You're wasting your time. I'm not interested. Leave me alone.'

'Think about it.'

'No.'

'You could avenge your father's death.'

She hesitated. 'Get stuffed.'

'Take my card.'

He leaned over, dropped it in her coat pocket, turned around and walked away. She watched his back diminishing and she half wished she hadn't left the Firebird in the cellar underneath the floorboards of the fisherman's cabin in Dungeness. Fuck him. Disturbing her peace. She had no interest whatsoever in being an informer. A spy. A bedraggled crow in a Larsen trap trying to snare some mates. What grubby corner of Intelligence did he work for anyway, she wondered. She reached into her pocket, removed the card the spook had forced on her. Plain white rectangle. Name and number. No indication of the office, address, anything. Just a quote. 'Confession is not betrayal.' She stared at the card for a while, then placed it in her back pocket. Confession is always betrayal, she reckoned, no matter which side you were standing on. She thought then of the bones of the informers spread out across the marshes, the ghosts of the waterlogged meadows, the saltpans and ditches, searching for their missing limbs, trying to make themselves whole again. And she remembered the witches, trial by water, ducked and ducked again until they squealed or drowned.

She took a deep breath, watched the marsh harrier sweeping across the headland before it gave up the chase, rose on a thermal and faded; nothing more than a speck of dust in the heavens. She made a decision, slid down the causeway bank, waded through the shallow lagoons and reed beds. Saltmarsh, shifting ground. Neither sea nor soil. Her legs were soaked by the time she had made it through the tidal creeks to the far side of the headland, but the sopping shoes and trousers didn't bother her. She was too hot to care about being wet. She found a suitable spot to sit among the thrift and sea blite, removed the cardboard box and Aston Villa mug from her rucksack and carefully funnelled Dave's ashes into the cup.

'I miss you,' she said as she poured.

She walked down the sun-baking mudflat, leaving a trail of dark footprints behind, scooped a cavity in the silt at the edge of the saltwater and buried the mug, up to its rim. She returned to her resting place on the firmer, grass-covered ground and waited. Watched the tide come creeping in and wash Dave out across the saltmarsh.

AUTHOR'S NOTE

THANK YOU OLI and Laura for your encouragement, and everybody at Head of Zeus for your support. Thank you to all the people who helped me along the way: Rosy for driving me around in the dark, Sal for unstinting enthusiasm, my mum for all sorts of things, Mary for sparking a memory, Jem for the biscuit barrel, Muriel for her advice on South Africa, Mark for the field walking tip, and Neil for helping me with radioactive materials. Biggest thanks to my family for sticking with me while I traipsed around the saltmarshes and for spending an afternoon in a nuclear power station.

Skell is a fictitious village on the north Norfolk coast. Dungeness and Romney Marsh form part of a Site of Special Scientific Interest on the Kent coast. The nuclear power station exists but the research lab is a fiction. The remains of some of the Lookers' Huts on Romney Marsh still exist. They are marked as sheepfolds on OS Explorer Map 125 Romney Marsh, Rye & Winchelsea. Most of them are on private land. There is a reconstruction of a Lookers' Hut at the Romney Marsh Visitor Centre.

Sources I used in various fictionalized ways include the following:

His Majestie King James I of England (1597). *Daemonologie*
John Allin's letters to Philip Frith outlining his alchemical
    experiments and details of the Great Plague (1663–1674).

The Keep – the East Sussex Record Office (Reference FRE 5421-5634)

Ralph Merrifield (1987). *The Archaeology of Ritual and Magic*. London: Batsford

Martin Bond (1992). *Nuclear Juggernaut: The Transport of Radioactive Materials*. London: Earthscan Publications Ltd

Anne Reeves and David Eve (1998). *Sheep-Keeping and Lookers' Huts on Romney Marsh*, in *Romney Marsh: Environmental Change and Human Occupation in a Coastal Lowland* (ed. J. Eddison, M. Gardiner and A. Long). Oxford University Committee for Archaeology. Monograph 46

George Crile (2002). *Charlie Wilson's War*. London: Atlantic Books

Wensley Clarkson (2012). *The Curse of Brink's-Mat: 25 Years of Murder and Mayhem*. London: Quercus